OWEN MARSHALL was born in Te Kuiti, New Zealand in 1941. His first collection of short stories, *Supper Waltz Wilson*, was quietly published in 1979. Since then he has written seven collections including, *The Divided World, Tomorrow We Save the Orphans*, and *The Ace of Diamonds Gang*. He is now considered to be the finest short story writer in New Zealand.

Marshall has received many awards, prizes, and fellowships. He held the University of Canterbury Literary Fellowship in 1981, the 1988 New Zealand Literary Fund's Scholarship in Letters, and was awarded the Queen Elizabeth II Arts Council Award for Achievement in 1990. He held the Robert Burns Fellowship at the University of Otago for 1992.

Owen Marshall lives in Timaru with his family.

Marvellous, unforgettable, world-class stories.
Gordon McLauchlan

We are in the presence of a regally gifted maestro.
Michael Morrissey

Owen Marshall is, quite simply, the most able and the most successful short story writer currently writing in New Zealand.
Michael King

By the same author

Supper Waltz Wilson
The Master of Big Jingles
The Day Hemingway Died
The Lynx Hunter
The Divided World
Tomorrow We Save The Orphans
The Ace of Diamonds Gang

OWEN MARSHALL

A Many Coated Man

LONGACRE PRESS

Acknowledgements

The author is grateful for the tenure of the
Robert Burns Literary Fellowship at the University of Otago
in 1992, during which the draft of this novel was written.

Published with the assistance of
the Literature Programme of the Arts Council
of New Zealand Toi Aotearoa.

ISBN 0 9583405 2 8

First published 1995 by Longacre Press Ltd.,
P.O. Box 5340, Dunedin, New Zealand

Typeset by Egan Reid Ltd., Auckland
Printed by Tablet Printing Co.

Book and cover design Jenny Cooper

Front cover painting: *Untitled* (*Watcher on the Shore*),
1982–83, by Tony Fomison. Reproduced courtesy
of the owner and the Fomison Family Trust.

'Like these, my many-coated man
shields his hot hunger from the wind,
and, hooded by a smile, commits
his private murder in the mind.'

Laurie Lee

'The three most intractable beasts; the owl,
the serpent, and the people.'

Demosthenes

*For Jacqueline,
Andrea and Belinda.*

ALDOUS SLAVEN hangs for an instant on the power line of his home; his fine, pale hair a brief nimbus in response to the charge. As a vocal context there is seared in place the lyrics of the Hoihos's *Half Moon Bay*, as a visual one see the blood clustered flowers of Kellie's Earl of Athlone rhododendron. He was aware of the danger, has warned himself to be oh so careful in his movements with the brush. When the ladder betrayed him, there was a brief struggle in his brain between the rational, longer term choice and the instinctive action. *Baby, baby, come again and live with me upon the shore of Half Moon Bay.* But the atavism of a million years can't be denied and Slaven's mouth forms a funnel of apprehension as he watches his freckled and hairy hand seize the wire. Another has the spouting. *Fouveaux storms are fading, baby, within the calm of Half Moon Bay.* In the Earl of Athlone's clotted blossoms are bumble bees which growl with ecstasy as Slaven's shadow flits past them.

Existence is never truly a linear progression: all overlaps, merges, partly conceals, as the scales of a serpent. So every moment is at once a beginning and an end as well as continuity, an assertion and a giving up, a revelation and disguise, a knapsack of the past trekked into new country.

Kellie hears first the clatter of the aluminium steps, then the more unpleasant thump and the impact driven exhalation like a grunt of savage laughter. *Kinder hearts are waiting still, amongst old friends at Half Moon Bay.* Habitual and trivial concerns persist even at the core of emergency. As she goes down on her knees to ease her husband's pain, Kellie sees with resentment that the ladder has sheared the laterals from her favourite lemon bottlebrush and that Slaven himself has destroyed a fledgling camellia with his buttocks.

In a garden also, Kellie would tell you, there is constant flux, with half the plants being given every aid and opportunity to prosper and the others being rigorously curbed to keep them within the bounds of the gardener's conception. The ideal is static and so always a season or two further off. And anyway that particular camellia *R. luteum* is always a beggar for leaf curl caterpillar and the petal edges bruise with the passing roughness of a breeze. *There's no near neighbours, no dismay, at our bach in Half Moon Bay.*

None of this prevents Kellie giving her husband immediate and practical help. She puts her fingers in his mouth to check that his tongue hasn't gone back to block his breathing and draws forward one of his knees so that he may be more comfortably rolled onto his side.

'Ah, Jesus, Kellie, what a thump,' he says. His hands shiver and the great burns there are the only signs of any damage. So he won't be a concert pianist any more, but a dentist too needs his hands. Kellie puts her fingers high on his right cheek and wipes back a trickle of blue paint which is getting into his eye.

'You're okay now.'

'Something's happened to my heart. And Jesus, my hands hurt.' Even lying amid the enveloping leaves and blooms of his wife's garden, the well-worked soil soft beneath him, Slaven has the smell not of those surroundings, but of paint and of the sickening current which has escaped by way of him. It is a scent compounded of the vast ocean's air — and the charnel house.

'I'll get someone. You just lie quietly,' says Kellie and she goes inside to the phone. 'I told you to be careful around the power lines.' Not callousness you understand, but utilising the customary tone as a protection against tears. 'I warned you.'

So she had of course: so he had himself, but that's no help. Slaven lies in the summer garden and he shivers with the shock — yes! — and the agony of his hands. Don't imagine any immediate neighbours to give succour. Pull back your mind's eye and see Slaven's older style house of the nineties on its four hectares of city outskirts as befits a middle-aged professional. And he has been made to pay for this display of course, Kellie's garden spread round them and the hobby Romneys further out, for no houses in the city have overhead power lines any more and the anachronism of his indulgence is almost the death of him.

The medicos differ in their opinions regarding the effects of electricity on the system; there are so many variables. Not just the nature of the current, amps to volts, and its intensity, but the point of contact, what you may be wearing, your physical condition, whether you are earthed and even the atmospheric humidity. Some people are hurled clear with a Batman KO punch, others seized to make complete a frightful circuit. There is a natural curiosity about our own afflictions. We become lay experts and augurers in wounds and diseases which we accumulate.

So it is with Slaven and his burns. There is even a support group for it, inclusive enough to accept burns from any source. Slaven finds that the burns are particularly difficult to heal by normal grafting practices. The neurological factors are even more interesting to the experts and Marianne Dunne is kind enough to spend time explaining to Aldous Slaven the modern discoveries of electro-chemical functioning and thus how subtle as well as brutal might be the repercussions of an accident such as his. There is a sympathy in this as well as a sense of mutual professional respect.

Yet Slaven doesn't share the whole of his experience. Even when Kellie makes her first visit to Burwood and tells him when he is still groggy and in the worst of it that she has taken the responsibility of arranging for the power supply to be laid underground at their own expense. A decision made on the analogy of having your Alsatian put down once the malice of its disposition has been revealed by an unprovoked attack. As Kellie goes over the quotes with him, Slaven nods above the cradle of his bandaged hands, but sees in tableau the simple landscape torn asunder as he hangs for that moment from the living wire and the angels of both allegiances chatter their teeth in his face.

'I'm going in to Evan at his office later on today. Don't you worry about a thing,' says Kellie. 'You just concentrate on getting better.' All his life Slaven has considered the visible world a mere dust cover, with the things of significant meaning hidden and there have been occasions when the real world was on the point of revealing itself to him, when through the fatiscence of the conventional guise he caught a glimpse of the true shapes.

'I should have almost the same dexterity as before, they say. Except for the thumb.'

'You're lucky that the left hand is the worst,' says Kellie.

The mountains on the western skyline had erupted to igneous whorls and his hobby sheep made snide comments amongst themselves as he suffered. Columns of the damned marched down to the eternal grave, but with no theatrical repentance. They persisted in their old habits, they scratched their arses, malingered, blamed the government and gossiped second hand of hell. Warrant officer second class Slaven was getting dressed in the foreground. Ties were then more popular than cravats, or nushkas. He held a paisley one draped over his left hand and with his right ran over his cheeks and chin to check his shave as he always did, blowing his cheeks out to increase their tautness. 'Let this be a lesson to you,' he said in the voice of his wife. A half windsor was what he usually tied. On the plains in such breathtaking, electric colours there for an instant and forever, Lucifer and Gabriel drew up their hosts to face each other and waited for Yahweh to arrive. Even in the real world there is some waiting around. Almost in Slaven's own space there was an ocelot which watched him with amber and limpid eyes and Birdy Knowles sat cross-legged with a smile before the hills, his hands on his knees as he leant forward for a better view, as if unaware he had drowned in the Wairau, his head caught in a driftwood fork below the surface and the soles of his feet pale in the moonlight when the searchers found him. *Kinder hearts are waiting still, amongst old friends at Half Moon Bay.*

'Kellie,' says Slaven, 'there's going to have to be changes.'

'Oh, I've worked that out.'

'I mean in my intentions from now on. You know?'

'That too,' says Kellie.

'I'm not talking about the tabloid thing; cheating death, realising each day thereafter is a bonus, something on trust. It's such crap.'

'But you want to come out of yourself more.'

'In a way I suppose — .'

'You want to be in the world more. I've seen it coming.'

'Not influence for any sense of power,' he says, 'but more like involvement. Putting a stake down on things you consider are worth some risk.' Slaven lifts his bandaged hands tenderly in some impatience that he hasn't yet a clear idea of what he wants and why. *All our troubles fall away when we're together at Half Moon Bay.* 'Anyway,' says Slaven vaguely.

'It's the same in a garden,' says Kellie. Slaven is pleased that Kellie looks classy on this visit; well, classy enough for who they are and their age. It is irrelevant and unfair he knows, but how nondescript, flaccid, Montgomery's wife looks when she comes. Her face has the soft creases and the fine hairs of a caterpillar. 'Often some sudden change in environment,' says Kellie, 'an extra wet spring, a prolonged southerly buster, an Indian summer, and the plants undergo a change in nature — profuse flowering when they never have before, or a sudden show of plain, green foliage when they've always been true to variegation before. I had arum lilies once which became tinged with blue after the stubble fires got out of hand and Elizabeth lost a wonderful maple after a hail storm.' Kellie smiles at Montgomery two beds away and at the boy closer to the door who has the dark, Italian hair and eyes she wishes her own son could have inherited. 'Who's that curly boy by the door?' she says.

'Vincent.'

'I meant to tell you that you've lost a patient. Valerie Pratt who had all that orthodontic work because of overcrowding. She hid under the grill of the storm water drain in her street and was drowned in the tunnel when there was a release of effluent by mistake.'

'Good god.' All the work he had done on that girl's teeth so that she'd have a winning smile. Slaven sees exactly young Valerie's teeth and the x-rays of them even more clearly. There had been typical overcrowding with severe displacement of lateral incisors.

Kellie sits companionably and enjoys the anticipation of her first tour of the hospital gardens before going home.

She knows that, like fools, even institutional gardens have their story. The more extensive ones she likes for their comparative possibilities, when you see in three or four plots say, a double dozen varieties of modern roses and establish preferences because of it. 'All that work done on Valerie's smile,' she says, 'and now she'll never captivate anyone with it. Her father is absolutely distraught.' She knows her husband's sorrow is at the loss of his artistry as well as Valerie. She admires Vincent's ear amongst his Italian curls.

'She was learning a poem by Frost for her speech exam and the braces made enunciation difficult. She said "walls" over and over to me, but never got it quite right. You'd better tell Heather not to send out the last account.'

'I have,' says Kellie. 'And I rang Cardew and Sarah last night. They send their love. Sarah was upset and said she'd fly back if she could help. They've had snowstorms where she is outside Prague and she hasn't been able to get a visa to visit Switzerland because of the troubles there. The Tell movement and so on.'

'People have such a small, selfish view.' Slaven isn't listening to his wife's talk of their children. 'I see that now. Their own farting is more impressive to them than thunder at a distance. When my head clears and my hands stop giving me gyppo I'm going to work out how to spend my recuperation time.'

'I'm going to have a look around the grounds as I leave,' says Kellie. Through the window behind his head she can see in the middle distance a bald-headed man in shorts and boots walking towards the lawns and the display of dwarf conifers. His legs are extremely muscular and brown. He seems intent on subduing his energy so that he can keep himself conventionally on the path and not spring into the ether. Maybe he is the gardener.

Kellie puts her hand gently on her husband's bandages as a gesture of affection and farewell.

Camille moaned softly, deep in her throat, and canted her hips for maximum penetration as her old mentor Count Glissor had taught her. 'I never thought it would be so good,' she whispered. Her tanned breasts trembled against the cream satin sheets in the Hotel Lumbar, but on the tiled wall above her head a gecko was a lapis brooch in the glitter of the Singaporean sun. She had been wrong; it was never too hot to do it.

Vincent puts *The Beaver Trade* face down in front of him on the bed and watches Dr Marianne Dunne coming through the ward. Her title is higher in fact, but her burns people always call her doctor. In appearance she is not at all like Camille, though her face is smooth and regular like a pattern within a glass ball. She is short enough to be remarkable for it, but in status is a big doctor in the hospital and a wider authority on burns treatment and therapy. Vincent knows that although she will check the compression dressings on his torso and make jokes with him about the nurses, it is Slaven she enjoys conversation with — and Miles Kitson in one of the private rooms off the corridor at the end of the ward.

'Well, Aldous,' says Marianne Dunne when she has given Vincent, Lloyd Montgomery and dying Norman Proctor their professional due. Yet Vincent does not at once return to the Hotel Lumbar for he wants to listen a while to her. As one whose language is little more than verbal gesticulation, Vincent is impressed when someone is able to give words their due. Dr Dunne has the confidence and ability to demand both attention and the time to articulate words fully, to conjure complete sentences, to give the form of language more than just a passing resemblance to the ideas it expresses.

She is also so short that as she stands by Slaven's bed her head and shoulders are at the sitting height of most other people. 'I gave some further thought to our talk about the persistence of ethnic centred cultures,' she says. She takes his hands in hers as she speaks, but resists the urge to flex his fingers through the bandages: it is too early in the treatment. 'The pundits thought technology offered the chance of a common understanding. A new mode for a new world. The sharemarket indices, computer sheets, semantic graphics, a pervasive language of the media which could make a drink logo recognised in places where the cross wasn't, but that sort of knowledge doesn't seem to hold when the crunch comes. When the USSR collapsed and then the African nations and China, the people went back to their most basic allegiances which were to race and the cultural identifications of race.'

'Perhaps even that's expediency and material success is all we're ever after. Notice how happily polygot a prosperous community can be. They're content to put their cultural priorities on the back-burner when there's a better standard of living to be had that way.' Slaven has an itch at the corner of his eye and as he talks he examines the strange bulk of his hands to find a point that he can scratch with.

'Come through with me and I'll introduce you to Miles Kitson,' says Marianne Dunne. 'You may take a fancy to his cynicism and he needs someone to talk to. I haven't time to be always arguing with him.'

Vincent rejoins Camille, who is able to hold her orgasm for just such a curly haired and dilatory reader, though her lashes flutter on the damask of her cheek with the effort of it and the pink tip of her tongue is compressed between her teeth. 'Nurse McMillan told me that he's a grumpy old sod who doesn't want to meet anyone; that fellow patients in particular depress him,' says Slaven. 'I can understand that. Mediocrity is unbearable when your wits are stretched by suffering. Anyway,' he says, his voice dropping in deference to the old captain of souls, 'isn't he dying?' Like Bushy Marsden in the Technical Gym class, trying to look up Angela Pruit's skirt on the ropes and crushed when she fell on him from that great height. Just before she fell, Angela had seen through the lightwell of the new gym a blaze of yellow gorse on the rough slope above the reservoir cutting.

'You just come on down,' Dr Dunne is saying. 'I think the two of you might make a useful combination. Your brain, such as it is, has been shaken up so much that you need conversation to stop it whirling and Miles has come to love inertia as a bulwark against further loss.' She helps Slaven from the bed. He puts a hand on her far shoulder and she seems tucked under his arm. Yet Dr Dunne is compact and strong, manoevring Slaven easily down the ward and she wears no white coat, but a plain, dark blue dress and her only ostentation apart from intelligence is a very large ruby and diamond ring aflame on her left hand.

'What are you reading?' Slaven asks Vincent as they pass.

'Poetry.'

'Anyone we'd know?' asks Marianne.

'Burns perhaps,' says Slaven.

'Nice one. That's a good one,' she says. Vincent is shy in his ignorance and draws the book to himself. There is a smooth nape to his brown neck where the curls rest that the nurses would not resist if pressed. Dr Dunne considers it a double shame that someone with such perfect skin should be scalded so severely. Slaven now, has the typical leatheriness of his countrymen although he is not outside to any great extent, and he is putting on weight. 'You're putting on weight,' she tells him in the corridor.

'Isn't it a reaction to the accident?'

'Ah well,' she says. 'One thing at a time. Your wife came in to see me after Tuesday's visiting. She was a little disappointed by what she called the evergreen regimentation of the lower garden. Your own treatment regime she endorsed, but she reserved judgement on that of the the succulents and hebes.'

'Kellie's something of a gardener.'

Miles Kitson can hear them outside his private room. Go on past, he thinks, go on past. He dislikes the sound of Slaven's voice, the elements of confidence and goodwill not permitted to enlarge themselves to arrogance. Miles repeats Slaven's comment with a wordless mimicry. At the end of his life he wants no new acquaintances, and even less does he wish for new friends, having grown weary of most of those he has accumulated.

Miles has been ignoring a nagging itch in his anus and composing the next letter to send to Georgina from his bedside computer. It is a recollection of their first meeting at Badmenheim fourteen years before, when he had been on his way back from inspecting a plastic extrusion plant in Dortmund. He had stopped at Badmenheim because a protest to save the Rhine had blocked the road further on and from the second terrace above the old town he watched the protestors attempt also to block the shipping of the river itself. They had a fleet of yellow and black inflatables with outboard motors and they endeavoured to link them together with cables across the broad river.

At the door, where they stop walking, Slaven becomes self-conscious about the familiarity with which he has Marianne Dunne tucked in for support. He lifts his bandaged hands gingerly away and thanks her, while through the angle of the partly opened door he sees Miles for the first time. He's predisposed to dislike him because of the man's exceeding wealth and his exceeding sickness. Science has never convinced us that death isn't contagious. 'I'm sure he'd rather be left in peace,' says Slaven.

'Oh, go on in,' says Marianne Dunne.

'I would. I'd rather be left alone, which isn't the same as being left in peace. That state departed with my health,' says Miles. 'I'm writing to my wife.' They'll come in anyway, he knows. People no longer recognise frankness; they mistake it for humour. He reaches out to the keyboard on his bedside table and with barely a glance at it, types in — meeting at Badmenheim — so he will have at least a starting point when alone again.

'Don't be a nark,' says Dr Dunne. 'I've brought Aldous Slaven who has been burnt too.'

'A pity he isn't twice shy then.'

'I'll stay just a few minutes to catch my breath and be the butt of your humour,' says Slaven. 'Whatever the company the healing process goes on just the same I'm told.' So they begin the talk, first three of them, then the doctor slips away, and Miles also for unfinished business though he leaves a face and moderate contribution to the conversation. It had been windy and the Rhine provided a large enough surface for choppy waves to develop which made it difficult for the protestors to get all their inflatables in a line. The Riesling was not enough in itself to dispel his irritation and he remembers that what annoyed him was not the cause for which the young people disrupted the lives of others, he could agree in principle with that, but the self-conscious, self-righteous zeal with which they worked, calling loudly to each other, gesticulating in their collaboration as if the whole world were watching. Wilde was right enough when he claimed that youth was wasted on the young, for not only do they lack an absolute appreciation of their state, but also a comparative one. In the living experience it is all animalistic arrogance, magnificent though that is and only in retrospect can the spiritual opportunities be somewhat wistfully discerned. As a rich man grown poor, or a winter's man remembering summer, it is having lived the contrasts which makes a true assessment possible.

Slaven begins to explain the state of his burns in answer to Miles Kitson's question.

What Miles hankers for is the oneness of youth; the fusion of body and spirit so that the failure of one is the failure of both and the triumph of either is utter triumph. Five times he had cut across Lockhardt's bull paddock and knew to less than a metre where that great, Minoan head would be when he somersaulted over the fence into the brown top and red clover. He was the only white business-man to fully gain the trust of Mr Ng of Hong Kong. He once shagged three sisters in one night, quite without realising it was the best he would ever do, and as a young businessman he could work to exhaustion, slip off his shoes and sleep on the office floor for an hour or two, then be up for another day at a pace which made his name and his fortune.

But now body and soul have ceased to be natural allies and are kept together only by a fading act of will. He has eleven physical complaints that he can give a name to and four others which he can recognise when pronounced by the doctors as part of his stable as well. Recurrent piles are making his arse itch right now, the burns weep and Slaven's voice comes to him through a whine of tinnitus.

And disorders of the spirit? For these he is reliant more on self-diagnosis, and self-treatment for that matter, though the disabilities which he suffers by them are just as severe and numerous as those imposed on his body. And as with them it is as likely to be one of the minor, irksome things, as any of the more calamitous failings, which causes him regret. Like his aversion to new people. Almost all new faces, new voices, new personalities, disappoint him with their callowness, even before they disappoint him he feels them tiresome, intrusive. Miles no longer has any wish to be viewed.

'You look as if you've had a fairly torrid time yourself,' says Slaven. As the possessor of a leathery skin, Slaven is appalled by the tenuous separation that Miles Kitson has from the world. Not that he is burnt on any visible surface, but his skin is opaque, shiny and forms fine, gladwrap wrinkles when he talks. Some blood vessels are visible as they surface, or dive, twisting spermatozoa of capillaries, larger ones lighter if arterial, or the dark, sluggishness of veins. The rims below his eyes sag forward slightly so that they make a pink underscoring for his gaze and above his ears in the sparse, dry hair are plaques of cradle cap.

'Yes, I'm completely broken down, as you see,' says Miles. His voice is husky as old men's voices tend to be, but there is as well an individual quality — a flat directness which can harden into derision.

'Don't humiliate me, Marianne, by examining my dressings in front of a stranger,' he says when she is back.

'There's no latitude for your self-pity today. Remember that I've brought someone with brains to talk to you. You won't see your wife and you've said you miss your friends.'

'Friends, yes,' says Miles with emphasis. He doesn't have much hope of Aldous, who has a general air of liberal good intent, a wife with the ridiculous name of Kellie and is a dentist. Who could be friends with a dentist for christ's sake. 'So what happened to you?' he asks when Dr Dunne has mechanically raised his pillow and gone.

'I almost electrocuted myself on the power lines while painting the house.'

'For me it was just a jug of water. Everything becomes a threat with age. I'd barely got mobile from heart surgery. There's a message in it I suppose. Marianne said that you've undergone some sort of involuntary revitalisation and have a vision to put the world to rights. Isn't that what they used to do in the funny farms years ago? A bit of the old electro-convulsive therapy. In my time in business I've seen a few candidates for it.' Miles remembers the stiff breeze there had been on the terrace above the Rhine and the yellow and black inflatables pitching as they endeavoured to stay in line. The barges had pushed past with angry exchanges and in the distance, up river, Miles had seen the old Marksburg Castle high above the town of Braubach. 'Have you ever been to Badmenheim?' he says. 'It's in the Palatinate.'

'Kellie and I have been to Munich and Augsburg in the south.'

'They make a fine hock in the old way, above the river on the terraces. I met my present wife there.' She had come back from the road-block, one of several English amongst the international group of protestors and immediately he had felt his cock stiffen. In those days he still received such healthy signs.

'Have we anything in common?' says Slaven. He surprises himself with this new directness which has come to him since his accident. His hands rest on Miles Kitson's bed like two huge cotton buds. 'Not that I don't enjoy a good Riesling,' he says. For the first time Miles feels some interest in him, not an interest that overides his wish to continue with his letter to Georgina, but a stirring nevertheless.

'Well then, Aldous, tell me some belief that you have.' His eyelids fall for a moment on the important word, an involuntary apology to himself for having mentioned it. Much further back than Badmenheim was the New Year's Eve in Bosnia's old city, with the special intensity of celebration which befitted both a new century and a new millenium. There were strobe lights, sirens, guns, fireworks flared against the snow and afterwards the relayed T.V. speech from the President which Miles had been unable to hear because of the marching bands and sky-larking in the streets. He had been forty-six years old, with thick, elastic skin that held his body in, and already rich.

'We are alone,' says Slaven.

'Yes, good.'

'So all the more important to have some links with others in an external life,' Slaven continues. Miles turns down his lip in disappointment and the lids blink over his slate eyes again.

'And?' he says.

'Since I've been in here I can't get politics out of my mind. Well, not politics so much in the sense of government as in the means of empowering communal will. A sort of pre-government consensus.'

'Tell me about it then,' says Miles. Well, it is one way to pass the time. His dying is so slow that it is almost a life of sorts. He leans over and turns off his screen, but with Badmenheim in the memory there and in his own: that exact chop on the Rhine splashing on the inflatables so that their surfaces of black and yellow are seen to gleam at a distance, other protestors coming back from the road-blocks, talking mainly in German and French, and the proprietor advising Miles that it is better to wait longer until the glut of vehicles has sorted itself out. Georgina's dark hair in cusps and her low-waisted denims. Maybe he will die thinking of Badmenheim where he first met her and with this dentist somewhat self-consciously laying out a humdrum metaphysic which is special to him because it has the scent of burning. The owl here is often calling names.

Norman Proctor has died before we have come round to telling his story. Let's just say that he had a good match temperament did Proctor. It used to be a treat to see him cope with the pressure at provincial, even national, tournaments. Oh yes, it's easy advice to treat each ball on its merits irrespective of the state of the game, but Proctor actually managed to do so on occasions which seemed important at the time. Had we started at the bed furthest from the door there would have been more of him and less of Montgomery and young Vincent I dare say.

Norman Proctor was dying anyway, but Kellie was the occasion of it, if not the cause, as the scholars say. Norman had very little movement and no woman. He had no enjoyment from watching Montgomery's wife when she came to call, but he admired Kellie's energy and sense of purpose. He made a considerable effort to watch Kellie inspecting the gladioli she had placed on his table the day before. Kellie's shoulder was brown and well muscled by gardening. Unfortunately the strain brought on a cramp in Proctor's neck and he suffocated in silence there as Kellie talked to

Vincent of the Mount Cook lily she had seen below the Hooker Glacier.

It is a Thursday, with a heat cloud pressing down on the city. The first trees and buildings from the hospital windows can be seen and then the white-grey uniformity of cloud like a well used sheet. The nurses wheel Proctor's bed into the corridor and close the swing doors to the small ward so that the others don't have to see Proctor being tidied away. For some reason there is a good deal of birdsong on such a day and in his room Miles can hear the throaty whistles of the thrushes as well as the voices of the nurses outside his door.

'And I've just spent an age changing the dressings,' says Elaine.

'Ssh. Mr Kitson will hear you,' whispers Jan. What happens to such an instant, Miles wonders, what record is there of the momentary coincidence of all the elements that are there. Proctor cooling in his transported bed, Elaine and Jan on the shift together only because Nicola is to be a bridesmaid in Dargaville, the white gladioli stems with five buds still to open, the slight vibrato whistle of the birds in the heat mist underscored for Miles alone from the faint orchestra pit of his tinnitus. Often after such a day there comes in the evening a welcome drizzle which drifts and trembles in the failing light without ever leaving any trace of itself as rain.

Miles presses a key and begins to dictate the corporate structure that he wants for his new business in Indonesia. He wishes to carry his Board on the principle that stand alone financial accountability is the best yardstick for measuring executive potential. Also he wants to be doing something unless the owl decides that it might be as well to take him while in the neighbourhood.

The orderly has arrived and Proctor is transferred to a trolley which squeaks cheerfully away down the corridor. 'Leave it to me, darling,' the orderly says. It won't hurt to follow him just a little, not to depress ourselves with the aftermath of Proctor's death, but rather see the misted grounds outside the corridor he travels. The corridor is long and narrow with many uniform windows on both sides, rather like a gutted railway carriage, and links ward seven with the main block. On the orderly's left — Proctor's too if you wish to be reminded — there are the dwarf conifers in the quartz pebble garden and on the right mainly *Scoliopius bigelovii* and ranunculus, which Kellie would tell us are prone to fungal blight after just such days as this. In the branches of a sycamore, just out of sight in the warm, gathering mist, is a canary which escaped from Mrs Wicks when she was cleaning the cage an hour ago. It adds nothing to the songs that Miles hears and Proctor is still relaxed enough about his death for his chin to quiver whenever the trolley jars over the joins in the flooring, almost as if he is attempting to join the orderly in 'a line or two of the Hoihos' hit of the moment — *Sure, all our friends are waiting in good old Half Moon Bay.*

Kellie is walking back to her car through the mist. Slaven goes in to see Miles. 'Fancy that,' he says. 'Kellie had just been arranging the flowers on his table and the next thing he was gone.' Jan stays a while in the ward to talk to Vincent and Mr Montgomery. Off-stage Mrs Wicks is weeping, because somewhere marooned in all the soft, massed vapour moving in from the sea, is her poor canary.

'Kellie came in before she left,' says Miles hoarsely.

'She finds you particularly interesting because of your money.'

'Is that it.'

'That's not quite how I meant it. To be fair, she hasn't any envious, or trivial, motive. It's psychological effects she finds fascinating; how it might influence a personality, a view of the world.'

'It means I don't have to be so accommodating, rather as some of those who have nothing decide they won't flatter, or appease anyone. At the two ends of the scale you see that, while the bulk of people are in between, oh, so very conscious of what and who can be to their advantage. To retain a conviction of freedom you should have nothing to lose, or so much that you don't believe it could ever happen.'

'That's what she senses, I think,' says Slaven.

'She brought me in two arum lilies and laughed when I said they had the stench of the funeral parlour. She said they weren't true lilies at all. I never knew that.' The two lily stems are on the bedside table, their great fluted, sari flowers more arrogantly white than anything the hospital itself can provide, their yellow, parrot tongues upraised and the scent indeed crass and heavy.

Miles Kitson begins to revise his opinion of Slaven. He has begun to look forward to their talks and not just because there are so few he would choose for company within the hospital. Almost anyone would come in at his request. He realises that he is seeing a man in the process of metamorphosis, a change of priority and intention, although Slaven's commonplace exterior remains just the same. Well, almost the same. More and more there are times when his long, dentist's face loses its expression of habitual professional caution, becoming animated with the intensity of new ideas. There are times also when Miles is aware of a greenish haze, an emanation, around his friend's head, incongruous as a background to Slaven's black, pig-bristle hair, as you recall. Miles can't decide if this is some illusion arising from his own illness, an aura, or the lingering consequence of all that electricity suddenly surging through Slaven's middle-aged brain cells. 'When do you go home?' he asks him.

'Within a week I think. Dr Dunne said that I would have to keep on making out-patient visits for a while of course, but there's no need for me to be taking up a bed here for much longer.'

'I'm going myself soon, at least for a time. You won't be able to return to your practice though. Not with your hands.'

'No. I'll have an enforced lay-off for some time I suppose.' The old Slaven would have been very concerned about that; not just for selfish reasons, but from a reluctance to let down the many people he regularly cared for. But now there is a new willingness to let go of some responsibilities and so allow other opportunities to come within his grasp. 'I want to find out a lot more about people.'

'You want to save them, perhaps,' says Miles gravely and his eyelids fall closed in his delight at Slaven's ingenuous ambition.

'Come off it. What I think is that we've got to revitalise social action, have some concept of ourselves that's clear enough for us to charge the politicians with its accomplishment. We spend far too much time proving to each other that the process is tainted, rather than ensuring that the aim is pure.'

'So this is what you're going to tell people?'

'Government is just a process, not an end,' says Slaven. It is in time to become the first Slavenism.

'I like it,' says Miles. It isn't quite worthy of the energy to laugh aloud, but his breath comes more quickly and commensurate with that the scent of Kellie's arum lilies more strongly, so that for a moment he feels unpleasantly overpowered. 'Do you mind if I rest for a while now?' he asks Slaven and as his fellow patient is at the door, 'Is it still foggy? Is it raining?'

Through the window behind the bed, Slaven watches the mist unwind and stretch in the hospital gardens. Some billows are thicker than others so that there are sudden scene changes, the grey forms of trees and buildings standing out for a moment and then so utterly erased. Where is the sycamore and the canary within it? Where in this drifting fiction, has the trolley borne our Proctor away?

When Slaven goes, Miles cannot sleep. Instead he activates his computer and begins a letter to Georgina — 'Aldous Slaven, the dentist, has decided to save the country.'

Aldous Slaven arrives home from Burwood Hospital quite ready to be a new man in respect of social involvement, but he's at something of a loss as to how to begin. He considers this as he steadies the new, wooden ladder with his left hip and elbow and Kellie putties and primes on the barge board where the power lines had been attached to the house — before the accident and before she had called in the private contractor.

'Be careful down there,' Kellie calls. Slaven feels guilty that he hasn't expressed the same concern for her, even though his hands are still paws because of the bandages.

'You're the one to watch out,' he says.

'I'm fine,' and so she is; effortlessly assuming all the extra responsibility since his accident as a simple extension of the planning skills she demonstrates in her garden and home.

'Lions perhaps, or Rotary, or Ozone Bak,' he says. 'Some active service organisation for a start. Then again, a more obviously political organisation, do you think?' They have many acquaintances, but the links are social; chances to relax, gossip, sublimate the tensions of maintaining a professional income and image. To do more than talk in passing of any issue unconnected with immediate self-interest is considered a bore.

'Or Astley School Board of Trustees, even your own professional organisation,' says Kellie. If Slaven looks up he can see the pale, ribbed soles of his wife's sneakers nine rungs above, if he looks down he can see the camellia and lemon bottlebrush which he damaged ten weeks before. Nowhere on the soil, the plants, is there any trace of the bright blue paint he was using. The garden is quiet, subdued and orderly in all its detail. He isn't high enough to see the hills to the west, or his sheep beyond the garden, but if he breathes in deeply there is a catch of some awful smell which was part of his ordeal.

'See the kelp and crayfish pots, beneath the rocks of Half Moon Bay,' murmurs Slaven.

'What's that?' Kellie doesn't look down. There is one splash of bright paint on the brickwork close to the ground. Now that he sees it, how could he not have noticed it before. His hands itch at such times. He hears a voice much like Birdy Knowles's, muffled now though by a more resistant present.

'Just singing,' he says.

'What? I remember now there was one call asking you to speak.'

'Really?'

'It was from the Civil Defence Officer, Ayesbury. I didn't really see how you being almost electrocuted was a disaster on that sort of scale, but I took his number for you on the hall pad.'

'Perhaps they want my views on how it feels to be a victim. The psychological aftermath that they'd have to deal with, but on a scale of thousands.'

'Maybe.'

When Slaven rings, the Civil Defence Officer is happy to

go along with this. He's committed to an evening seminar on the nineteenth and has been let down by a meteorological spokeswoman, then the Hospice Superintendent, his second choice, was called to a conference on economy euthanasia. So Ayesbury rather clutches at Slaven, who is a professional man at least and has time on his hands because he is unable to employ them for much else. Ayesbury had intended that Slaven talk about precautionary dental care, but victim psychology will do.

'Think of the management skills required,' he says in his introduction of Slaven at the seminar. 'Imagine the state of mind of a thousand earthquake survivors and we're asking them to line up quietly and then fill in an identification report which has twenty-three questions.'

Although it is only eight pm and daylight saving is in force, the Civil Defence Headquarters are lit by recessed bulbs, for they occupy what·was once the basement of a bank, protected there from fire and tsunami impact. The rent is also lower. Slaven can see lines of videophones and radio telephones in the communications room through a glass divide and the compact Controller's room all set to go, with its message pads and CD plan on the desk.

In the largest room, where they gather, the walls are covered with display screens, maps and flow charts. An operations room, says Ayesbury, from which he and his volunteers constantly practise the salvation of a city which largely ignores them.

Slaven has been a small part of that disregard, but as he stands up to address the twenty-three people in the bunker-like operations room, he feels a curious warmth towards them. They are here on a summer's evening, having put aside other duties, pleasure even, to come to a Civil Defence seminar. Slaven spreads his legs slightly to ensure a good footing, as he often does when about to begin a challenging piece of orthodontic surgery. Now for the first time he will put to the test his new compulsion to promote a cause, to influence others. He feels his hands begin to tingle, reclothed in skin and muscle from his thighs. He has nothing to say regarding the maintenance of dental health, or the management of disaster victim psychology.

He realises that despite his notes he never intended to follow them.

He begins with the irrevocable sense of isolation he assumes all to feel and the great act of will necessary if it is to be sufficiently controlled to allow a sense of community. He goes on to talk of personal and social conscience, the need for policies which cater not just for physical and material needs, but for the hungers of the spirit. Hungers for moral certainty, for the validation of love, for less parsimony in an experience of life and less secrecy in death. He speaks of his new faith that beyond the cumulative, sporadic, stultifying assemblage of experience which is life there is a secular redemption possible through empathy and co-operation.

'In the hospital,' says Slaven, 'I had moments of vision. Should I be ashamed to admit that? Ashamed of my convictions because I can't account for their origin?' Before him some of the small audience make unconscious movements of support. 'I was still fried I suppose.' Some laugh, uneasily. 'The best civil defence it seems to me is civil action, restoring the deliberative power to the people and insisting on a spiritual dimension in politics as in life. No citizen is dispensible. The most sustaining idea we have, surely, is that collectivism will work, and the most enduring fear that we have no part in the direction of our lives.'

Slaven has mulled over his ideas lying in his hospital bed at night and expressed them in conversational fragments to Marianne Dunne, to Miles Kitson and to Kellie, but he is himself amazed at the fluency which has come to him. He hears his voice ring in the operations room and feels himself the focus of the twenty-three people gathered there. He can stand a little apart from himself, regulate his breathing, calculate the ongoing performance and make the fine tuning adjustments, yet all the time a convert anew to the power of his own message.

He has tapped a new man within himself — born from the fire perhaps.

This first time, Slaven retains something of caution. He pauses only twenty minutes after he has agreed to finish. The applause is sudden and fierce, some of the audience almost embarrassed by the intensity of their reaction. They will be unable to account for it by any reiteration of Slaven's speech that they can manage. In the midst of the clapping a male voice cries, 'Yes, a message at last,' and Ayesbury's thanks are disregarded in the press and chatter. A red-headed woman takes the opportunity to seize Slaven's arm.

'How wonderful,' she says, 'to hear someone talk openly of practical Christianity again.' She is in middle-age, attractive in a horsey way: all nose and blunt, sound teeth. Her name tag identifies her as Marjorie Usser, Red Cross. 'In particular I commend your emphasis on gender equity,' Marjorie says, another aspect of his speech of which Slaven has been unaware. Several other people are grouped here, smiling, nodding in agreement with Marjorie's congratulations. One tall, diffident man has a half-smile of entreaty and a tear, surely, glistening at the bottom of his left cheek.

'Good one,' he says and all the while his entreating eyes meet Slaven's to say, you and I know, don't we, you and I know the workings of the bloody world.

Slaven feels a sharp gratification that he has moved them, but even with Marjorie Usser's hand on his arm and in the gaze of other admirers, his eyes slide away for an instant in defence against the unspoken, yet insistent, emotional demand. By the door, looking uncertain whether to join the queue for coffee, approach Slaven, or leave altogether, is a bald-headed man in shorts and tramping boots. Maybe he is a CD volunteer on stand-by, thinks Slaven. He wears a tartan shirt with the sleeves rolled up on his brown arms and the muscles on his legs would satisfy any life drawing class. On the wall behind is a dark glass square which can be activated to display a map of the city in any one of four modes — location of diesel and petrol stores, hospital services and GP clinics, supermarkets and grocery warehouses, warden posts and CD zone divisions.

'You must, must talk to us at the Red Cross,' says Marjorie. Her upper lip has the soft, pink fullness some horses' lips have and it is finely lined.

'Yes, yes.' It is the man with the tears on his cheek, wishing to register vehement concurrence without being sure of its object. At a distance Ayesbury raises and lowers a coffee mug as a sign to Slaven. A solid, plastic mug best suited to withstand the holocaust. Marjorie takes her hand from Slaven's arm.

'I mustn't take all your attention. But heavens, what ideas, and the time is right for them,' she says with a departing squeeze. Slaven, watching her go, sees also that there is no one standing at the door, just the dark glass of the map screen reflecting the lights of the operations room.

'Some of them took to it greatly. Very well done, but not quite what I expected.' Ayesbury's voice has a tinge of envy which adds to the sincerity. Slaven remembers those nights when he lay prone and his mind was prone also, to race unpleasantly. He would lie in the darkness looking towards the corridor light and hear Norman Proctor sighing with each breath, a sound of hopeless submission. How Slaven's burns had tormented him when the drugs were wearing off in the night and also strange, new imperatives which took possession and began to plan the rest of his life.

'Of course in Civil Defence it's not so much the theory of things that matters,' says Ayesbury. 'Logistics, communications, accurate assessment, decision making and deployment of personnel, they're really the concern when the crunch comes. What has happened and what can be done about it. Why isn't a priority when the shit hits the fan.'

'You're a counter-puncher.'

'Exactly. Good to get all the background settled beforehand though. There's no doubt about that. Last time I had along a missionary from Bangladesh who talked of the floods there and the different attitudes to disaster according to religion. She went down very well too, very well.'

'Of course I'm not talking about religion,' says Slaven.

'No?' says Ayesbury.

Slaven tells Kellie about it afterwards, not the Bangladesh business, but his own talk and its reception. The tall man's tears, the cheers, Ayesbury's envy and acknowledgement as a professional motivator. 'That's great,' she says.

'I moved them, Kellie.'

'I wish I'd been there,' she says. 'Did you get a fee?'

'No.'

'I think you should for other times. Everything needs to be on a business-like footing and then you can judge people's real feelings. To pay for something is to acknowledge its value.'

'But the two are distinct aren't they. The money and the value. What you say may be true, but still the two things don't equate.'

'That's a different point,' says Kellie.

They talk inside and the garden is hidden by walls and the night, but they know it so well that they see it still, the colours and shapes, perspectives and fragrances, those plants in health and those which Kellie has been ministering to with special care. Talk of the garden is never really an interruption in any conversation with Kellie and Slaven has become used to that. 'I'm thinking of extending the west bed somewhat, with a plot for tulips and a site built up for japonicas at the back. The lovely dark variety especially, rosacea.'

'Ah,' says Slaven, as if his own teeth have been probed and a weakness found. Slaven likes plants. He admires both the garden and his wife's ability as its creator, but there has been that one last spot looking westward from the patio from which a more primitive landscape could be seen. A strainer post at a distance on which his sheep can rub themselves, a grey trough amidst the clover and grass with a bright stain from the crack on its side, and further back three cabbage trees.

'You like japonica,' says Kellie.

'So I do.' Yet they might cost him his view of the strainer post and the leaking trough.

'And next?' says Kellie.

'Next?'

'What organisation are you going to approach?'

'I've no idea, but I feel a need to keep on with it. A need not just in me, but out there; a need out there. Tonight's shown that, even with only twenty-three people. I can see that I won't be at ease with myself until I've tried to give leadership and direction in the way which has become clear to me since the accident. Does that sound pompous? I'm not clear on what it all means yet. Perhaps it will be just for the time until my hands have healed and I can go back to the surgery.'

'A mission,' says Kellie matter of factly. 'You've found a mission, I'd say.'

There is a place, as you well know, quite close to the Beckley-Waite Institute in Wellington, but a private home, flats in fact with the Yees in the front one, the McGoverns in the back and Walter Tamahana in the bed-sit. The Yees have been out since the Democratic Reconstruction over thirty years ago, but have broken with precedent by not working the pants off their new countrymen and becoming rich. Instead Victor Yee tutors part-time in Cantonese at the Polytechnic, stoically looks after his wife who is a severe asthmatic and has the passing joy of a fortnightly visit to the brothel above the Tahitian tattooist. Very late and very often in the intervening nights he opens his window and plays his clarinet with exemplary skill while looking at the dark mass of Beckley-Waite. He does not, you will notice, spend a great deal of time rejoicing in his adopted country. Will he ever get to hear the dentist from Christchurch do you think?

Following the Civil Defence seminar Slaven has three calls. Ayesbury rings to thank him again and give him the address of the missionary from Bangladesh. Marjorie Usser proves that her enthusiasm hasn't abated and the entreaty man, whose surroundings on the vidphone appear surprisingly opulent, claims that at last he has a clear purpose in life. He says also that he has taken the liberty of mentioning Slaven's gift to a friend — the Rev Thackeray Thomas.

Enter then, Thackeray Thomas, when the first autumn winds whirl old leaves and seed heads and husks of insects into Slaven's double garage. He is sweeping it out clumsily because of his maimed hands, when Kellie comes in and tells him that a Thackeray Thomas from the Charismatic Cambrian Church has rung to see if he may come out and talk. Kellie says that the Rev Thomas has been struck by reports of Slaven's comments at the seminar and would appreciate the opportunity to meet him. 'Have you ever heard of the Charismatic Cambrian Church?' asks Slaven.

'Never heard of it. But he speaks well.'

Thackeray Thomas brings his two sons when he comes to visit: fat, freshly scrubbed young men who are determined to gain the power of rhetoric. 'Pay no attention to them,' says Thackeray after the introductions. 'They're here to learn.' So the sons sit with Slaven and their father in the autumn sun and listen to this conversation of their elders and betters — occasionally twitching their mouths as they silently practise some orotund sentence of their father's, or understatement from their host.

Thackeray Thomas is a man of average height who appears taller because of his bearing, the large Brythonic head, but most of all a voice which he wields as excalibur. New Zealanders remain suspicious of any pride, or skill, in words, but Thomas claims a heritage beyond his five generations locally — descent from the great Meyricks of Bodorgan who fought for Henry VII at Bosworth under the Red Dragon standard of Cadwaladr, and were rewarded for it.

'Positively we are a social church rather than an institutional one you see,' says Thackeray. 'The ideas which you have and which you express so succinctly are precisely those which our church and the Cambrian membership have been working towards in the development of our outreach policy.'

'I don't think of my ideas as being religious and certainly not denominational. In fact it's a sense of downing the barriers and classifications of all sorts that most interests me, the fellowship and unity of those people without any great power base of their own. I've never been much of a joiner. My profession has supplied almost everything for me as of right, but now I have this urge to attempt something on a public scale.'

'I'm not suggesting that you become one of us, that you have any obligation to adopt a religious stance, just that you might find it helpful to accept some assistance in support of your ideas. We have a community programme which operates nationally for example, and which tries to respond to the needs people have instead of being just a recruiting agency for a political party, or sectional interest group.'

'All I know at present,' says Slaven, 'is that I have a compulsion to speak out. I'm bursting with it and I don't understand why. Maybe it's some sort of folly that I'll regret.'

'Do you know Tuamarina?'

'By Blenheim isn't it.'

'We're planning a regeneration rally there in the winter. Us in conjunction with the Women's League and local rural fellowship organisations. I have close ties with both Maori and Pakeha in the area. Come and speak at Tuamarina — a wider audience for your ideas. We get hundreds of people often and they're just the ones you care most about I'd say. We think Tuamarina is appropriate for an ethnically inclusive meeting because of its history.'

The young Thomases sit patiently against the house side of the patio and their lips move as their father discusses with Slaven the forthcoming Tuamarina rally, but moving at this time not in a silent rhetorical preparation, but because they enjoy the fruit loaf which Kellie has put before them. They have heavy, luxuriant hair hanging very straight and Kellie finds that their names are Iago and Dafydd. The names are so correct that Kellie can't resist asking the Rev Thomas why his own Christian name sounds not at all Celtic. 'There's Anglo-Saxon in the family,' he says in a tone which shows that such honesty is painful.

Kellie asks him also what he finds in Slaven's views which he thinks should be brought to a wider audience. 'Fellow feeling, collectivism,' says Thackeray. 'An emphasis on the spiritual dimension in everyday matters. People can't understand the social and political systems any more. They feel angry and threatened and disappointed because of their own ignorance and powerlessness. Most have no way of expressing what's gone wrong, no concept of what can be done to correct things, so they fall back on isolation and selfishness, dog eat dog. But Aldous has the gift, you see. He's been chosen to speak on the behalf of others. It's a wonderful thing that.'

'I've only done it once, just to twenty-three people,' says Slaven.

'It's plain to see though. Most of those people are talking about it all the time. I've developed a skill for public speaking,

I'm known for it, but you have the gift you see. Quite different. You'll always be admired now, or hated, because people won't be able to ignore what you say.'

'Sounds as if it could be an albatross,' says Kellie.

'A phoenix, Mrs Slaven,' says Thackeray. 'Risen out of the arcing fire; the lightning.'

'The gift is it,' say Iago and Dafydd in unison as their only contribution.

See Kellie's garden spread around them, the sere birch leaves rattling a little on the paving alongside the patio, the anxious sound of the Hammond boy's remote control model plane from the next four hectare block, the tension creases on the trousers of Iago and Dafydd as they sit politely. Here is the trough to be glimpsed beyond the flowers and shrubs. It has that bright show of green moss and algae at the leak. And on the breeze which rattles the leaves comes the oil-wool-dry shit smell of the hobby Romneys which can be heard cropping grass close to the fence. In the close texture of such boredom surely nothing of significance can be said, or planned. Victor Yee prepares a meal in the front flat with no sense of release, Miles, who has forbidden Georgina to visit him, watches on video while she strips, Norman Proctor's memorial plaque at the Avon Crematorium dazzles the custodian with reflected sun.

'You realise that it's political action rather than any religious conversion that I'm interested in,' says Slaven.

'You want your aims to be spiritually and socially regenerative though. Isn't that so?' replies Thackeray.

'And I don't want to work within any particular party; certainly not yet. Just give people the opportunity to endorse a few basic principles, just give me the chance to gauge the opinions of ordinary people.'

'For that you'll find Tuamarina the ideal place,' says Thackeray.

'Is there provision for a fee?' says Kellie. 'Aldous has very little coming from the partnership while he can't work you know.' The minister spreads his fingers palm uppermost as if to make clear that he hasn't any golden handshake.

'Expenses though of course,' he says.

Kellie decides for the future that if indeed Slaven has

the gift then it will not necessarily be passed on as such. She leaves her husband and Thackeray talking, and the Thomas sons, adult, but not yet come into their intellectual inheritance. These two rise in courtesy as she goes. Kellie imagines them late at night, roaming the beaches and parks while they practise their rhetorical skills and await their chance. Will the Charismatic Cambrian Church, the country even, be big enough for two of them when Thackeray has given up? Will they be new Lloyd Georges from the glass caves of the other side of the world? Do they harangue the possum, rat and morepork with wondrous eloquence despite the pebbles beneath their tongues?

Thackeray and Slaven find that they can be straight with each other. There is in both a bedrock intelligence and good intention as a link despite the slightly gothic aspects of the Rev Thomas's personality and the reverse in Slaven's.

'I see you as the keynote speaker at Tuamarina,' says Thackeray, despite this role normally being his own. He is pleased with his insight in regard to Slaven's significance and he takes an innocent pleasure in the comfort of Kellie and Slaven's home, with its basking garden of colour and the hobby paddocks as a further privacy around it. He has no great wealth and possession and doesn't direct his talent in that way, but it sometimes occurs to him that there may be Meyrick estates in Penrhyn which are owed to him perhaps. 'Are you the gardener?' he asks Slaven.

'My wife.'

'What a talent she has. My own wife now, she's an equestrian. Dressage is the thing with her and I suppose that's rather like being a gardener in a way. A sense of fitness, order, the contained display of nature. My own personality is rather archaic to a degree, tempestuous even, but you can't deny your race. You're not Celtic are you?'

'More English and Dane.'

'It's of no consequence,' says Thackeray, 'but I do hope you'll come to Tuamarina in June. We're taking a risk in the weather, but the seventeenth of June was when the fight took place there — the massacre as it was once known. It's fitting in that way you see and our organisation is quite strong in the countryside there.'

'**I** rang Adelle and found out a bit about him,' says Kellie. 'Adelle's into religion and influential figures and so on. She says the Cambrian Church is one of the big things now throughout the country, but they believe more in regional autonomy and grassroots help than a high national profile. She says Thackeray Thomas even goes overseas to speak by invitation.'

'Well then, it seems reasonable to appear at Tuamarina. It's not as if we're joining up and it provides a ready made platform, a means of access to the people.'

It is late evening now and the colours of their garden are fading as the light goes. Bright, self-advertisements of distinctiveness are replaced by washes of shadow, blue and grey. Hedgehogs begin snuffling amongst the pea-straw that Kellie has laid beneath the shrubs, moths swerve clumsily towards the windows behind the patio where Kellie and Slaven have come out again. Kellie has a cardigan over her shoulders and as she sits surrounded by all the common-place reassurance of her home, she stifles any fears of where Slaven's new life will take them and how it will end. 'What does it feel like?' she says.

'Feel like?'

'To have yourself turned upside down, yet still look just the same. We're heading off god knows where, with scarcely a remark about it. I imagined more emotion, long discussion, declarations of commitment and intent. Instead it's just happening isn't it.'

Slaven makes a quick grimace in the dusk. He opens his mouth to make the impossible explanations to his wife. Even as he talks he is confounded by the realisation that the more urgently he is driven to influence other people, the more aware he becomes of an unspeakable and final isolation. There is no necessary sense to it, but consequences will be no less for that. Something has been burnt out of him, perhaps, or something exposed. *All our troubles fall away, when we're together at Half Moon Bay.*

It is cold and still when Slaven and Miles drive from Blenheim to Tuamarina on the Picton road. The grass is bowed down with the melt water of the night's frost and where any stock have disturbed it their tracks are clear within the milky paddocks. At the Tuamarina turn-off there is little visible to encourage cars to stop: a lay-by, the cheese factory and primary school beyond the railway line, the small cemetery on the summit of the first, abrupt hill which overlooks the plain. The new prosperity of boutique vineyards and lifestyle organic horticulture has passed by this part of the Wairau. The trees are motionless and from a weatherboard farmhouse a trail of chimney smoke gradually topples to one side. Two border collies bark them past, the heads jerking at each release of the sound. The sky of the grey winter morning presses over everything like a shark's belly.

Slaven carefully negotiates the few, steep bends of the cemetery hill, the granite and concrete of the graves repeating the colour of the sky. At the summit, behind the patch of graves there, a park has been bulldozed out on the ridge which runs back to the gathering hills. No one else has arrived, but some preparations stand from the day before. A line of yellow portaloos has been set behind a green canvas screen and flexible pipes from them snake down the hill to a large tanker parked on the flat. There are stacks of chairs to be set out for invited guests and the infirm. The dew covers the tubular backs with droplets and has pooled in the top seat of each pile. Angel Hire, is stamped on each backrest. There is one strung banner to identify the day's event, its vinyl background lighter than the morning sky and the blue lettering saying Praise The Lord. A cheerful, defiant banner, even if one end is held up by a manuka pole and the other attached to the eucalypt tree which grows over the grave of those Europeans killed in the skirmish with the Maori in 1843.

It is all so ordinary, so do-it-yourself, so low-key New Zealand. 'Perfect,' whispers Miles from the car. For him it is the best moment of the whole occasion. He doesn't want anyone else to come, doesn't care if no one speaks, if no issues are raised, or resolved. He doesn't want people gradually obscuring his view with their earnest, solid bodies and the equally solid belief in their own importance. The secret pride of New Zealanders is to be alone in their landscape. Miles wants to see the sooty fantail on the loo screen, the stacks of Angel Hire chairs amongst the grass drenched with the winter dew, the side-road bearing west to Waikakaho, the Wairau River in the middle distance and its plain, the modest monument to what in less sensitive times had been termed the Massacre, its concrete almost friable with age, and behind both Slaven and himself the hills in a jumble mounting higher; gorse, scrub and regrowth at first, but then the dark, true bush. And a banner in white and blue — Praise The Lord. Miles gives a shiver of joy. 'Perfect,' he says again. There are a few more recent graves, low plaques in contrast to the memorials of a more religious age. He could rest in such a place.

'What about the acoustics?' asks Slaven. 'You know, I've no idea how loud I should be for an outdoors group. I'll go further back a bit and you tell me how it sounds.' He walks up the hill another twenty or thirty metres. 'Thank you all for making the effort to join with us today. How's that for carry?' Miles has the car door open; his head lies back on the rest, but he lifts one hand in a gesture which reassures Slaven that his voice is fine for carry.

Two vehicles come up the track while Slaven tests his voice, one a truck so old that it still has two-way glass and Miles and Slaven can see the workman driving it. He has a green jersey with honest holes and he walks up to Slaven when the truck is parked. 'How many do you think I should put out?' he says.

'Chairs?'

'Yes. How many do you expect?'

'I'm not sure.' Slaven has taken no part in the practical arrangements.

'There's one hundred. The Rev Thomas says they're for old people and so on. I'll set them all out and we'll know where we are. Les Croad's the name.'

During the introduction four people come from the car which followed Croad's truck and stand at a sufficient distance to give the impression that they are outside the conversation, but in line for attention. Two men and two women. Slaven recognises only one, the entreaty man from the Civil Defence seminar. He smiles and endeavours to catch Slaven's eye as Croad moves away to do his thing with the chairs. 'I've brought some business friends to hear you,' says the entreaty man and he introduces them. Let's see the second woman that Slaven shakes hands with, for she draws interest by kicking her feet to shake the water drops from her suede boots. Her face has the soft shine of a complexion nurtured with the very best of creams and she tutors in the textile arts, does good by stealth, yet can never forget the mischance which led her husband to land in the boiler funnel of Grudgling Alloys while free-falling over Rolleston. The quiet words she uses are overlaid by the noise of Croad swearing and using his boots to separate the chairs, yet from his distance Miles, who has not been introduced to either, imagines how a slap on her round and naked arse would ring across the cemetery. In the east the grey of the morning sky has a dull glow from the sun behind it and in the first breeze of the day the banner puffs its chest for a moment, then is still again. From their vantage point on the hill, all can see small groups of vehicles turning off onto the narrow road to the memorial. The entreaty man tells Slaven that they won't intrude anymore, on impulse steps closer to clasp his arm.

'Good luck. Good fortune for the message,' he says urgently, before turning away with his eyes down once more. Slaven is flattered, but also disconcerted by the barely suppressed warmth, the heightened expectation, the distance they have come. What has he to give that merits such hope.

The Rev Thackeray Thomas arrives with his two sons; such splendid fat cheeks. With Thomas are three elders of the Ngati Toa who have come to lift the tapu on the site before any Pakeha speak. Thackeray Thomas seems as fluent in Maori as the elders and given half a chance will no doubt lift the tapu himself. It is an irony bitterly evident to him that he speaks virtually no Welsh despite his lineage. A Thomas related to the great Meyricks and he speaks only the two New Zealand languages.

Eleven o'clock and there are about two hundred people; some wandering over the site, some still at their cars in the school grounds below the hill. A few have claimed chairs, one or two are already slipping behind the screen to the portaloos. Thackeray Thomas shouts loudly that he wants to invite Paul Hurinui to make a start with the meeting, but people dislike to be called to order and so give their attention rather to a group of horse riders who come trotting up the track like a detachment of Boer guerrillas. Thomas walks down to welcome them, but finds that they have mistaken the Tuamarina gathering for the assembly point of the gay riders' safari to Nelson. Despite the Rev Thomas's charity in inviting them to stay, the riders don't want to miss the start of their trek. Several of the audience recall noticing riders heading towards Waikakaho and so the gay guerrillas move off again, some of the horses farting with the jolting of the slope. Despite the motive for the Tuamarina meeting and the example of Thackeray Thomas, not all those who remain are able to show toleration. Les Croad, resting by his truck, shouts that it's a good riddance.

Miles has been sleeping in the warmth of the car. The small excitement of the gays on horseback wakes him. It takes time for him to orientate himself, at first imagining that he is in old Otago. When the truth comes to him he is sad not to be accompanying the riders. Two or three days on a bridle-track across the Richmond Range to Nelson; the lower ridge-lines of scrub, the spongy trails through the valley bush which meets overhead and folds in sounds of the wood pigeon and bellbird.

There are other places you must know. Past the street of car yards — bunting and flags strain in the wind's gaiety, you didn't know that the purchase of a vehicle is so much a carnival, pink, green, yellow, red and blue, the pennon strings lead up to the central maypole. Then a side road and a place with a reduced showroom at the front to display the kitset furniture made at the back. It's close to the reclaimed harbour land, zoned light industrial, and across from it you will remember is the headquarters of the vintage car club and on one side is the crowd who import Persian rugs from Korea, on the other a large tin shed in which galvanised guttering is made for the trade. The kitset showroom was once the front two rooms of a cottage and the dull, tiled fireplace is still there at one end. They use mainly reconstituted hardboard and three-ply. You can buy your three-drawer desk built up and stained, or take the kitset and the single sheet of photocopied instructions in which the possessive its is apostrophied and a lacquer finish is termed most unique. Two men do the manufacturing, two men sell when necessary, two men are the proprietors. The same two. Perhaps Gavin Buttery is the one you knew better, killed by a monsoon bucket during the scrub fires behind the city. Quietus now.

'Tena koutou, tena koutou, tena koutou katoa,' Paul Hurinui welcomes the people, who drift to a loose focus around the Angel Hire chairs. He stands before the officials' chairs, facing downhill to the crowd. Seated behind him are his two fellow elders, together with the Rev Thomas, Slaven and Eula Fitzsimmons, spokesperson for Gender Plus. Hurinui, who for three years was Chancellor of the Iwitini University, speaks for only a few minutes in Maori, then changes to English to explain the significance of Tuamarina as a setting for consideration of policies to ensure greater unity and progress for all New Zealanders. He explains with a compassion as fresh as if the events were only yesterday, something of the Wairau Incident. The pressure on the Ngati Toa to sell land to the Company, the provocation by the Europeans in sending the survey team in early 1843 and the Maori repudiation of it. Then an aging Te Rauparaha interrupted at his breakfast of potatoes by the arrival of the armed party to arrest him. Hurinui says that the Ngati Toa were sitting at daybreak in two groups — heathen and Christian. He points out on the Tuamarina stream below, the place where a canoe was placed to allow the Europeans to cross. The arguments, the fighting, the deaths, make both a fine drama and a useful text and Hurinui does it well. At the end of it he gives Thackeray Thomas a shard of totara which comes from a Ngati Toa canoe.

There are not a great many Maori in the audience, but Slaven can see a group of Kurds who have come down from the Shipley refugee subdivisions on the Wairau. Most of the people here are heartland Kiwis whose accents prove that their families have been country people for several generations. A few smoke in contravention of official regulations, but there's no sign of more dangerous drugs. Some older people wear vinyl jackets with star signs on the back, maybe there is even an honest cardigan or two. Plaits are in again for women and pony tails for men. There are children as well, making no effort to disguise their boredom once Hurinui's rich history is replaced by more immediate politics. They kick at the still wet grass, test each other's strength and determination by pushing and wrestling, walk openly on the graves, even climbing the small, wrought iron surround of the memorial to stand on the cracked concrete and scratch at the names of those who were killed. One girl swings from the gum tree which overhangs the grave, and water from the leaves dashes on the concrete. Below the steep hill on which they're all gathered and beyond the sealed road to Picton, the last of the gay riders can be seen on the side road, strung out towards Waikakaho.

Thackeray Thomas speaks next, just a pipe opener for him of some fifteen minutes to introduce Slaven. His voice sweeps over the several hundred people on the hill at Tuamarina. In his easy, fat-cheeked eloquence he slips into Maori at the conclusion of his introduction and so Slaven misses his cue. While Thomas waits, half-turned towards him, Slaven watches the gray cloud stealing across the slopes of the hills and feels the cold June air take the heat from his face. He wonders about the weather on that Saturday, 17th June, 1843, when Thompson and Te Rauparaha talked through the interpreter.

'If you would like to speak now, Dr Slaven?' says Thackeray with another inviting sweep of his hand towards the people still less than compact and attentive before him. There is no dais, no lectern, no table with a water tumbler even, just the roughly levelled and gravelled park on which to stand, the patches of long grass and graves downhill and the seats awkwardly angled there, and his fellows waiting to be convinced that they haven't wasted a day. The entreaty man in a close row nods his head in agreement and support before even a word is said. Above the heads of his audience, Slaven can see the main road turn to the right towards the river and the willows which mark from a distance the

Wairau's braided bed. *Dropping southwards down the coast, baby, until the sanctuary of Half Moon Bay.*

'We are the living people in the scene of the moment,' says Slaven, 'and so we are culpable. Our own frame in the long sequence is for an instant lit by time, then we too wind to the reel which holds Wakefield and Te Rauparaha, Helen and Hector, the drift of Gondwanaland, a grandmother's face. Our turn at the front of life. Our chance to have some effect. There is an obligation that accompanies human continuity.' Slaven watches his audience as he speaks. Three hundred or so are not much of a crowd on the hillside, with a cold, winter sky and cars coming and going on the Blenheim-Picton road. Two Kurdish boys are having a stick fight with a younger kid amongst the parked cars. It is the ordinariness of the people that catches at Slaven. Their half-acknowledged longing for a community and a search for purpose as they recognise they have no particular, or distinctive, life to set them apart. Slaven sees their ongoing, patient humanity, the inarticulate desire to be part of some corporate aim which will make reason, even rhyme perhaps, of filling their bellies with food and babies, cutting toenails, watching the broom flower on poor country as if the yellow clay beneath has been sucked into the blooms, gathering the dessicated blowflies from the window sill of the bach, improving their keyboard skills, practising the retirement speech for inclusion in the *Laystall Gazette*, hearing at last the diagnosis always feared, winning a third division Sweepstake prize in a syndicate of seven.

Slaven has been until recently a self-contained man, but now he feels again the powerful stirrings that came upon him in the hospital and at the seminar, the flow of an implacable conviction, an imperative to speak out and a confidence that the words will come. He draws in the winter air more deeply and it bites deep within him, but the shiver he gives is in response to the grip of emotion not the chill.

'We have lost our way,' says Slaven vehemently, gratified by his words rolling down the slope of Tuamarina before him. 'We have abandoned the hope of inner life.'

'That we have,' shouts the entreaty man in support.

'We've no sense of national spiritual identity, no unity of purpose, no confederacy of care.'

'We haven't.'

'Each of us has retrenched into a personal life from which we are bitter in our criticism of anything that others do. We have lost true conviviality as an aspect of life and replaced it with drunkenness in crowds, with queues, with shouting at sport together. All the forms of our participation are chosen for personal gain.'

'Aiee,' shouts a ginger boy at a distance as he discovers another boy beneath a green sedan and begins to beat the protruding legs with his stick. The adults are oblivious however. Those standing move closer to Slaven as an involuntary expression of support. The entreaty man sees a green aura forming at Slaven's head and gives quick glances at his companions.

'I dare say our group today is the biggest most of you have been in this year,' continues Slaven. 'We've grown uncomfortable with the physical presence of our own kind, and not just because of the isolation of technology. We need to re-establish brotherhood and sisterhood, to accept a common rather than a personal cause.' After all the years of guarded living in respect of his emotions, Slaven feels a release of goodwill and compassion and something deeper, inchoate, besides. His arms lift in gestures never before natural to him, yet at the centre of his fervour is a composure which allows him to judge the responses of his listeners from their faces, to note a pair of wood pigeons scything the air in heavy flight from the bush, to calculate the pitch and resonance of his voice on a winter's day, the pauses for effect and for the calls which come back to him.

'Tell it all.'

'That's right. That's right.'

'This *is* the message.'

The banner doesn't flap, but every so often seems to swell of its own volition to display blue letters — Praise The Lord — and then relax again. If anything the cloud is thicker and lower; the sun behind it less suffusing. There is no drying and the grass still untrampled remains meek with dew; the stones of the carpark still darkened. See the cars coming from the plain pass on the smooth road below the memorial hill and vanish up the narrowing valley towards Picton. See a third row Angel Hire chair lose its back legs and pitch Vanessa Pringle onto the grave of Charles Hennessey, who had not been unaccustomed to women breathless above him in his time.

'How long since a government has been sensitive to the wishes of a majority of ordinary New Zealanders? Put another way, how long since we as a people had a real conviction that our views were of more account than the predictions of experts, the precedents of overseas experience and the computer models of our economy? The great success of the governing elite in this country has been to spread the notion that ordinary people are never capable of more than ordinary beliefs, even in consultation with each other. We have come in our hearts to despise democracy because we are contemptuous of our neighbours and unsure of our own worth.'

'Amen,' says Thackeray Thomas.

'What we have to do, it seems to me, is to give more heed to those parts of our selves and those parts of our lives which we share with everybody else, instead of always standing on our uniqueness, going on about being captains of our souls. It's the right sort of crew that we need in this country.'

'You tell us,' cries the entreaty man.

'Amen,' say Thackeray Thomas's sons.

Slaven talks for over an hour and a half without a glance at his notes. In his enthusiasm he advances step by individual step closer to the first row of chairs and further from the official party behind him. That Eula Fitzsimmons is meant to speak after him is forgotten, even by Eula, and the Rev Thomas, something of a demagogue himself, is enthralled by Slaven's power. 'We have a tiger by the tail,' he says to Paul Hurinui who is too carried away hefting his carved stick to Slaven's speech rhythms to reply. 'A power is rising in the land,' says Thackeray. 'This man has the gift.'

The meeting may well be set to burn itself out in another hour or two; there is only so much combustible emotion stored up in three or four hundred people. But Radio Charlotte from Picton send out a van and begin a direct broadcast for the region, part verbatim transference of Slaven's voice from the hillside at Tuamarina, part colourful asides and descriptions. So a new and steady tide of people begins to arrive. Farmers and alternative life-stylers, town people from Blenheim and Picton. No more vehicles are able to park on the hill, or in the grounds of the small country school and the farm gates are opened on the other side into the paddocks and the new arrivals push back the cows and sheep and then move towards the meeting on the hill. The new people form a fan around the original nucleus who are rejuvenated by such proof of their prescience in being with Slaven from the start. Some of them feel on display themselves and cry the more extravagantly, 'This is the message,' and 'The man speaks from the heart.'

Miles Kitson wakes from a dream of youth to walk carefully out and listen to his friend. The message is nothing to him, but the power of delivery is electric, yes, electric, and he sees some people so affected that their shoulders are tightening, drawing up. Even the children stop their play, standing with their slings and arrows to watch their parents shout, Slaven give his exhortations and the crowd swell. Something is happening. See the other world's over-lapping rim though, which no one there notices. Are there creatures trooping on the skyline, their brilliant and baleful colours glittering behind the mist and cloud.

Slaven speaks for three and a half hours and even after that must be persuaded to take a break. He rests in the privacy of his car with Miles, protected by Iago and Dafydd Thomas, has a chicken mayonnaise sandwich and a cup of tea. Paul Hurinui joins them and prompted by Slaven talks more of the fight at Tuamarina. Mr Howard the Company's storekeeper instructing his labourers how to fire a musket while the parley goes on, Thompson the magistrate giving the order to fix bayonets, old Te Rauparaha finally at the charge. The fury of Te Rangihaeata when his wife is shot. Twenty-four European names on the humble memorial at Tuamarina, and Hurinui tells Slaven and Miles that Thompson was found with his hands full of hair torn from his head in the agony of death.

Slaven sees that Miles is tired; his head rests on the

seat and his mouth is open as he breathes. Slaven arranges for Iago to drive his friend back to the Blenheim hotel before the crush prevents his departure and asks him to keep an eye out for Kellie along the way. 'You were good, Aldous, absolutely,' says Miles with his half-smile. 'You could sell anything with sincerity like that. No wonder Marianne Dunne is writing a paper for the medical journals on your case.' Yet of all the day he's seen he remembers best the arrival when they had the place to themselves and the intimate stories of Paul Hurinui of Ngati Toa.

Thackeray Thomas addresses the people, then Eula Fitzsimmons at last and all the time the crowd burgeons and with its growth comes a heightening of atmosphere, a strange, tacit awareness that something of significance is happening here. Some of the original supporters depart, but not many and only then if they can extricate their cars from the press and the chaos. A television crew arrives in the late afternoon when already the shadows of winter evening are moving out from the clouded slopes. The children have barely the light to gather the gumnuts which lie like the bowls of pipes around the memorial and on its cracked concrete surface. The mist presses lower and the cars turning off to Tuamarina begin to use their lights. The television crew takes footage of the people pressing steadily and insistently towards the meeting place on the hill where the Rev Thomas, Paul Hurinui, Eula Fitzsimmons and an informal Maori concert party all have their turn. Fires are started for light and warmth. The red flames leap and the sparks glitter in the darkening sky when new branches are thrown on. The fires are the particular focal point for younger people who arrive in greater numbers. They sing the old protest songs like *We Will Overcome* and newer ones, *Welfare Heaven* and *Remember Greenpeace*. Mobile caterers move in with pies, pizza, wontons, hot-dogs and kiwi juice.

Now that Slaven is rested and ready to speak again, even people from Nelson have begun to arrive, city people with knee-length coats who stand next to the clansfolk of Renwick, Springcreek, Koromiko, Havelock and the townies of Picton and Blenheim. There must be over six thousand people on the slope here at dusk when Slaven speaks again.

Thackeray Thomas has had Croad rig up a flat deck truck to act as a platform which can be seen by the expanded audience. Slaven is helped up there and his voice is hoarse in starting, but comes back to him once he has settled in. As he looks out from the back of the truck the detail of his view, so familiar during the day, is indistinct, features and demarcations fading in the night, or obscured by the press of such a crowd. The new, red fires catch rings of exultant faces, the media crews jostle for prime positions at the edge of the tray.

'What we're part of here at Tuamarina is a reaffirmation of faith in collective action. Even more, it is an assertion of trust in the existence of a collective will and sympathy which must precede action. The greatest fear is not death, but futility, not mortality, but inconsequence, not failure, but alienation. A united people instructs its representatives; a divided and selfish people are manipulated by their leaders.' There is still movement in the crowd and singing around the fires which grow brighter in the night and are far out from the original chairs from the Angels. Slaven has no microphone and for a time many don't notice that he has returned to speak, but his voice stills those before him with its unhurried insistence and they can see the aura forming at his head again. Attention spreads outwards until almost all are listening and voices which before had their own direction become individual or chorused exclamations of endorsement which fill the pauses in Slaven's speech, buoy up his delivery and gestures for them all.

'This *is* the message.'

'Power to the People.'

'Brotherhood and sisterhood is all.'

'Back to the heartland.'

Slaven feels a sense almost of exultation, not from personal vanity he assures himself, but because here in the gathering winter night of Tuamarina, individual, ineffective, disparate identities are being supplanted by a holistic mood, the personality of a community, a sum greater in wisdom than its parts. It's here only fitfully at first, a quick current through the crowd when the people are most united in their response. It is a change of aspect in accordance with a force, as the contours of a familiar face alter in a headstand because of gravity. 'Any cause which makes a good neighbour is a cause to uphold,' Slaven tells them.

'Here is our drummer.'

'A new start, thank God, at last.'

'Politics is not a party,' says Slaven, and they love to hear it. The mood is palpable, so that the audience even though now grown so much greater, draws together again, tighter, revelling in a unity of purpose. 'All we need is honesty and agreement. Anything shared benevolently with others bears interest. You and I know that for too long the centre ground of politics has been left to those of personal ambition and professional attitudes, while the rest of us have concentrated on our personal lifestyles. It's time for all of us here, and more like us elsewhere, to direct this country again. Isn't it? Isn't it time for spiritual values to be as powerful in the formation of manifestos as any other motivation. There's nothing so crippling in a citizen as a lack of self-respect and that self-respect comes most readily from involvement with our fellows.'

'It is time.'

'Politics isn't a party.'

'Remember Greenpeace.'

'We're getting to the guts of it here.'

'Fucken true.'

Slaven is still speaking at seven-thirty when the helicopter comes from Television South to hover with its red eye cameras which penetrate the dark to give home viewers an excellent picture, but the scene as viewed without augmentation is the more authentic. See the great crowd as a dark pelt on the hill and spilling to the paddocks beneath, Slaven on the truck deck lit by car headlights and the unstable, wheeling flames around which the people sway. Many children lift their arms and faces to the helicopter, trying for their moment of national exposure on the screen. 'Jesus,' says the pilot. The main road to Tuamarina is lit by a press of vehicles, a capillary in which the glowing cells flow, gather when checked and flow again. Picton is hidden by the hills, but on the plain of the Wairau the lights of

Blenheim just show. To the east however, where Cook Strait lies unpopulated and unseen, there is no movement, no light at all, no surface life to hint at what goes on beneath.

Rain begins: the finest drizzle which stirs and drifts like smoke and like smoke is grey and ethereal when caught in the car lights, or illuminated by the prancing red-yellow fires. So delicate and seemingly weightless are the drops that even when they settle the surface tension keeps them intact on fabric, leaf, hair, skin, on the cow dung slickered in the grass. As small jewels the droplets add their opaque spangles when caught in light. The mist gathers on the blue rug which Slaven wears over his shoulders as he speaks so that it becomes silver-grey in the headlights, and droplets tickle on the fine hairs high on his cheeks.

Slaven has kept the people pumped up for another hour, casting out his ideas again and again and drawing them back like a net through the crowd. Now the fervour leaves him and he climbs stiffly down from the truck against the great roar of supporters. He takes his turn along the beaten track to that portaloo set aside for officials, then sits in his air-conditioned car and watches new speakers who have been drawn to the meeting to capitalise on its vast success: the Actuarian Legislator for Marlborough, a celebrity herbalist from Pelorus, and Professor Marian Pesetsky who has retired in Picton, but won fame in the twenties for her successful campaign to outlaw male circumcision.

But it's over, isn't it, whatever held all these people in conviction. The singleness of purpose, the group identity almost all felt, yet none could adequately name, is no longer with them and despite the celebrities and the leaping fires, the media gunship overhead and the pizza stands, people are aware of the cold whisper of the drifting rain. They remember things neglected for too long — pets and children and lovers and nagging parents at home, seminar presentations and office meetings tomorrow, heaters perhaps unattended during all this winter day. So gradually the dispersal in the night begins, some in groups still singing to maintain euphoria, some couples, families, some singly, conscious that they are again alone and pleased that their state is inconspicuous in the dark. There's been no method, or supervision, in parking and people call out, sound their horns and flash their lights in exasperation as the exodus begins. Cars circle through the long grass seeking easier ways to leave. Thackeray Thomas displays a weeping, lost child on the deck of the truck and the informal concert party sings *Te Kuiti Dream.* Paul Hurinui and his fellow kaumatua are waiting patiently to give a proper farewell to their land.

Slaven watches from his car for a while, but is very tired. Has Miles reached the hotel without mishap and where has Kellie got to? He wishes she had seen his impact, his great success. He arranges the blanket around himself, damp side out, and lets down the seat back so that he can sleep comfortably. He begins to drowse, seeing the sparks dance upwards as the fire nearest to him is kicked to death. Tilted back as he is, he can see no people, not even Dafydd his protector, not even the body of the fire, just the tiger eyes of sparks gleaming in ascent. So, amidst continuing confusion, he rests.

Kellie wakes him the next morning. She hadn't got through until almost midnight and then only because of help from a bald-headed man, in shorts and tramping boots despite the weather, who pointed out a way against the flow. She has slept a few hours herself and while waiting for the late dawn considers the Tuamarina meeting as an exercise in organisation and finds it wanting. Sure, the numbers had grown quite beyond anything that could be expected, but there had been poor management nevertheless, too much left to chance, too few contingency plans made, too many actions taken as a response to events, rather than as an instigation of them.

She makes her observations to Slaven as she provides him with fruit and sandwiches and coffee. She has brought a flannel and a towel. She winds down the windows for the one-way glass has misted from Slaven's breath during the night and she wants to see the sun coming up, the sea of Cloudy Bay at a distance, the vineyards and orchards, the pasture land before Tuamarina and the hills rising behind. 'You'll feel dreadful,' she says.

'Not so hot. You're right. You get stiff not being able to

change position easily I suppose.' Slaven rubs his face. His trousers and shirt are twisted uncomfortably around him and the rug has begun to smell because of the dampness. He wants Kellie to tell him that the triumphs of the day before were as he remembered. She pats his hair down at the crown and folds his coat.

'We'll get back to the hotel and have a clean-up and a decent meal,' she says. 'Miles is being made a fuss of there because they know how rich he is.'

'And your sister?'

'A beautiful big girl. Born on the very stroke of three o'clock.'

'I think something was born here too,' says Slaven.

'There was something of it on the television before I left,' she says. 'You were standing on the back of a truck looking like a refugee, but speaking like a man possessed. Next time I'll be with you and hear it all for myself. God, it must have been something.'

See the cloud has gone, but its presence during the night has kept a frost from taking hold. The sky is a cool, slate blue, cleansed anew, the immediate environment beneath it soiled. On the hill around the isolated cemetery and in the paddocks by the country school and the minor cheese factory, whole areas of grass are trampled down, littered with pie wrappers and plastic kiwi juice containers. Some fire sites still smoulder and the hundred Angel Hire chairs have been taken late at night and set around them as the last of the crowd sought warmth. On the morning air a stench drifts from the portable loos which have been quite unable to cope with the numbers. The eucalypt tree in the graveyard has been partly broken down and Les Croad and a few helpers from the Charismatic Cambrian Church have already a pile of abandoned property on the gravel of the small cemetery carpark — coats, car rugs, bags and food bins, a hearing aid and a Panda Bear, a size eleven left shoe, a book of chutney and relish recipes, a Kurdish prayer belt with its crescents far from home. Cars are scattered over the lower site, some left because they wouldn't start, some not found before the offer of a lift, some stymied in a search for a new exit, some used to sleep in by people who like Slaven were too dog-tired to face the drive. Old Hurinui is a small figure walking down from the bush where he has seen in the new day.

'Ah,' says Slaven. 'Jesus, I'm stiff.' He arches and stretches as best he can in the car.

'Was it what you wanted though?' says Kellie.

'It's odd. Only since the hospital have I felt the compulsion to speak like that, of those sorts of things, and now I find that people do respond. Do you know what I mean? You wonder whether there's the possibility of real communication. I find I can do it.'

'What's the outcome, though. I mean if you can create all this enthusiasm for agreed views, how do you use it to make things better? What's the process by which the gathering of so many people actually gets anything done?'

'Political pressure, I suppose. We're just feeling our way, aren't we. At least now I know I'm not kidding myself. After all I could have had some aberration as a result of the accident. No one likes to be a laughing stock.'

'You feel okay when you do it?'

What can he answer. Does he tell her that when he gets underway, lifts himself and soars on the convections of expectation and identification from his audience that he feels too the stirring in the chrysalis of the world yet to be revealed. Look instead, then, on the reassuring texture of Tuamarina around them both, the exact physics of the kinks in the plastic of the kiwi juice bottles, the small, pale cross on the top of the Wairau monument and the cynicism in the lines of Croad's outdoor face as he wonders how best to deal with the mess.

'Do they remember when they all get home,' says Kellie. Like Les Croad she is inclined to be disillusioned by the aftermath of such magnificent and complete conversion. 'Perhaps it's like a rock concert, or an open air Shakespearean performance and they get it all out of their system and carry on just the same as before.'

'I guess we'll find out about that.'

Despite the stink of the latrines, the litter, abandoned fires and trampled camps and tracks in the grass as if a circus had moved on, Slaven is sure that an important thing has happened at Tuamarina. He has been given a sign, a mandate even. Croad is standing with Thackeray Thomas at about the place on which the speakers' truck was parked last night. Croad waves an arm despairingly to indicate the enormity of the clean-up before them and Thackeray is placating him, telling him that there will be a full Cambrian youth team out within an hour. His church is very big on conservation and ecological matters. Thackeray comes over to Slaven's car to congratulate him anew. There is no envy — he has his own achievements and is grateful to be part of what has happened. 'I've never before seen the like of it,' he says, taking Kellie's hand in a greeting. 'I can't get over the way in which the people kept coming and coming and the great sense of release and identification they had each time you spoke. The power to grip people, to make them give voice like that, now that's a special thing.'

'We were just talking about it,' says Kellie.

'There was a sense of hope, wasn't there?' asks Slaven.

'What's begun here — who knows the end of it.' Thackeray's voice is rich with portent. 'Last night when you were at the height of your powers I kept thinking of David Lloyd George. He had the gift.'

Croad is taking down the banner as he waits for the youth teams to arrive for the clean-up. Hurinui talks with Iago and Dafydd Thomas and a long, thin man comes to claim the panda with assumed confidence. Maybe in his withdrawal he covers the exact spot where a Ngati Toa lookout watched the special constables coming from Cloudy Bay: more likely the spot where tourist lovers from Alberta lay in the summer grass and cicada rhythms of 2007, to conceive a daughter who would show great talent in software development, but be killed by a bouncing boulder in Yellowstone Park.

'To be able to mobilise people like that,' says Thackeray Thomas and he leans in at the car window to squeeze Slaven's shoulder. Croad has the banner down at last and begins to roll it up.

'But mobilised for what?' says Kellie. 'At present it's all steam and no engine.' Thackeray is delighted with the analogy. He mentally files it for his own use.

'Precisely,' he says.

'Kellie is a born administrator,' Slaven boasts. 'She knows that efficiency is never the enemy of any worthwhile undertaking.' He looks her in the face and wonders if she has fears about his new life, as he does — snide fears circling in hope of misfortune. 'You can be the impresario. It will be like planning and planting a brand new garden, a landscaping of this political project we're beginning.'

In time the rally at Tuamarina becomes the recollection and the relics rather than the actuality: spools of video from the ground crew and the helicopter, the radio tapes, the selected memories of people who were there, the invoices for a double thousand beef mince pies, a lesbian thigh rocking to the movement of the horse's flank, the banner blue and white, the drifting rain which enveloped them, the sparks from the fires which dazzled and escaped, Slaven's oratory from the truck deck, the singing of *Welfare Heaven* and *Remember Greenpeace* as the noose tightened.

In time the place itself recovers from such thoughtless possession. The grass grows back rank in the sun and the wind so that the fire sites and the few juice containers missed by Thackeray's youth workers are hidden, the gum tree over the grave branches out again in directions not too obviously determined by the depredations made upon it, the broom flowers in summer and the stench from the latrines long gone is supplanted by a sweet wind coming over the bushed hills from Queen Charlotte Sound. And the words most likely to linger are those of old Te Rauparaha as he burst from the trees to fight. 'Hei kona te marama. Hei kona te ra. Haere mai to po.' Farewell the light. Farewell the day. Welcome night.

At night, after a campaign dinner, Slaven wakes at seven minutes past four. He can see the blue figures on the display clock by his bed. Slaven thinks that he has woken simply because he needs to piss, but when he has done this quietly and come back to his side of the bed he realises that his stomach is queasy. He has overdone it somewhat with the Australian shiraz and the pork and bacon kebabs and the marinated mussels and the cocktail onions with gruyere cheese. Altogether, it leaves him with a sour weight low in his stomach and an inability to rest comfortably.

He leaves the bed again, again quietly so as not to wake Kellie who faces away, just a sweep of hair showing on the pillow. By the drapes Slaven rubs his stomach up and down, not round and round. He grimaces slightly for his own benefit and looks through the narrow gap in the drapes to pass time.

There are people on the front drive of his house.

Seven of them, no, eight. All quite young; both sexes. The moonlight is not particularly bright, but he can see that they are throwing something from baskets at the house. Well, scattering rather than throwing, broadcasting with an action of the wrist rather than the whole arm and whatever it is they cast it makes no sound against the walls, nothing that would wake Kellie, or him. All of them wear pants and most the canvas jackets fashionable amongst the unfash-ionable, which show the dirt of constant use. They are dancing, rather perpetrating some parody, some travesty, of a pastoral dance, with the baskets hung on their arched arms and their bodies clumsily bending and swaying.

Slaven has an unpleasant sense of their conceit and affectation, but they themselves take it all with arty solemnity despite the almost total lack of grace and skill. And every few minutes they put down their baskets in an unsynchronised way, hang themselves like scarecrows, then shake and quiver to mimic electrocution.

Even though he can't be seen, Slaven takes a step back. He has the right to be here, yet the last thing he wants is to reveal himself, to challenge the dancers. He is afraid of them, but not in the immediate and physical sense. Far worse than that. They are the manifestations of his worst fears concerning his work, proof that from the rational, humanitarian ideas he upholds, mutants can be spawned. Slaven watches the figures in the ludicrous repetition of their makeshift dance, yet what faces he can see have expressions of fixed intensity.

Slaven knows that the Executive and staff try to keep such things from coming to his notice, yet he's aware of a whole range of half-baked responses to his speeches and his campaign. Half-baked! A grim reminder of the fryers who continue to electrocute themselves in his name and to make headlines at last with their death. There are people who have fits at his meetings, women who wish to bear his child, or claim they have already done so, fundamentalists who insist that the coalition prefigures the Apocalypse, people who demand large sums of money and blessings, others who are intent on giving both. Sarah has a group of volunteers who go through his mail bag and weed out the most disturbing letters, but Slaven finds others thrust into his pockets when travelling, or under the door of a hotel room.

At times the dancers go forward and bend in the garden close to the bedroom window — whether to pick, or place, it is difficult for Slaven to tell. He begins to feel cold, but won't lie down while the ritual goes on. One man is very fat and his serious face shakes as he parades in the dance.

Why don't they just all bugger off. Whatever they see in Slaven's beliefs he will never acknowledge. In fact he resents their appropriation of his name and movement even more than their appropriation of his drive and lawn before the sun has risen. In his heart he knows that the real source of his anger is a fear that his work could be corrupted, that what was so clear to him could still nourish opinions quite contrary to his intentions. The snake they say, hears nothing that the charmer plays.

Finally the dancers leave, after whispered argument, trailing down the long drive with their baskets. The fat man has an arm around one of the women who doesn't return his embrace. A more nondescript man waits long enough to secure a minimum of privacy and then pisses by the crab-apple tree, his shoulders hunched protectively. When he has pranced after the others the drive is empty and Slaven at the gap of the curtains is hard put to keep the episode in mind as any more than a sour dream. Before going back to bed though, he moves through the house and checks on each of the other three sides, in case like wagon pioneers he and Kellie have been surrounded by the basket cases with their ungainly dance. He must talk to Kellie about security.

In the morning Slaven says nothing to Kellie of all this, but he goes outside after breakfast and steps close to the bedroom wall. Kellie has musk mallow there and the gladioli which have seen off Norman Proctor without so much as a flourish. There are lines, small heaps even, of yellow-orange scraps set together by the dew. Slaven takes some of it to his wife. 'Safflower petals,' she says. 'I'd say that's what it is. Where did you get it?'

'In the garden.'

'I've never grown any.'

'A gift then,' says Slaven. 'Has it got any particular folklore associated with it? Is it lucky, or anything like that?'

'Not that I know. It can be used as a dye.'

Slaven yawns to prove to them both that he is at ease. At least his stomach is settled. In his mind however, he has an involuntary reprise of last night's dance. The earnest, self-absorbed clumsiness of it: bows and crooked legs, baskets dangling, hissed instructions, the fat man's jowls trembling in the fish-belly light. What else goes on at the far ripple remove from his intentions. What things are fed on tail first which he has sent out with a sense of true direction.

There are people, you understand, who are employed for the hypothetical. Dr Royce Meelind is one. He works in the Government Think Tank with a responsibility for the potential political impact of social movements and events. His most splendid career success was predicting the growth of reactionary regionalism as urbanisation intensified. He noticed such signs as the growth of country and western music in the lower part of the South Island. The media term it Hillbillyism, but Meelind refers rather to the Pancake Syndrome, after the great twentieth century West Virginian author, Breece D'J Pancake.

Meelind read all the reports of Tuamarina and watched the uncut film from the television station. At the Thursday morning briefing of the Think Tank he uses it as an example of nostalgic popularism which arises from time to time as a political expression of frustration and anxiety with the complexity of modern life. Meelind's colleagues expect Slaven to flare across the political sky briefly and then be forgotten, but Dr Meelind is impressed by the man's grip on an audience. He jokes about the prospect of a dentist with a mid-life crisis, yet opens a file on Slaven which includes the names of school friends, medical reports, his financial situation, his links with Thackeray Thomas and his recent friendship with that old power of business — Miles Kitson. To the file he adds the information passed on to him from sources within television, that Slaven has been asked to appear on the 'What's Up Show'.

I haven't burdened you with a full static description of Royce Meelind at this stage. His time will come. The large, pale ear-lobes for example, whitened with down, and the extreme length of his upper legs so that when he rests his elbows on his knees his body is almost lying forward, but you'll be interested that his brother was that paleontologist whose death was widely reported when he choked on a bumblebee while climbing in the Old Man Range.

Anyway, it is a staffer from the show who rings Slaven and invites him to appear on the 'What's Up Show'. 'Amand is very much hoping that you can see your way clear,' says the staffer. 'We're all very much hoping. You realise of course that there's no payment offered as such, but the exposure of views is absolutely enormous, isn't it.' Slaven has been slicing onions for one of Kellie's quiches and his eyes swim with tears. 'Just a few questions on your policies and reaction to the present political direction of the country.' Slaven thinks he would like time to consider the invitation. 'Of course. Look, as long as you let me know by four this afternoon. That's three complete hours. Remember, we're very much hoping. I haven't talked in detail with Amand yet; I wanted your initial response, but I imagine he'll be interested particularly in the angle of oratory, inspirational delivery, the democratic message. Quite extraordinary what happened at Tuamarina. We have a great programme mix in mind — with you, cartoonist Buffle who has just turned ninety did you realise and Marie Antoinette Smith, the first woman convicted of serial rape in this country. It's getting that balance, that cross over impact, for prime time TV you see.'

'I suppose so,' says Slaven.

He talks it over with Kellie and later she rings back to make the arrangements, insisting on a clear understanding concerning fares and accommodation for both of them, and being met at the airport.

Afterwards she takes the opportunity to point out to Slaven the need for a more businesslike approach to his activities. She reminds him that despite the thousands at Tuamarina he received no fee, nothing at all. Yet increasingly money is coming in, often vaguely identified in origin and purpose. She has been talking to Thackeray Thomas of the administrative and financial structures required as Slaven becomes a focus of attention. She is of course the best manager he could have. Her ability to organise and direct is no surprise to him, but her enthusiasm to do so humbles him. As they discuss the practical matters, the external things, he has a sense of both guilt and remorse concerning their marriage and yet finds as ever that he has neither the courage, nor the words, to speak. He can barely admit to himself what a falling away there has been; gradually, imperceptibly almost, the erosion of love's isthmus until they are quite separate again.

'Absolutely,' he says energetically, 'but not just the management of finances and logistics. What's more important is that we're sure of the true motivation of those people who want to be associated with us, who we allow to represent the movement. There's a real danger of exploitation in all of this, exploitation of the people that I know now I can reach, can influence. Oh, we're all of us used and users I suppose, but there has to be some scrutiny, some on-going evaluation of our purposes and our power. Don't you think?'

'Can you make yourself responsible for the opinions and actions of everyone who responds to your ideas.'

There should be a moment here when Slaven can admit that love has gone, and weep for that loss. Admit that he has admiration for his wife's intelligence and decisiveness, the lack of triviality, her loyalty and respect of privacy, the skill she has in the garden and the nimble way that she can keep all disappointment hidden. Say all of that to her and also that in the heart where love was, he cares not a jot for any of it. Instead he continues to talk of the contribution he hopes to make towards the general good. '— trying to return a measure of effective political influence to people who aren't interested in the processes of politics,' he says, 'but are interested in outcomes, some of them even in collective outcomes, but let's not push our luck too much on that last one.'

'Not on the "What's Up Show", anyway.'

Kellie and Slaven sit in the kitchen and watch the onion, cheese and pineapple quiche rotating in the oven. They talk of the formation of a Coalition for Citizen Power which they will invite the Charismatic Cambrian Church, Gender Plus and the union movements to join. Slaven remembers a time some nine or ten years before, when Kellie's younger sister came to stay with them, remembers the dreams he had each night while she was in the house, the frisson each time she came into the room, the profitless recital to himself of all the fortunate aspects of his life. Nothing was said, nothing happened. Miles once told Slaven of an affair he had with a South African nurse; how they would habitually meet during the late afternoon in a bungalow his firm maintained for guests. Miles said that as soon as he opened the front door he knew whether he had arrived before her, because his cock would stiffen if she was anywhere in the house. That's natural life, that's pure experience of a sort, surely, Miles had said.

They are met at the airport and taken to the inner city Hotel Hollandia, and later to the studios. There they are separated, Kellie being invited to visit a neighbouring series in production before joining the audience of 'The What's Up Show'. Slaven goes first to have the layout of the set, the format, explained to him, then to make-up and on to the small lounge for the panel guests where he joins the ninety year old cartoonist and the female serial rapist. Peter, the staffer, gives them a choice of fruit juice, coffee or scented tea and tells an amusing story to explain why they no longer provide anything alcoholic for panellists before the show. It concerns a noted bishop who disgraced himself while discussing the rites of adolescent passage with Mrs Van

Troon the painter in egg tempera. The serial rapist, who has paid her debt to society and is now recouping it through personal appearances and magazine stories, says that the Church is finished, anyway, more obviously irrelevant under capitalism in the twenty-first century than under communism years before. Buffle, the cartoonist, hems and haws with senile incredulity and asks by the way was she rapist, or rapee. Ex-rapist he is told, and presently a leading expert in herbal remedies.

When Amand Beardsley strolls into the room to meet his guests, Peter is quickly by his side. Marie Antoinette Smith doesn't rise for the introductions. Buffle can't co-ordinate himself in time, so only Slaven joins the staffer in courtesy, or obsequiousness. Beardsley has the ability to talk to them all at once, practising with casual confidence the information Peter has given him on each. He possesses a magnificent smile which appears with sudden radiance, but fades only gradually so that it can be lingered on by the cameras while his mind and eyes have moved on. 'We are most impressed by the Tuamarina rally,' he tells Slaven. 'Rivetting political theatre. Tonight, as Peter has mentioned, I wish to touch on the funding structure of your organisation and the ties with Christian fundamentalism.'

'Fundamentalism?' But Amand Beardsley has left only the Cheshire image of his smile as he turns to assure the cartoonist that there will be someone to carry his folio of drawings onto the set.

'Remember the parameters we agreed as far as the questions on my sexuality are concerned,' says the ex-rapist.

'I shall be gentle,' says the host. The corner of his mouth has the briefest of puckers which is then assimilated into the embracing smile. As they talk they can hear from the studio the live audience being warmed up and members of the production team appear in the doorway from time to time, not saying much, but giving signals and murmurs which Beardsley replies to by asking for more young people to be seated in the front rows this time, or deciding that the cartoon close-ups can be cut in later.

'Just relax,' says Amand Beardsley. His eyes jitter.

'That's what I always say,' says Marie Antoinette Smith.

'Arms are the difficult things to catch,' says Buffle, who is perfectly relaxed through obliterating age. 'Heads are easy enough, but it's difficult to caricature an arm. See?'

'We're thrilled with the mix for tonight,' says Peter. 'You'll all bounce off each other superbly.'

'Just be yourselves, relax and do yourselves justice.'

'I never expect justice any more,' says Smith vehemently.

'We're nearly off,' says the staffer.

Beardsley is to have a final few minutes of privacy. He pauses on his way out to light his smile. Peter takes up station at the door where he can see the floor manager while still able to talk to the guests. Slaven has a sure instinct that his appearance is not to be a success, that the technological constraints, the packaged indirectness, will prevent a message.

And so it is. There is no stage-fright, no particular ignominy, or slapstick confusion, no special malice of Beardsley's part, just the essential superficiality of the format and the medium which assumes that a few minutes of shared prime time television are sufficient to establish any viewpoint, or transfer a philosophy of life. A laugh a minute is considered slow stuff these days. The ninety year old Buffle goes down best. He is used to talking to himself and the cartoons when flashed up have the necessary immediate impact. He has a fund of scurrilous personal anecdotes concerning the celebrities he's satirised and Amand Beardsley, who knows a good stunt when he sees one, keeps him going at the expense of Slaven and Marie Antoinette. The ex-rapist is too nearly a match for Beardsley, Slaven too earnest, yet at the same time seeming evasive as his eyes slide away from the cameras seeking human contact. And the heat — Slaven feels his body prickle with a sweat induced by the great lights and his tension.

After all, as Beardsley told the staffers later, a dentist with a social message is not a sure fire cert, is he? And what reaction can be expected from a studio audience? They crowd in an arc of seating, mirroring on their rapt faces the play of expression of those on the set. Oblivious for an hour of their humdrum lives they cluster towards the incandescence of Beardsley's set, watch the clap board, remember the lucky number, glance at their neighbours in response to innuendo and trip their ready laughter.

Kellie and Slaven don't talk much about the panel on their way back to the hotel. He finds even recall is difficult, for the interviews recede at a greater rate than normal experience, like the implosion of the image when a television set fails. As he left the studio after taking off his make-up, Slaven hadn't been surprised when Beardsley passed him in the corridor with only a last minute muted gesture of recognition. Not avoidance, or even arrogance, just that it was history; gone for ever. Slaven's mouth had been open in readiness to greet the man who minutes before had been leaning towards him, diligent in pursuit of Slaven's inner self.

Slaven tells Kellie that after all he's fully aware of the nature of professional intimacy. It is his occupation to hover over people's mouths, working the plaque from their teeth, checking for caries, seeing the blood well from their gums, breathing a muted duodenal release, or admiring a set of eyelashes. Close as lovers, with his fingers in their mouths and their heads well back. Then the suction removed, personal distance resumed, and the relief of parting as strangers. As Slaven forgot the close-up of a nasal configuration, so Beardsley made public auguries in the display of faces and ideas then washed his hands of them.

'You just don't suit that type of television, that's all,' Kellie says. 'You need the physical immediacy and rapport of a meeting.' There is a sudden spray of saliva from beneath her tongue and the tiny droplets fall upon her brown forearm so lightly that she is unaware. She is watching the rowan trees which they pass in the taxi for they remind her of places in which she once lived.

'It'll put ten kilos on me, I suppose. They say that television puts ten kilos on you.'

'I thought the ex-rapist suffered a good deal more than you in that way,' says Kellie. 'You did sit with your legs splayed out somewhat, mind. The Smith woman's knees were like uncut cheeses. The very old guy, the cartoonist, had a wonderful profile, etched by the years. Was it true do you think, what he said about Winston Peters?'

'I can barely remember Winston Peters.'

'You'd think that they'd have a vase or two of greenery on that set wouldn't you. A few sprigs of japonica, or some Leucadendron.'

'Not a great success. Let's face it,' says Slaven.

'We've learnt that a TV panel show isn't the best thing for our purpose, that's all,' says Kellie.

There is a place — a narrow street in an old hill suburb. The rank hedges obstruct the footpaths as do the cars with two wheels up there to leave just enough room for solitary passage. There are no complaints for who else besides the inhabitants go there; not a cul-de-sac, but certainly a dead end. Sets of damp, concrete steps lead steeply up through aisles of weeds and shrubs to the street above. As windfalls the dog droppings line the hedges, the chronology of their deposit is a colour code with the most venerable the fine, white ash of a Churchillian cigar. There are wood pigeons on the telephone lines and the gates have been left open so long that the hinges have seized, even frames rotted where they stand. Almost every retaining wall is a Pisa, yet having made its threat apparent the angle is held for a hundred years. The fractures allow the walls to weep when the rain comes so that delicate fans of yellow and rusty clay embrace the dogshit. Houses here were never grand. Cottages mouthing directly at the roadway, a few wooden villas with verandahs beneath a bow of roofing iron. Old people live here in the houses they have owned for fifty years: young people live here, glorying in the antiquated loo and the one lead-light window for a few months on their way to a degree in French. Such a very narrow, a very quiet, street, only the inhabitants go there one at a time with their heads down against the slope and not speaking. In the soft rain of an autumn's evening the dogs trot along the hedges and there is an emanation of all the people who knew the place before and now have gone. Do you know them? There is a cherry tree with a canker over its branches and a board nailed to its heart to fix one end of the clothes line. There is a glass house with no glass two doors up, from which the convolvulus flows. There is an old lady who once had both musical talent and aspirations and now she presents her great bum to the world as she gathers chickweed for her canary.

In the summer evenings the cats of the street sit on the letter boxes and the leaning walls and the rowan berries are like blossom at a distance, clustered flowers which the blackbirds eat, shaking the fingers of the rowan leaves. In the winter the seepage of yellow and rust coloured clay and grains of dark top-soil spread over the footpath towards the water hurrying in the gutters, or the frost bears up in the shade of the hedges.

And all of this is the twenty-first century. The days, you see, have a trail of continuity as well as a cutting edge.

Slaven's *Tuamarina Address — A New Drummer* is printed for the recently established Coalition for Citizen Power by Pomegranate Press and Kellie keeps control of its distribution. It sells 173,000 copies in three weeks and provides the final proof of a target group for Slaven's beliefs. Kellie begins to plan a commercial strategy to tie in with the publicity for the Coalition — posters, stickers and cable ads utilising the more epigrammatic of the Slavenisms such as, 'Specialisation leads to alienation', 'People are the means and the end', 'Politics isn't a party'. They try to prevent the trappings of a cult developing, despite the swelling interest in anything to do with Slaven. Supporters want private articles as mementos and thousands of sightseers are disappointed that because of new security they cannot visit the home to see the precise place where Aldous Slaven experienced his near fatal shock and received his mission. There have already been five copy-cat electrocutions, including the twenty-three year old daughter of the Minister of Aviation and Technology. She left a note saying that she was determined to break through to the euphoric component of the human soul. The street term for these unfortunates is cracklers, or sparklers, and if the Slavenisms are the healthy and open publicity for the Coalition, the sparkler jokes are a strange underside. In the cities arises a skinhead cult with 'Shavin for Slaven' tattooed on their heads. God knows what inspiration they find in Slaven's message.

He talks about it with Kellie during one of the few spring

days he has had time to work with her in the garden. The early afternoon sun warms his protective gloves, but far to the west beyond the Canterbury Plains the Southern Alps still show white. Kellie is concerned by the number of wasps and fears an awakening nest in her garden. She dislikes wasps particularly because they force out the more passive, pollinating bees.

'A lot of this I didn't count on,' says Slaven. 'A lot of these things you don't expect when you start out. People hearing in my speeches a great deal that I'm not saying, or meaning, taking a word or two here and there, odd ideas out of context, confusing illustration with the point at issue, making them in some way evidence for the notions that they've been determined to push all along. Jesus, Kellie, fancy men and women deliberately electrocuting themselves and doing it in my name.'

'There's always a cost I suppose,' she says. 'Always a perverse element in a movement. It happened with feminism didn't it, and with euthanasia and republicanism, but the essential progress was made all the same. I imagine the more democratic the organisation, the more crackpots and salvation seekers it attracts.'

'But people killing themselves because of expectations they have of me. I dreamt of it last night. The thin, naked forms spread-eagled on the wires, convulsing in the blue flicker of the current. I even had the stink of it from the instant of my own agony.' Slaven begins to rub one hand with the other through his gloves. Are the Hoihos still playing do you think? *Foveaux storms are fading, baby, within the realm of Half Moon Bay.*

'In the end people must take responsibility for their own actions,' says Kellie.

'That's just it. What are we finding of the consequences of mine? Isn't there a temptation to make an impact just because you're capable of doing it? Pride and power must be in there somewhere. I can see that.' Slaven and Kellie take a heaped wheelbarrow of weeds each and in Indian file trudge to the shredder by the main compost heap. With the shredder on it's too noisy for them to keep talking and they feed the machine, watch the mulch whirl onto the compost heap, and carry on with their thoughts. This is something they have done many times, only the thoughts are different this year and Slaven's physical participation more limited.

'We need a break of some sort,' he says. The noise of the machine echoes for a moment. 'Don't you think? A chance to sort out our aims so that we're not just swept along by the publicity and the agendas of the other groups — Thackeray and the Cambrian Church, Eula and Gender Plus, the unionists, the egalitarians, devolutionists.'

'You want to be by yourself?'

'No.' He tells her that they could have a simple holiday; places and people they used to know, family members perhaps. Soon enough will be the point of no return.

'I can understand that,' says Kellie.

'I don't suppose that many people overall are born in one millenium and die in another.'

'Is that what it's about as well; some mid-life crisis?' she asks. Above the smoke bush which won't leaf again, the mountains seem so much closer than they really are. Usually at this time of the year she and Slaven would ski at Mount Hutt. His hands aren't good enough for it yet. 'You'll be suggesting that the power line was a subliminal choice next.'

'Hardly,' says Slaven. The portrait of all the landscape before him seems to buckle for a moment as if in the throes of metamorphosis and he checks his breathing, intent on the new forms which surely will come raging forth, but not today either is the time for the detailed sheen of the chrysalis to shatter.

Slaven finds his wife an astute counsellor. Their marriage is pretty much burnt out, but there are advantages in that — tolerance, familiarity, the ease of custom, tacit acknowledgement of disparity provide a basis for a bearable life of mutual routine and separate examination. There are betrayals of a sort, of course. Slaven nine years ago first persuaded one of his nurses to fuck with him, more from a sense of opportunities passing than any unbearable desire for her. The sexual pleasure quite astounded him at first, but the emotional obligation, the guilt, the planning of trivial deceit, the sense of limiting another's life, were in total too high a price. Instead thereafter he allows episodes which are both discreet and discrete, but mainly he enjoys the visual pleasure women give, without the enjoyment too obvious on his face. Among his patients, friends, passers by, to register the frisson of a nape, a forearm, the fall of an eyelid, a tremor of a lock of hair, a jersey's fold on the hip, the breasts' undulation as a woman hurries at the lights, the glint of a zip beneath the tuck of a taut skirt. A voice, lowered in trust almost to a whisper. Such quick, glimpsed things to flare in his mind and there subside as he offers an observation on the new shopping mall, or gives money to a fund which will send Wendy Parmenter to Los Angeles for new lungs.

For two weeks then, he agrees with Kellie, to make some reassessment of intentions, some scrutiny of the power he has discovered within himself.

Maybe you can't go back, that's true, because as Proust said you're looking for a time past as well as a place, but you can return which is a less satisfying thing. Waiouru is not on the tourist trail, a place by-passed by New Zealanders, let alone Americans, Arabs and Chinese. Slaven doesn't inflict this visit on Kellie, leaving her with his mother in Palmerston North. For him Waiouru speaks as much of family and childhood as civilian cities and provincial towns do to other people. JGs on the line in married quarters, the zenith note as RSM Glassey gets the battalion on parade and the tarmac shimmers in the heat, the MP's Landrover circling through the camp at night, helicopter gunships lifting off above the snow, the D Block Mess, the basic training confidence course with its walls, trestles, ropes and swaying logs which have been a playground to Slaven and his friends as swings and see-saws have to others. His father's dress uniform, warrant officer second class, carefully pressed and on a hanger in the window of the lounge, turning first one way a little then the other, with the insignia of rank a splendid crest on his sleeve. All such things the motifs of a way of life at once totally familiar and completely unknown, A child's view of a man's world and a woman's suspicion of it.

'I don't know quite when I'll be back. It depends on how the exercise goes and what sort of chopper support we're given. You know I won't be longer than I have to.' Slaven's father had been part of GAMD — ground air missile defence — which became important after the Gulf and Moroccan wars. On Slaven's study desk is a detonator case that he uses as a paper weight. It was used for the same purpose on his father's desk in the company HQ room at Waiouru and when Slaven was there with his father out of hours he would play with the defused detonator, flat and heavy, watch his father working at the computer screen, regard from the window the birds amongst the regimented lawns and shrubs outside. In the summer the sparrows foraged in the mown grass, or fluffed their soft, lower feathers in the dust at the base of the shrubs.

Outwardly the place remains the ultimate in clone development you might think. The repetition of barrack blocks, parade grounds, store and maintenance depots and its population walking in step, jogging in unison, saluting on cue. Uniformity in uniform, you say. It's not true of course, with any knowledge, anymore than all Asians look the same. Slaven had known each street and building, each restricted zone, each training area, each armoured vehicle park and loading bay, for the special character it bore. Just where he could dig the spent bullets from the butts, how to fry an egg on the base of the receptor discs in a Waiouru summer. And personality persists despite a uniform. CSM Slaven played badminton with intensity and grace and had a musical snore. His profession was to kill, but cruelty to an animal would rouse him to a fury and in his bottom drawer were hidden correspondence papers in torts and legal history. A man's reach should exceed his grasp, the poet says. Maybe his study was interrupted by service in the UN force to China, the Antarctic pickets some years later, or just the nights in the mess with his friends. Maybe he didn't have the brains for it. Anyway, quietus now. He would lay out his personal gear on the lounge floor before an exercise and as Slaven called out each item, his father would tick the sheet and say, 'check'. He died three weeks after Slaven graduated. Coddy Burns in the bar slipped a bottle top in his beer for a joke and Slaven's father downed it and choked to death. After the graduation he had taken a pair of blue handled pliers from his pocket and passed them to his son as the foundation, he said, for his equipment as a dentist.

A regular soldier knows how to keep himself spruce. The CSM could have undressed in the main street of Auckland and folded his clothes beside him to pass inspection. He despised a slovenly belly, or a grubby collar. 'You'll do all right, Aldous,' he told him after the graduation. He was pleased for his son even though Slaven tended to slouch because of his bookwork and his fitness was suspect. The CSM showed no sign of self-pity that he wouldn't be a lawyer, would choke on a friend's bottle top amid the benevolence of his mess. All his warlike skills, and he was undone by a bottle top. He would have seen the irony of that, given his quick smile which didn't show his teeth.

Slaven's mother lives in a retirement village in Palmerston North; a self-sufficient community with a Maori name which means landfall after a long voyage. The air is heavier here than in the outside world and each small house has the silence of a trap-door spider's lair. Even the garages are swept bare and the work benches in order, but it is a neatness which has the rigour of despair. It is close to the airport, but Mrs Slaven is deaf enough to be unconcerned by the planes angling in and out. She has played no sport during her life, taken no interest in her husband's badminton, yet as she talks to Kellie and Slaven in the cubby hole of her town house, her eyes slide away to the screen on which the Kiwis play England at cricket and she gives a stifled cry when her son is explaining his political plans, because a catch is put down in the slips. 'Yes,' she says without taking her eyes from the sport. Old age is past the need for pretence. 'I read all about it in the paper and watched the television that night. It seemed a very exposed place, that Tuamarina. I couldn't get over you choosing it.'

'I feel ordinary people should have a better time of it, Mum. Do you see?'

'Eh?'

'A better time of it. A way of life which is closer to the ideas important to them. Greater participation and control.'

Neetridge cuts for a couple. It's almost a drinks break.

'Everyone wants to have a better time of it,' says Mrs Slaven. 'We don't need someone to tell us that, do we,' and she leaves her chair to make tea.

'But doing something about it is a different thing,' says Kellie. Mrs Slaven pauses at the doorless entrance to the kitchenette, but instead of answering she looks past Kellie and Slaven to the screen on which the comments man is taking the opportunity to have a say. She likes his thick hair and his confidence.

It's easy to continue a conversation as she makes a drink and Slaven can stretch his legs out in her absence. 'How's Sarah and Cardew?' she asks. Kellie tells her that they are overseas and doing well, which is only half true.

'We get regular letters from Sarah, but Cardy, well you know him.' Mrs Slaven doesn't of course, and has over the years lost any great need to do so, but she just says that they will be all grown up, she expects. 'Twenty-four and twenty-six,' Kellie says. Mrs Slaven says they will have to put up with tea bags, because she doesn't like the new fangled powdered tea. She uses a tone of voice as if they have been arguing the respective merits of each for some ten minutes.

'I had quite a wander round at Waiouru. The old stamping ground,' Slaven says when his mother has come back and he has drawn up his legs to make room for her.

'Eh?'

'Waiouru, Mum. I went there.'

'I never want to see that place again,' she says.

'It's so bare and the seasons so extreme,' says Kellie. 'Hardly anything grows there it seems to me.'

'How many times were you stationed there?' Slaven asks his mother. 'How many years altogether did you spend in Waiouru?'

'We've fallen behind in the run rate,' she says and nods to endorse her own views. She holds her tea mug with great deliberation and talks to Kellie of her weekly finances, valuing her daughter-in-law's budget skills. She allows no access to the years her husband and Slaven spent with her as a family. All that has been closed a long time ago.

Simon Adderley and Slaven had taken her Staysharp kitchen knife to cut up stolen blanks for gunpowder which they used to blow up cans behind the gas hut. Lance-corporal Joux showed them his cock one Sunday afternoon in the old gym and afterwards on cue a hailstorm began which dislodged puffs of dust from the high louvres and heaped stones in the gutters like a whitebait shoal. In very different weather, Slaven met Sgt Hamate drunk and on his way back from leave and was warned in a comradely fashion of any surrender to women. Summer's dusk it was and the smell of Hamate's beer was rendered innocuous by the fragrance of the pines by the sports field and the acetylene and oils from the maintenance shops close at hand. 'Ah, the most beautiful of God's creatures, nevertheless,' said Hamate sadly. 'They fuck like angels and are almost human at other times.' He sat down to buff his dress shoes with a handkerchief and then toppled sideways on to the grass of the sportsground. Slaven left him sleeping there in the warm night and with the resinous pines breathing above him in the same soughing way. Slaven remembers his mother helping him with his school projects on photosynthesis, votes for women and David Livingstone, when no doubt she had better things to do. She came to the prize-givings and saw him take an award or two; some recompense perhaps for their mutual industry. In all his childhood he never once asked her how she was feeling. He heard them arguing half out of earshot, but neither would make a criticism of the other to him. Yet his mother wept when CSM Slaven left for China to join the international forces assisting Democratic Reconstruction. She is dry-eyed now as she watches the cricket and doesn't remark on the oddity that a man with such habits of neatness and with legal aspirations should survive in a land of over a thousand million foreigners and then choke on the top from a lager. There is a time in a relationship when intimacy is a possibility, but a failure to attempt it then means the opportunity will almost certainly not come again. So Slaven arrives at the end of this visit to his mother. A long life is lived in phases and for peace of mind it doesn't pay to straddle too many at a time. Blow the egg of misery well the first time and the thing is always lighter thereafter. 'I see you enjoy the cricket, Mum,' he says.

'Oh, very much,' she says.

Mrs Slaven is pleased to see her son and Kellie, but not disconsolate when it is time to part. She and Kellie wander from Slaven at the end, to see the gardens of the retirement village and talk of the plants there. It is the responsibility of someone else to look after them she says. Another plane comes down into the airport as Slaven stands by his car. He remembers that as he left Waiouru, he had passed a tramper resting on his pack. Perhaps his attention had been taken because it was the first civilian after many people in uniform, yet there was a familiarity wasn't there — a bald headed man with powerful, brown forearms folded on his knees and a calm, observant face. The plane seems to sink into a clump of dwarf bamboo that marks the division between his mother's small section and the next.

When his father was attached to the recruitment office they had lived in Auckland for a time — Takapuna. His mother was happier there. His father had less odd hours to work, though he was no less punctilious in matters of personal hygiene and organisation.

'Two video carousels.'

'Check.'

'Monitor.'

'Check.'

'Recruiting pamphlets for all three services.'

'Check.'

'Application forms; all three services.'

'Check.'

'Posters glossy.'

'Check.'

Mrs Slaven has been saying that there's a much better show in the spring of course. 'Is he all right now, after the accident?' she asks Kellie and is told what the doctors have said. 'Does he still say that his father choked on a bottle top?'

'Yes.'

'He made that up, you know.'

Quietus now. Any more is idle curiosity on our part. See the parting here, in the retirement village with everything in place for the spring and the northern summer already in progress on the television that Slaven's mother goes back inside to see. 'She's not interested in what I'm doing,' says Slaven tolerantly. 'She's got past it.'

'Also I think she's wise enough to know what she can cope with.'

'Not a word about my accident you notice. She didn't ask how my hands were healing.'

'She talked about it when you were at Waiouru. Lucky to be alive she said.'

'No blessing then to be received for the new venture.'

'Check.'

'Nothing either in his new powers to make the past explicable.'

'Check.'

'Just the mirror image memories which can't be read, though sharp and true as the scent of fennel.'

'Check.'

'Just the owl watching from the dark, evergreen trees.'

'Check.'

'Blizzards on the Desert Road and the white peak of Ruapehu.'

'Check.'

And in the summer the tar molten on the street and everything a shimmer so that his father's work day camouflage dress was even more irregular in outlines.

Slaven tells Kellie that, on the way back south, in Wellington, he wants to accept the invitation to call on Dr Royce Meelind, the political scientist who works in the Government Think Tank. 'I feel sure in my own mind now,' he says, 'that I want full steam ahead. I think that we need to get the Coalition for Citizen Power up and running in as many areas as possible, and our next big rally should be in Dunedin.' He uses the phone to reach Miles and get the financial backing he needs if they are to move quickly. Kellie has her turn then, making the appointments she wants in Wellington to set up an organisation there. It's easier, healthier, to concentrate on the future and external things. Surely if you build up some speed in life you're less likely to stall, and find yourself going down. Slaven is done with disquiet for the moment, with questions of what expectations may be aroused by the power of his message, with misgivings as to his health, with the loveless admiration he has for his wife, with his mother and his father. 'Full bloody steam ahead. What do you think?' he tells Kellie. 'After all, before you know it the election will be on us.'

You will remember that Royce Meelind is a top man all right. A top man in the sense of ability and presence rather than merely position. The greatest overt power will never be his because with all his talents and advantages he lacks the strain of personal bitterness and trivial curiosity which are necessary to understand the final one third of the world. He is a small, wiry man you will recall, with brown skin and circular nostrils, like a jockey perhaps, or a steeple-jack, but his voice without much bulk to resonate in is nevertheless deep and clear, full of masculine assurance. He rocks on the balls of his feet and his laugh, without being at all brash, sounds through the corridor, a succession of even, strong notes like a gong. Not a word is slurred and the grammar of his sentences rarely falters in impromptu conversation. Despite his brown skin, on the bridge of his nose and high on his cheeks, small, twisted, inconsequential veins are clearly visible, like crimps of red and purple cotton.

Meelind comes from behind his desk to meet Slaven and sits with him on the leather sofa of the executive suite. His smile has a sincere interest and he takes Slaven's hand firmly. 'Give me a place to stand and I will move the world,' he begins. 'Said in connection with physics, but it applies also in your case Dr Slaven. I'm amazed by your performance at Tuamarina, the tremendous sales of *A New Drummer*, the appearance of the CCP as a national organisation almost overnight. You've struck a chord all right.'

'But which one?'

'Alienation. Without a doubt. A very significant group of New Zealanders who feel exiled from their country while they're still living in it. They seek an allegiance.' Meelind rises to draw two coffees from the dispenser by his desk. The north side of his office has a large screen for presentations, blank grey now, but the windows on the opposite wall give a magnificent view of the harbour.

'Yes, we're having an overwhelming response in many ways, but for so many different, even contradictory reasons. If you could see some of the letters that flood in and some of the callers.'

'I'd very much appreciate any material for assessment.'

'Everyone has a grievance it seems and also a solution for it, but they're all different grievances and various remedies.'

'In toto though,' says Royce Meelind, 'you see they have a unity of opposition to what's being done at present, or not done. That's the beauty of political opposition, there's always an aspect of solidarity, even if it's lost in the very instant of success, the moment that power is achieved.'

'I can see that an analyst, or a campaign professional, would be fascinated in the workings of that, but I have to justify my leadership. What I say and support give rise to expectations. I don't find it that hard to arouse that sense of alienation, but the direction of it? Ah, that's it you see.'

'Exactly,' says Dr Meelind. They both realise that in the end people like Slaven take the chances and people like Meelind are commentators. Although Royce Meelind is in the Government Think Tank, although he will make both an assessment and a report after his talk with Slaven, they are not in direct competition. 'Proportional representation, then bi-cameralism, then non-legislative representatives were all brought in for just the sort of feeling that you have tapped. Despite it all people haven't any greater sense of identification, or participation. There are too many steps in the process, too many complexities. The earliest democracies were crude and direct, like the people who voted in them, and then as now they offered opportunities to the demagogues.'

'You understand that the Coalition isn't putting up any candidates itself. We're not attempting to become a Parliamentary party.'

'Yes,' says Meelind. Together they have their coffee and see through the large window the crowded street many stories below, people, foreshortened, scurrying about there. And buildings rising up to rival the one in which Slaven and Meelind sit at their ease. From the outer office is the sound of some noisy arrivals. 'There's nothing sinister in our interest,' says Meelind. 'In fact I openly push the politicians to pay more attention to what people think. Isn't it important for Government to be receptive to the public mood? The sort of groundswell that you create is exactly what we should be on to. Whatever we do receives a largely cynical response. If we take no notice of such movements we're arrogantly elitist and captured by our own bureaucracy, if we show an interest then we're manipulative and exploitative. I'm excited by what you're doing. The power to mobilise the opinions of the electorate is so rare. The flow for so long has been the other way that people have become the negative pole, given themselves up to apathy and malaise.'

'You're well in the shit, boy.' The voice isn't Meelind's, or Slaven's. It comes from the outer office and is accompanied by heavy movement and thuds. Royce Meelind smiles and lifts his eyes quickly so that the whites show in a brief mockery of the crass world's intrusion.

'The length of your Tuamarina address,' he says. 'An amazing thing when all research shows that these days people will not be talked at hour after hour. It proved me wrong. You must have the rhetorical stamina and gift of a Gladstone, a Luther King, or new China's Soong Shih.'

'Any strength in my speaking comes from conviction,' says Slaven, 'rather than art.'

'Like a pig in it, son. Yes, you're well in it. Jamie says you were supposed to come in on Tuesday and do it then. It's all on the roster and now you're really in the shit, see.'

'No one told me did they.'

There is a variety of workman whose voice becomes louder in proportion to the inappropriateness of his presence. Slaven imagines them amongst the soft carpet and monstera plants of the outer office. 'I'm not sure what it is myself,' he continues, 'but a rally builds towards unity if it's a success at all. You need actual physical proximity, personal decision becoming awesome in a mass expression. That's why I think it won't work on television. You saw me on Beardsley's show?'

'You were okay.'

'You don't mean that. I have to be there, with everybody.'

'The crowd as Leviathan,' says Meelind.

'When a crowd comes together like that it has a soul of its own and a resolve of its own and no conscience whatsoever, so the resolve must be the right one. Must, must be the right one.' Slaven wonders if Meelind understands.

'You hold the ladder then and I'll unscrew the sodding thing. I can't see anything the matter with it myself. Jamie is not happy, sunshine. Not happy at all my old son. Not happy one little bit and myself I don't like your chances. In the shit, my son. That's you and my heart bleeds.'

'Still, that gift for holding them, getting through. I mean, god, the news of the world these days is only fifteen minutes before the first game show of the evening isn't it.'

'For me it's still a success of ideas rather than delivery,' says Slaven. 'People become numbed by routine unhappiness and trivial compromise until they think those are the natural conditions of life, but at Tuamarina we had the exhilarating realisation that a great many people want something better and think it possible.'

'And is it?' asks Meelind.

'Let it down carefully, old son, or else we'll be arse over twat and in worse trouble.'

'Wait till I shift my fucken grip on the thing. It's cutting off the circulation. My back'll go in a minute.'

'You and me both, sunshine.'

'Some people see it as a freakish talent, and in the end doesn't it become a power thing. Where will you point the crowd and when release it?'

'You mean what side I choose?' says Slaven.

'Yes, what side you choose.'

'I'll come back for the ladder. Remind me.'

'Is that why you asked me to come.' Slaven admires the ease with which Royce Meelind does his job.

'It's my homework. I imagine that quite soon the Minister will ask about this Slaven chap and his CCP.'

'What will be your opinion?'

'Another rally or two like Tuamarina and you'll be shaking the political establishment by the throat. Then again, as you know well enough, you've got a tiger by the tail.'

'And if I can point it in the United Party's direction?' says Slaven.

Royce Meelind smiles. There is the impartial interest of the scientist in his eyes as well as the appraisal of a Government servant.

'Tuamarina is a long way from Auckland,' he says.

When Slaven leaves there is no one in the outer office; just an air-conditioning unit cover on the carpet and an aluminium ladder of the sort which makes Slaven wince with a memory of betrayal. Slaven parts with Meelind at the lifts and as he drops down floor by floor, he wonders if the Think Tank would be set against him if he and the Coalition presses the Government hard. As he comes into Bowen Street, Slaven sees the great copper dome of the new speed rail terminal glistening not far from the Beehive. In just a few months he has come a long way and he must be careful not to over-reach himself.

There is a place, known well to most of us, where the printers hum and the computer screen glows in fields of blue and grey and green, and on a field azure, say, is a profit graph rampant. The vidphones are just an under-growth in such a jungle, yet each has its time to bloom and blush, casting a glow while communication proceeds. A frieze screen is high on the front wall and words like runners chase across it for general announcement. All balances to the sync computer by 1650 hours, or, don't forget Anna Sledgley's farewell at the Goblin tonight. People never change. They are the same here as in Dickens's counting house, or the Minoan records room of the palace at Knossus.

See the finest grime of a thousand thousand finger applications that lies just below the pressure point patina of the high tech keys, the tape which holds up the continuous feed door on number twenty-three. Popperwell coughs to cover a characteristic fart and the women screw up their faces. Abbot glances from the inner office at the people who would like to change places. You are entitled to a short break of course and there are seminars on alternate Fridays in company time and a suggestion drawer on the main computer which is always a laugh to bring up. Allen is the sharpest programmer, but he won't get on in the firm, because he blatantly takes his sick days to renovate American cars.

The machines of each technological niche have their eyes of green, or yellow, or red. Dots, or strips, or obelisks that gleam, wink, alter hue and form and finally die at the day's end.

Whatever it is that is done here has always been done, and by the same people — informing and arranging and recording, letting people down lightly and with some profit in it. Only the means at their disposal alters.

Although Aldous Slaven isn't a member of any of the three categories of parliamentary representative, he sets aside an afternoon each week to be available to discuss the principles on which the Coalition for Citizen Power is established. Kellie provides him with a list of those who are to see him, with brief comments she has added, and Slaven drives in from the western hobby farms to the Rev Thackeray Thomas's Charismatic Cambrian Church in Armagh Street where the Coalition has rooms and secretarial services.

See him on this cool, spring day with a drifting easterly drizzle from the sea which encourages the gulls to come scavenging in the city. Read the list that he scans briefly before leaving the unsealed carpark to enter the Church Hall.

> *2 pm — Mr Nicholas Halley — offer of his talents (unspecified)*
>
> *2.15 pm — Ms Anna Fivetrees — thrilled to the core by* A New Drummer
>
> *2.30 pm — Anatasia — to discuss gay issues inherent in the Coalition's stance*
>
> *2.45 pm — Ms Polly Romains — freelance journalism graduate, wanting scoop I suppose*
>
> *3 pm — Mr Dean Talbot — long standing grievance with all about everything*
>
> *3.15 pm — Mr Murray Franca — wouldn't say*
>
> *3.30 pm — Mrs Jocelyn Piers — financial and thinks she remembers you from Te Tarehi primary*

*3.45 pm — Mr Bruce Anderson from Statos Nationalist
party — matter to your advantage*
*After — toast slice kibble wheat, margarine, penlight
batteries, prescription, don't forget.*

From the plain room that the Coalition rents, Slaven
sees a toi-toi bush and a neglected garden before the road.
Weeds are obviously assured of equal divinity with the
flowers here. Diamonds of water gather on the leaves of
dock, twitch and chickweed. As a background to everything
that is said are modest sounds of water dripping, seeping,
plopping, trickling and the sounds of the earth drinking.
Dafydd Thomas is talking in a room in the other wing, visible
to Slaven. Framed by the window he is obviously working
up a good head of steam, though no sound is heard and no
audience visible. He is counselling seniors perhaps, or merely
practising his rhetoric so that he's more his father's son.

'You might say that I've powers of plenipotentiary,' says
Bruce Anderson. 'Why restrict yourself to being a pressure
group, however powerful, when you could have direct
political influence as a representative. It stands to reason.'

Anatasia is well and comfortably dressed and comfortably assertive. Slaven notices that her legs are shapely and
that on one ankle is a small tattoo. 'I appreciate your wife
plays an important part in the movement,' she says, 'but
it's a matter of perceived stance and public profile. The law
is quite clear on equity in executive structures and if you
have a copy of Coalition appointments and responsibilities
I can quickly check whether it's in compliance. You know
how such things can be picked up for political purpose by
the unscrupulous.' A thrush is on the rough lawn, listening
for a worm that the soft rain will tempt to rise. How much
more delicate its colours than the greasy, pin-flecked dark
feathers of the starlings, or the full gloss of a blackbird.

'I mightn't have the qualifications on paper, not the
actual qualifications on actual paper, but then I always say
that's what they're worth, aye. Paper. No, but from the school
of hard knocks I've learnt a few lessons I can tell you. Aye?
What I see myself being able to bring to the CCP is
promotional skills that I've developed in the world of
insurance and bereavement support.'

'Form one with Ms Kedgley it would be wouldn't it. I said to my sister that there wouldn't be many Aldous Slavens. Fancy that. And there was that boy with us for just a term from the foster home and he broke into the school office and set fire to it, no, sprayed everything with the foam extinguisher, that's right. It all comes back to you, doesn't it. And he's copped it you know. Oh, yes. Locked accidentally in a commercial freezer and when they found him he'd built a snow cave of 1kg bags of free flow peas. It all comes back to you, doesn't it.' Jocelyn Piers looks at Slaven expectantly as if there has been a clear reward posted for Slaven's identification and she is here to claim it.

Slaven realises these are the people who come to Tuamarina and St Kilda. These are his people. He's not long back from Dunedin and he saw clearly there the thousands of people just like these. Standing high on the sealed road at St Kilda he had addressed the crowd on the beach and on the recreation grounds below him. The people had covered the ash-blonde sand on the seaward side and also the sports fields on the city side. He had seen the line of generating windmills on the hills behind the city and looking south along the beach where the great audience finally thinned he had seen a scud of white blowing up into the dunes from the beach — drifting spray, or the pale sand wind-driven. They had sung the protest songs *Capetown Races* and *Remember Greenpeace*; they had begun the vogue of the CCP's own theme song — *Half Moon Bay*. And all of them are the same people that write the thousands of letters, send money and policies unsolicited, come to the Cambrian Church Hall so that they can talk to him. Iago right now deals with a number who have come without appointments, but find they can't by-pass Kellie's system.

'You think about it. Don't dismiss it out of hand. We feel that you have all that it takes for a major political career and a place in Parliament would guarantee a continuing profile for your policies. Otherwise, you know what will happen once the elections are over.'

'And then when I first heard you,' says Anna Fivetrees, 'I could hardly believe it. After always feeling totally alone in my views, to find someone who has the same values and the ability to make them known. I talk to people about you all the time. They must think I'm terrible, terrible.' Anna Fivetrees puts both hands to her face in confusion at her own daring. 'That bit when you talked of the need in adulthood to regain the trust of youth. How true, how beautiful.'

Behind the chair on which each of Slaven's visitors sit in turn is a poster of platitudes and as each person's head comes to a different height, so from Slaven's vantage they have individual adages. There are no strangers here, only friends you haven't met, is Anna's halo; for Nicholas Halley, today is the first day of the rest of your life.

'The Council has given me a complete runaround, never mind that I've been a ratepayer and reserve fireman for over thirty years. They won't see me any more, because they know there's no bloody answer to my argument, Aye? The papers have refused to publish my letters now. The buggers have been got at I reckon, and I've been individually to every Christchurch MP. They all say they'll look into my case, but do nothing. Everyone's knuckled under to the big boys except me.'

'One of the things that interests people, Dr Slaven, is that apparently you weren't active in politics at all until the accident meant you had to stop working.'

'I went for days you know, before I plucked up the courage to ring and ask for an appointment. I kept thinking of how valuable your time was.'

'What I'm keen to do as well,' says Anatasia, 'is talk to your wife and Eula Fitzsimmons. Absolutely essential to get their perspective on what the CCP offers women. An issue you address often I'm sure.'

Slaven thinks he can hear the Hoihos — *Someday, baby, there'll be time for sailing, on the ebb tide from Half Moon Bay.* A radio in one of the other rooms perhaps, or one of those odd bursts he gets within his brain. Several of the people kindly rebuffed by Iago Thomas are standing in the drizzle to catch a glimpse of him through the window. Slaven hopes it's just idle curiosity, but knows there's more to it. 'When I think of everything we will achieve, it's almost too much for me,' says Anna Fivetrees.

Dr Dunne comes down from the Euthanasia Clinic after supervising the send off for a top-dressing pilot with inoperable cancer of the bowel. Such occasions leave her subdued, but thankful that the option exists. The pilot's wife initiated the sequence of injections and there was a video on the large screen showing the pilot working over blocks of the inland Kaikouras; virtually no wind and the plane banked into the evening sun at the head of the valley where the scree slopes led up to the divide. The pilot watched himself, the plumes of super drifted above that steep, lonely country. Dust to dust. 'Look at her go, the beauty,' he said to his family.

Yes, Marianne Dunne comes down from Euthanasia and thinks that she has fought her old enemy to a draw. A few quiet minutes in her office before she goes to see Miles Kitson, who is back in for a spell of treatment. She has videos for him too, but not terminal. One is from Aldous Slaven and covers the St Kilda rally. The other is from Miles's wife — the only access he allows her when he is at his worst and in care. Marianne has already seen the first, watched the vast crowd on the long open beach and the sports fields, wondered what is really happening to her patient and friend. Slaven with his burnt hands and a mind subject to magnificent alteration by the surge through all its circuits.

Miles watches Georgina trying on a selection of new clothes that are heaped on the window squabs of her bedroom. She talks to him as she does so, remarks sometimes occasioned by the garments which are reflected in the full length mirrors, or a commentary of her life without him. 'I'll go ski-ing with the Railles if you're not back by the fourteenth. There's been a final dump, Polly said.' Georgina is trying on a lace camisole. She shows no awkwardness, no posturing before the recorder that their housekeeper holds, for she is both confident in her beauty and familiar with such display as a form of communication in their marriage. She and Miles are perfectly aware of the sexuality; the slipping of a shoulder strap, hip rotation, the tightening of her breasts as she stretches her arms up, but transcending that, or at least complementing it, is the need for such display of grace in the face of illness and time.

Miles in a private room lies propped up on his pillows. The tears gather beneath his eyes. Marianne Dunne sits further towards the bed-end. She is so short that her legs won't touch the floor and she tucks them beneath her on the spread. 'I love the black dress cut low at the back,' she says. 'Georgina's back is very smooth, yet with little sign of the sub-cutaneous fat which gives that effect. One of the things with black is that it suits both a pale skin and a tan.'

'I read that everyone has a birthmark somewhere on the body. Is that true?' Miles can see the skin taut on Georgina's collar bone and hair falling over one side of her face. See how definite the hip is, how fragile the wrist bones raised beneath the skin.

'Maybe if you accept any minor blemish, and some that come out after birth. But there's no genetic imperative.'

'Georgina has one on her heel for god's sake.'

'Mulberry, wine, or bleach?'

'Oval and white as spider's silk.'

'A bleach mark then. Just lack of pigmentation. It's stable and of no consequence whatsoever.'

'I've told her that it's a reminder from the manufacturer that nothing's perfect.' Georgina, naked to the camera and the glass, pauses to talk to him. Her stomach has a slight forward curve with just the single navel tuck in its upholstery. She has the nails of both feet painted — purple almost.

'I spend a good deal on clothes in these sessions,' she says. 'So many of the things I try on, I like.' Miles gives a barely audible laugh. Money has become at last a source of humour for him.

'Lucky thing,' says Marianne Dunne, 'to look like a model and be able to buy what you like.'

'And be married to a package of disintegration,' says Miles. 'I imagine that the poor see mortality as their greatest ally. The one alternative to their lifestyle they can afford and the one thing the rich can't buy off. It's the only justice they can be sure of.' Georgina is trying on beige, linen culottes; through the window behind her, Miles catches a glimpse of his grounds and the view beyond. The wall of

Central Otago schist he helped to build, Christchurch city spread below, and the gondolas, reduced by distance, passing up and down the Port Hills.

'Don't take the morbid approach on me,' says Marianne. 'I may take you up on it. You've had a great time both rich and poor and you're still pleasing yourself. And Georgina wants nothing more than to visit you, you know that. It's just your pride that means you lie here and watch a video of your own wife.'

'Well, thank god I can indulge my pride. I can afford my own nurses, I can afford you, I can afford the periodic services like this which may give me a few hours a week when I don't feel like a bag of shit loosely tied. If I can't go back home in better shape than this then I'll be asking you to do a different job for me.'

'And what will you leave me in your will? I calculate that you're good for a new surgical annex at least.'

Miles turns the video off. He's interested in planning his death. 'There's a potion for everything I suppose, but the old Roman way must still have its supporters. I've always enjoyed a hot bath.'

'There are several appropriate parts of the body very poorly served with nerves, yet with large enough arteries. The side of the foot for example. Virtually no pain need be felt at all. You have to get special dispensation to use anything but the procedure laid down by the Council. Anyway, if the time comes I think you'll find our way the best.' Marianne Dunne is always quite candid with Miles; it is their way together. 'I still think you should let Georgina come to see you.'

'Once, you know, I was a man for women to reckon with. Confidence and humour are more important than looks. I learnt that.'

'I've always wanted to be taller, of course,' says Marianne, 'but thank god I was given a good brain.'

'I used to have that,' says Miles, 'but it's gone.' He watches the doctor swing her feet from his bed. When she is standing though, her head is not much higher than before.

'I'm serious,' she says, 'about asking for money for the hospital. I don't feel guilty at all about asking. You know what we do here and the value of it. I bet Georgina wouldn't miss enough to build the extensions I need.'

'We'll see. You're as bad as Kellie Slaven, who's conned me into bankrolling the activities of the Coalition until their financial structures are in place. I've had the bite put on me by people most of my life and many of them with better offers than you can make. So, an annex is it? Kitson Castle, or the Miles Mausoleum. You think I'm a sucker for it, because I'm dying. It's shameless of you. You need reporting to the Medical Council.'

'Why should dying be an excuse for not accomplishing things before it happens?'

'Now there's something worth arguing about if you had the time,' says Miles. 'It reminds me of old Roland Purcell who was at the university and was intrigued with a delivery van with the words Door to Door Transports. He became preoccupied with the semiotic implications and went out on to the road to determine if the van was signified, or signifier and was run over by it. Struck with his own research.' His own mention of Roland Purcell leads Miles on to recollections of Albie Purcell, the son, and he doesn't notice when Marianne Dunne quietly leaves the room.

Albie flatted with Miles in a converted garage by the Addington Saleyards and they went to lectures at the Canterbury Campus with the landscaped humps of smooth lawns, the streams through them, the faculty buildings in ugly and rectangular contrast. At every party, when he was sufficiently drunk, Albie would start to shout, 'It's frontal lobotomy time,' and thereafter talked with a lucidity and passion of higher things which were completely beyond him when sober. He scraped through a law degree and then went into local government. When he felt stifled there, he established a small farm in the Hokianga, raising frogs and mushrooms for the gourmet restaurant trade. Miles eventually became the major shareholder for old times' sake. The only tangible return Miles ever receives is in kind, cartons of frog pieces and mushrooms when Albie makes the occasional visit to indulge in undergraduate memories and ask for more capital. He thinks the glory of their early experience together comes from the poverty. Miles knows it is rather the recollection of youth. Unfortunately, no amount of drink now restores to Albie the frontal lobotomy of that time.

Miles lies alone in his private room and watches more video: not Georgina now, but Slaven at his second great rally. The huge crowd on the beach with their backs to the wind from the sea which hasn't been told of spring. The wind snatches at Slaven's voice and sends the words scudding and swirling away over the people packed on the beach, the top carpark, the recreation fields on the other side. The camera pans the sea to show the swell breaking white far out from the beach. The Rev Thackeray Thomas stands behind Slaven on the stage, wearing his red dragon jacket and hyped up in the turbulence of emotion and weather as if it is some great pit-head deliverance. Miles is at once appalled and fascinated by the energy, the conviction, the transience of it. What can they expect, all these Otago people — the worst dressed and least progressive section of the country's citizenry. They haven't grasped the essential premise of life; that nature has no sense of justice.

The soundtrack has a portion of the song ever more closely associated with Slaven and the Coalition. *Hear the secret night parrot from its booming grounds. Love has many calls to offer from the place of Half Moon Bay.* The video runs on, but Miles's thoughts move back to his own life. Even the sensational involving a friend is no competition for your own thoughts. The outcast is lonely, they say, the adolescent, they say. Lonely at the top as well and lonely in the face of grave decision, yet Miles wishes that much more of his time had been spent with no company, but his own. The weak and the mediocre cluster into groups. He has wasted years in total dealing with people of no interest to him. Miles lies in the private room darkened for his viewing. The changing colours from the screen play across the sheen of his face. He is flat on his back as he thinks, eyes to the ceiling, mouth opened by the slackness of his jaw. Only the arc of nose cartilage, clear beneath the waxy tissue of his skin, maintains his face as a living head, below it is all mandible, socket and brow ridges, the topography of skulls.

Miles is thinking of the chance encounters and opportunities which can begin success. His own first coup at Zapp Corp, which set him on the way, was the trip to Chile to investigate distribution outlets. He was too junior at the time to be anyone's nomination in the boardroom, but he had by chance come into the executive washroom only seconds after Jasons, the Chairman, had cleared his bowels and must still own the stench of his excrement in the confined, tiled room. Miles had with humble obstinacy blocked Jasons' way and asked for the opportunity to represent the company in Chile. With his passing and common mortality so blatantly in the air, even the Chairman was at some disadvantage. 'Oh, very well, very well,' he had said in passing, and Miles had gone and managed — very well. Such a recollection is a pleasant sophistry in part, for Miles knows that there have been a hundred chances of ruin which he has avoided by talent, hard work and good fortune, but all the same there's enough truth to prompt his soft, hoarse laugh. A career so well known and envied — launched by the trivial humiliation of Jasons in a latrine.

See Miles Kitson lying alone as he prefers it and the St Kilda video still on, the southern images of excitement and opportunity casting movement and colour into the hospital room. Slaven's speech although turned low has resonance and power. Yet Miles's pale eyes are on the ceiling and he goes back years for the replays that he needs. Two lines from the poet Alberto Valdivia come back to him.

Everything will go — afternoon, the sun, life:
evil, which cannot be undone, will prevail.

In the spring also, Cardew Slaven flies in on a hush jet from Sydney to see for himself what his old man is up to. He has received no invitation from home, rather the stimulus was Australian reports of the political backwoodsman setting the normally morose New Zealanders to bay at the moon. Also, somewhere in it all, Cardew gets the sniff of money.

His parents are pleased to see him of course. They say so as parents do, though Slaven's greetings are at second-hand. Kellie meets her son as he comes through customs at the overseas terminal. She almost kisses him, but at the last moment puts her hand on his shoulder instead and both of them are relieved by the restraint. 'Your father's preparing his speech for the Western Springs rally,' she says.

'Fair enough,' says Cardew. 'He's certainly come right after the accident. Bounced back and into the news and the big time. What on earth's got into him?'

'He can't go back to the surgery because of his hands and some emotional effects, but he's working harder than ever. He has this sudden passion to accomplish improvement and it's brought out this special leadership in him. It's a whole new life. Everything is topsy-turvy now.'

Cardew drives his mother's car towards the outskirts on the west of Christchurch. Going from the airport that way he avoids most of the city, although the suburbs continue to encroach, with subdivisions amongst the nurseries, orchards and horticultural units. 'Is there any money in it?' he asks casually.

'If he asks for money they give it. They've even been sending it in without being asked, along with every other sort of thing that's important to them. The Coalition's been backed by Miles Kitson you know?'

'Right.'

'But we've got our own financial structures in place now and money's not a problem. Anyway, we're not in it for that reason, though I think there should be prudent policies and reserves.'

'Yeah,' says Cardew. He was a partner in Placemate Personnel Agency in Sydney, but has come out of it with next to nothing. He looks forward to the eventual half share in his parents' assets, but the new activities offer the chance of more immediate returns. 'I could stay on for a bit and give some help. I'd say there'd be a good deal of pressure on you and Dad in all of this. Often it's sensible to have someone close to the family dealing with the business side of things.' Cardew's large fingers hang over the steering wheel as he drives. He has large, soft hands and feet like a bear, but despite the belief about the size of appendages indicating final growth, he has never grown tall. The suede expanse of his shoes covers most of the car floor in front of him. 'So what are the arrangements for Western Springs,' he says.

He sees the chance to do himself some good. A chance for once to be on the inside and to make that work in his favour. He thinks of the professional issues promoters, protest campaigners and political frontmen who have made it big and the managers and agents who made it big with them. Cardew wants some real money so he can afford one of the top blondes he admires in Sydney. S-shaped blondes with breasts like flotation devices and thighs which never meet. Cardew's bear paws tremble on the steering wheel; the world blurs for a moment. 'Who's setting up the Auckland thing?' he says.

'I am,' says Kellie. 'After Tuamarina — you heard about that?'

'Uh-huh.'

'In many ways Tuamarina was a shambles and not just because the numbers caught them out. Things are a lot more business-like now. Aldous and I worked all through what was needed. St Kilda was so much better; the first that the new CCP took responsibility for. You can't afford to have it any other way in a political movement. A lot of people make no distinction between method and message, you know.'

'Any organisation needs clear financial structures.'

'More than that; needs accountability in all it does. A weakness in the movement at all, anything goes wrong, and Aldous will be blamed. It's no use saying that ideals are distinct from the management of things. I said at the meetings, if we're going to be responsible for the whole show then we have to be able to influence the whole show. It's not bearable any other way. Responsibility for an outcome should be accompanied by authority to affect the outcome. The thing we can't control of course is the response people have. That's what your father worries most about. Anyway, we've some clever people on the team now.'

'I reckon family control gets around a lot of problems. Have you considered making a charge at Western Springs. People never value what they get for nothing.'

'Except sex, poetry and money,' says Kellie. Cardew doesn't answer. He thinks his mother's being a smart-arse and he doesn't remember her as talking in that way. These new activities of his father's though, this Coalition for Citizen Power rapidly developing a national profile. Cardew sees possibilities.

His asks his mother about the garden next, something closer to her traditional interests, but doesn't listen to her replies. Two years apart and yet within half an hour he is tuning her out. Don't talk too much of the power of flesh and blood. Cardew thinks of Steven Wybrow as they pass the street in which he had lived. He sees himself running down that street having punched Steven Wybrow in the face and making his lip bleed. It was the only reaction he had at the time to the humiliation of eleven straight losses at computer Galaxwar during the course of a Sunday afternoon. 'Another win to the Champeen of the entire, wide world,' Steven kept crowing. Cardew remembers the surprisingly firm impact with Steven's face and the sprint down the Wybrow's drive which seemed endless. He'd left a red anorak at the house which was never returned and Cardew denied knowing where he had lost it. 'Champeen of the world, aye,' murmurs Cardew.

'What's that,' says Kellie.

'Steven Wybrow thought he was Champeen of the whole damn world.'

'Sarah's with us,' says Kellie. 'You knew that?'

'How is she.' Cardew attempts brotherly warmth, but there's only jocularity. He is seized with a boredom sprung from return to what is familiar and unloved.

'She's come back for a while as well. It's been relatively slow with her freelance astrology, I think. She says she might do some psychology papers.' Cardew opens his mouth to make reply, but is not supplied with even the most banal of comments suitable for his mother to hear, and he is left with an expression half fatigue, half adenoidal idiocy as he turns off the main west road and into the fringe belt of four hectare blocks which includes his parents' home. Jesus, though, freelance astrology.

Something then of exposition from a distance this has been. A hush jet delivery, but no deliverance. A hand upon a shoulder and externals like a short order cook. A placing of each in relation to the others you understand, but you come right up close with me and meet the man. All right?

It is Cardew, evident by a distinctive bad breath in the air and a less explicable, but equally characteristic aura of physicality such as strikes the observer of an empty baboon cage at the zoo. Everything about him is too obvious, too carnal, as if a model *homo sapien* has been made in the flesh. So here he is: the nostrils drawing attention to their vital function, his moustache not quite the colour of his hair and offset a little because he always trims it with his right hand. His expression is one of ignorant presumption, of scrabbling for a living in the here and now because there will be nothing after death — not even brief immortality in the fond memory of others. No shadow of the spirit, no tincture of the divine, no faint stirring of apprehension at the potential of the mind.

So you see him. Cardew Slaven with no letters after his name and no approbation in its pronounciation. How like his father though in the hair which stands up from his crown and the way he shakes his wrist to bring his watch strap down, the way his big foot hangs from the ankle when he has crossed his legs, his dark, lacquered eyes. How like Kellie in the thin, lobeless ears and jawline. How like himself in that he looks away while he is talking and his mouth is tight with a barely suppressed yawn before people who have no immediate advantage for him.

So here is Cardew Slaven for you, the son, cast as the cast off in the list of company and deserving it. Not the villain because he lacks sufficient malicious interest in others, not the fool because he lacks the pathos of the true jester and any grasp of the symbolic utterance. Experiment with him in that dark laboratory which shuts down external stimulus in sequence and he will in stages close down himself, until he is inert there in the dark, only his blood coursing. For nothing sublime originates from within to motivate him, no sense of higher aspiration, no vision to which the metal of the world and self must be beaten — just the instincts of gratification, or survival.

Shagging is the thing he likes best. That's how he spent his money in Sydney. That's how he will spend the money the CCP will unwittingly supply. He has a cultivated appetite. He shags in hotel and motel rooms, in old villas renovated for the purpose, in chalets which never see the snows, in staff quarters reached by a narrow path with a tin fence hard beside it, in bean bag lounges and maisonettes. He shags with the glow of television casting bruises on the white arses of his loves. He shags in dormitories, changing rooms, vans, and after hours cafeterias with all the legs turned up to the ceiling; yes, all the legs turned up. He shags in the bed and breakfast which overlooks the croquet green and shags in the deep doorway of the St Vincent de Paul in Mitre Street while a group of drivers yarn at the taxi stand ten metres away. He is indiscriminate, except that he dislikes women who come to sex determined to enjoy it, as they might join a tennis club on advice to make friends.

He shags always with the same fixed, lacquered eyes, not looking at a woman, not registering the things that seem the object of his fierce stare, but shagging as if he is knocking at a secret door and in the greatest pitch of the act the flicker in his eyes is brief anticipation of the opening of that door. Knock, knock, knocking at Heaven's door.

If he isn't shagging in any of those places, then he's most likely shagging in his mind. Shagging Eula Fitzsimmons at the meeting of the Coalition Executive until his mouth slackens from its yawn, shagging the weather reader in her own deep depression, shagging the girl who comes with the keys for the rental cars until her breath mists up the windscreen, mounting the shapely shoppers and catching their exclamation from behind while a cool wind blows on his balls at the top of his stroke.

Knock, knock, knocking on Heaven's door.

Just an insight to ponder on as Slaven sweeps his double garage and sees the car approaching. He comes out to meet Cardew and the clumsy touch is only partly explained by the damage to his hands. They haven't seen each other for two years and Slaven hopes for some change for the better in them both, some lift within himself at the sight of his son, some sense of mutual goodwill even if attitudes and understandings must remain distinct. It doesn't come. There are only the physical resemblances and they're most remarked on by others.

'You've become almost famous, Dad,' says Cardew. He resents that as well of course, as he resents the example of hard work and moderate success that Slaven provides. Now though, a sudden, flamboyant success and therefore one that could come to anything. As they talk Cardew yawns in his father's face and his eyes slide away.

'Sarah will be back later,' says Kellie when the silence lengthens. They move inside. Aldous and Cardew carrying cases, Kellie leading the way. Slaven wonders why his new vision offers no insight in regard to his children, why he has nothing of urgency to say to his son, yet can speak with strangers about vital and personal things for hours on end. Some people are known so well that we can have no hope of them.

After St Kilda, and with the CCP establishing branches in all parts of the country, there are political approaches of course and discreet talk of possible accommodation. Eula Fitzsimmons was approached by Tonkin of the Democratic Socialists and there is a meeting. The Democrats haven't held office for fourteen years and are now mainly urban liberals with a rural fringe of alternative lifestylers. Gebrill, a former PM who came to grief over refugee immigration is here, Fassiere as well and Tonkin who set it up.

Gebrill sits next to the window and speaks little. He watches Slaven's face and finds there all he needs to know, but when his own colleagues have their say he tips his melancholy eyes to the grass and gardens two floors below and picks his lip. He hasn't been given very long.

'How do you think that your public support would translate, realistically, into votes?' asks Fassiere.

'The studies show the Coalition's reaching at least twenty per cent directly and influencing at least that again through family, or associate contact.'

'Yet our research indicates that over one third of the people attending your rallies haven't voted in the last two national elections.'

'Yes, but will they in this one? The point you see is that

we've got these people thinking politics again.' Kellie and Fassiere weigh each other's smiles and Gebrill, one long finger at his lip, watches the office workers from the bank and the legal firms enjoy the fountain, the freedom amid the lawns and flower plots. Beyond that he can see the wide, glassed entrance to the atrium of the South Pacific Bank, which he had once termed in the House, the Bubble Bank. The atrium is inviting now — pungas growing in the coolness, more delicate ferns below them, yellow Samoan orchids. 'Middle New Zealand,' says Kellie, 'that's where you're weakest isn't it. The heartland. And that's just where we have the greatest strength, the greatest control. Who can give you Dargaville, aye? Who can give you Tuatapere, Fielding and Becks, Greymouth, Ngapara, Bulls, Parnassus, the valleys of the Owen and the Hakataramea?'

'A lot of places, but few people,' says Tonkin. See the neatness of his collar despite the heat and the thin case with touchtronic locks.

'All right. What about the ninety-five thousand third quartile by income who live north of the bridge, or the sixty-seven thousand of the same group in the new sprawls beyond Porirua. What we did at St Kilda we're going to do at Western Springs.'

'We're not denying there is a constituency,' says Tonkin. 'We're here to determine the political cost of encompassing it within the Democratic Socialist Party. We have to be a very responsible shopping party. You understand that.'

Gebrill watches a young man below lean forward with his knees spread to eat an orange, careful that the juice doesn't dribble onto his clothes. The young man's hair is fashionably permed and his movements are supple and quick.

'There's no way that we can take on board full regional devolution, ostracism, or quantitative gender and ethnic equality in political office,' says Fassiere. 'Let's be honest about that.' Fassiere has some Chinese blood of which she is proud. A certain Deng came out to the Tuapeka goldfields in the 1860s. He worked through the tailings left by European miners; made less, but saved more. All that was long ago and would have been forgotten, except that Fassiere is now deputy leader of the Democratic Socialist Party and the journalists are delighted with a simplistic explanation for her financial acumen, her relentless industry and a complexion that all admire.

'Which of the demands could you accept as policy, then?' asks Kellie.

'Or, even more important, which would you like to include?' says Slaven. 'I believe that the ideal should be discussed before the practical.'

Gebrill perks up at that, swivels his face from the window back to the affairs of the office. The long, lined face of a gibbon with the area of his upper lip very full and semi-lunar. 'Ah, now there's the rub,' he says. 'None of them. Not one of your grubby arsed, popularist, minimally egalitarian and fatuous statements will be part of Democratic policy while I'm alive.' And Gebrill has a good laugh at that, because it is known that he is dying, like his old enemy Miles Kitson, and has no one to please now but himself. No voice says he'll be dead soon anyway, hopefully before the election, and that Fassiere, who is acting leader during Gebrill's illness, has the numbers in caucus if she has to use them. It is politic of course and a sign of new allegiance, that Tonkin is the one to hint at the true order of things. He smiles at them.

'All we can do is consider all the possibilities and report back to the caucus and the party organisations,' he says, 'but for myself, I must say that there are features of the Coalition's demands which appear to be endorsed by a groundswell of voter opinion and which aren't necessarily incompatible with our objectives. A mandatory plebiscite on the presidential term, a new ministry to promote emotional well-being, further curbs on party advertising; these things could well be runners.'

So Gebrill turns away from them once more, preferring to watch those happenings outside which are transient enough, but not with an end so imminent, so bitterly capping great achievement. He deserves better, surely, and he feels little concern for any politics which might come after, but not include him. He is tempted to speak to Slaven concerning the temper and the patience of a crowd, the onslaught of popular power and its equally sudden passing.

The Democrats are prepared to accept several CCP points into their manifesto. It becomes clear some political appointments for Coalition members could follow if the election is a success, and in return they would require public, sustained and exclusive endorsement before the poll. Gebrill takes no part in the discussion. Where he has torn a little skin from his lip, the bright blood grows, but he doesn't lick or wipe it away. So it spreads slowly into the creases at the side of his mouth. There is no point in standing up to Fassiere and Tonkin, for even if he won, he no longer has the time to take possession of the field.

Afterwards, Slaven agrees with Kellie that the Democrats will have to do better than this. If Western Springs goes well they'll have to cough a good deal harder, Kellie thinks. Slaven wishes he could take greater pleasure in the growing power of the Coalition, the consideration with which Fassiere and Tonkin treat him, but the image that he takes with him past the South Pacific Bank is the painful bitterness of the former PM's face and the blood from his picked lip.

Miles, on the other hand, is quite bucked up to hear of a once powerful adversary in such decline, and while in a good spell himself. Slaven and he have a beer in Miles's tower house on the hills above Christchurch. 'Like all lawyers turned to politics he had a fierce love of regulation,' says Miles. 'The satisfaction, the contentment, of a lawyer is achieved only by the knowledge that his influence is always growing. The process of reduction now for old Gebrill must be a torture worse than hell. I love to think of it. The bugger made business more difficult for years. His government was like a fat tick on every enterprise.'

'You mean he wouldn't let business go unchecked.'

'Or your CCP if he had the chance.'

Slaven enjoys this opportunity to leave the hurly-burly of his work, the meetings and decisions, the planning and consultations, the close itinerary for each day that Kellie efficiently provides for him, the ever more insistent emotional demands that come with great success. Such time as this in the tower, with Miles asking nothing of him, with silences, and prejudices, unguarded opinions, pettiness and innuendo. They laugh at each other, and with each other. Slaven's laugh a brief burst usually, Miles's little more than a hoarse rustle.

'The third richest man in the world has built a house from stone from the moon,' says Miles. 'Did you see that in the news?'

'I think I did.'

'Now that must tell us a great deal about human nature, but I hesitate to work out what. The Roman Emperors used to have ice brought down from the mountains for summer court banquets.'

'You take enough advantage of privilege yourself.'

'My chief indulgence,' says Miles, 'is to keep as many people away as possible. I buy privacy with my money rather than mountain ice, or stones from the moon. I don't find it proven that we're naturally gregarious.'

'You say that now because you've grown old. You're the rogue elephant turned out from the herd and making a virtue of it. When you could cut a dash you loved to do so. You spend much of your time thinking about it. You're full of bullshit yarns about your prime.'

There is a haze over the heart of the city on the plain below, mainly fumes, but a blue bowl of sky above it. Slaven pours them both another lager and almost wishes that he didn't have to leave, that he could claim some sort of truce with time and stay in the tower house with Miles. He says as much to Miles, but they both know he has prospects of achievement that are offered to one in a million. The gift, as Thackeray Thomas says. Just thinking about it, Slaven feels a tightening of awareness of things and a gratitude that he has been given the opportunity of having a life out of the routine.

'It's all set for Auckland and Western Springs?' asks Miles.

'Yes, we've got people up there now, including Cardew, but there's a lot of negative feeling at work. People who don't want us to come off well there, but won't publicly take that position.'

'You'll blow them away. I've never heard a better ideas salesman.'

'I'm raring to go, actually. I feel strong. I was better at St Kilda than Tuamarina and I'll be better again at Western Springs. We're getting a more specific programme together now. More down-to-earth objectives that act as a focus for all the pent-up frustration and sense of loss.'

'Stick it to them,' says Miles in his whisper. 'And so you're feeling okay?' Slaven smiles, but remains looking through the floor to ceiling windows across the Canterbury plains.

'You know me. I'm still slipping a few cogs now and then.'

Most nights they sleep in the same large bed and most days they have at least one meal together, ample opportunity to discuss private things, privately. Yet they find themselves reviewing their marriage while waiting in the airport lounge for their flight to Auckland, so that the expressions on their faces for public view are sometimes not in keeping with the things they talk about. Maybe, of course, the private places are by their very suitability, locations in which it's too difficult to begin, offering not enough excuses to draw back when the time comes.

Kellie asks him if he loves her and they both laugh a little. Partly they laugh at the incongruity of it, here in the airport on a rack of seats by the observation windows and with people looking at Slaven already. Partly they laugh in pain and discomfort that the question needs to be asked at all. Partly they laugh to placate one another, meaning as with a shrug, this is how it is, this is how it is.

And as they talk, Kellie wonders if the accident is the sudden imperative for new ways and new preoccupations that it seems, or subconsciously for Slaven the plausible occasion to turn away from disappointment with his family, his marriage, his profession and his image. Yes, people change, they grow apart emotionally perhaps while still in a tandem of routine, eating and sleeping together, supporting each other, attempting to make changes in each other purely from habit. And the emotion is gradually replaced by civility and forebearance and common sense so that the appearance may be much the same, as the real tissue of creatures is fossilised and replaced bit by bit with quite different particles in a perfect duplication.

Maybe too, there is a cowardice in it, but Kellie and Slaven don't get on to that. A willingness in middle age to jog along, a position taken when others try for some great passion and are made fools of almost certainly.

What they do talk of, with a solemn and reassuring intensity in the airport lounge, is the pressure of their new work, taking each other for granted, a greater need for open discussion, resolutions even, sincerely meant. You will know them from your own intimacy, or not at all, and each is a perilous promise as you become aware.

Even as Kellie and Slaven talk, with some part of their minds they seek diversion, overhear the news of Jan's death — suffering an implosion while lighting farts at Frankie Boyd's stag night.

Western Springs is going to mark the push on Auckland and the North Island as far as Slaven and the CCP are concerned and the political commentators as well consider it a crucial test. It's one thing to draw the people at Tuamarina and St Kilda, to have a wildfire organisation spring up throughout the country amongst those of little clout in the main, but to come to the city of over two million, to try to work the heart-strings of a truly urban population, now that's a different matter. Dr Meelind tells his Think Tank colleagues this is the test all right. It's all very well to gather strength and combat temptation in the wilderness — yes, there is laughter — but after all in a democracy power should be where most people are. Nevertheless, Meelind reminds them that there is a gift at work here.

It doesn't take Kellie and her team long to realise that there is an alternative plan to their own for the Western Springs rally, a plan to ensure the throttling of the Slaven phenomenon. Not beheading by outright opposition, which might smack of official fear of the Coalition, but more oblique moves to make the occasion the sort of half-pie success which will damn it. The media take the line that Slaven is a Rip Van Winkle come to the city, a back to decency small-time South Island liberal who thinks that the problems of government can be solved by returning to the handshake as the sign of a person's bond, and mandate politics. Preview television cover is scant, muted and vague, most of the 10,000 flyers advertising the event are never displayed despite the contracts signed and two days before the rally the Metropolitan Council revokes permission for a march from Victoria Park to the stadium via Williamson and Hepburn streets.

The CCP has a special meeting of those executive members in Auckland for the campaign — Eula Fitzsimmons, Thackeray Thomas, union representative Sheffield Spottiswoode as well as Cardew, Kellie and Slaven — and Miles, who has come for his own reasons and the hell of it, sits in. Kellie gives the evidence she has for the pervasive, but covert opposition. 'Who'd be behind it?' says Slaven. 'You think that Gebrill, or Gittings, even the Government, are doing it?'

'More likely the United Party machinery here in Auckland,' says Miles huskily. 'People with the Government's interests at heart and plenty of influence in the city. It's less obvious for them to do it. They don't want you to have the publicity either of success, or forced cancellation. They want it to be a fizzer. That doesn't go down well in Auckland. They have a nose for losers. That's my guess.'

'Is there still enough time to call it off?' says Eula.

'Perhaps Miles could indemnify the Coalition for any losses,' says Cardew. 'We've put over $250,000 into this as it stands.' Miles shows no more reaction to Cardew than a donkey does to a fly. He has said all he wishes. He runs a hand slowly over his head and envies Thackeray's extravagant shock of natural hair.

'Under the circumstances we could call it off I suppose, and issue a disclaimer. We might even get a good deal of sympathy which we could capitalise on, but it's a backdown isn't it.' Kellie uses the word she knows all of them in their own way are temperamentally unlikely to find comfortable.

'Surely we're committed,' says Thackeray. Kellie watches her husband.

'It's a test really, isn't it?' she says finally.

'Yes.'

'A trial of strength in the camp of the enemy,' says Thackeray.

'Yet,' says Slaven, 'they underestimate the friends we have here, or can make. If we have what we claim to have then we'll reach these people whatever disadvantages of publicity, or prejudice.'

'All the same,' says Kellie, 'I'm going to have our people provide and operate all the audio-visual equipment themselves. No outsiders at all. Nothing must be left to chance with that. Sure, we expect the audience to respond, but for that you've got to be heard.'

'Western Springs is the big one for us, if we're going to be able to put the screw on before the elections,' says Slaven and he feels a surge within himself at the truth of it, the challenge that bears down on him personally, the opportunity for achievement, or failure, on such a scale.

'Hail, Caesar,' says Miles. His baby bird head falls back with a smile. Everything that happens is for him lit richly with his own setting sun.

'The clubs and the pubs have their own newsrooms, don't you worry,' says Sheffield.

'Something like this can't be ignored. Not a CCP rally; it's too big.'

'Remember what happened at Tuamarina and Dunedin.'

Yet Slaven knows that unlike Tuamarina and St Kilda beach there will be actively hostile forces, a counter culture, on the night. It stands to reason that if he draws his power from the crowd, then the crowd is the best target. He wonders who is working against him and to what effect. Meelind perhaps and the dispassionate professionals, or the branch executive of the ruling United Party and its allies as Miles assumes. Maybe the Democratic Socialists because of the Coalition's move to their own strongholds, maybe the Statos Nationalists because his views are almost all directly opposed to their own. 'Not to be alarmist, but there could be an element of personal danger,' says Thackeray. 'That shouldn't be overlooked. You're becoming more and more a focus.'

'Aw, come on,' says Slaven, but Kellie is one to provide for as many contingencies as she is able.

'I want every precaution we can set up,' she says.

Slaven decides to go and see Western Springs the day before the rally; a chance to get some feel of the place by himself. The gates of the old Mill Road entrance are open because of the dog obedience trials being held inside. It is smaller than he expects. The more he had heard of Western Springs and the more significant the happenings there, the more impressive it had become in his imagination. In the quiet reality of this evening, and hosting only the regular obedience trials, it is a modest enough place, steeply contained on the side from which he entered and with concrete tiers there making something of an amphitheatre. Slaven can see the scaffolding on the grass which will be his dais tomorrow night. The pipes have patches of paint, red, blue, white and yellow as some code to indicate their length and position and they are held together by grappling nuts. Slaven climbs the new stand, known as Shafters because of the propensities of the mayor before the present one. He watches the Labradors and Alsatians crossing from the sunlight to the sharp-edged shadow that Shafters casts across the grounds, as they prove their obedience around the flags. Good dog, good dog. What is it in the convergence of time, consciousness and space that can keep the dogs, their owners, their quiet, circling tasks, apart from the press, the massed response to message and conjuror of another night — the next. Slaven's impressions of his future at Western Springs, the past of Tuamarina, may be aberrant fancies of his decline, or worse, and he might wake to the life before it all; the subdued talk of his nurses in the surgery, or Kellie's call from the garden when he returns from work. *Baby, baby come again and live with me upon the shore of Half Moon Bay.* But his hands, you see, still held half curled and the scars of the grafts raised at the join with original skin. Almost there, you notice. The dogs wheel at their owners' knees and trot with complacent obedience. The lake and the park are just a fence away. There is a clump of toi-toi on the fence line and finally the one golden retriever disgraces its breed by succumbing to the temptation of the fragrances and deposits beneath the long, drooping leaves. Bad dog; no biscuit.

There are other places, aren't there? There's the old place in the North Otago downs, where the pink road of crushed Ngapara gravel is bordered by gorse hedges with clay sods to fill the gaps and the road runs up the small valley like a stream and the shoulders of the downs are ringed with sheep tracks. Useless pines around the farm buildings heap the pig-pen, drill shed and fowl run with brown needles, and on the shattered branches which weep a whitening resin, the cones are fully open in the drought. There are single cabbage trees on the hillsides and rilled, limestone outcrops, grey where the weathered surface is undisturbed, yellow in the overhangs where the sheep pack in to find the shade. The yellow-ginger ground of the drought has only the thistles green. The house, see, has a red tin roof and a dish to suck a little glamour down from the satellites. Yet the letter box at the end of the track has a tin flag which can signal to the rural delivery in the same old way, the magpies squabble in the woolshed pines and in the copper evening skies the gulls fly slowly back to the shore. But you know all that.

And it comes of course, much as has been predicted and planned; the evening at Western Springs with rather less sun and no dogs, or training flags — instead the scaffolding skinned over with orange tarpaulins, the cables and the lasers for the hologram and the sound systems and a small, subdued crowd of less than three thousand people. Most of them are middle-aged and somewhat less than middle-classed. Some of them sit towards the front of the main stand, outnumbered by the flip seats behind them. Some of the people stretch, amble a few paces and return, speak loudly, all in a pretence that they are at ease here at Western Springs.

Thackeray Thomas begins promptly at seven thirty. He gets the big electronic speaker system up and running, but right from the start it's obvious that there is to be disruption. The heckling is amiable enough while Thackeray is speaking, almost as if the opposition are checking the acoustics, their positions in relation to each other, the mood of the small crowd.

'Move into the 21st century.'

'Where's the banjo, hillbilly?'

'Another holy roller.'

'Suck it up your arse.'

'There's nothing out there to feed on,' says the minister as he comes off. 'A dead mutton audience. I think Eula, or Sheffield, should go on for a while until things build.'

'We need to grab them early,' says Slaven.

'You're welcome to it.'

Slaven feels pumped up; more excitement than fear, but the fear is that he will let down all the people who have supported him in the past months, rather than suffer some loss of personal importance. He is determined to be as direct and forceful as he is able, and then just trust the response — isn't that what you have to do? The hologram is used for Slaven; it sets up his genie in three dimensions in the daylight sky. A huge figure in enhanced colour that revolves so that no part of the crowd always has his back, though the original Slaven on the platform faces only the one way.

He begins quietly, conceding that in some ways these are good times, with less chance of war than for most of the last century despite the predictions that we would blow ourselves away, with the oceans still not open sewers, with a comparatively high standard of living and less illness and physical suffering than ever before. And he makes little reply to the wisecracks at his expense. He seems open to any number of free shots.

'Then why bitch, fuckwit.'

'Boring. Boring.'

Slaven tells them how much he has been looking forward to this night in Auckland, how important it is for the Coalition if it's going to bring any decisive pressure for change on the parliamentary parties before the elections. He reminds the people that the CCP isn't in it for personal payoffs, that he's not running for office, that the Coalition isn't a parliamentary party.

'Damn right. More like a funeral.'

Slaven feels the compassionate power of his mission stir within him. A feeling he recognises, but which is never totally familiar, as if he is possessed by the best part of him- self and the rest held in abeyance for a time by inner compulsions which he has no conscious means to summon. He feels his voice begin to throb with the increasing pulse of his ideas. He is charged, yes, charged again. He says that the loss of conviction is what he is bitching about. The lack of confidence throughout the country that people have common aims and that these common aims and interests can be defined, can be championed, can be achieved through a new community of spirit and a new revitalisation of political will.

'Utopian crap.'

'Double crap.'

'Stick to drilling teeth.'

Some of the audience are drawn into laughter at the interruptions, not from any wit in the shouts, but as a sign that they are free agents here and not yet committed to Slaven's views.

Slaven's genie grows more solid, more glowing, above them all as the dusk intensifies and at a distance is the suffusion of lights from the suburbs of Pt Chevalier and Mount Albert. The genie's increasingly vivid presence makes it easier for the hecklers to be ignored, reducing the impact of their animosity by the sheer size and magnificence of the image and by the enhanced reverberation of the banks of speakers.

The full horror when a sense of individual and national purpose is lost is what Slaven wishes to convey. The genie in the gathering darkness has gestures which seem more flamboyant than his own, some compound effect of the enlargement. Slaven talks of the inner ache of inconsequence, of something missing.

'Yea, a brain in your case.'

'And balls, too, I'd say.'

The opposition is well organised and prepared. They shine powerful beams into the holograph to dissipate the image. They have portable machines to manufacture a distracting cacophony. The stadium is a dark mass beyond the central field. Still further back the gardens and the lake. To reach the lake a squadron of mallards on a set descent cut through the genie with their fixed wings. There are iridescent flashes from their wing colours and the drakes' heads as they pierce the hues of the twisting genie.

'Shit on him! Shit on him!'

'Most of our days are just lived through,' says Slaven, 'and if we've warded off misfortune we consider ourselves lucky. We spend a life getting by, determined not to be cheated, snatching at what we can, hoping it won't be us in the gun for tax evasion, hit and run, cultural insensitivity, or masturbating in Anzac Square.'

'That's you all right.'

But there is little laughter now as a response, an empathy is growing. It shows itself at first in small things, the heads tilted more steadily to watch the genie, the growing disregard of any distraction, the unconscious relaxation of personal distance amongst people most of whom have come as strangers. Slaven can feel the stirring of a unified will. As he speaks Slaven feels the first tears on his cheeks. The sense of any manipulation slips away and he is one with his spendid image in the sky of Western Springs.

'We all go down to the grave in the end,' he says. 'All go down to the grave, but before that there's an opportunity to have some unique experience of the world. A world unbidden by any of us, impartial beauty, random horror, which equally serve the immutable laws. And almost the only thing that we have power to determine in all this is our relationship one with another. The human fellowship. The collaboration amongst ourselves which is an act of trust.'

'Bullshit.'

The heckler has misjudged the changing mood and his shout ends in a sudden exhalation as he is punched hard in the small of the back. From now on those who have come to disrupt, turn largely to the roles of observers, although one woman who continues to shout is scragged, and runs weeping towards the carpark, drawing glances of mild curiosity from people on their way in.

The full night draws around the lights and words at Western Springs and so sharpens the focus on Slaven's genie. It is wondrously lit, translucent, yet with a pulsing solidity of form and as Slaven moves and talks and gestures on the platform, so it moves, gestures in the sky on a grand and luminous scale. And it goes beyond aping its master, for although Slaven faces the one direction, the genie turns in the sky so that no one is denied its shimmering countenance for long.

Slaven begins his exhortation concerning the need for spiritual values in private and public life, his vision of a successful community as an equilibrium of complementary personal and social forces. The crowd voices increasing approval at the Slavenisms familiar to them and draws closer. Slaven demands a new commitment from them, a pledge to the regeneration which manifested itself at Tuamarina and St Kilda. It is beginning to happen; the melding of the parts into a whole. Despite the deliberate lack of coverage by the media, despite the campaign of urban disparagement, the political put-downs, the hecklers, the bureaucratic obstacles, despite all, a growing number of Aucklanders are arriving. Some have been close enough to hear the singing of *Glasnost Galaxy, Remember Greenpeace* — and *Half Moon Bay.* Some have heard the speaker vans that tour the streets relaying Slaven's message, some tuned into the anti-establishment radio stations AK SOS and Blue Sky which are covering the rally, some put aside the cynicism and apathy of their daytime selves when night fell, some simply followed others because the pubs and garage parties bored them.

They come first from Grey Lynn and Ponsonby and Morningside and Mount Albert, but that only begins the capillary action which draws people from Parnell, Birkenhead, Onehunga and beyond. Slaven keeps speaking and the genie keeps turning, a gleaming titan in the sky above Western Springs, above the same grass on which the Alsatians and Labradors had answered to the whistles. Whistle and I'll come. The arc lights of the rally are selective, catching a face, a feature, a stir of movement within the crowd while other things are left in darkness. And on the fringe of the lights and sensed beyond them, the place is alive with dim, bobbing heads and shoulders of people moving purposefully to join the listeners.

Slaven takes a break so that he can stretch and drink. He goes down from the back of the scaffold stage and stands unnoticed in the night on the same level as that part of the audience on the field. Iago and Dafydd provide a bulk of security at a little distance. Most of the crowd and the genies of Thackeray and Eula are blocked by the scaffold and its tarpaulins, yet Slaven knows that he has brought about another success and he squeezes his eyes closed with joy and thankfulness in the darkness. Seized with the conviction of it, the drama and passion of it, he goes back up the steps and takes centre stage again. They are chanting his name and he lifts his arms as if he can encompass them all within the span.

'Tonight,' he says, 'we lay down another challenge in the name of the people. We make a pledge with our presence that the political establishment can't ignore.'

'Slaven, Slaven, Slaven.'

Kind hearts are waiting, baby, amongst old friends at Half Moon Bay.

Auckland is a large city and accustomed to spectacular activities, yet when the genie still hovers in the night sky at midnight, the speakers still sound, when people continue to flow in as if pulled by the moon, the Coalition rally can no longer be ignored. The police arrive to ensure that the Great North Road remains clear and that the stands are not dangerously overfull. Prodded by insistent and inquisitive callers the late-night talk back shows begin to provide coverage — the woman who has miscarried in the midst of the crowd, the man in the wheel chair howling in euphoria, the possibility of a breakdown in order as the audience grows. By one thirty the police estimate there are over 150,000 people at Western Springs.

Such a crowd develops an increasingly brazen self-confidence, a sense of potency. So in the small hours Slaven's audience has a narcissistic delight in itself. Here we are, see us, see us. Except that it is see ME, the single-ness, the heart of wildfire, the swaying serpent of anonymity which rose also in the Colosseum, in Savonarola's Florence, with Robespierre, Demosthenes, with Soong Shih when she brought down communist China. From the few thousand who came originally to Western Springs, the crowd has grown to a base majesty whose roar carries for miles across the city and is finally lost over the dark emptiness of the sea.

'Let this smug city hear the voice of its true masters,' cries Slaven. He hears his own words coming back from the speakers, with a half-echo because the system isn't quite in phase and he sees his magnified image in the sky turn and glint in electronic radiance. Slaven says there is a message going out from this place about a spiritual renewal in the country and that they must all insist upon a political manifestation of it.

The Hoihos sing. *Let the movers and the shakers of the day, heed the rhythm of the tide in Half Moon Bay.* Slaven begins to sing as the massive sound of the multitude rises up. Some in the crowd are swaying, some crying, some take the hands of strangers and raise them aloft to salute the genie.

Still the people gather as close as they can to Western Springs, as they gathered at Tuamarina and St Kilda, but here the numbers are so much greater. Kellie and her management team can no longer maintain estimates. The carparks are full, the people stretch beyond the discovery of the lighting across the park, into streets. All that can be done is to have the laser project the hologram at the greatest possible size and turn up the sound. Cardew has stopped yawning, got his mind from shagging for a moment and urges his unofficial collectors further into the throng.

Slaven has the holograph bring up the CCP's chartist claims across the lower portion of the genie. One after another they appear following his vehement submissions.

1. The right of two annual political ostracisations by plebiscite.
2. A return to one citizen one vote.
3. A reduction of the Presidential term to three years.
4. Formation of a Ministry of moral and spiritual renewal.
5. Increased regional devolution.
6. Proportional gender and ethnic representation in political office.

The Commissioner of Police rings his Minister when he can no longer control vehicle and foot traffic in the area of

Western Springs. Also more and more residents are becoming frightened. Alan Warden, whose appropriate name made it no easier for him to become Minister of Police, has his chauffeur drive him as close as they can conveniently come to the rally. He uses his influence to gain entry to a penthouse in Finch Street and the legs of his blue silk pyjamas show beneath his robe as he clings with some agility to a railing there. Warden can see the glow of the arc-lights and the genie posturing at a distance. The huge audience is invisible, but when it gives voice the sound rolls into the city. 'Jesus.' A lesser man may wish that he was not within his electorate; from Wellington he could have told the Commissioner that he must use his own discretion.

Warden climbs down and more comfortably descends the building by lift. As he is driven home to change, he talks on the phone to the Commissioner and says that he will join him in the operations room within the hour.

'Is it over yet?' he asks on arrival.

'Still growing,' says the Commissioner. It's two thirty-five. Slaven is just hitting his straps.

'What are they doing?'

'Listening, singing. I haven't heard anything quite like it. It's on the radio now.' The Commissioner turns up AK SOS and Slaven's voice is in the room with them. Into that room of watchful hierarchy, regulation efficiency and professional inhibition it brought a gust of soaring entreaty, elation, emotions cut loose. Slaven's voice rides on the crests of the crowd's tumultuous response. 'We've got people there,' says the Commissioner, 'but I haven't created any police profile very deliberately. No chopper, or anything, to show that we're concerned, though we could do with our own pictures. It's a tinder box.'

'Will they disperse from there do you think, or will they march?'

'No idea, but he didn't march at Tuamarina and St Kilda did he. He's pushing a list of demands though and they're shouting for them like crazy.'

'Will they all move off together somewhere, that's the thing.'

'We've had some reports as high as 180,000.'

'Jesus, ' says the Minister.

'Nothing confirmed of course.' The Commissioner takes a piece of grilled chicken from the pack on one of the computer screens. He feels a slight discomfort at eating in front of the Minister at such a time, but the food will get cold and besides he has been in the Ops room for an hour longer than Alan Warden. A man must live, even if there are 180,000 people at Western Springs howling at the sky. The Commissioner is a man used to crises, though not immune to their pressures.

'One hundred and eighty thousand. Christ Almighty. I thought there was some campaign to defuse this guy. It was all going to die a natural death, so we were assured.'

'Well it wasn't my brief. Local boy scouts again I suppose.' The Commissioner wipes his fingers with a paper napkin. He isn't in uniform, but the shoulders of his blue reefer jacket are inordinately expansive, as if for epaulets. This Slaven is really tapping into something that's hot, you know. Television won't keep out of it. Even if we get all these people home tonight without the top blowing off, Dr Slaven is the big news tomorrow and if he decides to march them somewhere, then we'll all be front page news.'

'We can't just sit around.'

'We can get a line through to Western Springs.'

'Yes, that could be useful. Have it laid on.'

Nothing human is ideal in conception, or execution. The Coalition's rally becomes what the street guys call The Main Course. The language chapters, the outre gays, the patch gangs, the royalists, the hoons who drive restored American cars with otherwise forgotten names like Chrysler and Chevrolet, the whatitiri and the vague population of drifting lassitude which eddies in the heart of the city until it feels a current, all have been drawn to Western Springs.

The police watch them go by and radio in again. The marginal elements don't alter the essential nature of Slaven's audience, but add an edge of free-falling irresponsibility. Some begin a predatory assessment of the crowd, some are genuinely responsive to the atmosphere, even the issues, some copulate, some masturbate, or down pills to the rhythm of the mass singing and Slaven's harangue.

It will be light in a few hours. The Commissioner and the Minister of Police are at the main window of the Operations Room. Its view is not towards Western Springs, but the downtown area and the waterfront — dark blocks of offices with occasional high lights still showing and the more numerous security, sign and street lights at ground level. One fat truck sucks litter from the gutters while it can do so undisturbed. Above everything is a scrubbed, moon grey sky.

'Get in touch,' says Warden. 'The dentist himself if you can.'

'Are you going to do the talking?'

'We don't want them to know we've got the wind up. You talk to them and say that strictly on grounds of logistics and public safety you think they should break up.'

'I'm having a check made on their permit,' says the Commissioner.

'Perhaps technically they're not entitled to be using the venue after midnight anyway.'

'Good idea. I'm going to have to ring the PM,' says Warden.

Kellie has been hoping for just such a call from the Commissioner. She and the others in the control booth recognise it as the cautious opening of negotiation. She has Thackeray change places with Slaven on the stage and while Slaven stands in the canvas wings wiping sweat from his throat and sipping mango and apple juice, Kellie talks to him on the phone.

The Prime Minister receives his call with no pleasure, but Alan Warden is a friend and supporter within Cabinet and so there will be good reason for it. The PM sits on the side of his single bed and flexes his back so that it cracks. He pushes a hand above his hip and rotates his shoulders as he listens. He can see Alan Warden, but has not activated his own visual. With one part of his mind he is assessing his Minister's appearance. Warden has both a good face and a direct manner for the screen. When the PM speaks he does so quietly, not wishing to disturb his wife who sleeps in the next room. 'Ah, god, Alan. There's always something isn't there. Not 200,000 though, surely. Not 200,000 up there at Western Springs for this. I heard a bit on the radio — the guy can't even sing for christ's sake.'

Warden laughs. He admires the PM's equilibrium, but out of view of both of them, one in the Ops Room of Auckland Police HQ, the other far to the south in Wellington, the great crowd carries the melodies of *Capetown Races*, *Glasnost Galaxy* and *Half Moon Bay*.

'We've made contact through the Commissioner and Slaven says he wants an orderly dispersal as much as we do.'

'Will they march?'

'Depends what we come up with. The Slavens say it would be enormously helpful if they could announce some positive Government response to their concerns right away.'

'I bet they do. Have they much control over all those people at three in the morning anyway. Two hundred thousand you say! Jesus, Alan, this man's surely the next Prime Minister.' They both enjoy that, particularly as the PM is under a lot of pressure from the ideologists in his Cabinet.

'I think we must respond. This whole thing has proved he can't be ignored. The media will be into this like big dogs.'

One more crisis, thinks the PM. One more bushfire to be dealt with at the expense of actually governing. The consistent, responsible establishment of policies and their implementation is what he imagines people require him to do, but most of his time is spent coping with political misadventure, rivalries, ambitious animosity, ignorance, overseas shifts of influence, lobby groups, the marital difficulties of his Cabinet colleagues and all the while the civil servants despair of quality political direction, form their own society and get through one day after another.

'There's that list of demands that Slaven's been pushing,' says the Minister. 'If we could make a gesture in regard to one or two, then maybe we could squeeze out okay.' The PM listens to them and in the glow of his bedside light looks with distaste at the flaky skin of his ankles, the veins raised across the tendons of his feet, the ingrowing, oyster-coloured nail on the left small toe which gives trouble. All done up the PM is still an imposing man, but a regime of health and fitness is becoming just another casualty of office. When he wears his robes to address the conference of university vice-chancellors, or sports tails at a banquet in his honour at The Hague, he is conscious of muscle wastage on his thighs, a mild hernia and persistent catarrh. He hesitates over the menu despite his excellent French, because he needs to find the best length of focus. It is so in all things: although considered a pragmatist and political realist, he is continually surprised at the gap between the appearance and the actuality, the symmetry of theory and the debasement of practice.

The PM touches the mute and clears his throat into a handkerchief. He decides again that he must make more provision for his own health. 'We could take up the reduction of the Presidential term,' he says. 'Who'd give a damn really. It's part of the preoccupation with the Executive that's popular now. And we could form a spiritual ministry, after all we've several with no substance already.'

'Right enough.' Warden has a surprisingly uninhibited laugh for a Minister of Police. Almost joyous.

'Nothing else though. Ostracisation. He's been on about that ever since St Kilda. Now everyone's started on about it and I'm sick to death of it. Caucus bristles at the very mention of it. Christ, it's too late now to be a Greek city state. The idea is bad pyschology and it's bad politics.'

You are a power in the land, aren't you, when the Minister of Police scales railings in blue, silk pyjamas to suss you out and the Prime Minister must sit swearing on his bed at three in the morning to find a convenient concession. You have come a long way from a bed in the burns ward at Burwood, from presumptuous dreams of a calling, from the one hundred Angel Hire chairs in the dewy grass of Tuamarina. Haven't you?

Slaven's voice is as hoarse as a rock star's, more husky than Miles Kitson's even. His eyes are red-rimmed and his linen jacket heavy with sweat which extends from the armpits to the buttons. He enjoys the PM's call. The PM says that he had meant to ring earlier to congratulate Slaven on the interest he has aroused amongst Auckland voters and on the succinctness of his charter points and he assures Slaven that the Government is always open to what he terms non-partisan canvassing of views. The PM says that he wishes to extend an invitation to the CCP to meet with senior members of the United Party Campaign and although he can't pre-empt the stance of the party, nevertheless the PM feels that there are at least two of the charter points in line with recent United Party policy suggestions. The PM ends by complimenting Dr Slaven on his oratory and saying how appreciative he will be when the great gathering has been brought to an orderly conclusion.

So Slaven is able to use the call and its concessions as a culmination of the rally. 'The Prime Minister, the Right Honourable Brian Hennis, has it seems woken early this morning,' he says and the crowd roars triumphantly. As Slaven speaks for the last time the others come out on the stage with him, led by Kellie, Thackeray, Cardew, Eula and Sheffield Spottiswoode. Slaven's genie is resplendent still and when Slaven has finished the crowd sings as it begins its exodus; the edge of the vast assembly fraying away, the centre swaying to the Hoihos' *Half Moon Bay.*

So Western Springs, having drawn them all in since early last night, now exhales and the people surge out into the carparks, the streets, the suburbs and the watching police and camera crews marvel at the seemingly endless passage of them.

Slaven and Kellie leave the aftermath to others of the team. Together they are lifted from the heliport atop the Tizard stand in the first light of day. Below them is still a huge crowd, but the noise of the rotors covers the singing. Who doesn't know the words? *Everybody finds they have a neighbour, it they come back to Half Moon Bay.*

'That was some experience there tonight,' says Kellie. 'Was that a success, or what! But the scale of it finally was frightening, didn't you find? I mean it's exhilarating and it's flattering, particularly for you, but in the end I had this feeling that something about the crowd had outgrown our reasons for being there, their reasons for coming. There was otherness freewheeling there in the dark and it wasn't bound by any logic, or conscience, and it might do anything at all.'

'Yes,' says Slaven, but he is too tired and victorious to talk of it. A physical reaction is setting in. Although the sweat is still a sheen on his skin, he starts to shiver, his fingers tremble. He becomes aware of trivial discomforts such as a sore throat, a shoe that rubs and a thirst simultaneous with a desire to piss. But he recalls the Prime Minister's voice which had a placating rather than a patronising tone, the tears and the shouts and the cheers, the passionate singing and as the helicopter banks steeply he can see in the first light the great amoeba of the crowd still breaking up beneath them. 'But I reckon we took Western Springs all right,' he says.

Yes, but this has been for us a sort of slip glaze of talk and action which has glibly covered things which might be pertinent if given space. See Slaven still sitting in Shafters in the sun and watching the dogs and their masters define their roles on the grass of Western Springs. Feel the blessed heat that tightens the face, hear the easy sounds of this accustomed activity. There is a clump of toi-toi on the fence line and finally the one Dalmatian disgraces its breed by succumbing to the temptation of the fragrances and deposits beneath the long, drooping leaves. The other owners display no derision, but rather a courteous sorrow at such a lapse and the Dalmatian's owner fingers the dog's ears in affection rather than punishment. The owner is very bald, very brown and strong, with the legs of his shorts completely filled by muscled thighs and instead of immediately rejoining the circuit with his dog, they stand together by the fence and the toi-toi enjoying the view into the park where there is a lake. And all these quiet, obedient dogs will have homes throughout the city though people never know of them and instead hear askance of a loathsome brute which menaced little Howie James. Good discipline, Slaven's father always said, is the same thing as self-respecting pride.

A party then, after the CCP's dramatic success at Western Springs; a celebration of the heartland over the complacent poseurs of the big city. The Auckland branch of the Coalition is turning it on in the state room of the new Burlesque

Hotel in the Waitakeres, with a view over the city, the spread, endless shimmer of the lights in the night and the black holes which mark the excursions of the sea.

It is of course a political event as well as a celebration, with some people of importance to Slaven and the CCP drawn out by the power the rally demonstrated. A certain amount of sizing up is taking place, the agreement of times for mutual talks and so on. All sorts are here — Royce Meelind of the Think Tank, as he happens to be up from Wellington, Marjorie Usser whom Slaven met at the Civil Defence seminar, Fassiere with her wonderful complexion due to the gold-rush, the Chairman of the United Association of Volunteer Unions, newly introduced to Slaven by Sheffield Spottiswoode. But not poor Norman Proctor of course, not Roland Purcell, not Birdie Watson who fell from the Cenotaph, or Buffle the famous cartoonist, not Simon Adderley, not Mrs Prothero's canary.

Eula Fitzsimmons is showing the northerners that she too knows how to dress and her fluting vowels give a sense of panache to every view she expresses. The echo of her Rangi Ruru laugh penetrates the airing cupboard door behind which Cardew has his knee between the thighs of the hors d'oeuvres girl and his hands full of her breasts. 'Believe me,' he says, 'I've just the filling for you.' Thackeray Thomas relaxes from hard campaigning by recounting a Cymric dream — mists, magicians, Anglesey and the roaring ghosts of Iago, Llywelyn Fawr and Madog. He swears it is a heritage of the genes, so real is it to him.

'We're each of us conglomerates, aren't we,' he says, 'or like onions that have all our forebears one by one a layer closer to the heart.'

Kellie is still tired from Western Springs two nights ago, but it's now a lassitude of relaxation and achievement as well. She delights in the party which is no part of her responsibility. Even she has had enough of that. What does she care if there's a problem in the carpark with thieves, that one of the sliding doors of the state room has jumped its track, that there aren't quite enough girls to hand round the hors d'oeuvres. Kellie discusses with Royce Meelind the evolution of the organisational structure within the Coalition, the special difficulties of a quasi-political party without a parliamentary wing and her envy of the ease with which people here can grow citrus fruits and great evergreen magnolias.

'It's an amazing achievement in so short a time,' says Meelind in reference to organisation. 'The only parallel this century I can think of is the Antarctic Movement.'

'Aldous's father served on the pickets there. He was a regular soldier.'

'Somebody told me that.'

'Maybe it would be better for us to be completely independent. It's only circumstance that linked us to the Cambrians and so on, but they gave us that early help and we won't toss them over now.'

'I doubt if it bothers your supporters at all,' says Meelind. 'Everything is so focussed on Aldous. Such a direct source of energy, yet in another way inexplicable.'

'Inexplicable?'

'What I mean is, none of the ideas are new, but it's his conviction that makes people want to take them up again. In some way he arouses their trust. Don't you think?'

'Or their hate,' says Kellie. 'Whenever you want to share a conviction, there's someone hates you for it.'

'That's for sure. There's only so much success available, isn't there, especially in politics. So when one person gets more, the others see themselves as diminished.'

Kellie and Royce Meelind are sitting on the long, cushioned seat of the state room, well back from the uncarpeted area where dancers move before the huge windows and make it difficult for Kellie to see the distant city. She is slim and well dressed, isn't she? She has brains and money and power in the CCP? Better to concentrate on all that, rather than being forty-eight years old and with a husband in emotional free-fall. 'Western Springs was way beyond my predictions and I was more generous than most,' Meelind is saying.

See a youngish man in a tailor-made suit and a tooled leather choker instead of a tie. See him talk to a simpering guy with unctuous, yellowed eyes and to a slightly buck-toothed woman with glasses and a creamy breast. They stand between Kellie and the rest of the room. On the squab to her left is a solid man with creased trousers. He's a member of the Auckland Coalition Committee and Kellie worked quite closely with him for several days before the rally. She recognises the face of course, but has let go on the name. He intones snatches of their campaign songs to himself. On the other side, beyond Royce Meelind, are two of Eula Fitzsimmons' supporters.

'An inexorable law, absolutely,' says the choker. 'It matters not a bit what one is wearing, the lint from one's belly button is always pale blue.'

'Ha, Ha.'

Angels on the 1am all singing, come on in to Welfare Heaven.

'What I fear is an essentially patriarchal structure, while you seem to be happy that the end justifies the means.'

'You must be both tired and proud,' says Meelind.

'I never have any lint in my belly button. I am most scrupulous concerning orifices,' says the buck-toothed woman.

'But the proportional representation aim, the sixth point, that's our salvation. You must give credit to Aldous Slaven there. Eula says herself that he was a supporter.'

The best new century policy, is the making of a glasnost galaxy.

'Oh, how he can talk, can't he. It just carries you away, and I thought we were supposed to be the ones with the gift of the gab.'

'You're bluffing. I bet fifty that your sweet button has blue lint like all the rest of the world.'

'Ha, ha.'

'Pull your blouse up just high enough to prove me wrong and there's fifty right here, right now. I tell you it's an immutable law. No kidding.'

Kinder hearts are waiting, baby, amongst old friends at Half Moon Bay.

'I've heard things, you know, about the son. Things about Cardew Slaven.'

Kellie can see Slaven, between the young man with the tooled choker and his friend with jaundice showing in his eyes and a ready, empty laugh. Slaven, glimpsed a distance away, amongst others and with the glassed view of the lights of the city spread against the dark pelt of the night. Slaven rocks on the balls of his feet the way he does when bored in the presence of fellows and unable to escape. He is the centre of attention for a good many people and they wait to have their say, each with a personal agenda which has little in common with that of the Coalition. Slaven hasn't acquired the skill of sloughing off the concerns of other people while still preserving a solicitous demeanour.

'And another is the indication of libido provided by the ear lobes. Absolutely. Now yours are fleshy to a marked degree.'

'Ha, ha.'

'When you come to think of it, though, why should quantitative gender representation be the last charter point? Oh, I know there's supposedly no hierarchy in the order, but many will make assumptions.'

'It should be looked at.'

'It should.'

Foveaux storms are fading, baby, within the calm of Half Moon Bay.

The elegant woman is feeling her ear lobes. In the concentration of the moment her mouth opens a little more and her white, slightly buck teeth emphasise the sheen of her lipstick. Slaven at a distance is dancing, more as an escape, Kellie thinks, than from positive inclination. She glimpses something fugitive of his younger self and it causes her a brief, sharp pang. She tells herself that she's feeling down because of the anti-climax after Western Springs. That's what it is all right, she tells herself.

Royce Meelind is a man to whom ideas are more important than anecdote, yet even his professionalism allows for a measure of curiosity. He has sat with Kellie for some time without further comment, listening to the conversation around them, following Kellie's gaze through the shifting figures of the party. Slaven is a fair dancer and Meelind is reminded of the story told by his cousin, Eric Tydeman, who as a second year commerce student took evening dancing lessons in the bare room of the Langar Dance

Academy above the Suzuki Agency. The dance instructor was a Polish woman of great vivacity and charm, and one warm March night she excused herself in the middle of a modern bracket, opened the old sash window and did a header onto the pavement next to the display of Suzuki tourers.

'How is he in himself,' says Meelind. 'How is he bearing up under the strain of recuperation and heading a national organisation that at present gets more attention than the Government almost?'

'Hah. Hah. You see. You see.'

'That's Kellie Slaven just two along from us. We should introduce ourselves.'

'He's been buoyed up by the success of it, swept along,' says Kellie. 'He's only recently beginning to think of the consequences of failure, or of losing control of the public feeling he's aroused.'

Everything around you seems to say, remember Greenpeace.

'Personal leadership's like that. The emotional demands can be appalling.'

'People don't make allowances, or put themselves in his shoes,' says Kellie. 'They'll distract him with personal pleas only moments before he has to speak to thousands. They'll walk right into the house if they can, sit down at the meal table without a blink and start on their life story, the things they want from him. I'm just realising how selfish need is.'

Some people who are implacable in withstanding all the forces of the working day, or week, are quickly collapsed by relaxation and a little fun. Sheffield Spottiswoode proves himself to be one of these and after a supper of cannelloni, giant prawns, and cherry gateaux the bubbly goes straight to his heart. He supplants the creased campaigner as the source of protest songs and Thackeray Thomas as the leader in a range of toasts to CCP success.

Thackeray can not normally be so easily deposed, but he has been smitten with a sudden Celtic melancholy and gone out into the night beyond the state room to wrestle with his demons.

Some considerable time after Slaven's speech, he and

Kellie find time to slip away, knowing that the younger ones will party the harder for their absence. Les Croad drives them back into the city and boasts of his part in dealing with a gang who were rifling cars in the Hotel Burlesque park. 'Have a go then, I says to them. Have a bloody go. Chance your arm if you feel lucky.'

'Hasn't the Hotel a security system?' asks Kellie.

'Plugged nickle,' says Les. 'All activated lights and cameras and such. No, you need someone there, don't you. Someone holding the line as we did. They've got to think twice about having a go then.'

'Royce Meelind said that he would be in touch to set up the meeting promised by the PM,' says Kellie. 'He said there's no denying the political impact of Western Springs. All the parties are taking the CCP very seriously. Electoral leverage, he said, that's what we have now more than ever. We'll need to sort out a time frame for the meeting and a shopping list.'

'And when we meet, when the heats off the PM a bit, we'll probably get the old run around.'

'That's why we need to be well prepared.'

So they are all three quiet for a while, travelling back from the Waitakeres through the suburbs. Kellie's thoughts and Slaven's include each other in their different ways, but Croad is the unperturbed epicentre of his world and is unaware of any arrogance in that. He relives the confrontation in the carpark of the Burlesque Hotel as the great event of the evening and already the roles of actuality are subtly modified to enhance his mastery. He smiles his batwing smile as he drives and the blips of the centre markings, the reflectors, flash by. Have a go then, he thinks. Let's see what you've got.

Kellie is impressed by Royce Meelind. Despite his government job, his Think Tank responsibility for evaluating political impact of new movements, she doesn't regret the candour of their conversation at the party. She likes his dark eyes, his intellectualism, the quiet efficiency. She wishes she had just such a colleague to assist her with the administration of the Coalition. Meelind is a gardener, surely. She imagines him a man committed to large plants and long term development:

maples and golden elms, Spanish chestnuts, limes and the skyward reach of poplars — her favourites.

Slaven is appalled by his lack of response to most of the people who came to him in the course of the celebrations. Many of them praised the depth of concern he had for his fellow New Zealanders, while their individual approach, their particularity as the people to whom he advocated service, meant little to him. He comforts himself with the idea that the people of greatest worth, the salt of the earth folk that are at the heart of all his effort, would be the last to push themselves forward for his attention. He had enjoyed a brief talk with Fassiere and the promise of further negotiation, but otherwise he seemed to be amongst a press of people who had nothing he admired and whose resolves were transparently self-promoting. His training gives him a certain objectivity of course with which to view his own reactions. He considers the warping power of the enormous stress he has had over several months and that so soon after his accident. Fierce revelation and joys just as much as racking doubts and momentous decisions. Trivial frustrations which could suddenly flare to epic proportions.

The poet Cummings said that the fear of insanity is an unfortunate display of self-importance, but Slaven since hanging on the wire in sparks has never taken a happy balance for granted. The sudden expansion of his vision and powers which has brought him fame might be counter-balanced by the growth of darker faculties which will have their expression when the time is ripe. Still at times, just before waking, against a low-lit skyline he sees bursts of fire where the arch-angels fight and hears the scaled and feathered reinforcements griping as they march by. There are inner views which have a sad finality, yet lack a surface credibility and sometimes when he talks to people, snatches of conversations from his past come between his words and theirs, as spots drift in our vision across the shapes of an observed world. It happened at the party. A man in very creased trousers, a campaign worker whose face he knew and whose name he has forgotten, had congratulated Slaven while in fact seeking endorsement for the position of Auckland publicity manager designate and as they spoke together, Slaven heard quite clearly his father saying goodbye as he left for China when the Democratic Restoration was in progress.

'Did you see Cardew at all?' says Kellie.

'Not since right at the start.' Slaven had noticed his son then, how he seemed to have an appetite for the hors d'oeuvres. Slaven is pleased that he hasn't seen him since. He never finds any comfort in his son's presence. 'I didn't meet the people I wanted to,' says Slaven.

'There's never enough time at parties.'

'No. I mean that the people who are really important to the movement weren't there, probably not invited even. You end up each time with people who are organisational masseurs, who keep the administration in shape, but who have no consciousness of the spirit within the movement. There was hardly anyone I talked with who had a sense of the individual benefit possible, apart from their own of course.'

'It's a party. Be reasonable. You can't expect people to show their best side all the time.'

'I heard dad talking.' Slaven's voice is quiet and matter of fact.

'Pardon?'

'When Bowman bailed me up after supper. Yes, that's who it was — Bowman. He helped with the setting up of Western Springs from this end.'

'That's right. Bowman,' says Kellie. 'He was the one singing all night. A god awful voice, too.'

'As he was going on and on, I heard my father saying goodbye again at the Wellington airport before he went with his unit to China. I suppose I was about seventeen and there was just this group of service personnel saying goodbye to their families and mum never wanted him to go and so she wouldn't make it easy for him at the end. She made it seem as if he was staying very late at the pub with the boys when he should be home. His high, laced boots squeaked as he stood with us until he had to go and in his eyes you could see that he'd left us already. "Well, off to the land of Nanki Poo," he said. "It can't be helped," and mum walked away without a word.'

'What did he do then?'

'He said he'd get it right when he came back.'

'And did he?'

'Not altogether, no.'

'I feel sorry for them,' says Kellie.

'It's not easy being in the services,' says Croad, not thinking she may mean man and wife. He has the firm opinion that comes from ignorance. 'Like back there in the parking lot of the Burlesque Hotel when I had just a few seconds to decide to make a stand. And it could've been heavy going if the passing bald-headed guy hadn't waded in with a will.'

'Do you think I need some counselling, or more treatment?' Slaven asks Kellie as Croad drives smoothly on through the night.

'Actually,' muses Croad, 'I reckon I've seen that bloke before, but down south of course. Sort of familiar he was, but he didn't stick around afterwards. I suppose he had stuff in his car that he was keeping an eye on.'

'When we get back maybe I should go and get some advice from Marianne Dunne. The name of a top person. I still feel scrambled at times and although I wouldn't swap what I'm doing now, I haven't been at it long enough to know what I can take, whether I'm pacing myself as I should.'

'I'll ring her as soon as we're back,' says Kellie and she will of course. Slaven knows it is as good as done.

Les Croad drives quickly on the motorway. The lights set into the island embankments wink past as regular as heartbeats. The lights beyond are a delicate shimmer which disguises the reality of the city — the main thoroughfares traced with yellow through the starlight private whites, the commercial clusters of flashing blue and green. And from the outside, on the one-way glass of the car is all this same reflected, except that in the windows the lights stream past like sparks of phosphorescence in a dark wake.

There is a place, in an arcade, or is it a mall. A cave in a main street and so out of the light night breeze, but still allowing sight of the main chance. A large, slot video on which the guys play permissible pornography, but they are so familiar with it that their eyes slide away to the clothed women walking on the main street. They want the real thing. At the entrance is a Pacific Bank distribution point and the wind fluffs the discards on the paved floor and the guys even as they laugh together watch sideways to see how much is withdrawn, who has good tit, who's well hung. They are the real thing. The laughter has no humour in it, just an act of territory and when they see good tit and arse the guys lift their shoulders instinctively within their yellow, leather jackets and laughter beats out to the wind at the entrance. There is a takeaway bar which helps to warm the arcade with tacos, burgers, fries and pizza. There is a video parlour and plastic pot plants used as urinals, dispensers for kiwi juice and condoms, a cubicle shop that sells posters of the video rock stars — Doctor Normie, Little Nell and the Hoihos. There is a bright, red arrow which starts, runs and disappears towards the parlour and starts again, except that in its length is one malfunction so that the moving finger vanishes for an instant in just the same place over and over. There is movement and light and heat. There is a crass energy which has its own appeal. An arcade, a mall, in the city you understand. It is the real thing.

Slaven. In the week following Western Springs, with the residual triumph of that underpinning the quiet sun and flowers of Kellie's garden. He has agreed to an interview with Ms Zita Lee of 'Here and Now' and he waits in a deck chair by the rose plots and the weeping willow whose skirts sweep the ground bare in patches. He has been so busy that to be at ease in the garden is a heady novelty, simple, external things a feast for the senses. After all, the recent advice has been not to lose contact with a physical reality. Kellie has mainly modern roses, but there is Annie Vibert with its small, white flowers prim amongst the less inhibited generations. Regensberg, Pot o' Gold are here and Blue Nile with the bruise tint to its pale petal. Kellie has a spray which will flush the buds at her whim.

They are in need of a different spray now. Slaven can see beneath almost red new leaves and clustered on buds, aphids, and on the thorn of a Kerryman with a red-purple flower nodding above is a mantis in a sheath of pea-green. Cicadas cry for their lives from secret places and there's the whiff of sheep dung and oil and wool on the drifting air. 'Actually I haven't had time to read *A New Drummer*, though the political editor gave me a copy before I came,' says Zita. Tipped back somewhat in the chair she is aware of vulnerability. 'But I saw some of the St Kilda rally on the television and think you spoke marvellously well.' Slaven wishes that he could ask her the most personal things — where she comes from, whom she first loved, the story of the small scar on her left ankle, does she bleach the fine hair on her upper lip, did she have a pet rabbit with eyes of jellied innocence, does she realise that her life is being passed in this way and that the sun liberates from her skirt a fragrance of washing liquid and wardrobe. Loving Memory, a hybrid tea, Kellie has told him, is such a beautiful bloom; dark, glowing red, rolled petals with just the suggestion of down. And he can smell the bleached canvas of the deck chair close to his face. 'Our readers are interested particularly in the human dimension of the celebrity I suppose. Does that sound trivial? I mean an impression of you as a person apart from your political image. Things about your family and your background and whether you restore steam engines, or velum manuscripts, as a secret relaxation. Can you cook, for instance, delighting your wife with an egg and pasta dish.' On the stem of the Kerryman the praying mantis slowly climbs, two sways forward and one sway back. The new growth of the weeping willow rustles on the earth and the cropping of his sheep is as scissors through fabric beyond the garden. 'I can see your point. That you don't want to be photographed by the side of the house where the accident happened,' says Zita, but she knows the editor will be disappointed nevertheless. 'You've been generous in tribute to the part your wife plays in the organisation of the CCP. That's something I want to cover as well.'

Several times Slaven's father took him camping in the Kaimanawa Ranges, using all army gear of course, ration packs of mostly dried stuff, plastic water bottles in lined belt carriers, stainless steel pannikins which fitted and folded tightly together, gossamer tents which yet had strength and so low that after a night the breath's condensation gathered and ran only inches above their faces. 'Would you say you're fully recovered from all the effects now?' says Zita, 'apart from the hands. You must have been very lucky.' Slaven would wake early in the mornings and from his tent hear, or see, his father already up, washing at the ablution point he had established in the creek, or fetching a pannikin of water from further upstream. From training and pride he kept a tidy camp, things tucked away after use so that the site was never strewn and he could be packed and gone when quick movement was required. Before they left a campsite his father insisted that they walk the area to ensure it remained as they found it. Always there were the flies that found them out however, loathsome, yet with bodies of iridescent green, or blue. What could they possibly feed on normally in such isolation. Even his father had no answer. 'You've said that you won't stand for parliament yourself and that the Coalition has a policy of not putting up candidates. Is that firm, or a ploy as some people have suggested, to gauge support before committing the movement?'

Only years later did it occur to Slaven that his father was something of an ascetic. It didn't sit well with the idea of a soldier perhaps, but nevertheless it was true. His father hated indulgence and any easy way, He loved a rigorous self-discipline and a challenge, whether in the plotting room of GAMD, on the tracked missile carriers, or a ridge above the bushline. And a practical joke got him in the end: topped him. 'Not that you're old of course,' says Zita, 'but it does seem comparatively late in life to become so intensely and controversially involved in public life when before you didn't even belong to a party. The PM was quoted as referring to you as a menopausal prophet. Any response?'

French lace is one of Kellie's favourite floribunda and Slaven picks a few buds for Zita as they go in. On the heavier stems are the sculptured thorns that Cardew and Sarah when small would snap off, lick and place on their noses so that they could play the rhinoceros. Cardew has his own horns now and ruts wherever he is able. His interest in Zita had been obvious when they were introduced on her arrival and no doubt he will be joining them for afternoon tea. He has been yawning over CCP accounts and arranging a rendezvous with a postal clerk in the Woolston branch. 'I don't suppose you've decided yet where the next CCP rally will be? It would be a scoop you know, even if I could say that it was to be within a certain region. The central North Island for instance.' Zita feels more confident out of the deck chair. A more upright posture suits serious enquiry. She begins to determine Slaven's star sign, the trials of his adolescence, his response to sudden fame, what regime of physical fitness, if any, he follows. 'I hear that you have a bodyguard at the meetings, because of the enthusiasm of supporters,' says Zita.

The warrant officer had a good feel for a route when moving over rough country. He always said that you shouldn't give away hard earned height easily and he would walk just below the ridge lines out of the wind, rarely taking what might seem like short cuts across the gullies. Slaven can't remember his father talking in an overtly emotional way, anything about relationships, or personal despair. His conversation was more likely to be about his time in China during the Reconstruction, what Slaven would be able to do after university, evidence of the damage that deer and possums were doing to the bush. Slaven could tell what a natural, unexamined joy he drew from his own physical prowess: the steady, uphill pace, balance on a fallen trunk greasy with moss and decay, a vault across a creek, the pack close and high on his shoulders. He told Slaven that the countryside of China was full of litter and none of them gave a damn about cleaning up, because there wasn't any money in it.

'Professor Wheeler in the *Horizons* article said that the CCP appealed to a residual non-conformism inherent in our society. He said that the Coalition's true progenitors were the anti-nuclear movement and the Prohibition movement a hundred years before that. Carbuncles that rise on the body politic, give vent to inner toxins, but disappear in better times.' Kellie has a drink for them and as they come across the patio, Cardew joins in. He has done his hair and decided to be one of the family. Already he is shagging Zita Lee on the flagstone steps from the garden. 'Do you feel like a carbuncle?' Zita asks Slaven.

Slaven's father told him that he had expected a hot country, but had suffered from the cold. He said that the bits of China he saw had been worn down, walked over and handled too much and that it would happen in time to New Zealand. The people were surprisingly tough and ruthless, he said.

'Emergency dressings.'

'Check.'

'Water additive tablets.'

'Check.'

'Attestation documents.'

'Check.'

'Calculator and Veeb. Issue.'

'Check.'

'We like a human interest slant to our profiles, really,' says Zita. 'It makes it easier for our readers to identify with people in the news. Some earlier photographs would be great. A wedding one even.' She thanks Cardew for his offer of a ride into Christchurch, but says she has her own car. 'I'm keen to do a follow up,' she says, 'after the elections when the impact of the CCP is clear.' The rose beds and the willow are still visible and the faded yellow and blue stripes of the deck chairs, but they have come too far to be able to see the oscillation of the praying mantis, the suckling aphids, or smell the combination of rose and dunging sheep. Slaven remembers the wilderness flies he hasn't seen for many years, the astounding glitter of their blue and green and gold as flashes amongst the subdued landscape of tussock and bush.

Kellie has a sure instinct of course as to what Zita's readers want and an equally sure knowledge of what it is advantageous to provide. The reporter's shorthand is tested more now than at any other time of the interview and Slaven abandons himself to the indulgence of this free afternoon. Even his son's presence cannot spoil it. The sun causes a slight and pleasant itch on the new skin of the palms of his hands. Tonight he and Kellie are going to visit Miles and Georgina in their tower on the Cashmere Hills. Miles's diet is restricted, but he still provides generously for his friends, but more than that, Slaven looks forward to the astringency of his cynicism, the disillusion without bitterness, or regret.

Sarah comes to the patio to make the family complete for Zita's interview. She claims an equality of journalistic achievement because she writes a horoscope page and she talks in great detail concerning her father's subjection to Mercury ascendant. Of all the family she has the lightest disposition, which made her first a sparkling child and now a shallow woman. 'People are coming round to it a lot again now,' she says. 'They're realising that as astrological science has been about for thousands of years, there must be something to it.' She is excited by the new life the family is swept up in, without worry about its origin, or outcome. She puts a hand on her father's shoulder and her face is more than merely pretty in youth and animation. Slaven appreciates her touch. He has all his fatherly affection for her, which Cardew has lost, but little means of other communication. Today it seems not to matter.

Slaven and his family interviewed on the sunny patio, with laughter, rapid questions and answers, Kellie's effortless management, Sarah's vivacity, Cardew's silence and lacquered stare, Slaven's certainty in his course, Zita's warmth and sense of professional opportunity.

We are several people within our one life. Slaven remembers his mother and father taking him to 'Cavaliers' on the evening of his graduation, the slick wetness of a Dunedin winter outside, the best of everything within, his parents dancing on the small floor amidst the tables while Kellie and he watched. His mother with a gentleness and ease which she lost, or was forced to sacrifice, somewhere along the way to the woman who lives in a retirement village in Palmerston North and who has grown used to the jets sinking below her window.

See them; Slaven, Kellie, Cardew and Sarah come out to the tiled turning circle as Zita Lee leaves them. 'There will be so much happening for you all, leading up to the elections,' she says. 'I hope you'll let me do that follow-up,' and she promises Sarah again that she will mention to the editor about a possible horoscope page. Cardew says he may perhaps call in a day or so just to bring financial figures concerning the CCP which may be useful to her. It is almost evening now and the Slavens' quiet four hectares of the western fringe of the city are all smiles of garden, trees and Romneys in their small paddocks. The light breeze makes a gracious passage and just a score or so gawpers at the road entrance watch Zita leave and envy her the time spent within.

The PM stands by his Western Springs promise of exploratory talks between the Coalition and the United Party. Slaven wanted Kellie to come with him in the delegation and she was drawn to the idea, but she decided that it would appear too much of a family thing and thought Eula could represent any special view of women. One private school voice being replaced by another, except that Eula Fitzsimmons is more conscious of her vowels, particularly when Sheffield Spottiswoode is of the party. Thackeray and Slaven occupy the middle ground in both elocution and ideology.

They meet in Royce Meelind's office and he is disappointed at Kellie's absence. 'What a flair for logistics has been discovered there,' he tells Slaven and goes on to explain that the PM will come in as soon as he can wind up an urgent meeting with the Heads of the Producer Boards. Slaven wonders if by chance the workmen may return to the outer office and punctuate the PM's deliberations with talk of sport and pig shit. Alan Warden is also here, not as Minister of Police, but as a member of the Caucus Policy Committee and confidant of the PM. Meelind is interested to talk of Western Springs and national development of CCP support since he and Slaven last met, the charter take-up in middle range urban electorates and what Meelind calls the South Island Breakout.

Warden is more openly and cheerfully pragmatic. 'Really though,' he says, 'you're just a set of policies in search of a party, aren't you. And in politics you find through experience that a party structure is the far more valuable of the two.'

'We believe there's a third element — a constituency, and that it's the most important of all,' says Slaven.

'The power of opinion, you see.' Sheffield takes up the point proudly. 'People standing as one.' He holds up a fist as misshapen as Slaven's, but made so by the more gradual distortion of physical work in cray boats and tunnel gangs.

'Coherence through leadership,' adds Eula. 'All groups and sectors fairly considered. That's how it can work.' So Thackeray must be given his own humour too and he runs a hand through his tousled hair as a preliminary to speech.

'The moving inspiration of the word,' he says. 'Ah, the power and the revelation that come from authentic gifts of vision. Who can deny what those so many thousands came seeking at Tuamarina, St Kilda and Western Springs.' The clergyman from habit stands up to deliver his lines and barely restrains himself from remaining upright and enlarging on his text. His words are always for an audience and ring in the confines of Royce Meelind's office.

'A parliamentary party though,' says the Minister. 'A thing of structure and permanence which provides for able people a context for a professional life in politics.' Slaven knows that Kellie would enjoy hearing all these views. She would appreciate, but not be convinced by, Warden's enthusiasm for loyalty, for orderly and efficient function, for continuity and structure. 'You're holding a lottery of sorts I understand, or rather an auction, at which the Coalition will sell its endorsement to whichever party will accept the greatest number of the charter claims.'

'All uphold the rights of working people,' says Sheffield.

'And others disadvantaged by a residually patriarchal system,' says Eula.

'The CCP is a means of restoring a more direct democracy.' Thackeray half rises and then remembers the place. 'One less distorted in its operation by political horse-trading. With no candidates of our own we're not subject to the corruption and compromise attendant on personal ambition and favours owed. We state the policies of sound and fair government and we demand the parties give their intention in regard to them.'

Warden aped the movements of a violinist and rolled his eyes at such naivety. 'Intentions,' he says with emphasis. 'Oh yes, intentions.'

'The thing is,' says Meelind, 'that I imagine parties such as the Statos Nationalists, the Electoral Revisionists, agree with all your points quite willingly. They know they're not likely to have to implement them even with your support, but they're dead keen to pick up a good number of extra seats.'

'Bloody right,' says Warden. He has a genuine, relaxing laugh. To be with Dr Meelind receiving the CCP delegation and with the PM due to join them, is a piece of cake compared with the tough decisions and aggravation that he's often called upon to take as Minister of Police and Gaming.

'Fair comment,' says Slaven, 'but the Democratic Socialists under Fassiere can win with our backing can't they. And for you people, our endorsement would do more than guarantee your retention of the front benches, it would mean that no coalition would be necessary, even allow the PM to have the purge of his right wing that he's been aching for.'

Gebrill is dead you understand: all his power and knowledge and bitterness gone and a fine funeral held with representatives from all those bodies who had respected his influence. And Fassiere, with her complexion from the gold-rushes never looking better, gave a stirring oration which served notice of her assumption of leadership within the Democratic Socialists. And Miles Kitson made an effort to be present so he could savour the delight of seeing another enemy put away. Two people shed tears when Gebrill was found toppled forward amongst the made-to-measure suits of his own wardrobe and we can imagine with a scab still fresh upon his lip. His mistress, who found him a generous man, his grandaughter, whom he loved.

The minister laughs again, Meelind asks Eula Fitzsimmons if the air-conditioning is comfortable. They are too practised to give any revealing reply to Slaven's observation. Instead they bargain on the pre-arranged topic of the inaccuracy of poll results taken before elections and the opinion that in the end voting is almost always decided on traditional party divisions irrespective of campaign issues such as the CCP's charter.

It's interesting to see them work together, which they do quite effectively. At bottom their mutual attitude to each other is contempt, but neither a malicious, nor a personal, contempt. Royce Meelind appreciates the Minister's stubborn loyalty to comrades, his courage and shrewdness, as you admire such things in a dog long bred for the purpose. Alan Warden admits there is usefulness in one who can remove self-interest from the analysis of events, but despises a zealousness for knowledge which has no practical use.

Meelind gives a survey of policy origins within the United Party over the past thirty years to illustrate which of the CCP's demands are ideologically compatible in historical terms and the Minister reminds Slaven and the others that politics is the art of the possible. Ostracisation for instance; Warden says that every Member of Parliament views it as a personal threat and that as well it would mean fewer would dare to champion just, but unpopular, causes. '*Vox populi* can itself become a tyrant, you see,' says Meelind. Eula Fitzsimmons has a good degree. She finds the point an interesting one for her redoubtable skills of debate. Warden and Sheffield Spottiswoode take no part in the scoring. The Minister sees it as mere sophistry. The union man is in over his head.

The great majority of us are conscious of ourselves from the inside out, we observe events in which we are invisible, but those few people who are cynosures have an additional view of themselves as the focus of the interest and regard of their fellows. Slaven has been disconcerted by it. The PM is accustomed to it and every impression that he gives, each change of expression, or stance, is as visible and predictable to him as to those who join in the observation. He inhabits his own image quite naturally and with assurance. He knows from thousand-fold experience the reaction of those he meets for the first time — the initial sense of familiarity, under-mined almost immediately by the realisation that he's a stranger to them after all.

Brian Hennis is concerned about his health you will remember; a hernia to be dealt with when there is time, some pooling veins, an ingrowing toenail, persistent catarrh, but there is only confidence, presence, in the entry he makes. 'I am sorry to be late,' the PM says as he is introduced to the CCP representatives. 'Give me a moment to adjust my mind from double dump wool exports to Korea and aphrodisiacal deer velvet and I will be able to take account of *vox populi.*' It's a pity that he chooses to use the term from his briefing by Dr Meelind so soon after the advisor has used it himself. The effect for both is diminished. 'I would say that I've rather less than twenty minutes before my executive assistant will bear me away to a diplomatic briefing and yet I regard the present meeting as the most important of the day.'

'Then I wonder, Prime Minister, how much of the CCP charter you can accept as policy to be implemented if you are returned to office?'

'I like someone who is forthright in discussion,' says the PM. 'Okay, let's lay it out so far. A reduction of the Presidential term, we can live with it. The setting up of a ministry for community regeneration. Well within certain resource limits we can go along with that. Your regional devolution is much the same in essence as a new policy we have arrived at through independent initiatives within the Party, so there's probably common ground in this regard as well. For the others the answer is frankly no, for reasons that I think Dr Meelind and the Minister have explained.'

'I hardly think...,' begins Sheffield.

'Three then, from six,' continues the PM, 'and as a sign of good faith we'd require a genuine CCP endorsement from you personally, Dr Slaven, within two weeks and a pledge that there will be no more rallies before the December elections.'

'Three out of six,' repeats Alan Warden, 'and that from the Government, not some minority party that will accept anything, but can deliver nothing.'

'Our Party has its integrity too. You of all people will be able to appreciate that, Dr Slaven. There are things that we aren't prepared to compromise on whatever the electoral outcome of that decision might be.' The PM is so good at this sort of thing. He has been seizing the moral high ground ever since he was Head Prefect and he has been salting that ground ever since. 'It's no secret our policy committee is most impressed with what the Coalition has achieved. Spectacular in its way. There's a feeling the energy and rapport with the public that the movement has, should be given direct access to policy-making. Wouldn't you say, Alan?'

'That was certainly the feeling.'

'There was talk of a joint working party after the election, or a Commission, to consider social issues in an integrated and bi-partisan fashion and I for one would certainly support a CCP convenor, when we're successful at the election and such a body can be formed.' The PM has an almost ingenuous enthusiasm and a most excellent, expensive, soft-collared shirt held by a red and blue tie. He pays the delegation the great compliment of giving it his full attention, when it is one important aspect of a day with several events of equal significance. The information from the Chairpersons of the Producer Boards is already filed below the surface for later consideration, the briefing to come on the ruction at the Pacific Talks held back from impinging on his present concern. Even the discomfort of his hernia and fear for his ailing mother, do not really distract him. After all, on such eternal vigilance does power depend. His smile encompasses the delegation of four. 'Don't feel you have to make up your mind immediately. There's no ultimatum here. We're excited by the possibility of coming to some arrangement.' Prime Minister Hennis gives a smile that both he and they know from a thousand photographs and television shots. A smile pulled off slightly to the left of his mouth with ironic self-awareness, his face lifted somewhat to the eternal camera in assurance rather than aggression, the good teeth, the straight, dark eyebrows and the greying, abundant hair swept back directly with just the odd tress straying to the side of his face. It is the hair of a mafioso chieftain, or an intellectual novelist of the 1930s, and is at once the cause of intuitive feminine response and the joy of his cartoonists. Slaven, Spottiswoode, Thomas and Eula Fitzsimmons watch as they would the screen, and even the Minister and Meelind have to make the small effort to break the common pose and begin again with discussion.

During it Slaven realises that the only thing at issue is priority. The Coalition, its charter points, the service of its supporters, are the entirety of his new and zealous public concern, but only one piece of the action for the PM, one item of the agenda on which he's engaged.

'My door is open,' says the PM. 'Don't hesitate to contact Royce Meelind, who keeps up with everything about your organisation and is impressed. I must admit I thought the time of the mass orator gone forever. The 21st Century would be against it, everybody said.' The PM's assistant is standing at the door as a reminder of the diplomatic briefing.

Why is it that the central issues of people's lives which seemed in the context of Tuamarina and Western Springs, the Coalition policy sessions, meetings in the Dungarvie community hall in Central Otago and the Te Tarehi Anglican vestry in the King Country, to be indisputable, are here strangely moved from centre stage and diminished by imperatives which have not figured before. And how can Slaven go back and explain it all. Every activity and institution is dangerously misunderstood if judged by the common statement of its purpose. A democratic Government is no more the expression of the people's will than is a Church the defender of its faith. The intention of things is finally subverted by the exigencies of day-to-day functioning. A process of getting by rules the world, for always in their hearts people know that any ideal, any whole truth, or absolute accomplishment is beyond them. Humanity's greatest skill always lies in just managing to shore things up.

Meelind has a moment alone with Slaven as the deputation is leaving, as the Minister of Police mentions to Eula Fitzsimmons that if she has no objection he will have his department invite her to be the keynote speaker for the plenary session of the Conference on Humour Clinics.

'You're not disappointed?' asks Meelind. 'It's a balancing act you know, trying to keep all the elements of the party on side. Impossible in fact, but the PM usually avoids having too many aggrieved at any one time. You could do a good deal worse than take what advantage you can get for the moment and then be in a position of greater influence following the election if things go well.'

'But it's the soft demands which he's willing to accept,' says Slaven.

There are twelve reporters and two camerawomen to record the outcome of the meeting. Slaven thinks how cleverly the PM has slipped away, as there is nothing conclusive, or advantageous, that can be said. Even as Slaven speaks he notes a certain pomposity and complacency in his manner, and the others also, despite themselves, are a little puffed up at having met with the PM and the Minister for Police and Gaming. Spottiswoode musters his most appalling grammar when his chance comes, Eula Fitzsimmons' vowels cause a feedback glitch in the sound system, and the Rev Thackeray Thomas, last to speak, wields his delivery like Excalibur for as long as the reporters will listen.

The October dusk is lapping at the Beehive before the PM has a chance to talk again with Alan Warden. The PM isn't on visual and so his face relaxes from its photogenic lines and he sits close to one of his windows so that he can see much of the city: the concrete cubes of the mid-twentieth century, the higher glass blocks of the eighties and nineties, the more ornate buildings of the new millenium. The addition to the National Museum on the waterfront has a splendid copper dome and the more recent speed-rail station close at hand has facings of Takaka marble and huge figures of Maui, Kupe and a northern taniwha in Mount Somers limestone. It is a pleasant thought for the PM that he had supported the project when a junior Minister in the second United Government.

'I don't warm to him, Alan,' says the PM. 'He thinks too much, as Shakespeare would have it.'

'Well, who ever really likes a dentist.'

'That's right. You're right. The thing is he's not political, it seems to me. I can respect the integrity and ability. Meelind gives a good account of all that, but there's fixation of purpose isn't there. You don't get far in public life with the blinkers on. He's stiff, don't you think? Can't see beyond his own ideas. He's driven from the inside, not by what happens outside. Now that's dangerous.'

'Then again, he's had virtually no experience, has he.

Amazing in a way. He's just come out of nowhere and taken the place by storm. The pundits all said you couldn't do it without televison and that the people aren't susceptible to eloquence any more. That they won't listen any more. Well he showed them, didn't he.' So he has, thinks the PM. The lights come on automatically at the main station, throwing sharp light and shadow on the great tail of the taniwha and the hewn figures of Maui and Kupe.

'The novelty will wear off soon though,' says the PM. 'If we all just keep our nerve, the people will tire of Slaven and move on to something else, serenity drugs again, or gender therapy.'

Life is a multiple exposure, so turn aside for a moment, see Neville Hambinder in the back of a garage overlooking Meola Creek kiss his cousin, while a metre away through roughcast their mothers watch the heedless salt tide from the harbour and talk of double knit and raglan sleeves. While the spiders' webs tremble with the cousins' breath, at the Beckley-Waite Institute so much closer to the PM's office, it's smoko for the Caretaker. He shares it with a sandy electrician who has come from J.J. Orme Ltd in Guy Street to fix the laundry thermostats. The Caretaker repeatedly stretches his left arm behind him as they talk. His shoulder gives him trouble after all the years of League. They have mugs so large that on the surface of the tea, ripple patterns form. The Caretaker tells the Orme's man of an inmate who just yesterday claimed there was a monstrous tsunami sweeping north to engulf them from a seismic catastrophe in Antarctica. It makes a good story. The inmate said he could hear the headlong rush of it in the night. The electrician has finished his work for the day. He is relaxed in the evening and laughs until the tears run over the freckles of his sandy face. At this very moment Athol heads his Harley-D turbine Hog westward from Christchurch with the last light catching the greenstone stud in his nose and with the goose girl in a dreamy swoon against his back and he's scarcely five ks from Slaven's place though that's nothing to him and he's thinking of a rendezvous in the state forest and a sack of good leaf grown there. He passes a closed roadside stall for mushrooms and organic pumpkin where Norman Proctor had made purchases in better days.

What's all this in the process of time passing I wonder.

Slaven is on his way to Governors Bay. The Christchurch office has set up a meeting there with a group of peninsula identities who want to know the CCP's stance on rural zoning and historic sites. Influential people in their own quiet way, Kellie told him. Les Croad drives past the high rise apartment blocks at the head of the Heathcote Valley and into the tunnel. 'In we go me darling,' he says.

The tiled sides have recessed lights which flit past with the regularity of heartbeats. For an instant it reminds Slaven of the bathrooms in Burwood Hospital; sanitary, shiny, impersonal. Slaven recalls Norman Proctor resting on the floor there one evening, just a day or two before he died while Kellie was arranging his flowers. The ruckle of his death so subdued that no one heard it you will remember. 'Hello,' says Croad. The engine surges twice, stops. Croad coasts to the emergency lay-by, close to the Lyttelton entrance. Slaven can see a reduced, postcard view of green and blue framed in the arch of the tunnel entrance as Croad uses the red phone on the wall. Norman had said he was buggered: exactly that word and he had sat with his arms straight and the palms flat on the tiled bathroom floor as if he wanted to take some weight from his bed sores. He was buggered he had said and he didn't mean just too tired to get back to the ward.

'Someone's coming in a jiff,' says Croad. He's keen to show that he's well able to cope with the situation. He lifts the bonnet although the light isn't good enough for inspection, let alone repair. 'She crapped out very sudden.'

'We've got a bit of time,' says Slaven. Croad closes the bonnet and leans on it, watching the cars coming past. The service car is prompt and the two men in it have powder blue overalls. They link the vehicles quickly and ask Slaven to ride with them for insurance purposes, while Croad is left at the wheel of the other car.

'The fourth today, oddly enough,' says the serviceman sitting with Slaven in the back. As soon as both cars emerge into the light beyond the tunnel the tow is dropped and as Slaven is accelerated ahead he glimpses only the dark reflection of the one-way glass which hides Croad's reaction. 'A little ride, mate,' says the man beside Slaven. He is calm and heavily-built and he puts a hand on Slaven's left forearm as a friend might to ensure attention to a joke worth hearing.

After a few swift turns to disguise direction, the car slides down to the wharves, the tyres vibrating on the heavy, uneven timbers. The breathing rise and fall of small boats as they pass, coastal freighters, fishing boats, a working launch or two. Looking out at such mundane things as the car slows, Slaven feels foreboding rather than sharp, active fear. He can think of nothing which he can do immediately to his advantage. He is reminded by the attentive grip of his arm that his is to be a passive role, though nothing more is said. The car stops close to the open doors of a landing building which has a sign — Wholesalers Only. M.F. Products.

The driver comes to Slaven's door and stands gripping the release while he looks down the length of the wharf. 'Now,' he says. He opens the door and the colleague within gestures politely to Slaven and follows immediately behind him. One each side of him, all three walk into M.F. Products without proof of being wholesalers, past the freezers and pallets and blue and yellow plastic box trays, down wooden steps until they stand on a landing less than a metre above high tide. The landing has gaps between the timbers and the sea can be seen moving there. The landing is hung in the shadow beneath the wharf and amongst the massive, hardwood piles while the water slops and sucks and the sunlight glitters at a distance on the swell beyond the wharf.

The driver is a slimmer man than the other, with eyes and nose very much towards the top of his head which gives him a supercilious, ostrich expression. He has also the scent of a rather pleasant after-shave, with fennel almost, amongst its complexity. There is a dinghy moored to the landing and Slaven assumes it's for their use, but instead the driver pulls Slaven back to face the stairs and hits him in the face: not with his fist, but with his gloved hand partly open and heavy, as if he holds a bag of marbles. Slaven begins to fall backwards, but the bulk of the second man is solicitously there and the driver is able to hit Slaven again without altering his stance, or the arc of his swing. Slaven feels a numbness of impact, then the pain and a prickling as blood begins to flow from his nose. He would have made a fight of it sooner, in better circumstances outside by the car, if he had forseen the landing below the wharf and the blows in the shifting shadows there. He attempts a kick at the driver, thinking it might be unexpected, but the man behind locks ankles with him and with an 'uh huh,' exposes Slaven's face again by pulling back his hair. Slaven does his best in the unequal struggle. It's not his thing though, is it, and even at the beginning he's more driven by the horror of likely damage to his balls, or his eyes, than any conviction that he can escape.

So is there noise and somewhat methodical movement? Are there the heavy sounds of the driver's filled glove, the footwork of them all on the landing with the salt water glinting as a dark oil underneath, the pleasant fragrance of the driver's after-shave, the frothy burst of Slaven's breath through his own blood? Yes, he lies dealt with soon enough and the driver kneels and takes his Cyma gold watch and the wallet from his jacket.

'I'd break a few fingers, but his hands seems pretty much useless already,' the driver says. His high, bird's eyes are sharp even beneath the wharf. The solid man takes one of Slaven's hands and turns it from side to side.

'Burns,' he says. 'Burns is what these are. Poor bugger.' The driver slips the watch onto his own wrist and passes the wallet to his friend.

'Let it be a lesson to him' he says, as they walk back up the stairs and through M.F. Products.

Under the wharf it becomes darker and cooler as well. Slaven regains consciousness and lies with his eyes and his mouth open, resting, and checking with small movements and messages which parts are okay. Nothing seems to be broken, but any movement brings pain. His face feels immensely swollen. He has become an elephant man. The greatest mistake is to cup his hands and take sea water from the rising tide to wash blood from his face — sharper pain than anything the driver dished out to him. The small mussels clustered on the hardwood piles are almost all submerged, the patches and strips of light from above the wharf slide and undulate like photographic paper on the surface of the swell. The dinghy is higher in relation to him, nodding and veering on its rope. The sound of a simple, repetitious diesel as a cray boat comes in. Drifting, querulous gulls. Though Slaven can smell and taste nothing but his own blood, the waterfront fragrance is always there, compounded of fish scales, refrigeration fluids, ozone, salt, rust and tarred rope, poor food, sneakers, mussels and the farts of god-forsaken creatures in the depths of the sea.

There is a place in the hills where no one wins farmer of the year; high up where the road is still unsealed and has bulges on its length occasionally so that if you're unlucky enough to meet something coming the other way it can be decided by eye contact and gross tonnage who will back down — and then back up. Much of the land has beaten its proprietors and so is given over to pine forest and if the stands are immature the pruned branches are rust filagree beneath the velvet green of the firs. The farm houses are weatherboard and the sheds mainly shot. The dogs are kennelled in a gully head where the mutton bones go to die and the white leghorns flap up into nooks of the equipment shed to roost, where they mute on the harnesses and the post-hole digger which have no other use. There are boxes and bags of apparently unused seed, but the birds and the mice have long since been in and all can be winnowed away. There's a tractor seat cover made from possum pelts and stirrup pumps that have never worked and refuse to start doing so now. In the shearing shed the wood is richly stained with fleece oil and dags and a little blood and sweat. A track winds over the gorse-covered top of the gully to the manuka country beyond and slopes of pigfern rooted over by the namesake, and screes of serpentine rock which make a cheap fence because the sheep will hardly cross and a high pond or two which you'd never know were there, but the stock tracks wind their way to them and the mallards which can be covered with a couple of guns. Pretty much dry country most of the time and the hack still better than the farm bike, but there are days when the cloud comes in, the gorse and briar glisten almost as much as the serpentine, the manuka stems gradually darken as the rain seeps through, the pigfern is bowed down by the weight of the drops it bears.

There are ridges and faces and gullies and spurs that don't appear on maps. They're given names by the family who have to climb them and when the people go they take away the names. There's a place where beech were sledded down to make their first houses and there's a place in the creek, a small falls, where the biggest boar was stuck whose tusks hang over the shearing shed and glint in the evening sun. No matter who does the muster, no matter how keen the dogs, there are a few old woollies on every place that never come down to the yards. But you know all that.

Kellie and Marianne Dunne arrange for Slaven to be admitted to Burwood. There is no strict medical justification, but Dr Dunne, like many in her profession, is not convinced that all medical practitioners have equal skill and also she wants the opportunity to see how things are with Slaven in other ways. After all the genesis of the CCP policies and the Slavenisms which are now heard everywhere, lies in those first talks in her hospital — Miles Kitson, Aldous Slaven and herself. Just a day or two then, so that she can be sure that his injuries have no complications and in this time she will appraise his mental health and hear of Western Springs, of the amazing growth of the CCP and the meeting with the Prime Minister. Even a celebrity needs reassurance following an afternoon beneath the Lyttleton wharves. 'Some people don't like a prophet. I told you that when you were here,' says Marianne. She inspects the nasal passages with the flexoptic and gives him a scan in case of more deep-seated damage. Stitches had been necessary below his right eye and in the corner of his mouth on the same side. There is fracture and compression of his cheekbone. 'Most of the discomfort will come from your mouth and the bruising and you'll find that the neck muscles are very sore. You didn't get kicked lower down?'

'No. Just a feathering, the driver said.'

'I'll be able to have a better look when the swelling subsides, but you'll heal surprisingly quickly. Don't be alarmed by the spectacular discolouration as it happens. Burns are a different matter. There's a far more complex response from the system to burns. You can't just sew things together with burns.' Talk of burns leads Marianne Dunne on to look at Slaven's hands. He likes to feel her touch. She always does the same quick, professional things, like a seamstress checking a garment join, care and pride combined. She bends the fingers back from the palm to check the tension of the new and grafted skin, the time of renewed blood suffusion. She follows the raised lines and checks the muscle replacement at the base of the thumbs. 'Are you doing the exercises?'

'When I have time.'

'Make him do them,' she says, turning to Kellie, 'otherwise he'll end up with hands like a fish eagle's.'

And his mind? What grafts and seams and fractures are there? He may resemble worse than a fish eagle; some creature that takes flight only in the internal sky. Even Marianne Dunne knows precious little of that. She has read Esterhaub and Browne of course and the more recent studies by Langbein in Sydney, but her professional responsibility lay with the outward signs of searing. Even now there is little understanding of how electro-convulsive therapy does the trick, although still used for the very elderly because unlike the drugs it has no side effects. The psychiatrist Hans Berger established much of the early knowledge of the brain's electrical activity, but the realisation of his increasing mental illness drove him to hang himself in 1941. Ugo Cerletti was the first to undertake experiments with shock treatment on humans. In April 1938 the police brought to his clinic in Rome a madman who could not even be identified. Cerletti gave the man a brief shock and the man jolted, fell back on the bed and began singing. While Cerletti conferred with colleagues about a second treatment, the man said clearly, 'Not another one. It's deadly.' But he was given another one — 110 volts for 1.5 seconds — which brought on a typical epileptic attack from which he slowly awoke, peaceful and smiling.

Maybe it has been beneficial, that accidental charge while Slaven was painting his house. Extra connections could be made, new pathways, shortcuts even, stored treasures of the subconscious spilled to the light. There are parts of the brain which by physical stimulation have been proved to hold exact recollection, of which conscious recall is only a dim precis, and activation of the visual cortex will result in a visual sensation, phosphene, even in the totally blind. Slaven has read of people who have had their life again: every colour, every word, every random scent of the passing wind, every ache of their deepest grief and the most individual and piercing joys. At the cost of probing the brain of course.

'Things have been done inside, of course,' Slaven tells them. 'A lot of myself I'm not in touch with anymore, but there's new possibilities in return.'

'Such as?' says Dr Dunne.

'Not this last business, but the accident, the shock. It must have been close to a complete meltdown upstairs, you realise that.'

'Are you still having the syncopations and the loss of emotional identity?' asks the doctor.

'Some odd effects persist,' says Kellie. She has discussed them with Marianne Dunne and Mr Garrity before, as well as with Slaven. The singing and the marching, for example. Slaven can sometimes be found marching on the spot, his knees lifting quite high and a look of pride and resolve on his face. He might continue for ten or fifteen minutes at a time if not interrupted and has no recollection of it afterwards. And sometimes at night she is woken by him singing *Half Moon Bay* — softly, brokenly, with the tune gradually being flattened out as he repeats the verses over and over. Occasionally one of a series of movements in a routine physical activity is omitted; the motor syncopations that Marianne Dunne refers to, so that Slaven might take out his handkerchief, but not raise it to his nose as he blows mucus on to his top lip and chin.

Not often you understand, and for Slaven blips of consciousness which pass with virtually no recall. Set against the sustained power of understanding and expression they are nothing, surely. Such things will almost certainly disappear of their own accord as the brain recovers from trauma. Just circuitry problems, the jocular Mr Garrity has assured them, though even Garrity can make no guarantee.

Dreams however, Slaven can certainly remember, not for any Freudian topics or events, but the association of certain colours with intense emotions. A Van Gogh yellow for instance becomes a whole world of pathos and he wakes with tears free on his face. A high-sky vellum blue stiffens his cock. Purple crystals glow with the malign intent which drives him to an awakening with his limbs jerking in an act both of escape and denial. As Garrity told Kellie and Marianne Dunne though, it was most unfortunate that Slaven went through the Lyttelton thing so soon after his accident. 'It's set you back again,' says Marianne.

'You've got to start taking more care of yourself,' says Kellie.

Cardew claims that the police are doing little to track down the driver and his mate. He's sorry for his father he says, but emphasises that the greatest threat is to the standing of the CCP. He argues that the situation has been partly created by allowing the organisation to become too closely identified with Slaven personally rather than the principles for which he stands. It would have an element of plausibility from any source other than Cardew. His father's charter points are to Cardew completely negotiable, as is the faith of all the Coalition's supporters, as is the fortune of all in life except himself.

Cardew's title within the organisation is Financial Assistant, his job specification to help Kellie with the financial side of the administration and his resolve to assist as much money into his own pocket as he is able. Everything in life is a scam as far as he is concerned, from the Government down. Cardew sees no essential difference between his father's Coalition for Citizen Participation and a second-hand car yard.

It's not easy though. Kellie runs a tight ship despite the

range of her responsibility and Slaven runs an open executive structure with full disclosure and consultation policies. And the old gasper, Miles Kitson, provides expertise from his management team from time to time as a favour. Corruption doesn't thrive in the open, at least not at the stage of germination. Cardew wants a more close-knit, family business. One that is of course entailed and he has his supporters from amongst those in the CCP most opportunistic and from those outside who see change to their advantage.

At Slaven's first appearance following the Lyttelton attack, he suffers a mild convulsion while addressing a combined local bodies seminar in the Pocock Lounge of the Civic Administration Block. His face strikes the lectern, his notes are dislodged and flutter in the air briefly after he himself has reached the floor. Cardew is present at Kellie's insistence and takes his father's place as speaker while Slaven rests. His theme is not, however, a greater bureaucratic responsiveness to public opinion, but an appeal for official ratepayers' institutions to contribute to the Coalition's funds. His reception is less than rapturous.

So Slaven must cut down on his commitments for a while. It's the advice of both Garrity and Marianne Dunne. 'It's what I've been saying,' Cardew tells his mother. 'We've got to take more of the load off him by playing a bigger part. He's the last one to want some sort of personality cult. You know that and it only makes him a target.'

'Who else can make it work? Who else can speak like that?'

'Yea, well, there's that, but the organisational things, the policies and the supervision should be left to you and me, mum. We're the ones who understand him.'

'You feel you're that close then?' says Kellie. Cardew has the grace to let his eyes slide away.

'I reckon I'm closer than Thackeray Thomas, Eula, or Sheffield and that lot.'

'God help us,' says Kellie.

Cardew goes out soon afterwards to the Hello Dolly Escort Agency and then a motel complex with a Maori theme. He shags on the second floor by a window level with carved figures on a pole. He can see from his fixed examination what a sham it is. The pole has long cracks which show pale wood beneath the stain and the eyes are white plastic instead of the true irridescence of paua shell. 'What a have,' he says above his partner of the moment's rise and fall.

'Tell me about it,' she replies.

The Chairman of the Coalition's Wellington branch rings him later that night, saying he has heard that Slaven isn't well, that there's been an unfortunate incident. The movement as a whole has to be safeguarded he says, there are people just waiting to pick on anything suspect, to discredit the principles for which the Coalition stands. All the work, the commitment, the faith, the political capital gained, can be lost so quickly. He tells Cardew that some influential members are concerned that Slaven hasn't had enough rest since the Lyttelton affair. A rest for a while, the Wellington Chairman says, an opportunity for others to run with the ball. There's a group who would like to talk it over with Cardew; just a quiet discussion for the moment. There's a room booked at the new hotel in Island Bay, built by the Koreans. The Chairman is so glad that Cardew appreciates their concern.

Something of drama should follow perhaps. We think that evil of necessity comes with a heightened significance, don't we? That triviality is erased by betrayal, and boredom incompatible with cruelty and malice. It's not so though. Cardew and the Chairman meet with Messrs Pollen, Marr and Aristeed in the Chairman's suite overlooking Island Bay and they move cautiously towards agreement that Slaven is best taken into professional care. For his own sake, for the Coalition's sake, for the sake of Cardew, the Chairman, and those represented by Messrs Pollen, Marr and Aristeed. Mr Aristeed has a bad hip and from time to time he gets up and walks around the chairs of the others for a little respite. Mr Pollen speaks very highly of the Beckley-Waite Institute and gives a brochure on it to Cardew. The essential point emerges in regard to Cardew that a close family member will have to agree, almost certainly sign something to that effect, says Mr Pollen and the Chairman murmurs something about resolution and imposing oneself on reality.

Mr Pollen says that there are excellent medical people who know what's required for Slaven's well-being and are prepared to say so, but nevertheless there is this about a close family member, and some record of Slaven's little problems since the fall and the power line will be helpful. Mr Aristeed stops limping about the room and says that his hip is unbearable. Before he leaves he shakes Cardew's hand and says he's convinced that a secure convalescence is the best thing for his father and for the CCP, just until Slaven is strong enough not to be his own worst enemy. There are media hounds who crucify people just to keep their hand in, he says.

Cardew sits with the Chairman and Messrs Pollen and Marr for another hour or so and they talk about the amazing success of Slaven's Coalition. Cardew says that what's needed next is a corporate financial structure with the emphasis on subscriptions, donations, pledges and endowments. No doubt of it exists in the minds of the others. The Wellington Chairman thinks that he's had a small bucket of ice sent up, but can't find it. Mr Marr isn't much older than Cardew. He leans towards him and tells him that as soon as Slaven goes to the Beckley-Waite for a spell then they're in business for sure. No doubt of it at all.

These are a few of the other things that are said in the hotel in Island Bay, though not necessarily in the same order, or with the same intonation that you, or I, would use.

'Mr Aristeed is a former Minister of Community Equity. No one knows more about minorities. Ramon, Ramon, come and meet Cardew Slaven. It's his hip. It gives him absolute hell.'

'Pardon me for that. It's the amount of rabbit food these hotels serve. We'll all be like cart horses.'

'Yes, Miles Kitson. Now there's a man to watch.'

'I'll ring again. Have some sent up.'

'It would be a well-earned rest for the old campaigner, that's all. Christ, what a thing in Lyttelton. Ugly business.'

'Pardon. It's the fodder here, isn't it.'

'A small one then.'

'Absolutely freakish luck. One day before the appointment and while working in the research library a book of Gaucho ballads fell on him from a great height. Broke his neck the poor bugger.'

'No, no, I'll be down there anyway next week. Gives you a chance to think about it.

The Regional Chairman is down and Cardew has thought about it. They understand each other sufficiently for Cardew to ask for the Beckley-Waite people to come on Thursday, when Kellie is in Invercargill.

Slaven is supposed to be resting at home; not taking on too much until his face is fully healed and the small behavioural abberations have subsided. It's wet when Dr Eugene rings from the airport and Cardew tells him the best way to the rural sub-divisions amongst which Slaven has his few hectares. Not a dreary, or unpopular, rain however, for the plains need every drop of it. The ground seems to puff up as it drinks of it and the lines of vines, ranks of fruit trees, squash plants, nut bushes and boysenberry have the colour of stem and leaf fresh again. The rain takes the traffic film from the road seal and it gathers in paisley whorls of green and violet on the puddles along the verge. The rain deepens the colours of the tiles on the homes on their private blocks and darkens the old tyres on the sides of the pony jumps in the front paddocks. The rain releases essences of growth which drift in the humid air.

'There's a doctor coming out to give you a check over,' Cardew tells his father. They stand in Slaven's study and look out on Kellie's garden in its glistening variety.

'What doctor?'

'Marianne Dunne's asked a specialist from the Beckley-Waite Institute in Wellington to have a talk with you seeing he's in Christchurch for a few days.'

Slaven has been working on an article for *The Australasian* in which he draws parallels between the electoral systems of the two neighbours. He thinks that much of CCP policy has relevance across the Tasman. He's annoyed to find the doctor's visit landed on him without consultation, or warning.

'Mum's been so busy she just forgot all about it I suppose.'

'It's not like her at all. I'm not even changed.'

'I wouldn't think he'll want you to take your clothes off.' The rain is heavier so that the dripping is no longer audible. The rain can be heard striking the leaves outside and on the tiled path below the study window. There is only natural light in the study and in places on Slaven's face the vestiges of bruising are the colour of clay. 'Pretty much a formality I would think,' says Cardew.

Dr Eugene's rented car turns in at the road gate. The wipers are on full and the car pitches a little on the long, uneven drive up to the house. Each time there is a spray of water from beneath the front wheels. The cloud is not dark: it is difficult to see where all the rain is coming from, but it is low and the skirts of it trail in the willows of the creek and make indistinct the architect-designed and gabled home on the block to the south. Cardew goes out to meet them.

Dr Eugene is a very hairy, clean man who smells of soap and lotion. His chin and lower cheeks are gun-metal blue and only his palms startlingly free of growth. Whatever more is necessary will become evident, but for trivial curiosity there is the nature of his death in good time — smothered in the Totara Rest Home by an Alzheimer patient who mistook him for the adulterer in a daytime soap. Dr Bliss is his associate. A very tall man who threatens to topple forward when he walks and who shows his even, capped teeth often in affable smile. Slaven appreciates the teeth when he is introduced, for the work has been well done and with the latest bond polymer which gives a first rate finish, but is testing in the execution.

Dr Eugene expresses a considerable admiration for Marianne Dunne and is particularly interested in any psychological changes and eccentricities since Slaven's accident — the marching on the spot, syncopation episodes, sudden changes of colour intensity in vision and so on. Dr Bliss makes notes while Eugene and Slaven talk and the rain drums down on a receptive Canterbury. Dr Bliss takes the initiative only once, to say how impressed he was after listening to a tape of the Western Springs speeches. His senior colleague doesn't encourage the topic and carries on with the professional gathering of symptoms. Cardew goes unnoticed upstairs to pack a case of his father's things.

Dr Bliss finds him there and says there is no doubt that Slaven would benefit from a residential period of treatment at Beckley-Waite and that he isn't the best person at this time to make the decision for himself. Bliss has a form and Cardew signs it twice — once on behalf of the family to certify a fear for his father's health and safety, once to confirm a list of symptoms and incidents.

Cardew returns with Dr Bliss and is present when his father agrees to give a blood specimen to finish the examination. Slaven grips a red rubber plug from Bliss's bag to bring up the vein on the flat of his right arm. The tourniquet hisses to inflation, but Slaven doesn't see Bliss take a specimen, because Eugene obscures his view and draws attention to one of Kellie's beloved drum lily clumps, sleekly beautiful in the rain. 'Do you know,' says Dr Eugene, 'I would very much like to live here myself. Who isn't drawn to privacy and a garden in which to enjoy it.' Dr Bliss adroitly places the needle home and gives the injection. Almost immediately Slaven feels a relief from customary care, the welling up of a passive, but comforting ease and goodwill. 'So welcome to the therapy of the Beckley-Waite, Dr Slaven,' says Eugene.

'Yes, how beautiful the lilies are,' says Slaven. He is moved almost to tears. He can see Cardew waiting by his chair and for the first time in over a decade he has that bedrock love for his child, with the spoil of disappointment and contrary personality stripped away. He reaches out his arm with the small adhesive strip at the inner fold of his elbow and he takes his son's hand. 'Have I told you how much more I want to do for you?'

'No.'

'How much closer we'll become again. I'm determined on that.'

'Why not,' says Cardew.

'Welcome back,' says Slaven. Dr Eugene smiles to one side. Dr Bliss topples towards his bag as he packs up.

The rain rebounds from the roof of the car as it returns

down the long drive to the gate, the drops kicking back up from the surface in glints of fractured light. The water dashes from the wheels and Cardew sees the raspberry of the brake lights through the drapes of rain as Dr Bliss pauses at the gate before turning on to the road. The one-way glass makes it impossible to know if his father is looking back from the rear window. Cardew has an exhilarating sense of being on the threshold of something momentous. He enjoys being alone on the property, no one to gainsay him, no one to remind him of past failures, or demonstrate the deficiencies of his schemes. It's almost as if he has come into his inheritance. He can see some of his father's Romneys with their full fleeces parting along the back as the wool becomes heavy in the rain. The house waits empty, all his. 'Bugger me,' he says. 'Easy as pie.'

Cardew goes back into his father's study and he swivels the desk chair so that he can see the phone screen and the rain at the same time. Kellie is available immediately, which surprises him. She is tired and the fine lines of her face show more clearly because of it.

'We've had a really positive response again,' she says. 'Most people understand exactly what we're on about.'

'Something's happened here. Dad's had a bit of a turn. No worry, but the doctors think that he needs rest and observation.'

'Oh, my god, what is it.' Kellie's head enlarges on the screen, as if by coming closer she could learn more.

'He's okay. There's no panic at all, but we thought that you should know right away. He needs a spell without any pressure; without people pestering him, always drawing from him. You said so yourself. He's just dog tired and after the Lyttelton thing too.'

'Where is he?'

'We were lucky that Dr Eugene from Wellington happened to be in Christchurch. There's a really top place up there, just like an ecclesiastical retreat, Dr Eugene said, a chance to leave the world behind and bounce back stronger for it.'

'I'll come straight back.'

'There's no need. Nothing to worry about at all, and I'll ring Sarah at the Cambrian rooms so that she won't hear it from anyone else. Don't worry about anything. It's an opportunity to check up on some of the symptoms that concerned Dunne and Garrity.'

'When can I talk to him?' The rain is methodical, restful. Cardew wishes the conversation over. He works at keeping his voice patient and cheerful.

When she is rung, Sarah says she had a premonition. When she last talked to her father he had no aura at all and the tic was bad beneath his eye. Cardew looks away into the steady rain and the low, pale cloud which closes down a longer view. Next he will talk to the Wellington Chairman. Having paid the piper he now wishes to call the tune. Sarah says she's surprised Cardew managed to persuade him to go in for a rest. 'Where is the Beckley-Waite?' She's never heard of it she says, but the horoscope is for change.

Slaven should have all the trauma of being taken into Babylon, an evening of loss and hatred and fear, but in fact the ease and goodwill do not rapidly wear off and are no less real to him for being chemically induced. As companion it's not Bliss who most impresses him, or deputy-director Eugene, but the fellow passenger who remembers him from Tuamarina and who has been seconded to Montana to study the regenerative conservation of high country grasses. Vivien Castle. Dr Bliss is pleased that Vivien admires Slaven and shares an interest in the activity of the CCP. In the economy class also there are many who would like the opportunity to see and hear Slaven, but they make do with the small fame of having travelled on the same plane. Slaven talks for some time very freely about his own background and intentions, then is keen for Vivien to evoke Montana for them. She describes the high plains in both summer and winter, the small and mid-size towns with their distinctive culture, but most passionately the lonely, quiet places beyond Epsie and Sonnette in Powder River where she has done research for months at a time. The Montana air is the closest to our own South Island high country she says.

Ms Castle leans across to see the alps from the window and so make comparison. Slaven enjoys the fragrance of her and reaches a hand to stroke her hair, but finds Bliss restraining him. The doctor knows what he is going through and encourages Vivien to become more technical in the discussion of her grasses. With Bliss between them, Slaven's encouragement can be only verbal. He asks questions himself, then listens to Vivien and Bliss. If he turns to the window side he finds Eugene as observant as ever, though not entering the conversation. Eugene watches carefully the face of each person who speaks, as if to determine the psychological workings behind the sounds. Finally he leans to Slaven and says quietly, so as not to interupt Bliss and Castle, 'How fortunate to live in old Montana.'

'Why old Montana?' asks Slaven, but the plane is coming in to land at Wellington. The runway extensions are like vast and empty piers under which the waves disappear.

'I very much look forward to your campaign speeches in the run up to the elections,' says Vivien Castle. *Baby, baby come again and live with me upon the shore of Half Moon Bay.*

'*Upon the shore of Half Moon Bay,*' repeats Dr Bliss, who can hold a tune. Slaven feels tears well up.

Down from the sky. Slaven begins to feel both sick and tired, with tremors which flood his mouth with saliva. He can hardly bear the sight of the sleek fur on the backs of Dr Eugene's hands. A car from the Beckley-Waite takes all three quietly away. Slaven can hear Eugene and Bliss talking of Vivien Castle. 'Old Montana's the place,' he says. The others take no notice, except that Eugene tells Bliss that at one point he thought Slaven was going to saddle up their Ms Montana.

'Anyway, he's coming down with a bump,' says Bliss.

See ahead of them spatially, chronologically, epistolarilly — the Caretaker, though the arrival of yet another inmate is no immediate concern of his. The Caretaker is removing a branch from a sycamore tree which has been keeping the sun from the second storey window of the east wing secure day-room. See the women and men standing close to the large window to watch. In their affliction most have lost an awareness of themselves as possible objects of desire, even scrutiny. Posture, appearance and expression reflect the change. Their stomachs are allowed a natural slump beneath the dresses, or over the rough tuck of waistbands, their noses are ripe for picking, they watch the Caretaker with open-mouthed solemnity, or release sudden, secret smiles for no earthly reason. The Caretaker is working high up, on a plank he has locked between two ladders and his movements are both steady and cautious. It's not an ideal day for the job, but he committed himself before that was apparent. The large branch is constrained by two strung ropes so that the Caretaker can ensure at least the approximate path of its fall. He wears goggles and the racing chain of the power-saw doesn't disturb his smile. In a quiet spell, when the Caretaker is planning ahead and the women with their uneven hems are a frieze at the window, Ovens, the Beckley-Waite dentist, calls out as he passes about desecration and sparing a tree. He is a hard case. 'Dont' you worry,' says the Caretaker. 'I'm the bloody native here, not the tree.' He and Ovens shout with laughter and some of the women at the window are startled into joining them.

At the entrance to the Institute the car stops long enough for the window to be lowered so that the deputy-director can be recognised, then carries on to the admissions suite. There is nothing auspicious, or impressive, concerned with Slaven's arrival. The rain which in Canterbury was welcome and steady, is here just another blustery drizzle which stains the stonework and plasters litter to the ground.

'I know you're not feeling great,' Dr Eugene tells Slaven. 'We want to make you comfortable as soon as possible, but if you don't mind we'll just get you registered and make a quick admission check as the procedures lay down. Our Director's known as a stickler for the rules.'

Dr Eugene has his own key and lets them in to the admissions area which is well lit, but deserted. Slaven is becoming confused and angry as the induced goodwill wears off. He isn't sure of his surroundings, his companions, even his immediate past. Who uses these computer monitors during working hours? Who looks from the glassed offices? Who walks the strip of moss green carpet with the wood tiles polished on each side?

'If you'll just come into one of the interview rooms, Dr Slaven, we'll get through it all as soon as posssible. Then

I'm sure there will be a meal for you,' and Eugene ushers Slaven in and pauses in the doorway to thank Bliss for his help and tell him that he needn't stay.

'I'll say goodbye then,' says toppling Dr Bliss. 'I'll tell whoever is on duty in the wing that you're here. I trust the rest will be beneficial.' He shows his excellent teeth in a final affable smile and is gone.

'We don't need to do a lot,' says Eugene. 'Most of the questions I've already put to you, but there are a few things, rudimentary physical tests mainly and response notes that need to be covered on admission. Procedures snowball for everything these days, don't you find. In dentistry I mean.'

Slaven begins shuffling his feet, then marching on the spot; the spot being beside a walking frame which has been left in the interview room to save anyone fetching it from stores. Dr Eugene carries on taking Slaven's blood pressure and asking questions — has Slaven ever suffered from a communicable disease for example and has any member of his family committed suicide.

'Discipline is a form of pride.'

'Check.'

'Eventually the body betrays the mind.'

'Check.'

'Never rat on a mate.'

'Check.'

With one part of his mind, Slaven is able to view the scene quite clearly, see himself marching nowhere in a room unknown to him and before a man who is a stranger. He feels great pity for himself, but as he would feel it for another. An embracing Russian pity for the plight of all as one.

There are one and a half trees in the quadrangle outside Slaven's window. One and a half are all that he can see even with his face pressed to the security pane and so he hesitates to assume more, whatever logic and experience on the outside might lead him to expect. They are kowhai trees, not particularly thick in the trunk, or very tall, but a roosting place for sparrows in the evenings. The last dull, yellow blossoms litter the cobbles like heaped corpses of bees. The sparrows come careering in over the west wing and jostle for perches in the top kowhai branches which are almost bare as a result. The birds are slow to settle and move from one tree to the other, or swoop out of sight to a different place altogether. They make a great chorus of sharp, high cries which go on into the dusk. The conviviality of the birds makes Slaven more aware of his isolation, the long night which is coming, the next day when he will wake to find the sparrows gone without chance of flight himself.

The ceiling is lined with baffle squares, to cut down noise and conserve heat. Each one has a myriad of holes like a chinese checkers board, yet he has done all the calculations many times of course as he lies on his bed. Thirty holes on each side, but those in each corner are counted twice in that reckoning and he spent a good deal of time initially deciding how that would affect his sums. And the dimensions of his room aren't determined by the ceiling squares and so there are thirteen hole part-baffle boards along the window side of the ceiling and a six hole sequence at one end above his bed. And there is one individual square, just one, which has one row of dots less than all the others which are complete. Slaven thinks perhaps that's where the microphone is.

If he takes his stool into the extreme corner of his room by the window, he is able to see, as well as one and a half kowhai trees, a thin strip of the cobbled courtyard, an azalea equally captive in a terracotta pot and something of the city beyond. Such a narrow strip, curtailed by the blank bulk of Beckley-Waite wings, that it is like a road lying very straight and still before him. In the daytime he watches visitors at the courtyard entrance, few enough, and beyond is one, brief turn of a street on which he can glimpse cars passing. Sometimes Slaven makes guesses as to what colours will come next. Red is the most common, if he allows some latitude in regard to shades.

At night the cars are all far lights alike, each making a curlicue of beam and then snuffed out, but the band of courtyard closer to his window has an infinite variety of slight graduations. Slaven has the time to see nature go by on such a small stage. Moonlit nights reveal slight irregularities in the cobbles by hyphens and brackets of sharp shadow and the slaters can be seen questing out from beneath the terracotta pot. Winds test the aerodynamics of the place according to their origin, so that the southerly bluster sweeps his view clean and the nor'wester eddies leaves, bunion dressings, cats' fur, cellophane, grit and old kowhai blossom into the lee of the azalea and the bluestone wall. Here the water lies longer and deeper so that worms from lawn plots never seen are drowned trying to escape across the cobbles. If the wet weather persists they turn pale and flaccid, reminding Slaven of those things preserved in bottles which had been familiar to him as a student.

Slaven is unable to see the flats where the Yees and McGoverns live and has no reason at all to be aware of this disability, but often late at night he listens to a far clarinet expertly played and thinks what he has come to. He doesn't share our knowledge of the nights without this music, when Victor Yee tends his ailing wife, marks his Polytechnic Cantonese, or visits the rooms above the Tahitian tattooist.

Slaven is having his swimming session with the others. The Beckley-Waite prides itself on an holistic approach to patient welfare. The pool supervisor has a large body the colour of butter and is a man of hideous good cheer. Slaven listens for his laugh, ducks below the surface to evade it and wishes he could breathe the tainted water rather than surface to that sound again. The great, crass, braying laugh of a man with no claim to the attention of his fellows, but with the determination to impinge upon them nevertheless. A humourless, interrupting, vulgar laugh, that reeks of ignorance, shallowness and unwashed opinions despite his occupation.

'Come along, Aldous, see how Helen and Astral keep their heads down in the glide at the completion of a stroke.'

For many years Slaven has been accustomed to respect; for some months adulation even. The people in the Beckley-Waite don't seems to care who he is. They are impervious to eloquence, should he try it, and fame from any outer world is a flickering shadow here. Slaven swims as one of the frumpish group, showing no aquatic skills to distinguish himself. He dances in exercise before a giant screen, is chided for his weight at the sensor plate, is humbled by the vast butter man's praise of other members of the group. Slaven, who drew almost 250,000 to Western Springs and has taken the PM's hand in a sense of equality, picks up his thin, issue towel and is harried down the corridor to the changing rooms by the instructor's laugh. 'What a guy. What a hard case,' says Mathieson in front to a friend. Slaven wonders why Kellie hasn't rescued him. Why the world that thinks so much of him isn't at the gates of the Beckley-Waite Institute.

'Cheer up, Aldous,' the instructor says. 'You look as if you've been pissing in the pool again.'

In warm nights, Slaven pushes up his window the few centimetres it will travel. He sits by the grill and enjoys the air from outside. A relief from the dehumidified atmosphere of the air-conditioned rooms and corridors of the Institute. Tonight he notices again the fragrance of tobacco smoke: not the light, doctored brands which have given the habit a new impetus, despite regulation, but the coarse, lung-catching fume of the old days and with it some other fragrance that's unknown to him, but which causes his eyelids to half fall in satisfaction.

Slaven has never been a smoker, but finds himself inhaling with more than sufferance: a need for variety to compensate for the bland institutional routine which is itself calculated to be a sedative.

It's the sound of a cough and a tearing strike of a match which make Slaven question the source of the pleasure he shares. It makes him quieter in his corner at first, the knowledge of someone out there, down there. To be at ease, smoking in the courtyard means you are a free person. To be a free person within the Beckley-Waite means surely that you are part of the mechanism which restricts the freedom of others. Yet it's natural to be curious. Slaven begins the effort to see him, or her. By standing with his head against the grill, he can see almost directly to the courtyard one floor beneath, but in that metre or so hard against the wall which he misses, the smoker chooses to stand, unseen, at the very start of that narrow road of view which takes Slaven's eyes over the darkened cobbles, the terracotta sanctuary for the azalea, the entrance, foreshortened grounds and the brief, recurring headlights at the crest and bend.

No good, no go. Slaven thinks of making a noise to let the smoker know that he's above and not far away. A non-specific sort of noise which won't signal awareness of the smoker's presence: some humming say, or a companionable cough, but even this might be enough to lose him the drifting, occasional smoke and the sense of another person close at hand. They cannot see each other, yet share a greater intimacy — the breath of one drifts to the nostrils of the other.

A man's voice comes up to him. 'How you going up there?' A quiet voice with the slightly slurred, understated evenness of a working man.

'I'm fine.'

'Good on you.'

'I've been enjoying the smoke from your cigarettes for some time now. Evenings when there's not much wind. It's something against the sameness of the nights here.'

'Pipe actually. I know. I'd let you hoist a bowl up, but it would stink out the room and they'd get you for it sure enough.'

Some ploy maybe, some indirect means of assessment and influence. Slaven isn't going to be taken in as easily as all that, but he feels his spirits lift here at the window in the darkness, responding to the impartial goodwill he senses in the voice. 'My name's Aldous Slaven.' He says it without much deliberation. Silence for a time, the tear and flare of another match and then after an interval in which Slaven imagines the smoke lazily rising, he has the complex flavour of it again. 'What have you got in that stuff,' he says. 'It doesn't smell like any tobacco I know.'

'I was at Tuamarina.' When Slaven hears that he sees the place again, but not with any of the transient dress for which he and Thackeray Thomas had been responsible. The bare, scrubbed Tuamarina — as it truly is. The squat gum tree spreading above the memorial for the European dead, the quiet, gravel track winding up the hill from the turn-off, the little school of Tuamarina on the flat below and with the paddocks around it. There's gorse, broom and manuka on the ridges running up from the graves and the dark New Zealand bush way back. The same bush that watched Te Rauparaha as he watched the newcomers. High on a far hill towards Picton is a very large tree, quite dead, and its bare branches are like a drift of smoke against the green which surrounds it.

'I have relatives at Mahakipawa,' says the voice. 'We all came over the hill to hear you at Tuamarina.'

'So how come you're up here. In this place?'

'I'm the Caretaker.' Is there a hint of a pause longer than usual between the parts of the compound word. 'I take a break about this time at night, and sometimes I come out and smoke a bit of mixed weed. A nice spot when it's warm enough and I can have a think about things. It's different at night, as you probably know. It has a logic of its own.'

'What, sadness.'

'No, nothing like that,' says the Caretaker. 'I mean you can get close to yourself. You can nut things out with not too many distractions. I'm a slow thinker, see, and I need a fair bit of time to get my ideas clean.'

'Clean?'

'Yeah. Clean of all the crap that hides the real outline of what people are telling you, getting you to believe. And your ingrained self-interest, your assumptions and the beliefs you take up because you admire something about the people who have them, rather than the ideas themselves.'

'Some research suggests that at night the pattern of our brain is different; other insights and feelings are possible.'

'I wouldn't know about that, but it's clean thinking time, the night, it seems to me.'

They are quiet, as if neither wishes to put too much pressure on the contact they've made after several hours and nights of being close, invisible, sharing the smoke of the Caretaker's pipe, but saying nothing. Slaven doesn't move away however, lest the Caretaker thinks that he's bored. He remains at the window, seeing the flashes of the car lights at a distance. He draws in his breath carefully, but there's no smoke on the air. 'I'd better get on,' says the

Caretaker and after a time in the silence that follows, Slaven knows that he is gone.

Miles also experiences a Beckley-Waite of a sort, his ailments cutting him off not just from what is going on around him, but from his own life at times. Times of pain and discomfort, of trivial endeavour to eat, breathe, or defecate. To pass piss without blood is more important to him than Slaven's six points, or the massacres in Mexico. There are times when he sleeps without meaning to, times when he might as well be asleep although his eyes remain open. The worst is when his past is denied to him and he can't refresh himself in recollection. He comes close then to exercising his right to take his leave. No fears deter him from that, just a reluctance to abandon his influence, his memories, his friends, his wife, when there are still good times in which they may be enjoyed.

Today, for example, is one of his better days.

From his tower study in the Cashmere Hills, Miles can see across the city of Christchurch and the Canterbury Plains towards the mountains. He savours the taste of his orange juice untainted with pain and is trying to find out who is responsible for the Lyttlelton attack on Slaven, the Beckley-Waite committal, and if the two are connected. He is speaking to a woman who until recently was an inspector in a branch dealing with corruption. Miles is surprised how young she looks. The world has quite abruptly been filled up with young people who are unfazed by their lack of experience. Miles of course doesn't allow the inspector the similar advantage of viewing him.

'Anyone in the public eye to that extent is a target,' she is saying, 'but we can exclude the individual crank in this case — too practised, too well-planned and resourced. From what we've found out there are three main possibilities. The first is within the CCP itself; a group including Pollen and Laucoux, who's the Wellington regional chairperson. They want to diminish the Slavens' personal control and have a more corporate leadership. I do know that Laucoux has met Cardew Slaven at least once privately.'

'They might beat him up, but how the hell would they

pull this Beckley-Waite stunt by themselves. That's been set up within the system wouldn't you say?'

'Yes, but how I don't know. There's also a good deal of apprehension within the United Party about the CCP's impact on the coming elections. The Parliamentarians won't visibly support any dirty tricks of course, but within the wider party there's people been pushing. Gittings in particular, who has the deputy PM's ear and has been touting what he calls in private a pre-emptive strike. And he's got other Cabinet allies of course.'

'The very ones who want to dump the PM. It's difficult for them probably. Do they wait and hope that Slaven will undermine the PM without costing the party the election, or do they have a crack at the Coalition now and deal with the PM in their own way.'

The investigator is interested in the possibilities, interested also in the circumstance of Miles Kitson being her employer. She hasn't admitted that in her time she's done a good deal of research on his own power base and affiliations, and he hasn't admitted to being aware of it. He is sick now, she's heard, but can see only the blank phone screen. Miles admires her hair, which is dark, loose and long. He thinks that it has only been worn thus since her resignation from the force.

'What I'm looking for,' she says, 'is the link if there is one between that bunch and the CCP Wellington chair. Someone like Ramon Aristeed.'

'And the third possibility?' Miles sincerely wants to help his friend, but also while feeling well he wishes to spend time with Georgina — he could arrange a chopper and they could fly to their bach at Le Bons Bay.

'The Statos-Nationalists. Of all the main parties, theirs is the support which most closely approximates the voter profile that Slaven's been drawing to the rallies. And they've got plenty of sympathisers at the top end of the state service.'

'But the least likely?'

'Yes.'

'Could we get hold of the Beckley-Waite records and see who was pushing this thing along. A clandestine mission, is that what it's called?'

'I wouldn't advise it,' she says. 'There won't be anything in writing to point to political involvement, you can bet on that. No, just the case as set up and Cardew Slaven for the fall guy. Push too hard for the reasons for the committal, admission, whatever, and the whole thing blows up in the Coalition's face. The son's doing a lot of harm. He's easy to use; the weak link.'

'He's driven by his prick,' says Miles hoarsely.

'Something to get hold of him by then,' says the Investigator, who is used to working with men. Miles enjoys the sight of her shrewd face, her hair, her smile. It's not a bad way to pass time in your eighties — some jock talk with a handsome woman.

'Aldous isn't in any danger is he, in that place?'

'I'd say if they wanted that then it would have happened under the Lyttelton wharves, or a pot shot at his workplace.'

'Something else that might be useful,' says Miles. 'Find out where that Pacifica article came from, with all that business about his health and only three days before he's taken to the Beckley-Waite. A little conscious preparation it seems to me.' Miles begins to find it difficult to concentrate on the welfare of anyone but himself, because the pain in his mouth is bad again. Illness is a great isolator. Already the mountains against the sky seem less admirable and the investigator's hair folds with less appeal upon her shoulders. He has been told that an operation is the best thing and then a prothesis, less gross than Freud's. These days science does marvels, but he doubts if he will loiter when such things become necessary. 'Anyway,' he tells her, 'there's the more important question of what's for the best right now. I want you to go to Wellington and talk to friends of mine and someone trustworthy will need to go to Mahakipawa. It's time we took the initiative.'

Miles knows that Slaven will be hopeless in the Beckley-Waite, having almost no understanding of how to manipulate people except in the mass and for the general good. As he takes the medication for his throat, he imagines Slaven in the Beckley-Waite: that considerable intelligence and trust in a rational response under attack from both within and without. Miles has learnt that self-interest is the quickest and staunchest place to start.

Miles has a famous cellar, stocked with care and enthusiasm over the years. He has considered the merits of drinking himself to death. He's close enough that half a dozen first class reds would perhaps complete the process — go out on Chateau Lagune, or Mouton Rothschild '99. Oh, there are a variety of ways to move from one room to the next. Miles uses them as a blackmail against his illnesses: push me further and I'll be off, and parasitic pain draws back then, just a bit, apprehensive that it might lose its host. Anyway, he is only camped on the divide. A chance to look back, to savour the journey in case even memory is stripped by the arrowsmith on the other side.

He is amazed that he has done so much, experienced life as a treasure house, and it is served to him again when fortunate, in such completeness that he feels the quick sweat of a younger self, hears voices of utter accuracy, weeps for joy at the sight of friends come freshly back from sixty years.

Ah, he feels better now. The medication leaves a light, mint taste as a disguise upon his palate.

In 1974, when most of his friends were on the Ilam Campus, Miles had a courier business — himself and Izzy Paycock and two Honda 125s. The dispensing receptionists and secretaries were scrupulous in their insistence that Izzy and Miles signed for every item and the partnership in return insisted on acknowledgement of receipt. It was a statement of their commercial equality. Izzy finally became quite a big cheese in the union movement, but neither held the outcome of their lives against the other. Izzy died years ago. He must have been well into his seventies and he stumbled at the lavatory and fell headlong into the bowl. Mutual friends said he drowned, but Miles thought that just the process of trivial mythology. He considered a lavatory bowl, the constriction and the level of the water. No, not drowned, but there was no doubt that the hard, white circumference would deal a fearsome blow. Miles imagined the event with all its attendant bathos. So clearly he saw it and no less true because the lavatory was his own and the dead Izzy in it still barely twenty. The top grade mushroom carpet with Izzy's feet and shoe soles uppermost and the powder blue tiles as a surround for the lavatory bowl and bidet. Izzy always wore their company jacket, which was red vinyl to stand out on the four stroke Hondas and keep out the wind. Payson Couriers the lettering said, though Miles and Izzy always wished they had the daring to amalgamate the surnames in the firm as Kitcock. Izzy was as local as they come, but wore his long, fair hair in a pony tail like a Swedish tourist and his knees would stick out absurdly on the bike which was too small for him and his pony tail would stream out from his helmet as he raced through the traffic of Riccarton Road, or Bealey Avenue. The pony tail, sun bleached more at the end, spread over the back of Izzy's red jacket as he lay in the lavatory. Without the helmet his fair hair could be seen to be darker at the roots and on the side of his face turned up from the tiles, Miles could see the moles on his cheeks and the line of his long, nordic chin.

They kept the company records in a 'Warrior' exercise book and at the end of each week Izzy entered under incidental expenses enough for two jugs of DB and they went to the pub. They accepted the trust and comradeship of that first business because they knew no other and after they had gone their separate ways they never wanted to meet again and so trammel what they remembered of each other.

Izzy would smoke as he delivered around the city and in the bursts of acceleration the sparks would fly from his cheap cigarillos and pit his face between the moles. Miles could see the pale, sponge soles of Izzy's shoes as he lay there with his head under the lip of the bowl. Quietus now, Izzy.

Miles had first boarded with a de facto couple in Spreydon. The weatherboard house was surrounded with rank grass which pressed up to the wooden sides and swooned on the concrete steps, though from a distance there were just sufficient changes in the contours to suggest past garden plots, as stone age fortifications can still be seen from the air beneath a modern pasture. The woman was Suzanne and she called her man, Ger. Miles liked to assume it short for germ, but the rare letter was addressed to Gerald.

It was eternally winter in Spreydon and from time to time Ger tore palings from the road fence to start a fire. The grass turned an odd shade of blue in the winter and the smog seeped along the flat streets and all the world was in a slow-moving semi-hibernation of cold and poverty, which included the imagination. Ger was rarely able to manage a complete sentence, but he would say things like, 'is it ever', 'fat chance', 'bout fuck'n time'. He had a most wonderful, lolling, gap-toothed smile when Murphy's law caught up with him, as it invariably did. The smile of the holocaust victim: the candid look that the sparrow has pinned by the sparrow-hawk. Ger could outstare a cat, or a piece of furniture, quite unwittingly. A blank, aching scrutiny until the cat walked away, or the armchair blinked first. His feet smelled always of cheese and despair. He sang to himself in the bathroom where he masturbated during those considerable periods when he was out of favour.

Suzanne's lineage was one that equipped her well for poverty. She was small, pale, wiry and of a rattish intensity. Her white nose tinged with pink in the winter cold and her hair had no more suggestion of a curl than has Spanish moss. She had no sense of community, or nationality, but a congenital determination for personal survival. A rat-hole, white trash, come and get me philosophy of life, which meant that she defied all demands and tariffs, tax returns, licences, honesty boxes, all trust and all compassion, and she lived a fierce struggle for what little she could command. Chinese takeaways she loved, hotdogs, supermarket chocolate which she would devour with head-jutting urgency while a crystal drop hung from the pink tip of that sharp nose. Miles imagined her in a minehead village in West Virginia, or a Glasgow tenement. When things pressed her particularly hard she had a friend home and dressed as though she had breasts a man could get a grip on. They would spend a good deal of time in the main bedroom, set another mug by the takeaways and Ger would spend more time than usual singing to himself in the bathroom. There were other times of course of great rapport and delicacy, when Suzanne said sharply to Ger at the door of the bedroom, 'Get in here,' as if he were a bad dog, yet one forgiven.

Miles was never introduced to any of the temporary lodgers, never part of what passed for life in the eternal winter of Spreydon. Not once did Ger, or Suzanne enquire as to his life, or his views. When he stepped over the fence with so few palings to walk to the pub, or took the plastic cover from his Honda in the long grass behind the laundry so that he could go to work with Izzy during the day, or the Polytech night courses, then he stepped beyond their comprehension. Often he felt that even inside the house he was invisible and that if he were to walk directly in the way of them, there would be no contact, no collision, merely a slight visual flux as they passed through each other on different planes.

Just occasionally though, occasionally and no more thank Jesus, as Ger and Miles sat in an atmosphere of cheese and despair in the only room heated, Miles thought that in Ger's gaze was something intentionally sardonic, from the holocaust, or the sparrow-hawk. Maybe when there was the sound of the regular working of the springs in the main bedroom, maybe when the neighbour's winter cheer rhododendron gathered the stains of coal fires to its blossom bosom, maybe as cats squealed in the black judder of the night.

Miles remembers a cold May afternoon and the only story that Ger ever told him. Whole sentences of it. His lolling, Murphy's law expression as he said, 'Some cunt in front of me today found two hundred dollars, and me one away from it. That's my life though, one cunt away from finding anything.'

Miles can see over most of Christchurch, even the new sprawl beyond Orana and the airport. Spreydon must be down there somewhere, even the house itself, though Ger may have continued with it as he began with the paling fence. Izzy used to come round, quite unnoticed. They sat shivering in Miles's room where the most delicate of mildew rosettes gave botanical ambiguity to the bamboo-patterned wallpaper. Izzy would jiggle his knees for warmth, draw up the zip on his company jacket of red vinyl and discuss prospects for the firm's expansion.

Miles finds his mouth much better. Is he doing all that

he should for Slaven? He likes the man and fears for the effects of the strange talent which has seized him. Even as he talks with the investigator, he recognises that part of himself has only an academic interest, that as real to him as any hardship Aldous Slaven may be enduring is the pungency of Izzy's cheap cigarillos and the memory of the fine mist which gathered like amoebic insects on the visors as Izzy and he couriered their dreams about the city.

'**S**ome reluctance to commit in the pool, I'm bound to say,' says the butter man.

The dayroom of ward 37 opens on to a fully enclosed, grassed compound which has many seats around the outside, and some, by a bed of dwarf conifers, brown, green, yellow and grey, in the centre. The gardens of the Beckley-Waite, like the inmates, are essentially low maintenance.

Only Marianne, the salad lady, sits in the centre, content to consider herself the cynosure, or oblivious to it. She has a blue knee support, but never talks of sport. She keeps several small sores raw by devotion to the backs of her hands. Any movement directly in front of her draws cries of zucchini, shallots, garni, mushrooms, lettuce, or Russian bolds. Her lips are finely wrinkled and pout tremulously. No one takes any notice. High above the compound in the sky world are the trails of jets. No one takes any notice. Slaven is one of those sitting at the edge and with his tongue on the roof of his mouth he follows the mint trail of recent medication. There is occasional shouting, endless repetitions from some, catatonic peacefulness, restless shufflings caused by even the new generation anti-psychotic drugs. Mr Wormold has a habit of blowing on his fingers if he is prevented from circling and Roger Fielding charms the nurses with Italian verses when he's not gripped by thought broadcasting. Vivien Catanach was one of Dr Collett's successes until two days before planned release she choked on a ping-pong ball, thinking it one of the Satsuma plums of her happy, happy youth. Quietus now, in the green shade.

Chives, lentils, cucumber, onions, red peppers, baby peas, radishes and mangetout.

'He is never any hindrance to the satisfactory routine of

the ward,' says the Charge Nurse. 'He's never been put in the colour spinner yet.' Slaven experiences a gratitude of absurd proportions.

The category of ward 37 is chronic and the placement here more a matter of similar treatment and compatible symptoms, than commonality of illness. The schizophrenias predominate, Slaven finds the paranoid awake disconcerting possiblilities in himself, but there are those who must put their hand up for major depressive syndrome, for bipolar disorder, for Korsakoff's syndrome, for Huntington's chorea, for the old Maupassant penalty and new consequences of the very same pleasure. There is even ancient Eddie Lime who was for too long a boxer. Collett sees him as a special gem in the collection, so much a rarity since the fundamental changes in the sport.

Slaven has of course sought his own place in all of this. Post-traumatic stress disorder he has been told, but no glib explanation as to the posting — a chronic, a secure ward? Come, come gentlemen, there is more at work here than meets the eye.

The Therapy Aide and Slaven have reached an accommodation — mutual good-will without any demands of each other. 'Aldous does very well considering his hands,' she says. 'Mostly he likes to do things in his own room.' Nothing, is what he does mainly in his own room. The Therapy Aide has been well-cured of idealism and has dark, clean hair in her favour.

Violence is no more common in 37 than in the outside world, less in fact, and when difference is brought together it becomes the yawning commonplace. Insanity is like war; mostly discomfort and boredom, but that shot through with horror. Except that in the Beckley-Waite the assaults are launched from within.

Red cabbage, parsley, tomatoes, leeks and avocados.

What thrives is isolation and preoccupation. When you cannot trust yourself, then to place any reliance on others is a fearsome business. People share the ward almost unwittingly, and clumsily deflect contact when they come face to face, or turn away with indifference.

Yet Slaven is excited despite himself. Today he is to have

his weekly full-case meeting. Each time the experience disappoints him, yet each time the anticipation of focus on himself in all this dreary, time-dragging, throttling world, inspires a hope that from the limbo he will be taken out and dressed in a life again.

Tarragon, salsify, endive and artichokes. Mint and carrot slivers.

Dooley Shaw has his face pressed into a corner of the glass at the nurses station like an aquarium squid. Dooley weeps whenever he sees the moon, and he can see it in the midday sun.

The case meeting is held in the largest of the counselling rooms. A room with a window door through which the chronics can see which of their number have been chosen by the great — those with colour coded keys and language besides which fits perfectly into the locks of what others say. The Charge Nurse is there, the butter man from the pool who is in charge of recreation, the Therapy Aide, the psychologist, and Collett who is Slaven's case supervisor. Slaven struggles to keep down his anger when discussion moves from his treatment and progress to more general ward concerns, or the damage to staff cars in the special park. After all anger is not an appropriate response. Change the responses and you change the mood the behaviourists used to say.

Chronics blow like thistle-down through the polished barrels of the Beckley-Waite. Chronics rattle like chrysalids against the full-length glass. Both true, both true, hey nonney no.

'What comment have we then in regard to inter-action?' asks Collett. He begins a good deal of the discussion if Morris the psychologist is present. In this way he underlines his position as the clinical psychiatrist.

'Not great on the physical front I'm afraid,' says the butter man. 'Not a lot of outreach, I'm bound to say.'

'Fennel, cress, beetroot, celery, aubergines and corn,' shouts Marianne as Philip Mathieson passes in front. She will remind them all of their salad days.

Let us suppose for Slaven then, that which will not be — leave from the Beckley-Waite Institute to visit Kellie. A compassionate parole of some kind, so that instead of lying on his back listening to the sedulous whisper of the air-conditioning and regarding the pock-marked firmament of his room, Slaven is by choice walking up the long drive from their road gate, through the colours and fragrances of the paddocks and garden, determined to speak honestly. Honesty is a tall enough order don't you find, so let's not make any reference at all to truth. Honesty is self-referential and so subject to some degree to individual judgement.

Kellie watches him come, looking just the same as he has always looked, though she knows that can't be true. He has a slightly awkward action, almost as if his large feet must overcome some suction as he walks. Off the stage there is no show with Slaven, no special effort to impress, rather an absent-mindedness, as if he's still thinking of his surgery, of his beliefs, of the diminishment he suffers in the Beckley-Waite. So see him in this rather absent-minded way trail his hand among the red and purple hydrangeas as is his habit

Kellie comes to meet him, doesn't she? On the paved circle in front of the garages they kiss and weep and the last few petals flutter from his hand. It doesn't matter what they say of course. Words are of little consequence between people who are truly familiar. She understands by his touch, the colour of his face, the tone of voice, what he experiences within the Beckley-Waite Institute. In the past it has always been his good fortune to be valued, in at least a modest way to be sought out and distinguished, yet in the Beckley-Waite he has some sort of rat-arsed existence of no hope and meaning. Even Mrs Wicks still has hope perhaps, though which of us will tell her of the clotted, yellow feathers in the mottled light beneath the coral japonica of Burwood Park. Can anyone live long who sees the world unmasked?

The most ordinary things of his own home seem matters of tender regard to Slaven after the Beckley-Waite. The kitchen clock with animals on the dial, picked out by Cardew when he was seven, a magnetised ladybird on the fridge, a kauri tea caddy, the top worn dark and smooth, the green container for his gemfibrozil capsules close to the dining table. Kellie sits with him as a reassurance and she doesn't talk of her own troubles, but gives of her strength and care. She tells him of all the things that are being done on his behalf and of which he's been unaware. He looks just the same, but she wonders what's happening to him. She wonders how it has come about that at this stage in their lives he addresses mass rallies with abrupt vehemence, is beaten beneath a Lyttelton wharf, is treated at the Beckley-Waite for threats to his sanity. What she talks of though, is the vitality of the Coalition and the enduring support of his friends. She takes his hand. She knows so much about him that she's able to judge that there are parts to him she will never understand.

When first they were married, Kellie had been the nurse as well. On Sunday afternoons they would ready the surgery for the week, Slaven making professional preparations while she tidied the waiting room, sterilised the instruments and cleaned the single window overlooking the Sooper Doop Market. No premonition in such days of the new millennium that a great mission and the Hoihos's *Half Moon Bay* were on the way.

So they comfort each other in this meeting. A constancy of affection, a willing assumption of obligation, may be in their own way as valuable as passion. Kellie is determined to have him free and tells him so. She thinks for his welfare it must be soon, but doesn't tell him so. The rest for orisons.

Some time together then we have allowed them, but no more, or else we will confuse our point of view.

No one comes with the thumbscrews to the small individual rooms in the Beckley-Waite Institute. There's no bare-bulbed basement with a chair clamped to the floor. Slaven hears no drumming of frenetic feet on the ECT table, sees no bruising on his fellow inmates, no root canals are arbitrarily drilled to encourage right-thinking views — how could he miss the signs of that. It's not a sense of focused malevolence, or sinister agendas, that marks the masters of the place, but instead, pretence, and the burrowing, assiduous self-aggrandisement tempered with defensive duck-shoving which is the inevitable atmosphere of bureaucracy. It circulates invisibly within the air-conditioning more surely than Legionaires' disease.

The great fear of those who are official admissions is that they might be forgotten: NOT sent for, rather than the reverse, abandoned in the hard disc computer memory, missed from the counselling roster, or limited visiting list through weary inefficiency, randomly doomed because they happen to be among the case-load of Dr Burlapp who spends much of his working day ecstatically shafting young Penny Ambrose while the going is good.

This brave new world is not a victory for the positive forces of either Lucifer, or Gabriel, but a stalemate of malaise and triviality. What undermines the character of those within the Institute isn't a fear that they might be broken in renunciation of fierce allegiances, but an awareness that no one cares, that they are a part of no one's vital life. Slaven decides that he could be vacuumed out of society and kept in a bag somewhere, a victim of nothing more than house-keeping on a national scale. Do people ask about him? Do the thousands who had wept and applauded at Tuamarina, St Kilda and Western Springs look up from their counters, crops and desks to demand information and explanation of his whereabouts?

Two days following Slaven's first conversation with the Caretaker, he has another session with Dr Collett. There is no connection between the two events, is there? Wednesday, hopefully at eleven, Collett had said. Slaven has some status in the dayrooms because of it, as do all who have contact with professional staff today. 'I have my appointment with Dr Collett at eleven,' says Slaven to Philip Mathieson and Neville Kingi. He can't help it, yet despises himself for the comment and the tone just as he despises others for much the same on other days. 'It's quite a thing, isn't it, to get medical confusion on these matters sorted out.'

Slaven, who thought little of keeping people waiting in his own practice, is kept waiting by Collett. He idles in the cream dayroom, does some exercises in the corridor, has a sudden burst of tears in his own room, before the intercom requests him to come to Dr Collett's office. Of course Collett is apologetic about the delay, tells Slaven that he knows how these things work, how difficult it is to have rigid time-frames when you are in a people-intensive profession. 'I understand,' says Slaven. His eyes still strangely brim with tears and he wonders what Kellie is doing. He thinks of Sarah, Thackeray and Miles.

'Now,' says Collett, 'I'll just have a flick through your file and the matters we discussed last time.' He should have done it before Slaven came in of course. 'It's been a hell of a day actually,' says Collett, 'and it's only morning,' and then ah-huh, yes, yes, ah-huh, that's right, ah-huh at intervals as he reads and he runs his thumb carefully under the edge of his tie, up and down without looking, as if testing the blade of a knife. Aldous Slaven, who has recently discussed the direction of national policy with the Prime Minister and who has become a face almost as familiar in the media as Amand Beardsley, has to sit and wait as his file is skimmed. Each time it's the same though, isn't it. He has high hopes of the interview, yet feels only mild humiliation and rather greater anger. Collett, this inefficient guts-ache, who patronises him, a man who won an open scholarship and the option to do medicine himself. Collett removes his hand from his tie and takes his own nose between thumb and forefinger instead. He alternates the pressure quickly from one nostril to the other, as if attempting to make bird noises. 'How have things been with you in the meantime, in yourself that is,' he says after considerable thought and acoustic experiment.

In the meantime? How has he been. in the meantime, when he cannot sleep for the sound of the swell sucking through the mussels of the Lyttelton wharves, the scent of Cardew's carnal breath, the feel of the wire as he hangs there, the flavour of the Beckley-Waite medication at the back of his mouth coming through the mint camouflage, a vision of himself returning from his great, new enterprise with the black sails hoisted. 'I'm still wondering why I'm here,' he says.

'Aren't we all. Wondering about ourselves, I mean. Do you know I'm supposed to ensure the well-being of over a hundred of the patients here. We've faced a deteriorating medical staff-patient ratio for years and now reduced provision for sabbaticals and course-leave. I should be in Vancouver now — Comparative changes in the etiology of bipolar illness and I was invited to give a plenary session paper.'

'When can I leave? When can I go home and get on with my life? I have a wife and a political organisation which depends on me. I even have a profession of my own, you know.'

'You never did a Wellington rally, did you. It's a pity that. To have pulled out all the stops here, in the capital, would've been a most interesting thing. Wellington people are more canny of political issues than Aucklanders. It would have been an interesting thing.'

'I can't find out in the Beckley-Waite, can I.'

'Quite. The thing is, Aldous, that while there's no doubt of the underlying stability and coherence of your mental state, there is concern about the temporary, cumulative effect of the accident, the unfortunate attack, the enormous demands on your emotional resources in the public work that you're not accustomed to. I'm amazed in fact that more extravagant symptoms haven't been manifest.'

'What has been manifest?' Slaven thinks of Collett's suppositions concerning a rally in the capital and imagines a great outdoor meeting on the expanse of the waterfront, or Telecom Park. The stiff wind from the harbour raising the hair of thousands of people and causing a whining feedback in the sound system. Collett and his fellows in a rather self-conscious group, come to see crowd dynamics at first hand. Slaven is cut off now, however, from an audience to command and sits before the desk of Collett's authority.

There is a place, looking over the Clyde Quay Boat Harbour to the city and the curve of mostly concrete wharf to it. The foreground has the bobbing, monied dreams called Wavelength, or Broker's Rest, the shore is lined with lock-ups in Liverpudlian uniformity, each shaped like a Victorian bathing shed drawn down to the sea. The harbour is no millpond — ever — and the wind snatches each word from your mouth and flutters it away. Joggers trot from Oriental

Bay past the few black and rust ships and overtake the business people also on the shortcut there. Where the old Odlin Timber and Hardware Building used to be, spirals the Naismith Computer Complex. Central is the Gotham City face of the BNZ Building with its aging cohorts stepping down to the harbour. There are a few gaps where the bewildered ground sees the sky at last, but only temporarily and only through the cross-hatch of the counter-balanced, derek cranes which are the city's crucifixes. A steep hill to the skyline, with the remaining bush there under sentence and the buildings scaling with ever-increasing confidence.

'**W**e've been over this ground before,' says Collett.

'What is it that keeps me here when I want to leave?'

'Do you want to see the videos again?' Some mild degree of impatience is caught in Collett's voice. He too experiences a sense of capture despite his training. A keen department head not much his senior blocks promotion, the golf club's championship will never be his, he has begun to suspect that beneath the jargon of his profession will be found an equivocality and growing inconsequence. It's not yet lunchtime, but already Collett is thinking of the end of the day.

He and Slaven look at the video again. The interview room at admission with Slaven and Dr Eugene. The odd angles that the video seems to catch, like those of a chimpanzees' tea party. Slaven's face still stained with fading bruises. He is standing on a chair and rotating slowly as his own genie. 'Do you know why you're here, Dr Slaven?' Eugene is saying in the warped, off-stage, sort of voice such videos produce and Slaven's voice comes back.

'I am here to raise the dead.'

'I'm showing you this again as objective evidence for our concern,' says Collett. 'It's part of your condition you see that ideas of conspiracy, or persecution on a minor scale, are quite likely to occur. A more structured and inter-active routine of the sort I've suggested has a value.'

'I'm zonked out in the video of course.' If less conscious of why he is with Collett, the on-going assessment, Slaven might argue that the man they watch on the screen isn't him. Why should he admit to the yellow face and the King Chimpanzee crouch upon the chair, or a voice that stumbles in delivery. His own hands though, indisputably so in their damage and awkward carriage.

'Come on now,' says Collett. 'Your own family made the request. You're an important man these days. Bringing you to the Institute wasn't decided lightly.'

Slaven asks if he can have copies of his assessments so that he can send them to Garrity via Marianne Dunne and have an independent opinion. It is of course not possible in quite that way. Slaven is amazed at his powerlessness, his inability to be a greater threat to Collett, who has a quick glance at his watch and then a surreptitious one at the file of the patient he is to see after Slaven. How easily is Samson shorn. Collett offers however to pass on an appropriate report if Slaven gives him a name. He bears no particular grudge towards the CCP leader, but he is concerned with keeping to time, with the work he's doing — could be doing — on bipolar etiology, with the solid kauri beam that he purchased during the demolition of the Lower Hutt Catholic Church and which he intends to fashion into a mantlepiece for his holiday home in the Rimutakas. Forest hideways are now just the thing. He needs some positive way to finish his interview with Slaven. 'Over some evenings I've been giving your case particular thought,' he lies. 'It came to me that you might find it worthwhile to assist our own dentist, Dr Ovens, in his surgery.' Brilliant, Collett hadn't realised that he is still capable of such quick thinking. 'I've been very aware of your complaints concerning boredom, but I wanted to sound you out before approaching Dr Ovens.' Collett decides that he will sand it back himself with assiduous care and then bring up the grain with a little linseed oil, the way it had been done in the nineteenth century.

'Oh, easy,' says Slaven and holds up his hands.

'There's more than using the laser,' says Collett, 'however, it's something for the future, perhaps.' His face is oddly tight from the suppression of a yawn. 'Is there anything else, to finish with?'

'Why can't I have visitors. More access to the outside?'

'It's part of the depth therapy that's been drawn up for you. You'd have to see the Director for any complaint about that.'

Slaven makes his request, but well before he is informed of any outcome, he has more conversation with the Caretaker. 'A corker of a night,' says the Caretaker. Wellington has been known to have such a night. No wind at all to set the stars swinging and the scent of the Caretaker's pipe rises undisturbed and so more pungently than usual. Slaven has his face to the window grill as if at confession and watches the car lights turning beyond the darkened courtyard. They are talking of places far away from the Beckley-Waite. Slaven recalls fishing in the southern shingle rivers. The Caretaker describes his boyhood at Ruby Bay and Mahakipawa.

'It said in the paper you had a breakdown because of emotional fatigue.'

'I'm here to leave the field clear for others,' says Slaven. 'Nicely parked until after the elections, I suspect.'

'Your wife and others are kicking up a fuss.'

Yes, how easy to imagine Kellie, so resolute in facing the threat of things gone wrong. As she uses stakes to train the branches of a weeping cherry, she makes plans to counter the massive working of political enmity. It is her habit to wear no socks with her gardening shoes and so her hard, thin legs end in thinner ankles with the bolt of bone which secures them there set to whiten the skin. She will be mobilising the massive verbosity of Thackeray Thomas and the influence still traceable to Miles Kitson. Kellie never knows when she is beaten and perhaps you can't be beaten, until you admit to it.

There is still not a sign of wind, Slaven can hear only the subdued hum of the air-conditioning at a distance and the Caretaker spitting onto the cobblestones beneath. Slaven has a long breath which carries the aroma of the Caretaker's tobacco, part direct from the pipe and part from the very lungs of the Caretaker: moist, mottled with the blood flow and swelling or sinking with a rhythm less dramatic than the heartbeat, but equally decisive.

'Are you true?' asks the Caretaker.

'True?'

'True. You mean what you say, but will you remember to be true to your views when the chance to do something comes. Seeing what's wrong doesn't take much brain, it seems to me. To know what needs to be done to fix it is a talent of sorts, but the big one is having the guts to carry it out when you have the chance.'

'You make it sound like a Western,' says Slaven.

'It's a shoot-out all right. No bullshit about it.'

'Except that when you're in the situation it's never as clear-cut as the onlookers assume it to be. There's obligations, compromises, half-truths and all.'

'I reckon that once someone is comfortable with power that's when it's most likely to be abused,' says the Caretaker, 'but what do I know.' He is quiet for a while and Slaven also looks into the night, says nothing. It is however, a companionable silence and now the Caretaker continues. 'My great grandfather came back to Mahakipawa and built another weatherboard house there. He hunted Captain Cookers again despite leaving an arm at Monte Cassino, and told my father stories of the Italian women.'

'I need some help,' says Slaven. 'Someone who will take messages to my wife and friends. An inside man.'

'Yes,' says the Caretaker. Slaven hears him spit, tap his pipe on the wall which separates them. 'See you,' says the Caretaker quietly.

When he knows he is alone again, Slaven leaves the window and lies on his bed. He is so still that he can feel the slight vibration that is through all the Beckley-Waite and comes from the air-conditioning. He wonders about the unfamiliarity which is all about him and if he will survive it. Slaven has always considered himself an equable and self-sufficient person, but he hungers for the reassurance of customary, individual things. Here he is bereft of authority and achievement, of a past almost. He desires the evening light filtered through Kellie's garden, the chimes of their wedding clock, the Van Gogh swirls in the walnut of his desk top, the shower with sides of amber glass far enough away so that he can raise his elbows. Where are the sycamore leaves and their winged seeds? Where are the comfortable friends who needn't be impressed? Why do his most sincere principles seem suspect, trivial, in this place? The Beckley-Waite is a menagerie in which the inmates have been gathered from their habitats and those that maintain an identity hold fast to small, padding repetitions of the mind, or body. Kellie has sent him a photo and he has it by the bed. It includes even the son who has betrayed him. Slaven wakes sometimes with the elusive fragrance of warm grease and dung from his hobby sheep in the Canterbury sun, and sometimes to the receding protest songs of his great rallies— *Welfare Heaven, After Tiananmen Square, Glasnost Galaxy*, or the Hoihos with *Half Moon Bay. The Foveaux storms are fading, baby, within the calm of Half Moon Bay.*

Amongst all that is despairingly new, Slaven seeks only the pipe and company of the Caretaker. The man from Mahakipawa with a great grandfather who went to Monte Cassino with the Maori Battalion and invested an arm there.

See the Caretaker clean the grease trap in the kitchen of the east block. It has been negotiated that the women won't have to do it. The Caretaker has negotiated this, because he does not feel demeaned by it and also if it's not done well then in due time the more troublesome job as a result of the negligence, will be his. See him withdraw the heavy tray with a bale hook. In the centre is a space kept free of fat by the detergent and constant warm water — just some beef strings there, peas, chewed gristle, plastic top liners like coins, twist ties in blue and red. The rest is a polar bear's armpit of ridged white and yellow grease which folds in a visible menu for the past two months, as the more enduring amber folds in the prehistoric fly.

See the Caretaker — at the instant in which the model dips her bosom to the camera and the talk back host — thrust his arm strong despite his great grandfather in to the gap of the boiler flue and see the bars of soot like rasp files fall so much blacker than his hand.

'Lovely,' he says and coughs.

See the Caretaker put the mower up while it's still warm so that the oil flows easily from the drain hole and as he waits he cleans the spark clip to make a better contact. The very moment can't you guess that the driver loses Slaven's gold watch in a poker game and Dr Burlapp at Shangri La Motels shafts young Penny Ambrose while the going's good. Yes, the very moment as you've realised that Ayesbury decides to accept promotion in his field to Wellington where the disasters he plans for are more likely to occur, the moment as the goose girl sleeps in a warm afternoon and the reflections of the passing water move on the pale arch of her neck.

See the Caretaker use the carpenter's square as nimbly as a salesman does his biro and the saw bite the particle board evenly for the sides of a doll's house for the Director's daughter. From redundant stock you understand. Before the dust has lightly met the floor, Miles feels a chemical boost which permits him to escape the dreary gravity of his body and gather his wits in a free orbit. All he asks of life, or death, now is that his mind be not entirely party to the decay of flesh. There is a place at the crest of Dansey's Pass — ah, Jesus, so there is — perhaps you know it, for the wind comes up the hillside as a long Pacific swell and the tall snow tussock flails beneath. There's not a tree. Not one tree as far as you can see, just the snow tussock plumed before the wind and a catch in all your breathing as you watch.

See the Caretaker fit the speakers for the dignitary's address in the corner of the large Waitangi Lounge. He lays the cable to the skirting board and attaches it in places with squashtac so that it can't be caught up in people's feet. The drapes of therapeutic yellow shiver at the windows as the Caretaker checks the mike. 'Lovely,' he says and it echoes from the panels of the empty room. In the time it takes to die away the entreaty man has his diagnosis confirmed and Natalie Lyons in the suburb of Johnsonville determines she is born to be a poet.

Miles decides that he's useless now, had it. He has blamed age and illness, but they haven't stopped others from worthwhile involvement. Perhaps the thing is that he's become a believer in futility, and loss of resolve is the first step to death itself. He finds it difficult to feel passion for this rather than that, for this woman rather than that man being elected to some post or other. Everything that doesn't immediately concern himself has become the same size, assumed a neutral aspect. I'm journeying back into myself, he thinks, and have become more avid for a slice of gruyere cheese with lunch than the salvation of humankind.

See the Caretaker setting the poison trail for the rats which don't officially exist and stacking three hundred toilet rolls in a cupboard which smells of marmalade and horse sweat. See him adroit on the fork-lift tractor as he trundles the pig food drums to the ramp. The slops have a merry oscillation, the drums groan as they touch, at the very moment that Slaven sighs at the pock marked ceiling and Mrs Wick's canary takes its life in its wings once too often and flies in the face of a Mack. 'That'll do,' says the Caretaker, almost loud enough to be heard by the bald-headed man with tramping boots who is warming down with the aid of exercises on the wrought iron fence.

Slaven is allowed one outside, sightless call each week. It is the judicious decision of his doctors that more will jeopardise his cure. Slaven looks forward to each enormously and at the same time is upset by it, as a new school boarder is tremulous when ringing home — the real horrors only hinted at. The reaction confirms for him the pressure he is under; the bobbing of his psyche at the mooring of his control. But he says nothing of that to Kellie, having no doubt that the calls are overheard and could be used as snares against him, and there are factors which make indignant challenge of his kidnap more difficult. Imagine the media with his admitted oddities and the part of his own son in the committal. A certain amount of subtlety would be needed against the forces which were utilising the Beckley-Waite.

'... and Miles has made all his resources available to us. He's a very powerful man. All the others too, there's a great deal going on.'

'If I'm not out before the elections then they've got us beaten.'

'I've had a meeting with Dr Meelind and he's trying to

get a time for me to see the Prime Minister. And Thackeray and I... . Can we talk freely do you think?' asks Kellie.

'No.'

'Rest assured then,' she says. Slaven bends forward to accommodate the laughter which comes and goes abruptly and with no reason for its passage other than the mild oddity of what Kellie says. He is in the middle cubicle of three, all painted a therapeutic powder blue and with a glass ledge on which to rest an elbow and a digital display for the directory and a slot for his permission card. No graffiti on the sky like walls, well just one word, evenly written and of a modest size at eye level — Charon. But rest assured then, rest assured.

Without consultation it's accepted that the Caretaker always begins. Even on the nights when Slaven is drawn to the window by the fragrance of pipe tobacco and its additives, he says nothing till he's addressed and there are times when the wind bears the smoke away before it can rise to him and he might be alerted by a short, steady whistle, or 'Are you there, mate?' and he goes over for a chat, never seeing the Caretaker, but speaking into the dark, or the moonlight, smiling at times to a strip of night sky. It seems to Slaven that the Caretaker is at pains not to pass his window in daylight, but at the same time he recognises such interpretation as an inmate's delusion.

The Caretaker likes to tell Slaven what things are reported in the newspapers and cable programmes, and personal information from Mahakipawa. His people had free-range leghorns and donkeys for years as a main earner, but then went into partnership with a Dalmatian family and planted a good many hectares in Sauvignon Blanc. All the soil and climate research promised success, as did the first vintages, even if there was the slightly wild-card effect of years of free-range chooks and donkeys bred for side-shows, treks and carrying children over the sands of Nelson and the Marlborough Sounds. Slaven and the Caretaker also discuss their views of life. Not literally face to face, they feel less embarrassment about their apple-barrel philosophies. After many hours of largely solitary thought, the Caretaker has reached existentialism independent of the literature and years after the rest of the world has moved on.

Slaven tells the Caretaker that he hopes his coming interview with the Director will result in his release from the Beckley-Waite. He has spent several days in putting down on paper his reasons for immediate discharge, concentrating in a constructive way, he thinks, on his present health rather than claims of wrongful diagnosis and committal in the past. Such claims can only reflect adversely on the Director and make unbiased judgment less likely. 'Better you than me,' the Caretaker says. 'This place is like a crayfish pot.' The quadrangle is quite dark tonight and the wind which dissipates the Caretaker's smoke before Slaven can enjoy it, also makes litter scamper back and forth on the cobbles. The lights still turn at the end of his narrow vision.

'I wonder how long some people stay in this place,' says Slaven.

'Some get carried out,' says the Caretaker and he goes quietly away.

A Thursday afternoon is the time chosen for Slaven's interview. At 2:10 Dr Collett comes to accompany him to the Director's office and he enters with him so that he can be available for comment about Slaven's current treatment and prognosis if the Director requires it. 'I think in theory too,' says Collett, 'that it's a good thing to have a third person present as a sort of earth wire, to use that analogy. Know what I mean?'

'Not really,' says Slaven.

'I'm not saying neutral in a strict sense, but someone within the Institute who knows you, has an investment in your case. Your goal and mine are the same — to have you fully recovered as soon as possible.' Collett checks his zipper quickly at the Director's door, his back to Lisa at her desk and he runs a finger down his linen tie to ensure it's neatly tucked beneath the lapels of his suit.

The Director is much concerned with appearances. He sees the outer man as pretty much a deliberate replica of the inner one — no fat man can have his department guidelines in trim, the morality of a woman with scuffed shoes must always be open to question. Had the Director lived a hundred years before, he would have made an excellent battalion 21C. There is a confidence and zest for life in those who live it by the book.

'Come,' says the Director and he sits straight backed at his desk to smile at Slaven and Collett. The Director shaves twice a day and is fresh from the second this Thursday, the lower half of his large face as smooth as the hull of a racing yacht. 'Dr Slaven,' he says, indicating one seat with his left hand and, 'Michael,' he says, indicating another with his right hand. He takes in the complete arc of his office, checking that nothing is out of place, nothing more prominent in the scheme of things than it is entitled to be. For himself, having granted the interview he is quite content for it to go no further, for Slaven and Collett to occupy the requisite chairs and he able to remain with a triggered smile of condescension behind his desk. The surface has a sensual sheen and he moves his finger tips so slightly upon it. He could play a tape of murmured pleasantries perhaps and one wall could be replaced with sound proof glass so that the visitors could file past and see the tableau — Director of the Beckley-Waite Institute in interview.

The Director's office has a view of fountain and ornamental pond and the judder bars on the drive so that everyone will have time to enjoy such scenery. A northwesterly aspect so that the Director has the sun which draws flies to the window drapes, but there's not one with its toes turned up there — Lisa knows better than that. She has even lined the bottom of his waste paper basket with a napkin so that all rubbish can be dismissed without trace. No noises penetrate the Institute sorrowing its way through the calm of another day, but then such noises are intense rather than obtrusive.

'I understand that the environment and treatment must seem very subdued, very quiet, after the tempo of your activities in the public sphere, Dr Slaven. Even as a spectator via the media I was often astounded at the demands that your role, your aspirations and your supporters imposed.

To speak with passion for such length, hours and hours — my goodness.'

'Thank you. I'm very eager to know when I can resume that work, or at least my life outside.'

'Of course,' says the Director. Thumpety, goes a metallic green car on the judder bars. 'Michael, would you run over things as you see them as supervisor. A basis for discussion. Be quite frank. We're all professional people here after all.' Collett has expected the request, in fact he and the Director have already determined the course of the interview, but he is disconcerted as he crosses his legs to begin, by the smear of dog shit that he has left on the Director's green and gold carpet. Maybe the considerable expanse of the Director's desk prevents a sight of it from the window side. Thumpety.

'Complete rest has been a wonderful restorer of course,' he says. 'A drastic reduction in emotional stimuli and responsibility was a key part of the treatment in this case and I must say that the indicators all point to the correctness of that course which Dr Eugene and myself agreed upon. I know Aldous has found it very difficult to come to terms with the restriction on contact with family and colleagues. It seems tough, I know, very tough, but a half-hearted approach would negate the treatment regime. As it is, medication has been reduced and recent evaluations have been in the main positive. Very much so, I'd say.' The Director smiles; he hasn't noticed the shit on his carpet. Thumpety, thumpety. He is pleased that Collett hasn't become too technical, for he's forgotten most of his training — too imprecise, subjective — and made his name in administration where he can go by the book. Some sections of it indeed he has written.

'So when can I be discharged?' asks Slaven. He has a premonition that the Director's preoccupation with form, with symmetry, with accountability, is more of a threat than Collett's selfish disillusion and malaise. A man who believes in himself is the greater adversary.

'Oh, a little in the future yet,' says the Director. 'In fact, too soon and our progress will be jeopardised.'

'So what is it that makes me such a threat to myself, or others.'

'Oh, not others, certainly,' says the Director. He admires the afternoon sun on the polished flanks of his liquor cabinet which is never opened in office hours, but which holds some pretty good stuff and without admitting it to himself, he enjoys having this Slaven who is such a talking point, such a crass celebrity, now under his jurisdiction. 'Despite the very real progress,' he says, 'we don't consider all is entirely right as yet.' Thumpety.

'Socialisation for example,' says Collett. 'Staff agree that there's a marked disinclination on your part to form meaningful contacts with the people around you; people you're living with.'

'I don't want to live with them. I want my own life back.' He could tell them about the Caretaker, their night talks mind to mind, if not face to face. The trust and gradual ease between them, because neither expects anything of the other except confidentiality.

'Write down as many people as you can. Those in your wing I mean and something about them. Their occupations outside, or interests that are dear to them.' The Director slides paper across the smooth surface of his desk and as he does so keeps a biro steady on it with his finger. 'You see we want you to be objective about your own state of mind,' he says.

Well, there's Philip Mathieson and Neville Kingi, isn't there. Neville has the habit of lifting his eyebrows up and down if he is left with no one to talk to and Philip has a dark, slightly raised lump on his lower lip, like a blood blister that has never healed. Slaven knows nothing about them. Apart from that what is there? He makes no move to use the biro and paper. Collett, who is covering the carpet stain with his foot, catches the Director's glance of approbation that the device has succeeded so well.

'So when I've become firm buddies with all around me, I can expect to be allowed to leave and forget them?'

'We're trying to illustrate a point of some significance in emotional rehabilitation,' says the Director.

'I asked Dr Collett for my case notes so that I could have them looked over by a doctor of my choice outside the Institute. He said I should ask you.'

'You know we can't release case notes to the person they concern, but give us the doctor's name and I see no reason why we can't be in touch. This is a hospital and your best interests are our motivation.' Thumpety, thumpety. 'On the positive side, the staff and I are very hopeful that if your present progress continues then you should be able to cope without institutional care in weeks rather than months.'

'Yes,' says Collett. 'Weeks rather than months I'd say, definitely.' The Director catches again the whiff of recent dogshit from Collett's shoe and his eyes roam the manicured interior of his office seeking an explanation, then rest with questioning impartiality on staff member and patient. He is reminded of the nasty business of Dr Burlapp's resignation which is yet to be dealt with.

'Say about the time of the elections,' says Slaven.

'I don't follow,' says the Director. All by the book after all, exactly. His blunt finger nails are slightly milky, but scrupulously clean and the hands that bear them lie relaxed on the blank paper provided for the personal details of Slaven's fellow patients. Like Ransumeen for example who is being suffocated by understandable enemies with a cellophane industrial wax cover in the alcove beneath the stairs for cheating at Ludo. Thumpety. What is that smell, thinks the Director.

'I mean that if all goes well I should get out about the time the elections are over. An odd coincidence perhaps.'

You may be interested that the dog is a Labrador cross, with a liking for carrion. The smell of shit grows more pervasive in the Director's office despite the pressure of Collett's foot on the rich green and gold carpet. Thumpety.

As Slaven says to the Caretaker at night, amidst a gentle, soughing, dark wind, the interview was effectively over then, despite the continuation of a conversation without communication, of nodding heads, of stylised goodwill, of cars at the judder bars, of afternoon sun across the lily pads of banana black and yellow, of the impeccable inside of the Director's office whiffed with dogshit — and all done precisely according to the book.

'Surprise me,' says the Caretaker with a chuckle. 'Some

bigwig's bloody got it in for you. There's no doubt of that. Everyone must take orders from further up the line, or else the whole system breaks down I guess. Anyway, your friends have been kicking up a stink. Not just your wife and the CCP, but the medico from Christchurch.'

'Dr Dunne.'

'And Miles Kitson himself. You know I could have sworn that money bags was dead. There's been marches and so on, but not enough to cause the Director's masters to lose their nerve. It doesn't help when some in the CCP come out and say that the message must be larger than the man.' It's a belief which Slaven himself holds, but he's beginning to see it as a matter of degree. So Kellie and his colleagues are still working on his behalf, yet he imagines Miles using his considerable power while always reserving at the very centre of his support an utterly sardonic observation of all parties and views involved. 'You still there?' says the Caretaker.

'Yes.'

'I'll tell you what. You said that Dr Collett was keen for you to help out Ovens, the dentist here. Something for you to do.'

'Yes.'

'Say you'll do it then. Say you'll do it and let me work on the possibilities it offers to get you out of here. There's a lot in common you know, between your friends and mine. Just let me work on it with no promises made. There's one thing you see, I know my territory. Okay, I've no great say around here, but local knowledge has its uses too.'

Slaven's face is pressed against the window grill so that he can hear the Caretaker's unhurried voice through the night breeze which bears away any smoke he may be creating. For the first time in many days, Slaven enjoys a feeling that people are active on his behalf, as if he can hear slight tappings and scratchings at the walls of the Beckley-Waite.

Ovens has a modern surgery and an old-fashioned approach to dentistry. Both can be witnessed on the second floor of the Stewart Wing. Ovens has a magnificent, compact laser breach cauterising unit donated by the Friends Of The

Beckley-Waite, informally referred to by the staff as the cuckoo club, yet still persists with amalgams, polymers, and with capping instead of enamel reconstructive techniques. In appearance as opposed to professional practice he is impressively progressive; plaited fair hair, chin tucks and chrome expanders to hold his sleeves from his wrists. 'Do you know,' he tells Slaven on the first visit, 'I provide the only therapy of fear that the poor buggers here experience. In all this desert of bland, distanced and professional reassurance I give them something to worry about. A cogent threat without which there's no mental resilience, no contrast to plant their feet against and strain. My small theatre of cruelty is responsible for more cures here than all the drugs and fatuous blah that goes on. The buggers love it, Aldous my old son. In their heart of hearts they love it.'

Slaven can hear them expressing their love as he assists by the couch. Their eyes roll back in ecstasy, the tendons of their necks are ridged with pleasure and their hands quiver and clench in an abandonment of joy. Ovens denies himself painkillers for his patients' sake. It's an opportunity for them to grapple with life on more equal terms again. 'The buggers love it, Aldous my old son,' he says, 'but don't expect any gratitude from them. At Beckley-Waite they're taught to cunningly disguise their affection.' After observation, Slaven considers that they have learnt their lesson well.

Slaven goes to help two afternoons a week, usually Tuesdays and Fridays and Ovens is pleased to have him. Slaven is adept at stock-taking, preparation of amalgams and polymers, although his hands prevent him from surgery itself. Ovens comes to value his superior diagnostic opinions, particularly when they coincide with his own penchant for extraction. 'There is a salutary rigour in the loss of part of one's self, even a tooth, a portion of gum, blood,' he says. 'The buggers come to see that a prerequisite for mental health is to be reconciled to inevitable and progressive physical loss. I've cured heaps of them here exactly that way.'

For the first few times, Slaven is accompanied to the second floor dental surgery by a nurse, but then he's allowed to go by himself. It's still within the basic security perimeter.

The Caretaker has begun schooling Slaven as to the various rooms he passes on his way and now he knows each by its relationship to others and the corners of the corridors he turns. Most of the rooms have no names, though one is labled Emergency ALW, which the Caretaker says can be used to gain access to the lift well. 'Two along on the same side. That's the one for you, see,' says the Caretaker from the darkness below Slaven's window. 'Be absolutely sure you know it, for that's the one for you when we're ready.'

'When will that be?'

'Very soon now. Don't go fiddling with any of the doors as you pass in the meantime though. Some of them have alarm locks you see. You just make sure that you know which one's for you when the time comes.'

Slaven has doubts of course. He's never been able to see the Caretaker's face, his eyes, when he's talking and so deceit is the more possible. Maybe he's being set up to do something outrageously stupid and so provide the Director with reason enough to keep him longer in the Beckley-Waite, or discredit him with the media. Maybe it's the women's sick-bay behind the door two along from the emergency ALW and he could be captured there as a sex fiend, or is it a drug store with video surveillance? All he has against such apprehensions is his faith in the character of the man from Mahakipawa. Yet that is strongly felt and Slaven knows that the more suspect life becomes, the greater is the part played by faith.

'I talked with some of your friends and my friends in the weekend at Mahakipawa. Someone reckoned it was good on me for being pro-active.' The Caretaker's quiet laugh comes up from the courtyard and then the puh-puh sound as he draws strongly on his pipe which is almost out. Slaven closes his eyes as after just a little delay the fragrance rises up to him, a harsh, lovely nosegay of old defiant ways. 'Ah, well,' says the Caretaker. 'This isn't getting anything done, aye.'

'If I do get out,' says Slaven, 'I'll pay you back in some way.'

'I'm pretty right here. This is the best job I've had. Don't you go drawing attention to me in any way when you're out. You can see that? If we get you through that door and away, then I'll come and hear you speak when no one dares stop you. More important is that some good things happen for us, like you've said at Tuamarina and in your articles. This place here is full of talkers isn't it, but none of them know what to do for the benefit of anyone but themselves. You can do more than that. That's right, isn't it?'

'Right,' says Slaven. Moonlight of mushroom on the tiles of the yard, the building with edges as sharp as playing cards, cars at the end of his narrow view with their lights twisting at the corner and then gone. That's it, isn't it. Justifying any risk, any expenditure of talent, friendship or effort, by a proclaimed future and knowing from the large history and also the lower case record of your own life that fine expectation spins to coarse reality.

So is it night again within the Beckley-Waite Institute. The air conditioning hisses in its work. The dry air is forced to every corner so that a controlled climate is achieved which will preserve them all until the morning, or the millenium perhaps. Each night is a small advance in the process of mummification. Slaven wakes at three and lies with a wet flannel over his face, or pouts for fresh air at the slit the window allows. He has a sense of levitation and he turns as he drifts so that the walls go panning past. Has he ever been more than he is now, cut adrift from family and society, from the complacency of professional status, from more recent fame as an orator. What is there to substantiate his opinion of himself, even his account of existence? On some nights as he sucks life through a flannel, drifts on a level with the door top and mourns because the Caretaker has not called to him from the yard, he's assailed by the idea that the Institute is all that is real. That the Beckley-Waite is an asteroid which whirls in a phantasmagoria of black chaos with the symmetrical, close windows on floor after floor like the myriad facets of a gadfly's eye.

'A measure of conceit.'

'Check.'

'A counterweight of self-abuse.'

'Check.'

'The certainty of having received compassion, if not deserved it.'

'Check.'

'The determination to sell one's soul dearly.'

'Check.'

There are footsteps in the corridors, aren't there? Not of axe murderers, or limping droolers, but people like you and you who have lost the confidence to decide what is right, what is rite and what is written. Footsteps which hesitate for a security they don't receive, so move on and hesitate again. Slaven gets up and takes his flannel to the door, opens the door and looks into the passage, but there's no one there, or at most a heel-down slipper disappearing at the corner, a slack pyjama arse, the last, forlorn backward twist of a creased head with the dry hair of a dog tufted on it.

The Beckley-Waite has no need of any more extravagant enforcement than confinement itself and patent, impartial mistrust of the sanity of its inmates. The most bitter mockeries are those of malaise, misunderstanding and mundane neglect. A touch of egg yolk within the tines of Slaven's lunch time fork is a golden snarl of death and the supervisor's perfunctory chat, in a voice just louder than that he uses with his peers, hollows the soul until the place is merely an ache of one's inconsequence. When Philip Mathieson is selected to be the buddy for two new arrivals, Slaven can't repress tears of rage and self-pity at such injustice.

There is mould along the bottom rim of the aluminium window frames and a video eye follows the night visits that he must take for a piss. Dr Collett asks him how he enjoys his time with Ovens in the surgery, laughs appreciatively at the reply and glances at his watch. Dr Burlapp's resignation has added to the case-load of them all. Not one patient mentions Slaven's fame on the outside and a boy like a stick insect approaches him in the day room to accuse him of farting to excess, demands that he keep to his own room and quit farting in the common space.

Stimulating reading is kept from him. All he has are magazines with brief articles on actors who have put on weight, or lost it, and popular auguries which Sarah would enjoy. How to interpret the character of your loved one by the way he does his hair, cuts his toenails, or the manner of his walking in the snow.

Ovens is right perhaps: the only way to salvage a sense of self is the sharp pain of extraction and the taste of your own blood.

The Caretaker's voice is no different on the night he fore-warns Slaven of escape. 'Are you sill going up at the same time?'

'Tomorrow, yes.'

'Do everything just as usual, except that this time you go into the room two along from the Emergency ALW, on the same side, just as I've told you. And if someone goes with you then walk on up to the surgery and forget about it.'

'What if the door won't open?'

'Then forget about it.' There is the strike and flare of the Caretaker's match below. The darkened courtyard strip, the deeper shadow that he knows is the terracotta pot, the narrow view through the archway — they are different even as the Caretaker speaks, losing a unity of opposition and becoming just a collection of things within a set night-time view. 'Aldous.' Slaven has no name to use in reply. 'Aldous? Now remember, mate, don't try to take anything with you. You just go up to Ovens as usual except that you duck into that door. That's the one for you. Leave the rest to us.'

'I'm not going to forget this.'

'I hope not. After all it's the elections soon. Anyway, who knows, some day we may be together at Mahakipawa, take a bottle of Sauvignon Blanc up the hill and look down over the Havelock mudflats. My brother says we should call our wine iwi juice.' The Caretaker's laugh again, low and even and Slaven joins in. 'Okay, now I'd better get some work done, but you remember about tomorrow. You'll be all right. We got it organised.'

'Okay,' says Slaven. 'Thanks.'

It isn't hard to keep to the usual routine. There's no one apart from the Caretaker whom Slaven wishes to farewell. After all, although he has enjoyed late at night the drifting melodies of a clarinet, he has never met Victor Yee as we have, knows nothing of his asthmatic wife, or the passing joys of the rooms above the tattooist. Nothing in his possessions either, that he minds leaving behind, except his Hoihos disc. Slaven allows himself just the petty malice of ignoring the stick insect at lunch, and congratulates Philip Mathieson on how well the new chums are learning to stifle their weeping within their own rooms.

He does feel pressure in the half hour or so before he is due to go to the surgery. He dreads Dr Collett having such a lapse into concern, or efficiency, that he might come to accompany him, or send a nurse. But no one cares, or remembers, of course and Slaven makes his way somewhat self-consciously past the security check, on to the second floor, down the corridors, through the swing fire doors, until he can see the door marked Emergency ALW and his entrance two beyond. That's the one for you, he seems to hear the Caretaker say. No one walks behind, no one advances from the opposite direction. The corridor is as ever quiet and yellow — a therapeutic colour you understand. Slaven grasps the knob. The coolness slips on the sweat of his palm, but it isn't locked. He steps into the room, closes the door behind him, resists the urge to look back and see if he has been observed despite the silence.

It's a narrow room, sunlit unlike the corridor and obviously one of the supply dumps of the Caretaker's domain. The two longer walls have shelves of toilet tissue, cleaning fluids, folded drapes and large chrome teapots. There's an orbital polisher blocking most of the way and on one shelf a line of boxes with word processing identification; out of date titles such as *Word Perfect Corporation* and *MS DOS User's Guide*. Slaven has expected a reception less mundane and less cryptic. Something of a let-down perhaps. He steps over the polisher and stands at the window to see scaffolding not far below and two men and a woman using it to paint the roughcast. The woman is closest to him and she walks easily the grey planks laid on the scaffold pipes, comes and halts in front of Slaven's window so that her head's almost level with the sill. She motions to him to open the window, but waves him back when that's done and hauls herself in with strength and agility.

'Good on you,' she says. 'I heard you speak at Western Springs. Marvellous.' She stretches out a hand and Slaven has his half extended in response when he realises that she's picking up a bag from the shelf beside them. It has grey overalls within, like those she wears and when he's put them on, he climbs down to the plank on the scaffolding. He waits for her to follow. 'No,' she says. 'I'll have a breather here till you've gone in case there's some joker watching who can count. You go quietly down the end ladder and wait by the van for the skipper. And listen, make sure you give the buggers heaps before the elections.'

At the end of each run of worn boards is a small ladder and Slaven climbs down two of these flights until he's on the lawn close to the staff carpark and can see the contractor's van and the other cars in the bright sun of the afternoon. From the second tier of the scaffolding comes the Hoihos' *Bound On The Wheel*, their biggest hit since *Half Moon Bay*. A black Labrador cross with a grizzled nose looks innocently into the blue as its haunches draw up and quiver in the making of a deposit. Yes, the very same, as you have recognised and the tribute lay beneath a lovely, dark rose — Crimson Glory, a hybrid tea, Kellie would tell us.

It is impossible to believe that anything dramatic is taking place; that the Institute is at all sinister, or Slaven's escape from it is seriously opposed. As Slaven looks back at the tall sides, already he's unable to tell which room it was he entered and left.

'Time for a cuppa, I reckon,' says the skipper as he comes up to Slaven at the van. He has the seamed, square face of a prop and he pulls the zip of his overalls down to cool himself. The green singlet beneath is spotted white, pink, yellow and blue from previous jobs and the skin of his hands is dry from many cleanings with turpentine.

'Relax,' says the skipper and he lifts his right hand from the wheel in a lazy salute as they drive past the gate house when the bar has been lifted. Within a few blocks they're in the traffic of downtown Wellington where life hums by in ignorance of the hesitancy and introspection of the Beckley-Waite. 'Whip off the overalls,' says the skipper and as Slaven does so the skipper talks into a hand phone as he drives. 'A mate of yours wants to say goodbye,' he tells Slaven. 'Press the red one to talk back.' It is the Caretaker, telling Slaven that he'd find they knew all about him at the hydrofoil and that the evenings wouldn't be the same without their chats.

'I couldn't be there to see you go. You'll understand it was better for me to be clearly somewhere else at the time. Be careful on the way south. The word will be out soon.'

'In more ways than one, perhaps,' says Slaven.

'Go for it and good luck,' says the Caretaker.

The skipper drops Slaven at the private hydrofoil terminal in Oriental Bay and goes back to work. He's asked no questions, sought no contact apart from that quick, strong handshake at the last and a proffered barley sugar which was dwarfed by the large finger and spatulate thumb which held it.

Les Croad is waiting for Slaven, wearing the same scuffed moccasins and twill trousers. 'So here you are,' he says conspiratorially. 'Turning up like the proverbial.' He leads the way to the craft and the transparent hatch is closed behind them. Almost immediately the engine rises in volume and pitch and the hydrofoil noses out into the harbour. For a time it labours in contact with the full area of water beneath its hull, but then lifts with a sense of release, striking the occasional crest with sharp vibration.

Now at last Slaven feels the emotional reaction to his escape, mundane and all as it has been. He finds it hard to talk to Croad without his voice breaking, so he breathes deeply and looks across the harbour to Ward Island and down to Port Dorset. Croad is no soul mate, but he is an envoy from Slaven's own people, a sign of the active friendship which has reached out even to the Beckley-Waite Institute and countered its disillusion. As he listens to Croad, glances sometimes at his unkept face, Slaven thinks of Marianne Dunne in her hospital beneath the Port Hills, Thackeray Thomas and his stalwart sons, Eula and Sheffield, Miles Kitson putting off death awhile to help a friend. And most of all his own Kellie, who has a sure judgment and a loyalty quite undeterred by the disappointments of which they rarely speak.

Slaven leans on the cushioned backrest. His head nods

as Les Croad gives what he considers a shrewd overview of the past weeks, though the nodding is more in response to the movement of the hydrofoil than any affirmation of what Croad relates. 'We'll be in Picton in an hour,' says Les. 'In two shakes of, in fact.'

Slaven has a dream in which he gives his most emphatic and heartfelt speech to a great gathering at Mahakipawa and as he talks to them he is buoyed up by the audience's complete goodwill and agreement. Who can doubt that a better life and a closer fellowship are possible? And the Caretaker is sitting close to the stage. Slaven feels such pleasure to be able to see the Caretaker's face at last. He knows with the absolute certainty that a dream may have, that it is the Caretaker. The face is brown, calm and quizzical, just as he has always expected it to be. There is a rich smell from the tidal mudflats at the head of the sound and large patches of pig-fern on the hills, not yet dispossessed by the donkeys and vines.

Like a water beetle on the smoother surface of Queen Charlotte Sound the hydrofoil skims towards Picton. The drumming caused by the waves of Cook Strait dies away and Slaven can again hear Les Croad rebuilding life to his scale. They are passing Waikawa, the old batches clustered by the beach and the high rise hotels behind, built by Hong Kong investors at the turn of the century. Les examines Slaven's face with care. 'It's healed up pretty well you know. Any effects still?'

'My teeth aren't so good.'

'You're probably just too fussy there, being a dentist and all. Jeez, was I pissed off afterwards. They used remote electrical interference you know and I should have twigged to something when those two wanted you to ride with them.'

'You weren't to know.'

'All the same, a nod is as good as.' Les watches the small slipways and docks at the left of Picton harbour. He's making the most frank apology he finds possible. 'The police haven't found either of those bastards,' he says.

There's an old inter-island ferry laid up for the tourists to view and the hydrofoil slips behind it into a private berth.

Les and Slaven climb from the hatch and apart from a group of primary kids heading back from the ferry, there's no one about. Les leads the way to a utility with its tray full of boxes of fir seedlings and with a Parks Board motif on the door. 'We'll have to have a bite as we go, I'm afraid,' says Les. 'The sooner we're out of here the better.'

'From what I know of the Beckley-Waite they won't even miss me.'

'They have their masters though.'

'How far is it to Mahakipawa?'

'Right over towards Havelock,' says Les as he drives up the hill out of Picton. The vehicle has been chosen well. Les Croad is a natural in a ute with a load of seedlings. 'Mahakipawa. Whatever made you think of that. There's nothing at Mahakipawa.'

'For me there is. I'll go there some day.' Slaven thought of a broad hill with native bush on its crown, rough pasture with yellow-flowered gorse and bracken, then the carefully-tied rows of vines. The Caretaker's hapu would be working amongst them and the free-range leghorns would come from fluffing in the dustbowls beneath the windbreak pines to take grapes in their beaks so that the bloom on the dark skin was marked as if with pencil lines.

There's a tin of sandwiches and a carton of fruit juice in the cab. Slaven can tell that Kellie has made the sandwiches — egg and parsley, and tongue — for the crusts are cut from them as is her way. Who else but Kellie would think of it amongst the mechanics of escape. Slaven is eating as they pass Tuamarina and he looks up to the hill where he knows the cemetery to be. Almost he expects to see his meeting still in progress there, but all the people, all the rhetoric, the pies and publicity, have had no lasting impact and now he's a fugitive from the Beckley-Waite, sliding by in a utility driven by Les Croad. Will anything alter if he stops and adds himself to the quiet landscape? Will the hedges be less impenetrable, the Friesians less shitted at the tail, will the Scotch thistle mitigate the wonder of its purple, or the angles of the cheese factory be less definite against the sky? The backdrop has both the message and the last laugh.

Slaven has the taste of a beast's tongue in his mouth. The afternoon shadows give definition to the land. The old eucalyptus tree will be making its pipe-bowl nuts above the Wairau memorial and through it the mottled light will make the record of 1843 even less distinct. From the green schoolground below it are cries of joy from country children playing.

On then, across the Wairau Plain, with time for just a final backward glance over the firecely- waving seedlings to the hills of Tuamarina and the white memorial there.

Les Croad's phone buzzes and he answers with a voice of conscious conspiracy. 'Things are on the move,' he says to Slaven, 'but we'd better not have you talking to anyone. The snoopers will have their gear out. We mightn't be able to get right down to Christchurch tonight, but we'll be told of the best place to make a stop. There aren't any checks at Blenheim as yet, so we'll get through there all right. I used to work here you know. I had a seed drier and used to handle a good deal of small stuff, clover and so on.'

'So what happened.' Slaven knows that he is to be told in any case.

'My wife caught me shagging the babysitter and I had to sell up the business when the family broke up. I reckon I would have been mayor of Blenheim now if it hadn't been for that girl.'

'Who came out of it the best,' says Slaven. 'The babysitter, the town, your wife, or you.'

'Six of one, I reckon, but I never look back. It's all water under, after all.' He drives through the town which seems to have prospered under the leadership of Mayors who haven't been sabotaged by babysitters of either sex. Above the central shops is the huge, plastic bunch of grapes which can be lit up at night and which is decorated at Christmas time instead of a communal tree.

Perhaps indeed that's the secret — don't look back. Don't look back across the waving seedlings to Tuamarina, don't look back to the spinning eyes of the Beckley-Waite, don't look back to Waiouru and a father chinning effortlessly on the back-lawn bars that held the swing, a mother of special smiles, don't look back to Kellie on her wedding day with a face as serene as her expectations, don't look back to the blue paint of the barge board, the wire in his grasp and Half Moon Bay.

The present also may become with examination as unhelpful as Les Croad confirms his past to be. The dry hills before Seddon will be the same dry hills when Les and Slaven have passed, the frogs will bulge their eyes from the stock dams when the wind alone is before their stare, the genetic pattern of the harrier hawk will have it lift awkwardly from guts upon the road on the day Les surrenders his bitterness, and long after. What happens to the spools of incessant occurrence; insistent yet trivial patterns of sight, sound and fragrances which net the heart and hint at some explanation for consciousness.

There's a place, not far, sweet country if only it had summer rain. The sheep seek shade and in these camps the loess clay of the ground is smooth and hard, or pooled to dust and the droppings of the sheep are thickly spread, but dry and inoffensive, baked in the heat. In the odd sink hole the briar seeks moisture and gorse blooms brighter than the clay. The ridges are worn almost bald, like the heads of the lean, brown farmers who ride farm bikes too small for them across the paddocks of their land. The creek beds are marked more by rushes and willows than running water and the mallards come only in twos or threes. An easterly is always up after midday and burnishes the arc of pale, blue sky. The shelter belts close to the road and the macrocarpa before the farmhouse are dusted with a false pollen drifting in off the road. The rural delivery boxes are large so that stores can be left there as well as mail and each has a name painted by hand. In the evenings the sheep come to the stock dams and troughs to drink, the magpies gather to imitate the noise of poets and the barley grass and browntop ripple at the sides of the shingle roads.

Is that so far away?

Les Croad is on the phone again. He fully accepts the urgency of the present. He lowers his voice at moments of greatest decision. 'I'd rather not leave the visitor alone,' he says. And, 'Yes I see that, but I'd rather not leave him alone.'

'What's this,' asks Slaven.

'They're making checks before Kaikoura. Miles Kitson's people want you to spend the night at Lake Grassmere to be on the safe side.'

'Then we do it.'

They turn left from the main road towards Lake Grassmere. A deadend road with the old salt works almost at the finish of it. Les has a key to the works' gate. 'Plan B,' he says with his flat grin and they drive to the old buildings with the wide sea-pans beyond them, then the ocean. Solitude and dereliction have worn the buildings down in relation to their surroundings and drawn one building further from another so that there are conspicuous spaces between one gaunt barn and another. Only the remains of a viaduct conveyor system sticks up thirty or forty metres, its raw, solid parts expensive to dismantle. There are still slumps of unprocessed salt like old snow and the long grass is untrammelled at the loading bays alongside the rusted railway lines. Les takes a backpack and the food from the truck and pushes past the door of what may have been the administration block. Slaven can make out, in large letters on the outside — 'Cerebos'.

Inside there are stairs without a railing to the upper floor. 'Tomorrow morning I'll come back in a green van. Don't come out for anything else,' says Les. He's attaching a thin, metallic sheet, almost a foil, as a shelter. He strings it from warped partitions there, despite a roof that seems serviceable enough. 'If a chopper comes over you'll be all right under this,' he says. 'I've got to get the ute out of here pronto, but I'll be back quite early tomorrow and we'll have you in Christchurch lickedy.'

Slaven watches the Parks Board vehicle go back towards the main road, skirting the downs. It has left no obvious tyre marks within the gates, and as Slaven turns back he has the inconsequential hope that the seedlings will not suffer for their adventure. He's never been to Grassmere before, yet his first careful scrutiny after Les Croad has gone brings to him a landscape of utter familiarity; as if he has been assembling it in his sub-conscious during the long, air conditioned nights of the Beckley-Waite and now is able to visit his creation at last. The wooden and corrugated iron buildings are dry and whitened by wind and sand and salt. The sea has long broken into some of the pans closest to the coast, but from the others the setting sun still catches crystals and pond surfaces between the low rubble causeways and the wind casts grit and sand against the old buildings. In the concrete loading ramps and retaining walls the iron reinforcement has burst out in furled half-blooms of rust in response to the salt sea air. The skeleton of an industry remains — those things too large, or uneconomic to cart away. The sun shows through the ribs of the high walls and much of the heavy, simple machinery is still in place.

The people have drawn off to find a life elsewhere. A tribe of Croads; sunburnt, stubborn, bitterly humorous, clinging to a host of work-related perks of doubtful legality as they drove loaders and skimmers, alternately let in and held back the sea. Then in other jobs and places they would mention briefly that they'd worked at Grassmere by the sea, but not take the time when passing to come back to see the shallow, discoloured water, or feel the salt rind their sweat in the way it always used to do.

Slaven sits on the warm boards of the blank second story of the administration building. By the glassless window is carved —'here Tigger did the deed with Alice'. The night hills are one dimensional serrations against the red and yellow of the western sky and the closest pans have glints of flamingo pink. Slaven wishes the Caretaker could be with him so that they could talk some more and he could share the tobacco in a more substantial way.

When the sun is down, Slaven lies on the sleeping bag and beneath the foil which will keep his living heat from detection — all being well. He has no artificial light and lies listening to the building creaking as it cools, feeling the wind move easily through it. He is completely safe, free of the hum of the Beckley-Waite air conditioning and able to breathe the wind flowing in from Lake Grassmere. There is a rat, or a cat, maybe, scratching a reply on the tin, but no tight walls, no acoustic ceilings, no padding futility in the narrow corridors, or surreptitious unwrapping of chocolate, no soft weeping, or levitations of despair.

At three he wakes because of the chill and a need to piss. He urinates in the corner furthest from his camp, not trusting the stairs in the dark and he makes sure that he climbs within the sleeping bag when he comes back. Despite the hard boards, he's quickly asleep again; just enough time beforehand to hear the wind in the gaps of the old timbers, the ocean at a distance and the flexing of the foil strip above him. Also the drip of his own piss to the ground floor beneath.

Gulls wake him and the sun through windows rimmed with shattered glass. He is nailed to the floor with stiffness, but manages to dress clumsily and go down the stairs to stand in the doorway and flex himself. It's a wonderfully empty world and Slaven finds it hard to imagine that his presence is of concern to anyone. There have been no helicopters, loudspeakers, or dogs, not even a local policeman come to have a nose around. It will be a piece of cake from now on. Slaven thinks.

A green van comes while he's having a cursory wash in shallow and discoloured water of the nearest pan and stops by the old building and Les Croad picks up the kit which is already packed. Slaven hears the tyres in the grit and salt as the van comes towards him. 'No problems?' asks Les.

'Fine.'

'We haven't been all that far away. Better sure than,' says Les. He has brought coffee and a bag of apples and Slaven is able to balance the cup better once they reach the main road.

'Things get just a bit dicey from here on in,' says Les. 'There's a good deal of surveillance as we go towards Christchurch. They know they need to get you quickly, or the publicity will be too much for them. You're going to become a veteran cyclist to be on the safe side. I hope that's okay?'

'How veteran?' Slaven has never liked cycling.

'You won't be on the road that much. There's a group riding in turns to publicise Australasian Union.'

The Australasian Unionists have set up a pit stop at Ward and Les drops him there. 'Don't you worry. We won't be that far away,' he says. A grey-haired, whippet of a man takes Slaven into his care, arranging for a shower, a completely vegetarian meal and a shave which includes the legs.

'So that we can give you an instant tan,' says the whippet man, 'and you won't stand out from the rest.' From the outside maybe he doesn't, but he feels foolish in the large back-up van travelling on: lycra shorts and top, helmet ready and yellow elbow and knee pads in place. Rather than the threat of recapture he's worried about his own clothes and his possible inability to ride fast enough when his turn comes.

Certainly the six in front are slow enough and Slaven has ample time to watch an iceberg being towed north off the Kaikoura coast and to see the crayfish speciality stalls and tourist boat trip operators as the town grows closer. The handler is told that there's a checkpoint ahead, so he has the van pass the riders and flag them down for a change of personnel.

That's how Slaven comes to enter Kaikoura on a Torricelli touring bike with a thin, uncomfortable seat. He sweats in the morning sun and some of his new tan stains the fold of the white socks he's been given. There's some apprehension when the road-block is sighted, yet since the very beginning of his escape things have been so very much in the hands of others that Slaven has become fatalistic. Having no part in the planning against threat, he finds it difficult to believe in the threat itself. The sweat moves, tickles in the short hair by his ears. The sea breeze evaporates it on the side of his face and so there's coolness there. The breeze comes from the direction of the iceberg which is in plain view directly offshore. How marvellously out-of-place it is. Vast and with touches of the milky green of the lightest jade, it is towed captive far from its own world.

Miles has chosen his men well. They know that the best disguise is not to change a person's appearance, but to alter the context. Slaven and his fellow riders barely put their feet to the ground at the check-point before they are waved through. They are urged on by a bald-headed man in shorts and tramping boots who uses a megamike to extoll the virtues of Australasian Union. Rather than fearing a last minute shout of recognition as he moves through, Slaven has to concentrate on keeping up with the woman in front. Her bum swallows up the seat, but her brown legs provide a seemingly effortless propulsion. Slaven puts in a special effort as they climb the hill behind the town centre and he wonders when the whippet will order another change. At all his meetings, Slaven has spoken out against sexist attitudes, but sweating on the coast road he prays to a male god to deliver him from the humiliation of not being able to keep pace with a woman. He lowers his head so that his effort can't be read and he counts each thrust of legs as an encouragement — 702, 703, 704, 705. The tremor of small muscles in his thighs is a warning of cramp.

The back-up van overtakes them while still on the flat of Goose Bay. Slaven has no wish to be cycling over the Hundalees. 'I thought that just a small stage would do you,' says the whippet. 'Though it might pay to have you back on if we strike other checks. Just one other thing; you actually had your helmet on back-to-front.'

'I'll get it right next time.' Slaven is aware of the irony. He has never been on the run before and he's becoming aware of an aspect of it which he has never suspected — it is demeaning.

The others in the van are a cheerful enough lot, though by no means all youthful protesters. Nor is there any reprise of the advantages of union which is the reason for them coming together. Slaven could talk to them regarding that. Hadn't he been completing an article for *The Australasian* when Drs Eugene and Bliss called. Rather the talk within the van is of stage distances, muscle massage, energy foods and the reason for the police checks. The ample woman whose fitness Slaven found a threat, says they were after the man who tried to assassinate the Maori King and the manager, thin as a whippet, says that's it and catches Slaven's eye.

Slaven rides only one more stage — through Cheviot and the yellow downs immediately beyond — because there is a second check made by the police at the crossroads which you come on suddenly around a left-hand sweeper. The whippet however is constantly and well-informed. With his helmet on correctly, Slaven feels quite at ease during the short pause and breathes deeply only to ensure he'll be well oxygenated when he resumes.

In the van again, eating a parrot mixture of dried fruit, seeds and nuts, which the others relish, Slaven thinks of the weeks before the elections and how they can best be used. He wonders if he will have to operate undercover, if it's possible even, or if once he has a following around him again the authorities will accept his presence.

He goes over his six points in case there are things in his experience since Lyttelton and the Beckley-Waite which necessitate changes, but finds his mind circling back to the person most responsible for recent weeks — Cardew. For years his son has been both puzzle and disappointment; complete in all corporeal respects, but lacking character, having in its place only an instinctual drive for self-gratification. Slaven accuses himself of failing to pass on any of the values which guide his own life. Perhaps he proclaims, rather than exemplifies. Gradually Slaven's dislike of his son has sapped the love that can for a long time exist with it in paradox of parenthood. They have sat in the bath together. Slaven has carried him on his shoulders and can remember the joy in Cardew's face at the modest enough prospect of a video game. But soon he must be dealt with for the common good.

The stop for the night is a church hall at Amberley and Slaven's fellow riders are almost euphoric at the thought of rest and recreation, then their triumphal ride into the city the next morning and the official presentation of their petition. The whippet promises savoury sausages and mashed poatato, but when Slaven climbs stiffly from the van and makes to follow the others, the manager gives a whistle and raises his eyebrows and points to the quiet end of the hall where Les Croad is waiting in another vehicle again. The manager says nothing, just gives Slaven his clothes within a supermarket bag and squeezes his arm with thin fingers. The manager whistles and makes his way to sausages and mash, for he's done his bit.

'Almost there,' says Les. Slaven follows him to the car, flexing his arms and back as he does so. Les rather enjoys the cloak and dagger stuff, enjoys also the sight of a stiff and absurdly-dressed Slaven, with eyes reddened by the wind and borrowed white socks stained with the false tan sweated into them.

'We were going to have a hot meal here, you know,' says Slaven.

'Hotter than you bargained on perhaps. When people have satisfied their bellies they start taking an interest in other people, start asking questions. I'm afraid we can't take you home either, or to anyone you know. No visitors even until things quieten.' Les is grimly pleased by the inclusive isolation for it prolongs Slaven's reliance on him. 'I've an address though. You could say a safe house, I suppose. Famous last, eh?' When the glass has Slaven invisible within the car, Les Croad takes his time, even a few paces back to the corner of the hall so that he can see down the path towards the rooms where the supporters of Australasian Union are relaxing. Their noise is unmistakable in quiet Amberley. There is no apparent surveillance. 'I smell sausages,' says Les.

'Tell me about it,' murmurs Slaven from the car.

The Christchurch place that the advisers have arranged for Slaven to lie low in. An old house divided into flats, and the back flat where Les Croad leaves him has an addition which juts over the Heathcote stream. A banana-passionfruit plant grows all around the door, its fluted flowers lit like candles there in the low evening sun. Les puts a case for Slaven on the step and gives him several letters held together with a rubber band. 'Better I shoot through, now,' he says. 'These people don't know who you are. They're not well up on politics and national happenings, but Kitson's guys are sure you'll be okay. The boy is called Athol and he understands that you need to be quietly out of circulation for a while. But we won't be far away.' Les shakes hands with Slaven vigorously, then raps on the window and gives a thumbs up to someone inside. He leaves before the someone comes, cutting across the rough, brown lawn and perfectly at home. His shrugging walk and jutting, restless face seeking stimulus. The close-crimped, almost yellow hair, the creases of his grubby twill trousers well-suited to the movement of his legs. This is his happy hunting, thinks Slaven. What does he wish from the Coalition except a wage. Les Croad would have been born and grown up in a succession of back flats on railway and river sections. He would have crouched with his mates in the macrocarpa when he should have been at school, smoking and spitting on the spider webs and starting to resent those people who had it better. Les should stay by the less-than-crystal Heathcote and Slaven should cut across the lawn and away. Slaven opens his mouth to say so, to call Les back to natural surroundings, but he realises how absurd it all is, how weary and confused he has become, how hungry, how unwilling to meet more strangers who will constitute yet another interlude in the scheme of his escape from the Beckley-Waite.

Does the woman painter still relax in the room two along from the Emergency ALW, the skipper still gun the company van at Oriental Bay? The derelict buildings at Grassmere — are they still there? Have they ever been? Has his piss dried at the top of the stairs with no sides and is there a flamingo flush on the abandoned sea pans? Has Tigger done the deed with Alice? Does the woman cyclist with powerful legs and hair held back with a simple green band now deftly test the skin of a gravied sausage with her teeth and imagine the presentation? Does the road manager, that whippet of leather and feathery bone, rest in Amberley and peace? Where do the seedlings wave and where have the few children gone who shouted to each other at Tuamarina? Is the owl once more on the wing?

There is a fragrance of kerosene, or boot polish, in the calm air and Slaven's aware of the sliding feel in his left hand as the plastic bag of clothes slips, the sharp feel of the letters in his other hand. The residue of a day's sweat is on him, the salt of it drawing the skin tight and brittle. His leg muscles twitch with the poisons of unaccustomed strain and the banana-passionfruit flowers only inches from his face have a pearly, yet slightly yellow sheen, like the gloss on a pelt peeled from the steaming beast. A duck with one leg is swimming upstream in the Heathcote — he can tell by the compensatory movement that its body gives to each surge of propulsion. From an upstairs flat comes the Hoihos, but not *Half Moon Bay*. A huge Harley Hog leans on the wall and the richness of it contrasts with the surrounding neglect. Upwards, through the corroded grin of the guttering, Slaven can see the jewelled dazzle of the western sky. Ah, the mockery of indifferent precision.

So no discriminatory initial description of our Athol, as he first glances from the flawed window then opens the door and blocks it with his spread arms. He leans there, tilted cheerfully forward and he looks at this guy who has come as a windfall. 'You'll be okay here, mate. No sweat,' he says. So Slaven comes into the home and lives of more people when he has home and family of his own. Coming back from the dead, in a manner of speaking, isn't as easy as he had imagined that morning at quiet Lake Grassmere. 'You need somewhere to crash for a while,' says Athol and he takes up the case and leads the way through a living room of mismatched furniture into a bedroom of obvious femininity — shadow curtains at a window which overlooks the Heathcote and the smell of kerosene and boot polish overlaid with that of deodorant, fabrics and pot pourri in bowls of glass.

'Get your head down for a bit. I can see you're almost knackered, and then we'll talk about a feed.' Slaven has nothing in reply. He can't be bothered with the emotional effort of acknowledging yet another stranger. He undoes his cycling shoes at the side of the bed and lies on the blue covers with his arms spread out. The Heathcote's sluggish water idles by outside, but by some trick of evening reflection there is a rippling pattern on the ceiling — so ethereal and chaste in its silently breaking then coalescing flow that Slaven feels his essential self drift upwards to join it. 'Absolutely knackered,' says Athol as from habit he hefts the small case to assess its contents.

While Slaven sleeps there is an opportunity to make free with those tinctures of verisimilitude which he's in no condition to record. The greenstone stud, say, in Athol's left nostril, a blue, folded handkerchief — yes, to match the cover — between the lamp clamp and the bedhead as padding and across the Heathcote in an overgrown backyard is a netting compound in which unregistered pit-bull terriers are hidden from the world. See each of these, and the things which link them are just as certain and as clear to you as they are to Slaven when he wakes. The purple plums, say, each of which has been pecked by the birds sufficiently to be a token of possession and the hair in the portal of Slaven's facing ear, little cutlasses which catch the light and which he cannot describe even when awake. The goose girl's closest friend of earlier days was brained with a baseball bat at the back of the Gethsemane Hotel, but his pueblo carving from New Mexico still hangs on to a life on the wall. And ah, the comforting, orbital repetitions which knit up the world we know, for as you say, it is indeed a sticker for Australasian Union on the mirror of the goose girl's duchess. It hides a glass flaw there, rather than showing political awareness.

So Athol leaves us to it and goes back to the kitchen for a jar and to count the first of the money which has been his without delay. The poor, old bugger's completely knackered, he thinks, and will need a good feed when he wakes. Something to stick to the sides of him and put lead in his pencil. As Athol stands at the bench, looks through the window above the dishes in the sink, it doesn't occur to him that the one-wheeled trailer askew in the long grass is an eyesore, or that the landlord's brother-in-law would have done better not to mix his paints on the concrete path. Some things just are: a one-legged duck chugging on the Heathcote to match a one-legged trailer in the grass, lunar paint stains in orange and cream to walk upon, a battery of pit-bull terriers in a neighbouring yard, a pounamu nose stud, a pueblo carving whose expression changes with subtle reflections of the stream and the banana-passionfruit flutes with the most delicate tinge of purple at their base.

Live and let live. Do any of these things ever prevent Athol from going round his man on the outside and scoring a good one for his Heathcote League side, or threaten his concentration as he steadies the goose girl with a hand behind her buttocks?

So here she is then —the goose girl — who has been visiting her sister in Hoon Hay. She has boots despite the heat and an Azerbaijan patterned skirt, very popular since the planned immigrations. And her short, white hair and her long, white neck and her features gathered to her mouth. Athol has a hand on her shoulder as they stand at her bedroom door and watch Slaven asleep on her bed. His socks are stained on his thin legs, his hair prickled with a former sweat, and the stubble a salt and pepper scatter over his chin and throat. Now that his face is relaxed, the creases that he had drawn in against the wind and dazzle show as pale lines in the sunburn.

'Who is he?' says the goose girl.

'Some rich, old bugger who matters. I think he's been in the clink and it's all very bloody hush-hush, understand. We look after him here for a while until his cobbers pick him up. And it's money for jam; easy money by Jesus.'

'Why here then if he's a bigwig? Why stuck with us?'

'Because no one will find him here, will they. No guest lists, or sign in, no credit cards, or cleaners with keys to fossick around, no nosey people at the desk to recognise a photo. We'll let him sleep and then he can spruce up and we'll have a feed. A big bloody order of pork nuggets and chips is what we could do with and a bottle of plonk for him to down with it.'

'Perhaps he's one of those lawyers who's got off with millions from some outfit that's collapsed.'

'No idea, and what does it matter. The thing is that some heavy people are behind him and he's a bloody good meal ticket while he's here, so you look after him. You treat him better than your own dad, better than me almost,' and Athol pushes his hand over the breast of the goose girl. The swell of her skin is firm feathered and the curve of her neck is almost classic beauty despite the closely-gathered features of her small face. She smiles and tilts up that small face as she does when things are going well. Her long throat shows to best advantage and her short hair shivers as a crest shivers.

'I wonder who he is,' she says. 'I reckon he's one of those business guys with all the money and they've got onto him.'

'Anyway, you be good to him. A goldmine to us is what he fucken is.'

Slaven sleeps until after ten o'clock at night and then wakes because of the changing temperature and the constriction of his cycling clothes. He comes back to himself slowly from a landscape which fades only just before his recollection of it. He's a stranger here and so begins to orientate himself by a cautious process of deduction, before giving himself away by movement. The initial alienation means he's nowhere in his own domain. There's no angle of Kellie's garden, or their spacious bedroom, no round adjustable light of his surgery. Is it the hospital then, with the cover of *The Beaver Trade* to Vincent's face and Norman Proctor to his left, if not already dead? Is it the Beckley-Waite and his hotbed of insignificance there, with the whine of the air conditioning preventing the quiet voice of the Caretaker from being heard? Is it the chinked vastness of the old building at the salt works with a sea mist wreathing in, or the rocking motion of the protesters' van slowing for another check-point. No?

It is a bedroom unknown to him, partly lit by a passage light, so that he can see the blue of the duvet on which he lies, the cluster of the goose girl's bottles on the duchess and her slippers bottom up by the wardrobe door. And a young guy with his hair in a bun, a stud in his nose, and the balance of an athlete in his walk, coming in from the passage.

Athol doesn't introduce himself, but smiles at Slaven so that the stud lifts at the side of his nose and he asks Slaven if there's anything he wants and just to say if there is.

'A bath if that's okay.' So Athol leads him along to the bathroom and then sends the goose girl for the pork nuggets, the chips and the wine. The cold tap gives a forceful stream, straight from the Heathcote beside them perhaps, but the hot tap coughs and pants steam and is easily overpowered, so that Slaven has to leave it full on, yet turn the cold down. He hadn't realised there are places still without a mixer.

Even when he has the taps off and is soaking in the narrow tub, the pipes keep arguing and rattling in their sockets. Pale green the walls are mainly, but at bump level the chips reveal flashes of other colours which once held sway — lemon is well noted, mushroom is here and the deepest injuries disclose a pre-cambrian gloss white which is close to the bone.

Slaven dries himself with a large, thin towel which has the odours of a locker room and combs his hair with his fingers as best he can. He knows no other place to go than the goose girl's bedroom and so he walks back there in his trousers and carries the lycra gear in the supermarket bag. The small case brought for him by Les Croad has been packed by Kellie. He should have opened it before he went to wash, for the comb, towel, shaver are all there as well as a change of clothes, pyjamas and a tube of ointment for his lips. On top of it all is a single sheet of notepaper — 'You can't keep a good man down,' she's written. What will come of her loyalty, he wonders.

Slaven shaves at the goose girl's duchess with all its bottled promises and Athol keeps a cheerful check on progress and when he thinks the moment right comes in with the food. 'Grub,' he says. The goose girl follows with her head down, but still curious. She has the wine and mugs. The three of them begin to eat and Slaven feels the rich bite of the pork nuggets. Athol can make an anemone of chips between thumb and forefinger to dunk in the organically grown tomato sauce. The goose girl can tilt her head and clack her teeth in satisfaction. And no introductions are made, none necessary, or at least too late, for Slaven's slept in the goose girl's bed and drawn across his back the bow of the communal towel. His fingers have locked with Athol's in the pursuit of a nugget in the box and his eyes found easy rest on the whiteness of the goose girl's arching neck. Her legs are folded beneath the hem of her Azerbaijan skirt as she sits on the bed with the men to eat and her shallow, bright, goosey eyes are alive with the novelty of a man with money, on the run.

'A few more hours in the pit and you'll be back to par, I reckon,' says Athol. He clumsily pours Chardonnay into three mugs and tasting it is privately convinced that it's gone off, but gone off from what he hasn't the experience to say.

'But I don't want to take your bed from you,' protests Slaven to the goose girl.

'No sweat,' says Athol. 'She can doss down with me.'

When they leave him, going out without any fuss, Slaven

folds his trousers at the end of the bed and settles beneath the blue duvet in merely singlet and fresh pyjama bottoms. Athol has turned out the bedroom light and again there is just that from the passage, too faint for Slaven to read the writing on his small wad of letters which he idly turns before his face. Everything can wait until he's enjoyed more of freedom's sleep. There's a small hollow in the pillow where the goose girl's head often lies and a scent throughout all the fabric of down and chips and cologne and the light perspiration of sleep. How different from the Beckley-Waite and the air conditioning unit which there seemed to service all of the world, but is silent here.

Athol and his flatmate finish the pork nuggets in the kitchen and he pours the remaining wine into the sink. They have no idea who Slaven is and no interest in the public world he represents. The only television they watch is cable sports and Afro-rock. Conventional society has no advantage for them, no means of access and no contact with their lives apart from their necessity to know what money they can claim and to keep a watchful eye on the enforcers of the law. The goose girl, I assure you, couldn't give us the name of the Prime Minister.

'His friend called again,' says Athol. 'They want to know if he's happy here and I said of course he was, but he wants to sleep most of all. You remember to be good to him. These people aren't fucken short of a few dollars, I can tell you.'

'Enough for a knee-length calf-skin coat?'

'Maybe piss in,' says Athol.

So when Slaven wakes at last, the goose girl is here beside him and although she doesn't look at him, but watches the abstract ripples on the morning ceiling, her left hand gently holds his cock and moves sufficiently to keep it of a size to be gripped. The goose girl lies with her head back so that her throat is taut and white. There is a ridge almost cylindrical along the centre of her throat and the faintest of lines diagonally across it, which form creases when her head's forward. It is a throat so long that it possesses a sinuosity between shoulders and head, like the smoothly muscled body of a snake, and Slaven, looking past it at her tilted face can see her eye-lashes as serrations, because of the odd angle of his view. The small, smooth head of a goose and that muscular neck and one hand lying gently on the surface of the duvet while the other continues, enquiring, solicitous.

'I've only started doing this in the last year or so,' says the goose girl.

'Why?' but such is the pleasure of the engrossing present that he has no real curiosity of motive.

'I was saving myself.'

'From what?' says Slaven and the goose girl laughs. The muscles move in her powerful neck.

'Not from anything. You know; for something. Saving myself for the right man, person even.'

'Are you having me on,' says Slaven.

'Dead bloody right,' says the goose girl.

Well, it has been a long time in the Beckley-Waite even for a mature man and there's the sense of dislocation, of hiatus in the principles which he would conventionally accept. Of other things, Miles has told him that political correctness is the side door to hell. As well there's the unsought opportunity, but we can agree to make that secondary. There is the adjustment of the bed in time with their breathing and the river light dappling, sliding, convections and fronds of movement on the ceiling. The whine from the bull terriers, as if they too have a scent of gift.

Slaven closes his eyes with the joy of entering the goose girl and feels tears run down his nose. The goose girl's breathing is hastened and a feathery loop of her white hair caught on her damp forehead. How beautiful. Slaven experiences a welling affection for women — their strength, humour and steadfastness, the slight forward curve of their bellies, the movement of skin on their collar bones. As he holds the smooth-feathered goose girl, he loves also the young Kellie and Rebecca Maitland from a New Year's Eve and Charlotte his first crush and Paula who tasted of chlorine from the town baths, Shelley who drew blood with her teeth, Miss Carlisle his standard four teacher who leant over his poster and aroused in him a longing for he knew not what.

Slaven isn't able to make any of this explicit to the goose

girl, or shape it fully within his own consciousness. Instead he follows with his finger the white curl on the goose girl's temple and feels the tears slide down his nose. Is release a form of beauty?

Some other place then, for privacy's sake and it may be in your own town with the Lotto sign and the stars of the BNZ, with the arcades of specialist boutiques and the large shops that have a score of active screens so that you may order a life on any scale which suits. Buskers in the street who can't sing, or play their instruments, but will be paid by all of us flattered by a sense of the cosmopolitan. Shops of window stools, gossip and coffee; shops of exquisite lingerie in case you get knocked down in the street, or knocked up at the office party. See those friends of yours who have made professional careers and wear black shoes. Tell me why it is that they are grey at the temples in a distinguished way, while you and I are bald. See twenty-three pastries in the one window and not two alike. See seventeen cold meats, including four in jelly, eleven vertical and nine pastel horizontal blinds, a turnstyle of flashy books, the price and product expressly uniform. See power tools that have the masculine appeal of automatic weapons and the creams and ferns in the window of the naturopath. See our mutual friend who has been diagnosed as possessing a most obscure and terminal disease. See the joy on children's faces as if they travel through a different world.

'Lovely, lovely,' Slaven murmurs. On the bedside table is a digital clock, a ginger nut and a pork nugget, a box of lavender tissues, an owl made from blue and emerald felt and embroidered with golden thread. They look very settled together, comfortable in their accustomed spatial relationship. They and the pueblo carving are part of the exact scene and company for Slaven's climax with the goose girl, as they had no doubt been exactly present even if at a distance while he lay in Kellie's flower garden beneath the power line, while he galvanised 250,000 people at Western Springs, while he was beaten beneath the wharf at Lyttelton. Well, perhaps not the pork nugget.

The goose girl smiles at him in a surprisingly maternal way, considering her age. 'There now,' she says.

'Ah, Jesus.'

'We thought it would relax you. Athol reckoned you'd probably been missing out. That's not prying, or anything.' She props herself on an elbow so that she can see him better as she talks and her white breasts move to one side. They are full and the nipples still gleam pinkly from the wetness of Slaven's mouth. 'A guy brought round a special phone,' she says. 'You're going to get a ring about midday.'

'Thank you. I haven't been welcomed to the morning in that way for years.'

'I didn't mind it slower for a change. Young guys are so bloody quick, aren't they. Athol's very strong, overpowering. He comes off with a hell of a rush.' She gets on to her hands and knees and then stands by the bed to put on her dressing gown. The harp swing of her hips, the heft of her breasts; there's a sensuous ungainliness in her movement and her long neck, her too small head with compressed features, aren't beautiful in any conventional way. 'You like it here don't you?' she asks. The phone guy brought even more money and she likes Slaven's formality and all the words he uses without swearing. And she likes his gratitude.

'You know,' he says, 'I've been trying to change things for the better in our country. There's been too much separation, too many categories for too long. We need to be more a part of each other.' Slaven has particularly strong conviction of this at present and his voice has a rich vehemence which comes only when he begins to fire up. The goose girl enjoys how he talks rather than what he says. She sits back on the bed, watches the Heathcote flow on the ceiling and wonders if he's one of those extra rich guys who has been kicked out of Mexico by the Hispanics and hasn't a permit to be in New Zealand. When she looks at him she's not sure he's like a Kiwi and he doesn't speak like Athol and her.

'Your poor hands,' she says. Maybe he's been tortured.

'A work accident,' he says.

'You haven't even read your letters,' the goose girl says

and leaves him to do so by taking a handful of clothes to the bathroom.

'Has it been too awful for you?' Kellie writes. 'Miles has been a tremendous help at this end and so have Marianne and Thackeray. I just hope that we're doing the right thing this close to the elections. It's all such a risk isn't it. Miles's political friends don't think the authorities will try a public arrest once we get the background across to the people and Marianne's been questioning the medical grounds for the original committal. I've tried to keep the CCP on track, but of course all sorts of factions are making a bid now. We need to talk about Cardew. Anyway, soon there'll be time for all that. I'm worried about you. What about your hands and face?'

Slaven takes time from Kellie's letter to check his hands. They had shaped themselves to the goose girl's bosom well enough. The seams like lashes, the colour differences, will never go completely of course. 'We must make a strong public move soon, if we're to be effective before the elections,' Kellie has written. 'The main parties consider we're neutralised I think.' The goose girl leans into the doorway of her own room, her nose concave like a bill and her eyebrows darker than her hair. She has packed away her full-feathered breast inside a jerkin with indigenous motifs and has an amulet of Inuit design.

'Athol and me are going to have a feed of garlic bread and chilli beans,' she says as an invitation.

'I like hot garlic bread, thank you, but I'll give the beans a miss if you don't mind. A cup of coffee, though, marvellous.'

'I'm off then,' she says and Slaven doesn't even know her name. See her journey then to the Fabo Fast Food Centre, taking her slightly ungainly steps, her white hair, her kindly and shallow intentions, her arched neck, her curving breasts beneath the jerkin with the nipples washed by Slaven's tongue. The goose girl knows nothing of mythology, metaphysics, or populist ideologies, god bless her, but she knows something of a man's needs perhaps and is a ready judge of garlic bread and chilli beans.

Miles also has sent a letter. 'You may yet regret your refusal to accept the solace of hibernation in the Beckley-

Waite, that cave in which no one need look directly at the real. Why would you want to return to what we have around us at present. Perhaps you still believe you can change it. I begin to think that you have developed an appetite for fame. If so you will be consumed by it in the end. Anyway, I've enjoyed the hugger-mugger preparations for your escape and imagine your great daring in the execution of it. When you surface, come and see me if you have the time. I crave distraction, having used up all my memories, and dying is either a painful, or boring, business.'

Slaven grows hungry waiting for the goose girl to return with the first food of the day. He puts a finger first on the pork nugget on the bedside table, then the ginger nut there. The nugget is corpse-like and so he eats the biscuit with no great satisfaction as he has a feeling that it's been dunked then left to parch again. Surreptitiously he dries his cock with a squeeze of the goose girl's sheet, then dresses in the clothes which Kellie sent. Fresh clothes, freedom from the Beckley-Waite, a loving awakening to the goose girl. He hasn't felt this good in months. Slaven is determined to take up his mission again; to succeed in it.

The three of them eat together in the kitchen. Athol has the non-snoop phone as the centrepiece on the table, not just as a convenient proximity, but because to him it is a novelty. Time isn't money to Athol and the goose girl. Theirs is still a life of direct contacts and the day's agenda working out bit by bit as the day itself determines it in casual development. Athol likes to ride his Harley Hog to an address and knock on a back door beneath sloping wooden stairs, or a workshop window behind the auto tuning shop. He needs to see a full-sized, three dimensional face when he's speaking. How can you deal with people, reckon them friend, or threat, if they're not near enough to reach out to and touch, grasp.

The call from Kellie comes as Slaven finishes his coffee. It is right on time, of course. The goose girl shifts her position with innocent curiosity so that she sees Kellie's face on the small screen. There is a slight double image which relieves the sharpness of her features. Slaven is determined to be more deserving of her loyalty and talent. Kellie tells him that they have a recuperative cottage at a hospital not obviously connected with Marianne Dunne which will do the trick for a few days. 'Can't I stay here?' says Slaven.

'People coming and going in any number would soon be noticed. We have to have meetings, but without it drawing attention. An institutional cover is best now — privacy without isolation.' He knows that she is right and agrees to be ready when Les Croad comes. 'See you soon,' says Kellie.

'She speaks nice,' says the goose girl.

'You come here anytime you want,' says Athol.

Athol and the goose girl take a spin on the Hog to check out the neighbourhood. Just in case there are uniforms, Athol tells Slaven, who hears the barking of the exhaust as the patrol is carried out. Athol and the goose girl return as Les arrives and so the farewell is made there by the side of the house — Slaven and Les on the path amongst its coloured crescents, Athol and the goose girl on the wide cherry leather of the Hog. What would you say at such a time, I wonder, which would not be completely glib, dismissive even of such brief acquaintance, such ignorance of each other's motivations, such purely convenient mutual favour and passage. Just such does Slaven attempt and is aware as he speaks that the banana-passionfruit retains its set scrutiny. So do the felt owl and the tissue box now, so does the pueblo carving, but Slaven has borne the ginger nut away so that there's left merely the faintest ring of its drying on the goose girl's bedside table. Why have you this appetite for the bewilderment and joy of others? Already you have been told more than you would otherwise have known. There now. Is that it then? And the stud in Athol's nose dips and glints as he smiles. 'Go for it,' he says.

'Banzai,' replies Les Croad who knows them not at all.

At the recuperative cottage, one in a deliberately random distribution of cottages just the same, Slaven finds he has become Croad, yet Croad remains himself. 'Just as a precaution,' Les says. 'Answering the phone, any mail, things like that. Just a precaution. Better sure.' Slaven considers the convolutions of his escape. Perhaps before he can be himself once more, he'll be lost in all the subterfuge, his identity shucked and then what's left mislaid, or hard put to make a claim to what once was his. 'I've seen a damn sight worse than this,' says Les. He wanders uninvited through the cottage. It is after all to be the home of a titular Croad. 'Small, sure, but such a crafty, modern little place. So cheap to heat.' Fittings are tested for adherence to the walls and the body dryer activated in the bathroom. 'Kellie and Miles Kitson will come round this evening,' he says after satisfying his curiosity. 'They'll bring more stuff for you.'

With Les gone, Slaven has an opportunity to think things through. He leaves his one small case and the shopping bag of cycling clothes on the floor of the only bedroom and lies looking at a very clean, white ceiling on which nothing moves at all. Soon he will be caught up in the onward rush of the Coalition and publicity again which will blur the end to which they are the means. Just for a few hours then, free from the Beckley-Waite, from the mechanisms necessary for that escape, from the distractions of the goose girl and the mundane assistance of Les Croad and before Kellie, god bless her, Miles, Thackeray and the others, before Cardew's continuing betrayal and the fatuous auguries of his daughter. And in that time an earnest question for himself — where to now?

He will take the platform soon enough, raise his genie above a great rally to dismay the powers of politics, and all for the good of others of course. He will be the leader of ordinary people and made extraordinary because of it.

What is it then that prevents Slaven from a complete confidence in the future of it all? When the people have been most united and vociferous in support, still he's seen the snake's head forming. The great owl spreads its wing as a shadow backdrop to the genie. Why in his dreams do the archangels' reinforcements still troop to a lurid horizon? Why does he lie amid the Earl of Athlone's clotted blossoms and the bumble bees where it all began.

Baby, baby, come again and live with me upon the shore of Half Moon Bay.

Kellie and Sarah and Miles come when he's asleep, using their own card in the door and carrying cartons of food and clothes. After all, Slaven is repossessing his life. Kellie's long hug is all sincerity and comfort — and nothing more. 'How are you feeling?' she says and Slaven has a selfish guilt that in fact how he feels has always been in the forefront of his mind, but rarely how things might be with her. 'You look so tired,' she says. 'Your colour's odd. Most of your skin's so white, but your face is windburnt. Good heavens, I suppose it's all been horrible has it?'

'Not really. If you mean the getting away, then more confusing than anything and if you mean the Beckley-Waite, well the worst thing there was that no one cared a damn for you and yet you couldn't go anywhere else. I've come to realise that for a lot of people that's their life, but I've been used to better. You made me feel someone. You spoiled me.'

'Of course I did. And there's a big job to do now if you're up to it. You know that it's less than a month before the elections.'

'The parting of the ways, or the parting of the waters,' whispers Miles. The red inners of his lapsed lower eyelids glisten. 'Great things are expected of you as a sort of political Lazarus; a Lear's clown to our rulers.' Miles is protectively stooped. He looks about the small bedroom for a place to rest, but as there's no chair he walks slowly away into the living room and sits out of sight, but not out of earshot. 'I'm so pleased to see you, Aldous,' he says.

'Your face has healed up. It's really come on. Don't you think so, Sarah?' Kellie runs a finger down the side which had been more damaged.

'I knew you'd be all right, because there were no black fantails on the bush walk last Sunday. A black fantail is the really bad omen as far as signs go.' Sarah looks over her new surroundings. No fantails of course, but maybe there are other auguries.

'Let me see your hands,' says Kellie and she takes them in her own as if they are fabric samples and tests them thoroughly, bending the fingers back and running her thumb firmly across the palms to see how quickly the blood comes flooding back.

'No, I'm feeling fine,' says Slaven. 'Everything's working okay.'

Haven't Athol and the goose girl seen to that; primed him with pork nuggets and Chardonnay and ignited him in the grasp of the goose girl. As Sarah puts clothes in the drawers and wardrobe and Kellie outlines the background for the Coalition Executive Meeting, Slaven has in recollection the wondrous cherry leather sheen of the Harley Hog, the Heathcote gliding, turning on the ceiling, the quick switching muzzles of the pit-bull terriers, the tremble of the goose girl's breasts, the dazzle of blue sky through the guttering rusted right away.

'There are several options really,' says Kellie. Indeed there are. His father despised indecision. Take what you want — and pay for it, the sergeant-major always said.

'Four green issue singlets.'

'Check.'

'Two woollen draw-neck and leather-reinforced jerseys, issue.'

'Check.'

'One draw-neck bushshirt.'

'Check.'

'One stainless steel dog-tag set.'

'Check.'

'One reticent affection.'

'Check.'

'One bottle top for swallowing, personal.'

'Check.'

'Not everything's been Cardy's fault,' says Kellie.

'Come on now, Kellie,' says unseen Miles.

'Well, it hasn't either.'

'But he's behind most of the trouble. He's a hopeless little bastard, I'm afraid.' When you're very rich, very influential and dying as well, trenchant expression of the truth can be got away with. Kellie is hurt of course, and Slaven pulls a face for her sake, but shares the realisation that his son is as Miles describes him. It's a feeling of sorrowful awareness, rather than anger, for the only continuation for most of us is through our children and as well there's some responsibility for what they become, isn't there. 'Aries is never kind in Cardy's horoscope. Things are stacked against him,' says Sarah.

'I read one of your columns when I was in the Beckley-Waite. In some magazine. I understood that success was going to come to me through some imminent sporting triumph. I'm still waiting.'

'You need an individual chart done for any precise indication. You know I've always said that.'

'Some time soon, Sarah, we must sit down and do it. A full personal horoscope and we'll find out all sorts of things about each other maybe.' Slaven sees that his daughter's pleased with the attention while knowing his scepticism for her interest, and he wishes that he had been more welcoming, more often.

'I want my stars read, too,' claims Miles, 'but backwards, receding. Bright constellations which will light up patterns in all the rushing hitherto. The past is always more interesting than the future, because you have first-hand knowledge of it, but no idea what it means.'

All in all though, Cardew is dangerous sure enough, as has already been shown. Slaven knows someone close to the centre offers the best opportunity to opponents. A sort of palace revolution began with his admittance to the Beckley-Waite and though Kellie and Miles were too strong for it to be carried through at once, the division is real.

The simple meal becomes a reunion in a quiet, understated way. Kellie and Sarah, Slaven and Miles, shoulder to shoulder at the small table. Miles has brought a Schloss Fustenberger from his cellar and for the first time in weeks, Slaven has the sort of food he likes and is accustomed to. He realises how much of his former comfort in the world has been the result of Kellie's mediation between him and it.

'Are you up to it all,' asks Miles. 'It's not essential to have a meeting tonight, or to push on with anything unless you're up to it.' Is he up to it? Well, he is up to it in the sense that presumably it is the next thing to happen and up to it also in that he can cope with any of the pressures it will bring. What however, Slaven asks himself more keenly, is he UP to? What is it that he wants? Why is it that a conscious effort of concentration is needed to bring his mind to the CCP, the elections, the policies which have aroused the expectations of thousands of his compatriots? Just a delayed reaction, surely. The culmination of the psycho-logical pressures of the Beckley-Waite and then the bewildering montage of his escape. He just needs to place himself again. Just needs to be set.

'I'm up to it all right,' he says.

'Paul Hurinui, Eula, Sheffield and Thackeray are coming, that's all. Not Cardew of course,' says Kellie. 'We can't take the risk of telling him anything. He's speaking at a meeting in Ashburton. We're only just holding on. Things don't take off the same without you, even though Thackeray's been giving some fine speeches. A lot of people can't understand what happened to you. They're not sure what to believe. We must get back up to steam by doing something spectacular soon. A city rally, here, as soon as possible I reckon, so that the government and the other parties get the message that we still have the electoral power and are prepared to use it. A real jolt and then demands.'

'Dr Slaven back from vengeful exile,' says Miles. 'Certainly the moment's right for a big one.' Miles is having trouble with Kellie's meal, so much of it is uncooked. A line of cottage cheese and chives underscores his bottom lip and he finds the salad difficult to corner with his fork. Things that were second-nature have become of plodding con-centration. Yet he looks shrewdly at Slaven, wonders what has happened at the Beckley-Waite, what overt and covert treatment, what resistance on his friend's part. Their eyes meet.

'When we were coming here,' says Sarah, 'I saw all these intersecting snail tracks across the paths and we haven't had any rain. In the pattern of Aquarius, which is good. And your aura's out again, dad. I said as we came in and you were still sleeping that I could see it.'

'There you are then. Mighty portents.' Miles gives his caustic grimace which has once been a smile. 'However, I must mention the emperor's new clothes.'

'Thousands saw his aura at St Kilda and Western Springs,' says Sarah. 'That's what I mean.'

Kellie told the others that they would start at eight, but all four arrive early, hoping for some time before their fellows to welcome Slaven and slightly aggrieved at the similar intentions. They crowd in to pat and grip him. Thackeray Thomas, the broad beam of his face as openly evangelical and loyal as ever, Eula Fitzsimmons, with elegance and so many organisational allegiances that she has a cross reference at hand for any proposal, Sheffield Spottiswoode, who leans forward seriously with his hands firmly on his splayed knees as a union man should, Paul Hurinui, who finds a brief opportunity to tell Slaven that the Caretaker still enjoys a night pipe in the courtyard of the Beckley-Waite Institute.

'Tell him that I'm going to Mahakipawa when I can.'

See the Caretaker doing his stores inventory at the beginning of the month. He can calculate to within a score the total of the toilet tissue stack by just the first rank towards him and the colour code of the light bulbs needs no reference. See him judge the detergent which remains by one quick heft from the floor and alter on the order form the source of tinned stock because he hasn't forgotten the last outfit's refusal to help him hump it in. See him interview for new cleaners; what compassion for those who are halting and inarticulate in what they say, yet have character. In the summer nights he smokes stuff from his own land during his legitimate breaks and listens to Victor Yee release his soul. He values a multi-sourced heritage and claims no chiefly descent. One ancestor he admires was born a slave. See the Caretaker in his workshop fashion a tool of his own specification to gather leaves from the spouting of the Beckley-Waite and have a laugh with Ovens, who goes up to the surgery to dispense his gift of pain.

Sarah leaves them to the meeting, clears the table, begins the washing up. Maybe they have left some augury in the cups. Slaven feels a pang to see his daughter so surely know her place — to go away because she lacks the ability to be on the Executive. He leaves the small living room, takes the few steps into the kitchen where she is at the sink. He feels a helpless goodwill towards her and a turning of a father's love. This rather pretty woman with a plain mind. Does she deserve any less than if she had been dealt subtle understanding, but a plain face? 'I'm so glad you came tonight. So glad to see you.'

'Oh, me too.' She puts a wet hand to his face and smiles. Kellie watches from the other room. 'Do you know,' Sarah says, 'we were ever so careful coming here not to be followed. It's like a mystery video isn't it. Everyone with some sort of secret which might save the day.'

'That's exactly what it's like,' says Slaven. The Beckley-Waite has had at least one positive effect. He has no impatience now with his daughter. He has learnt the value of natural affiliation and affection by being deprived of them.

Slaven wants to talk with Kellie and Sarah, to hold their hands and feel that he's come through. The others however want all of his Count of Monte Cristo memories. Even Miles has an appetite. 'Was it so terrible at the Beckley-Waite place?' asks Eula. 'Was the escape a dangerous thing?'

It's an understandable curiosity and Slaven wishes for a more gripping and charged story to tell: direct and personal malice, rather than indifference and disavowal of responsibility, a series of racy events in which he has a decisive influence on the outcomes, instead of being handed on from one supporter to the next and with sunburn the most apparent threat. He knows how to conjure a tale of course from Ovens's surgical technique, the closest thing to explicable terror in the Beckley-Waite. So he makes the most of it and as the subject is one in which he's professionally adept, he knows he won't be caught out. Maybe in time he will be able to spin all of that place into travesty.

He listens to the others in their turn. The difficulties, the indecisiveness, the faltering of the Coalition. Kellie outlines her idea for a last great rally before the election, with the parties challenged publicly to state how many of the charter points they will support.

Miles gives a hoarse whisper which is his laugh. He has a tale which takes his fancy. 'A woman at Makara said you appeared to her in a vision with a directive to climb to the old pa site on the headland and when she did she found there five bags of stolen groceries and newly-born twins. She was on the news yesterday.'

'There's a crowd again at the house,' says Kellie. 'At the road gate and they say they want to welcome and protect you. I've had to get security again. I've talked with them, but it's no use. They're trampling the shrubs there and doing their business behind the liquid amber and smoke bushes.'

At the table in the cramped kitchen they agree on the great Christchurch rally. Kellie is well-prepared and sets out the priorities. She has made this new garden of politics her own. Slaven determines to tell her how proud he is of her ability.

He will play his full and essential part of course, but even as he works with his committee there is momentarily revealed to him the great cobra of the crowd which he can raise up, but which settles at its own whim. He has caught the stench of its vintage breath, the glint of its mocking eye even as it coils beneath his genie in the night. There are fleeting, facet images there of Colosseum Christians, Jacobin ecstasy and stadium hooligans.

There is a place, isn't there? There is a place in the old school by the sea, where the boys gather to fight. Past the fives courts as you remember, and the boiler room, and the old prefab used for cadets.

'Web belts.'

'Check.'

'Prismatic compasses, one per section.'

'Check.'

'Rifles, drill only.'

'Check.'

Two oak trees in the brown grass there and the staff room far from mind and view. Just the ring of the dragon and two boys of blood within, and the shouts of insensate satisfaction and the tossing of the sea beyond the foreshore. Each of us has been in the dragon's maw.

Slaven doesn't find the cramped, recuperative cottage easeful, despite its artful planning and modern fixtures. He prefers the ruins of the salt works at Lake Grassmere, or the back flat suspended in both time and space above the

Heathcote where Athol and the goose girl live for themselves. But now he has taken up responsibility again and wants to be in his own home and at the head of his organisation.

The authorities have become more amenable now that he is free to manoeuvre and the publicity, the searching questions of Dr Marianne Dunne and the CCP lawyers, the pressure of Miles Kitson's contacts, the union stance, all strike near the bone. So, a sort of stalemate compromise is reached with Slaven allowed freedom, the documents signed by Cardew not released, and in return certain key questions not pressed to the Director of the Beckley-Waite.

So Slaven goes home, openly, but with more precautions taken by the CCP after Lyttelton and the visit of Doctors Eugene and Bliss. Les Croad drives him from the cottage complex through the city and they are shadowed not by the amateur car of Dafydd and Iago Thomas now, but professionals acceptable to Miles. And what a clamour at the entrance to his driveway, where Slaven gives a brief and fiery speech for reporters and supporters. Some of the latter weep at his resurrection and sing *After Tiananmen Square* and *Half Moon Bay*. Slaven hints sufficiently at the great rally which is planned and the cheers of his followers cause a flush of emotion which covers all doubts for the moment. *Let the polar squalls go bowling by, as long as we're still seeing eye to eye.*

Les drives Slaven to the house amid the splendour of Kellie's summer garden — the Chinese ground orchid, butterfly bush, yellow dahlias and showy red justica, the crepe leaves of the golden elms. Les has an air of complacency as if single-handedly he has been responsible for Slaven's escape and return. 'Here you are then,' he says. 'Safe and sound. Where the heart is.'

Kellie has a drink for Slaven set in a part of the garden invisible from the road, though the singing can still be heard for a while. She wishes to keep difficult issues from him just long enough so that they can have their welcome alone. They sit together surrounded by flowers and leaves, they kiss lip to cheek, and as they talk Kellie prepares grapefruit and oranges for a salad. She has all the skills. Slaven thinks of this as he watches her deal with the citrus fruit with absent-minded dexterity. Just as she can effortlessly shuck the shell of boiled eggs, catch things that start to topple, recognise acquaintances by name when confronted in the street and eat any variety of food in all places without leaving a stain down her front. She can ask for the proprietor and deliver a complaint without appearing at all a bitch, put three blooms in a vase and have a talking point, succour Helene Corkery on the phone after her husband has suffered abrupt dementia in Dubbo, Australia, while on a sales trip for computerised cookery manuals.

Kellie has her diary planner and when she's satisfied that Slaven is up to it, they begin to go over the plans for the next few weeks. She has a flair for logistics, but even more valuable she has a flair for management and the two things are by no means the same. She has become the object of interest and admiration in her own right. She features in magazine profiles and has twice been more successful on television than Slaven managed in the 'What's Up Show.' Sheffield says she's a born union negotiator and Eula considers her a wonderful role model for her sisters.

Slaven admires her efficiency and loyalty, her lack of selfish ambition, and he knows he hasn't in him the sort of love that she deserves. In the year so much has happened. He's unable now to maintain the old, comfortable deceits. He cannot love his wife, he dislikes his son, he's disappointed in his daughter, and he's the leader of a national movement based on fellowship. Neither does he love himself — at least he can say that in all fairness.

Slaven and Kellie agree to reorganise the finances of the CCP. An unimpeachable audit so that Cardew's damage is contained, and their enemies won't find corruption to publicise. 'And we'll have to move against those Wellington Executive members who've been undermining everything. Miles has got it all sussed out.' She is neat, wiry, attractive, accepting middle age with the common sense typical of her. Slaven could want no better ally, nor does he, but love is burnt out. If Mrs Boss's horn sounds for her this instant, can he grieve as he should?

It must have been different once; if not then why does he feel the present loss and guilt. But the change has been imperceptible, all of the one thing, so that now he's unable to contrast what was then with a separate now. The accident has not caused, or even accelerated the process, but just made clear to him the point which has been reached.

'Yaa — aa — eech!' Imagine it very sudden and shrill, with just a slight falling away in the middle and a vehement end. Kellie has seen the ginger stray which terrorises her own cat and scratches in the seed beds. A burst of finches in fright from the smoke bush. Maybe even the CCP enthusiasts at the road gate are startled by it. 'That beast of a thing,' she says. Even a minor stampede of some of Slaven's Romneys which have been resting close to the fence in the shadow of Kellie's garden. There are just a few clouds like basking sharks, close to the horizon and a ladybird, reverse orange spots on black, in the hair of Slaven's wrist. What careless beauty. Perhaps he must learn that if you don't love life itself, then no great affection for the separate parts is possible.

'I suppose it's a free-range cat,' says Slaven.

He thinks again of talks with Marianne Dunne concerning the almost complete recall that is possible if the brain is surgically, or electrically, stimulated. Experience complete in all respects, the very sounds, hues and fragrance extant and the impressionistic, emotional responses welling up anew. What can be the reason for the memory having such a store and releasing so little, except to force the organism to go on striving for stimulus and not too readily fall back on time past, in the way that Miles seeks that escape. What has Slaven left of his first schoolroom except the smell of felt pens and the blue of plastic chairs. Thousands of family meals are only a multiple exposure and all the hours in his surgery spun into oblivion except those few moments of danger, or eccentricity, as when Danny Fougerie stopped breathing under anaesthetic and Mrs Wybrow pissed in the chair and claimed that her waters had burst.

Our life recedes to vanishing point and we're left with a small grab-bag of cyphers to represent it. A smack in the face, a lightening storm, a betrayal, Melanie's tartan skirt, the appalling threat that is the sound of the sea wind in a stand of pines, smoke on the winter mist, a text book once known almost by heart and still the title an open sesame to the faces of student friends.

A moral view of responsibility has been replaced by a pharmaceutical one; bulking up, or bulking down, stress management, rape, gambling, anal and mortality fixations, hearing choirs of angels, or the snort of the unicorn when others know there's only traffic noise at a distance — all can be dealt with by delaying the reabsorption of serotonin and norepinephrine in the synaptic gap, or the blocking of the enzyme monoamine oxidase. Pills to prevent life, or prolong it, or end it, have become customary, now too there are drugs to justify, explain and excuse it. The molecular biologists have in the end made a divinity redundant.

Slaven can hear his sheep coming quietly back into the shade. 'What's the story with Cardew, though,' says Kellie. 'We must do something there. It's the one thing that can blow up in our faces before the election. I think we knew all along that he'd be working against us if we let him into any position. There's no doubt about that now, is there.'

'It's hard to believe all the things Miles found out. I'd say he's up to all that and more. Cardy got a whiff of advantage for himself and that's all he cares about. All that happened to me at the Beckley-Waite is up to him in the end. He's been letting us down for years of course. Now he threatens the chances of thousands and thousands of people he's never met.'

'He's ours though,' says Kellie.

'I reckon he's stunted in some way,' says Slaven. 'Maybe it's not all his fault. I don't know.'

'But he's still ours.'

'I don't know what it is about him.'

'I can still hardly believe he brought in the Beckley-Waite doctors.' Kellie finds it difficult to talk of Cardew, to make any decision against him. But it must be made. Although her voice remains controlled, she gets up and touches the foliage of her plants for comfort.

'We tried with him, didn't we?' asks Slaven. 'Did we do such a rotten job? Fed and clothed him, took him to the doctor and the park, helped with his dinosaur projects — well you did, watched him play soccer, put up with his mates coming round, suffered his adolescence petulance. I didn't secretly sodomise him, or thrash him with a dog collar, and I don't suppose you did either. Sarah turned out all right: turned out very well. I bought him a car when he first went to Australia for god's sake, after he didn't want to go back to varsity.'

'It disappointed you.'

'He pranged the damn thing within a month.'

'I mean about going to varsity,' says Kellie. Slaven is arching his back to ease the stiffness he still feels as a result of his cycling escape on the Kaikoura coast. He almost starts talking about Cardew and university, then checks himself and comes back to what is important.

'So what are we going to do?' he asks. From the road gate they hear faintly the querulous discussion as another group of devotees is firmly prevented from approaching the house. Will there be more infiltration of the grounds in the night? More dancing beneath a gibbous moon and the casting of spices against the wall? The CCP supporters sing the anthem, *Half Moon Bay*, while Kellie and Slaven decide how to rid themselves of their son.

'It'll have to be right out, cut off, not just for our sake, or the Coalition's, but for his own. He'll do something really stupid and they'll arrest him to get at us,' says Kellie.

'It'll come down to buying him off. You know that. There's no better nature, no sense of responsibility, or guilt. It'll be a combination of threat if he doesn't go back to Aussie and reward for doing it.'

'A form of exile really, I suppose,' says Kellie. She is still moving amongst her plants. 'For his own good and essential for the run up to the elections.'

Kinder hearts are waiting, baby, amongst old friends at Half Moon Bay.

'Sla-VEN, Sla-VEN, Sla-VEN.'

'Who are these people all the time?' says Slaven.

He remembers a holiday in the Queen Charlotte Sounds, not all that far from Mahakipawa perhaps. The four of them in a dinghy at the point and instead of blue cod, both Cardy and Sarah hooked up a starfish and none of them had caught one before, or did after. Cardew insisted that his be stuck on his bare back and he wore it there all the way to the shore, even though it slowly crawled over his skin. The brightness of its orange colour still burns in Slaven's mind. Cardy bent forward on the wooden seat to encourage the starfish to stick, grinning as the centre of attention and daring Sarah to stick hers on as well. The colour of an old-fashioned pumpkin and all the myriad feelers writhing underneath. 'So you'll see him soon then?' says Kellie.

'I've asked him to come tomorrow. He pretended that there was nothing we needed to settle of course, that he's been going great guns on my behalf all this time.'

Those within an organisation often base their personal opinion of their leader on the extent to which tough issues are faced, which is quite a different thing from the public conception of how successful, or unsuccessful, a person may be. Slaven knows that the people in the Coalition he most relies on are watching to see if he's prepared to tackle Cardew's corruption, faithlessness, opportunism. For every–thing that's been proved there's almost certainly a double betrayal, but between father and son special, extenuating circumstances are always in force, aren't they? Isn't it a son's function to usurp his father's powers and shouldn't the father despite all disappointment and provocation in the end present himself as pelican? A son who supplants his father by any means assures his own future — a father who defeats his son destroys the future of them both.

'Sla-VEN, Sla-VEN, Sla-VEN.'

'Maybe you should go down and talk to them. Capitalise on your return.'

'Once I did that, there'd be ten times as many. They'd swarm over the paddocks despite the security and hide in the garden here. They'd garrote themselves with trellis ties, make sacrifice in the bird bath and flatten their faces on the window panes. Thackeray said there were three more electrocutions yesterday; one here in Christchurch. A retired Harbour Board navigation instructor who said that the world was to end with my deliverance from the Beckley-Waite and climbed into the Addington substation.'

'I hoped you hadn't heard,' says Kellie. She sits beside him again. She puts one hand over one of his.

'So you'll talk to him tomorrow?'
'Yes.'

So he comes. They don't touch, but Cardew says how pleased he is that his father's looking good and that he'd been working closely with the others to put pressure on so that Slaven would be released the minute he was well enough. A few sentences is all that Cardew needs to include some sort of lie. Slaven notices his son's big feet and the way he walks with his hands busy — trying to occupy a little more space than he can naturally fill. The distaste between them is heavy on the air, a reason perhaps for them both to prefer their meeting outdoors.

'Let's not try to fool each other,' Slaven says.

'Cut the crap you mean?' Even his language he knows, is a way to antagonise his father.

'Okay, cut the crap. You see I know what you've been up to. All the deals and little scams. The money that's ending up in your pockets, the kick-backs from some of the parties, the women you kindly interview on the Coalition's behalf, you and Pollen and Marr and others in Wellington.'

They argue in the double garage overhang and it is raining, as it was raining when Dr Eugene and Dr Bliss came down from the Beckley-Waite at Cardew's invitation. This time it is his turn to take a trip into the rain. The garden in which Slaven and Kellie talked yesterday is bowed with it, blossom and leaf drenched and so drawing the slighter stems down. There are puddles on the broad, paved turning circle in front of the garages and the heavy rain impacts there, forming clear bubbles even, which drift for a moment and then are gone. The worked soil of the plots, always fertile in Kellie's garden, is darker, richer, in the rain and seems to breast up.

'Miles tells you all this stuff, I suppose. The old stoat. The stinking, old stoat. Got a finger in everything, including up your arse.' Cardew is still young. I'm young, his look says and the voice beneath the words also. He's guilty of every accusation made and more. He's selfish, weak, ignorant and unimaginative; less than his father in all the things that don't matter as much as that he's young, and

Miles old and dying and Slaven ageing. What has right, or wrong, got to do with a sense of life.

Neither Cardew, nor his father, express anything of this as Slaven lays down the deal that Cardew must relinquish any connection with the CCP, go back to Australia and in return he'll get enough money to start some sort of business there and no action will be taken on what he's done. 'So I'm wiped off like an arse,' Cardew says. Yet he is young, see, young.

'You're still part of the family. Kellie and I will stick to that,' says Slaven and Cardew's eyes slide away with a boredom as absolute as if the subject has become non-penetrative sex. Slaven sees his son's face in all its unleavened physicality. Slaven has been disappointed — more, betrayed — so often by his son that the original love has become detached and persists only as a less specific, nagging pain, rather like a stomach ulcer.

'How much?' asks Cardew.

'How much?' Is it affection he wishes to quantify.

'How much will you give me to get started?'

Kellie maintains precise boundaries between lawn and garden and the water begins to collect in the small moats there, stretching back like a line of quicksilver in the light of a rainy day. It isn't the parting that either of them would have wished. 'I suppose you have your own beliefs,' says Slaven.

'Yes, you're a long time dead is what I say.' And he is young.

So see him off, yes, certainly that, with the rain still heavy and the two of them standing in the garage doorway. 'We'll come out with Sarah to the airport when you go,' Slaven tells him and Cardew gives his smile which turns down at the last moment. They glance into the rain which hachures the sky and sounds on the garage roof.

'I never liked this as much as the old place in Allen Street,' says Cardew. 'It's too far out of town.' People say they're alike physically in some ways and in some mannerisms. Judge for yourself as you watch them. The small, but fleshy, ears perhaps, the narrow wrists which make by contrast their hands appear large, a way of dipping a shoulder when they are called and turn back. Cardew has lost somewhat more of the dark hair than his father — yet he is young, young. Baldness is inherited through the mother, Slaven has told Kellie with some complacency.

'Two hundred thousand isn't that much,' says Cardew, 'when you're talking about a business. Anyway, I hope that the big Hagley Park rally goes off okay. I really do. Just remember that the blue bird of happiness can so soon become the chicken of despair.' He has turned back from his car to say it with a laugh and his shoulder dips; the rain already wetting down his hair exaggerates his young baldness and the two of them look just past each other as they make farewell.

'See you later then,' says Slaven as he sends his son into exile. And so epigone is, yes, gone.

Kellie and Slaven go on to the ostentatious house on the Cashmere Hills after talks with the Regional Council officers in which civic apprehensions concerning the coming rally are quietened. Miles has a German housekeeper and a Chinese gardener, gathered somehow in his business travels, though Georgina claims the roles should be reversed. He has a nurse, too, all Kiwi, who leaves Slaven and Miles together once the latter's artificial kidney has been replaced. There is a brief spiral of life blood in the catheter. Miles chooses a green silk shirt to cover it. 'Just like an oil filter really,' he says. 'I can wear it strapped to my stomach. There's a knack to everything you know, even dying.'

They have their meal in the tower, with the city of the plains traced with lights of pulsating, jewelled colour. Miles especially loves such evenings with his wife and the Slavens. He calls them his patient reunions and is intrigued by the irony of his support for Slaven and the CCP when he is utterly in disagreement with most of the beliefs they have. He has a sneer of pure delight to hear Kellie talk with conviction of the common interest as a means of gaining support, for he has long understood that the common interest is far too broad and too just an application to make anyone enthusiastic. Only personal and factional advantage provide an urgent motivation. A notion of fair play, justice, is unknown in nature and one of the most recent masquerades in human society.

'He likes to play at cynicism,' says Georgina, 'because somehow he thinks it appropriate for his success.' She is fully-dressed, and just as lovely, at the table tonight so as not to scandalise the guests. They are having venison for the main with a burgundy and ginger sauce. Miles is not allowed the sauce. They are having a turn-of-the-century Haut-Brion. Miles is not allowed the Haut-Brion, but has it all the same. He drinks it as a libation and his old face smiles.

'Until you are determined on a thing which runs counter to the wishes of everyone else,' he says, 'you never understand the force convention has; just as you don't realise the menace of the crowd when you're moving with it.'

'If what I was determined on was opposed by everyone else, then I'd question myself again,' says Slaven.

'The great majority of people are fools, as Ibsen said.'

'Present company excepted,' says Kellie.

'We're not supposed to think it of course,' Miles continues, 'but it's true. You only have to look at their entertainments to recognise that. Comparative programme ratings and the response to the most fatuous advertising are the best indicators of the real mentality we exhibit. The welfare of a fool is as important as the welfare of a non-fool in a democracy no doubt, but unfortunately the mass opinion is unlikely to achieve it for either. Most people are in a community because they believe that they can get more out of the association than they put in.'

'I suppose you have to put up with this hog-wash whenever he starts to drink?' Slaven asks Georgina.

'No, it's something he tries to impress visitors with. Most of the time he watches the programmes he says he hates, or tells me stories about his prime.'

'Lies,' says Miles in delight.

'He's like so...'

'Georgina has a marvellous pair of tits, but she slanders me all the time.'

'You're like so many really successful people,' says Kellie, 'because in your own way you've excelled, yet secretly consider yourself mediocre, you assume that all those who haven't done as well must be stupid. It's not like that.'

'Mediocre. Mediocre,' says Miles hoarsely. He has long since become sick of deference and loves any abuse from his friends. 'I bring you into my house and feed you and you turn on me. You've become a very proud, authoritarian woman since the CCP has made celebrities of you both.' The artificial kidney is only a slight bulge beneath his green, silk shirt, his wife is happy, the Haut-Brion is a pleasure and Slaven has told him of the strange, off-hand way in which Cardew went. So little passion, or action, in it as is his way.

'It's your generalisations which let you down,' says Slaven. 'You've been away from the people you categorise for too long. Most are this, some are that, such and such a percentage are something else. That's where you go wrong. Individuals aren't constant, they show a range of vices and virtues from time to time. Today's judicious person is tomorrow's fool. Maybe a majority take a wrong view, but the significant thing is that almost all of them are capable of seeing their own error. I'm in touch with that you see. I'm able now to bring the best out in people.'

'You do,' says Kellie simply.

'I know it sounds arrogant like that, but if I didn't believe it I couldn't keep pushing myself forward.'

'You're a power-hungry dentist,' says Miles. 'You've this secret ambition to be a pop star.'

Baby, baby, come again and live with me upon the shore of Half Moon Bay. Georgina begins the singing of it and Kellie then Slaven and Miles take it up. *Kinder hearts are waiting, baby, amongst old friends at Half Moon Bay.* It's not likely to rival the Hoihos' original, particularly with the respiratory deficiencies that Miles has, but the four of them enjoy it around the walnut table in the tower. The city shimmers on the plain below them and a constant wind adds a hollow whistle as a backing. The German housekeeper, who is agile and dark, smiles from the doorway and holds off on the Black Forest Gateau for a while longer. Slaven leans to his friend.

'You know, I've never actually been to Half Moon Bay,' he tells him.

'Most of us haven't,' says Miles, 'that's why we've taken it so much to heart.'

'What motivates all these people who come to your Coalition rallies?' he says. 'What do they imagine will be the consequence of such a show of electoral solidarity?' He himself is always uncertain of the degree to which one person is able to comprehend another. The link between signified and signifier seems both multifarious and tenuous as he grows older. What is loaves to one, is fishes to another, what is leadership becomes subjugation, what is intended as testimony becomes interpreted as confession. 'What do they want of you?' he asks Slaven with a sudden seriousness which prevents them continuing the line of conversation. For both know that the supporters, whatever slogans they endorse and whatever programmes they march for, want from Slaven all the fierce, private glories which they're unable to provide for themselves.

'I'm coming to the Hagley Park rally,' says Georgina. 'I've warned Miles that he'll be left here. I want to see Aldous's aura that they talk about and watch him whip up everyone's feelings. Sarah said she'll go with me.'

'You'll need to improve your singing,' says Slaven.

'The Government's got the wind up about it, I think.' Kellie's sharp face is eager in the candle-light. She stops eating at the thought of this final, great rally. 'Royce Meelind rang me to get details. He had to say it was all routine of course, but I could tell there's a good deal of anxiety about what's going to happen. Locally they're raising various obstacles of one sort or another, without admitting they don't want it to go ahead.'

'It'll be a real cracker,' says Slaven.

'It's nearly all set to go,' says Kellie.

'I wouldn't miss it,' says Georgina.

Miles in the exchange is able to pour himself more wine, without Georgina feeling the need to notice. He is relaxed, enjoying the present well enough, also allowing his mind to range beyond it. In recent years he has realised that some of his time was wasted in doing too much. Last night he had a dream about his life having taken a different turn. He was voyaging on a forest river where everything was new, the fruited jungle crowding to the slow water's edge and parrots in livery of flashing yellow and red, criss-crossing as heralds of his arrival. And he had an absolute and benign assurance that he was coming home. 'I had a dream last night,' he says,' about my life having taken quite a different turn.' Miles thinks most people miss the real significance of dreams. They're confused by the distortion of incident and appearance without realising that the emotion is always true. In dreams the quiet person may be paid that admiration so often due, and adulterers may awake in tears because they have restored to them the early joy of marriage.

So Miles shares his dream. There is laughter and ease. Cardew's jet far above the Tasman, the lapping of the jetty water amongst the hair of the mussels, might seem a world away. Yet there's no linear progression you remember and our own future is going on now, except that it's happening to someone else.

Slaven is very busy revitalising the Coalition and preparing for the rally. Kellie plots his time for him in a diary; designated sections for all the day and a good part of the night. Even rests must be consciously provided for, and she won't have them pushed out by last minute demands on his attention.

Slaven is having a rest between eight thirty and nine, when he's to be picked up by Les Croad and taken into the city to do a talk-back with Pamela Greene, Mouth of the South. So he lies on his study sofa with his belt loosened and his shoes off. There's still light, but it's not a harsh light and after rubbing the bases of his thumbs awhile, a habit which persists from the time they were healing, Slaven falls asleep.

Sarah wakes him by coming into the room. In the moment that comes with his awakening and before his attention is fully-focused, he knows that he's been dreaming. All of it has fallen immediately beyond conscious recall, except the last thing spoken. 'The Caretaker will see you now, Dr Slaven,' and there was the fragrance of the weed. No context at all remains for the line, but the voice itself is there and the vestiges of the pleasure with which he received the invitation.

He sees that his daughter has been crying. 'I just want to say I'm sorry,' she says.

'Sorry?'

'I'm not able to give you much support. I know you're disappointed in me and in Cardy too and I'd like it to be different, but I haven't got the brains. I see the things that happen to you, but I can't be there in any way that helps. Do you see? I'd just like to be able to say the right things, but I haven't got them in me. I haven't got the brains enough to get alongside you.'

For a moment the pain of love is such that he can't speak, and having woken suddenly, the more calculated defences against emotion are down. Slaven sits up clumsily; his feet smell he thinks and this embarrasses him. He takes her left hand in both of his and he looks with longing into her face. 'Not at all,' he says. 'Don't say it. Don't ever say it. It's just that we're two adults now and what comes between us is the ache of having once been father and daughter in that special, original way. You see what I mean? You can't go back to it and what you move on to is always something less, isn't it. Even with Cardy I suppose there was a bit of that and there's nothing can be done. It's a metamorphosis and a different thing entirely comes out of it, quite beyond our control. So there's no blame in any of it.'

'Tonight I'm going to listen to all of the talk back and get a proper grip on your ideas. Then I'll listen to the Tuamarina, or Western Springs, tape. They're so long aren't they. I just don't know how you think of enough to say. And mum said the best article is probably the one in Pacifica. Maybe I can help then.'

'I just want people to have a better deal, that's all. More influence on what happens to them and a sense of dynamic community.'

'In my full horoscope for this month, November's the best time for renewing old ties and friendships. It's a very definite indication. Isn't that a spooky thing, just when I've decided to do more for you.'

'That's a spooky thing all right.' The tears run down the back of his throat. He wishes his hands more sensitive to touch.

'I think it's wonderful, all the things you're doing now with the Coalition and that, after the accident. In her book, Anastasia says that illness — not that yours was, but you know what I mean — can be a spiritual redirection. You know? That it's the body's way of responding to the imperative of the psyche. I'm convinced that's so right, absolutely so right. Don't you just think?'

'It may be. May well be.' He has in his life believed more with less foundation, for causes not as precious to him.

'I'm getting so much more interest in my work now that people realise who I am.'

'Just make sure you always have an optimistic prognostication for the CCP and your dad. I'm counting on your skills. With the Zodiac behind us, how can we go wrong.'

'I know you're having me on,' she says, 'but you'll see.'

'I'm ignorant rather than sceptical.'

'You're having me on.'

'Just a bit.'

She seems quite happy again, and why not? It's all a lottery isn't it, or read in the stars. She could have been born with a harelip, or as a Down's syndrome baby. She could have swollen out to be the school fatty, or closed up in autistic isolation. To be both pretty and shallow may be a cause for celebration even, after all the unexamined life is often the happier for that.

'How does it feel when you really get going with the speaking,' she says. 'When you take off the way you do.'

'It feels as if at last I'm able to give of myself and there's both release and refreshment in that. Strangely enough, the more people there are the less self-conscious I am, as if a totality of fellowship is made stronger and stronger by weight of numbers.'

'Not even speech notes, though.'

'It's odd, Sarah. I trust energy and passion that comes to me when I get up to speak.'

'Mum says something may have been gained even out of the accident.'

'Or something burnt away,' says Slaven. 'Some people at religious conversion say they felt their hearts strangely warmed, perhaps my brain was fried.'

'It's not something to joke about really,' she says. 'I read in this magazine that we only use about one tenth of our brain and all the rest is there to be drawn on if we knew how to do it.'

'I think something's going on, but it doesn't always let us know.'

So they are talking there, father and daughter, when Les Croad comes to collect him and Slaven gets a real kick out of it, even if he knows that their interests are far apart. It's the mutual intention he finds comforting. He sees himself briefly in the long mirror, insubstantial in the waning, natural light. How should we describe him then, as he goes out in a pleasant frame of mind to the talk-back? Quite a sizeable, omnivorous mammal with upright, bi-pedal gait, a large head and life expectancy of three score and ten.

The helicopter comes suddenly over the dark, pine shelter belts with the sound of a dog being sick. Over those buildings of the old Burnham Camp which remain to be used from time to time in transit by refugee immigrants — from China, from South Africa and Kurdistan. The down-draught seems immense to Slaven and together with the retching noise bewilders him momentarily so that he sways back and gives a laugh of nervous release. The long, summer grass swirls beneath the wind of the rotor as the helicopter puts down on what has once been a close-mown parade field with stones painted white, with the cries of NCOs and squads in perfect time. WO2 Slaven has been there too, in a more junior rank, has carried a gonad half of his son across the place to which he's come again. The self-same son, the self-same sun, the same radiata pines grown taller from the same pale yellow loess and shingle.

'One lined parka.'
'Check.'
'One housewife kit.'
'Check.'
'One Johnny Walker, illegal.'
'Check.'
'One standard-bearer of resilience.'
'Check.'

'One father in the hereafter.'

'Check.'

On the chopper's side are emblazoned the words, 'Muche Safaris', which is one of Miles Kitson's firms. When the blades finish turning, they droop as if for rest. The pilot wouldn't switch off at all, except that Miles is to board as well and as he's a hesitant walker the climb into the machine is a business of considerable care and complexity. Also the pilot knows full well the deference that the old guy is due. The last echoes of the motor and rotor flee like receding wingbeats through the pines. The pilot rotates his helmet to see his passengers, ant sheen to his head, and slips his harness. Slaven and Miles walk slowly out into the field, the small and harmonious noises of the natural surroundings gradually reforming around them. The brown top rustling at their feet, sheep coughing from the paddock beyond the trees, cicadas coming back on song, a high bird too bright in the sun to look at, the half whisper, half whistle, of the easterly through the wind breaks and the fence wires.

Miles's breathing is as audible and persistent as any of it. His mouth is open to make it easier for him and as Slaven takes his arm he feels the skin sliding directly upon the bone. Miles has nothing physical that he can trust anymore and every trip is a calculation and deliberate effort and awareness of body diminished. Yet he still has the frame and power of his mind and thanks fate for that. 'What a companion for your only rest day before the rally,' he whispers. 'Thanks, thanks. Just see that I don't fall backwards when we're getting in. I've lost any quick reaction to my own failings and to think that there were nights when I could leap and pluck the moon one-handed from the sky.'

Both the pilot and Slaven would be surprised if told that the cockpit was familiar to Miles, given a few more technical advances since he was accustomed to fly himself from plant to plant, but he says nothing of it, can't be bothered with the effort of getting it out, or the element of personal vanity it would reveal. So he sits quietly and seems impressed by the skills of the best man that his 'Muche Safaris' can provide.

As they rise up, Miles remembers his first meeting with

Mr Ng, sixty-plus stories high in old Hong Kong and the whole restaurant rotating slowly so that as Miles talked with Mr Ng they could see the skyscrapers of the island around them, then the bulk of Mount Victoria, then in its turn the sea and the towers of Kowloon and the ferries going back and forth. Mr Ng had explained gently how concerned he was about the takeover and the faith he had in Miles as a potential partner for New Zealand investment. He said that he knew there was respect for Miles in Germany. Miles remembers how few hairs were in Mr Ng's eyebrows, scarcely three or four above each eye, how perfectly absorbed and still he was when listening, how scrupulous he proved to be in all his business dealings.

The chopper does a long arc before it sets direction and on the camber Slaven and Miles tilt their necks slightly and unconsciously to remain level-headed. The patchwork of the Canterbury Plains in subdued summer tones lies beneath them, marked in the gravel soils with a myriad sinuous contours of the old waterways which have built it up and the lines of willow, lupin and gorse which follow those braided channels which still have intermittent flow. Over Methven, Mount Somers and the moraines until the mountains rise abruptly and the Rangitata lies in its great glacial valley. The Havelock, the Clyde and the Lawrence are its headwaters and beyond that the perched snowfield known as The Garden Of Eden. Miles points it out to Slaven as they hang like a gnat in the clear air. Miles climbed there years ago and now he has lost his strength while the snowfield endures, glistening as an ermine pelt among the black-sided peaks. 'Look at that then.' says Miles in his rueful, hoarse voice. The westerly is blowing cloud up the other side of the Alps and it begins to show as a white, breaking surge at the divide, but for the present the sun still glitters on The Garden Of Eden, on the snow of the eastern mountain sides and the outcrops of rock, dark and gleaming because of the thaw. Even the pilot, whose livelihood is commercial scenery, cocks his head back and nods to affirm the impact of such country.

The helicopter hangs above the Rangitata like a gnat and Slaven resists the thought that it might fall, topple from its high point to the rock and tussock below. Miles has the same thought in his own way — and welcomes it. Instead the chopper lets itself noisily down, dog-retchingly efficient, until it is above the Erewhon Alpine Camp which has those words painted on the roof of the recreation centre for skiers. There is a line of single family chalets, quite modern, and the old dormitory block for budget accommodation. And the scale of it, almost the very existence, mocked by the endless landscape still going its own way.

'There's some group in at the moment,' says Miles as they sit with the rotors flagging and the noise dying away. There's a cluster of cars and vans in the park and a few people coming and going around the restaurant and recreation building. 'An ecology tour party, probably. They're very popular with Europeans. Where they come from you can't see a horizon for the haze.'

'Muche Safaris' has an interest in the Camp, which means that Miles is a part-owner in effect. He climbs out cautiously with Slaven and the pilot in attendance. Miles thinks finally to introduce them and the pilot says he's a CCP supporter; been to meetings even, addressed by Thackeray Thomas and Kellie while Slaven was in the Beckley-Waite Institute. 'I'll be at the rally. You can put a ring around that,' he says.

The pilot heads for the office. Slaven and Miles walk slowly towards the new chalets to visit Mr Ng. It's hot, yet on the mountain slopes, seeming closer in the clear air, the snow still lies despite the sun, and the west wind, unfelt here, still drives cloud to the top of the range and it builds there, ready to spill over. It will be pissing down on the coast.

Do you know the place? Sure you do. Up Lizard Gully there's that bit of stunted native bush, barely hanging on, but bush all the same. The creek choked with boulders and its catchment just screes and bare, eroding spikes and ridges. And you cross the broad scree fans at a trot so that you don't get caught in any slide that you start and the stone that was the mountain rattles away beneath your feet — another process of dissolution. Dark sedimentaries, slates and shales, some of it with fossils laid down beneath the sea and now it lies thousands of metres up beneath The Garden Of Eden.

Mr Ng and two of his staff are staying in the chalet with the best view across the flat expanse of the glacial valley and the braided channels of the Rangitata with the white-grey of the greywacke shingle. On the other side is Mesopotamia station and the sudden mountains behind. Mr Ng knows all about Slaven, all about the leadership gift discovered by accident — yes — in middle age and the political power as a consequence of it. As a business man he sees the possible advantage in it, but he's too polite to talk of matters which Slaven and Miles don't themselves raise. There will be time perhaps when Slaven has shown that his grasp more nearly equals his reach.

Since the change in China Mr Ng spends much of each year in the south there, not far from Macao. He has a grey brick home built in the style of the old double-level farm-houses and from the upper windows he can see the people making pilgrimage to the family home of Dr Sun Yat-sen. Most of the carpets sold at the gates there are from one of Mr Ng's industries. He is in retirement he says, but has agreed to act as an advisor for what has been termed the protective modernisation of the region.

'This for you must be one of the few quiet times amongst many busy hours,' Mr Ng says to Slaven. His English carries a variety of influences, most strongly that of Hong Kong in colonial times. He is much the same age as his friend Miles, but showing it less, because there has always been little flesh and bone on which age could take effect. He's a very slight man, very tight and instead of a face sagging outwards. Mr Ng is in a process of gradual dessication, with the skin moulded to the fine bones and no sign of moisture in all the glitter of his eye.

'I've persuaded him to have this one break, one quiet day in the preparation for the Coalition rally, then he's back in the cauldron,' says Miles to his old friend.

'The election makes it all doubly hectic,' says Slaven. 'It's got to be a king-hit affair. I imagine that you've had a good deal to do with politics yourself.'

'Only as an advisor,' says Mr Ng. 'Someone else must then make a decision and be publicly accountable for it.' He and Miles smile together: men whose power is quietly exercised in the main and not dependent on popularity, but practical matters like supply and demand. Spiritual hungers they tend to avoid.

From the chalet they can all see the bare mountains on the other side of the river and nothing seems to move in all their view. 'What a contrast this must be for you,' says Slaven. 'All this towering, empty country.'

'Amazing certainly and very restful, contemplative. Yes, very different from Hong Kong, or Wuchow, but in China there's a great deal of very high, cold country, also bare. It's this inland China that Erewhon reminds me of, except that here the country is not so strongly marked by the signs of people's persistent failure.' A small group of figures has come from the main building below the chalets. Several remain there talking. Three others walk slowly in discussion up to the dormitory block.

'What's the group in at the moment?' asks Miles.

'I'm told they are enthusiasts for one of the great writers of your country,' says Mr Ng. 'Is it Button, Bustler? I'm sorry.'

'Samuel Butler, I suppose,' says Miles. 'Erewhon.'

'That'll be it,' says Slaven. He has read nothing of Butler's, knows nothing of his life except that he lived briefly here and that Erewhon commemorates it. 'Erewhon, right,' he says.

'Ah, Samuel Butler. Butler.' Mr Ng is pleased to have it right. 'It is some special time for Samuel Butler,' he says.

And what would Samuel make of it? If he could look across from his hut at Mesopotamia and see the zig-zag road up to the ski-fields, the new chalets of the Erewhon lodge, the hard shell of the helicopter winking in the sun and a gathering of enthusiasts for his later work. Seminars on his Italian travels and his discovery that Homer was a woman; toasts in his honour. Vindicated, wouldn't you say, is how he'd feel. His bitterness assuaged after the sustained contemporary neglect. And he'd notice perhaps that despite the one road, the ski-track, the few buildings, the modest gathering of his fans, the great Rangitata was unchanged. 'That torrent pathway of desolation,' he called it. From the Mesopotamia hut of course he would not have heard the three of them in Mr Ng's chalet — two men of great wealth and a renowned political activist — even though they're talking of him. Maybe you yourself know something of the man and his friends. Jones, whom he visited in old age bearing bottles of turtle soup, Pauli who was the handsomest man god ever sent to San Francisco, and Hans Rudolph Fäesch, murdered by a discarded native mistress in 1903. Quietus now.

Maybe of course Butler would be surprised and delighted to hear that there's been an unauthorised release of snow leopards in the High Country and that they've become quite established.

Slaven leaves Miles and Mr Ng to their reminiscences and walks in the sun towards the communal buildings. He has a feeling of both release and relief.

He meets up with the group of three, two men and a woman, all middle-aged and with intelligent faces which show no immediate recognition, or expectation, as he joins them. They stand with their backs to the warm wood of the dormitory block and Slaven introduces himself just as Aldous. There is scattered gorse and briar on the river bed, glints of water in the channels, the abrupt mountains beyond with the great bench marks of ancient glaciers well up their sides.

Yes, they're members of the Samuel Butler Society they say and here to celebrate his association with the place. Forty-two of them apart from the three talking with Slaven and including some from overseas. Professor Hankie from the University of Swansea has come even and a deaf woman from Beth Car whose family once lived at the Butler rectory in Langar.

'When was he here?' asks Slaven. These people want nothing from him. They have no barrow to push apart from their love of a didactic Victorian writer with a tenuous New Zealand connection. Slaven finds it a luxury to talk of anything, anything, but the CCP and the coming rally. The taller of the two men has the wonderfully gaunt face of a prize-winning physicist and tells Slaven that in 1862 Butler did a pen-and-ink sketch of his hut at Mesopotamia and clearly labelled Mount Potts and the Jumped Up Downs on the Erewhon side of the river. The other two enjoying the sun are the McElries, husband and wife. Mr McElrie is a great repository of quotes from Butler's works and he intersperses them amongst the conversation of others whatever the subject. He smiles to himself in a preparatory sort of way before delivering each gem and usually looks away modestly in the act of it. 'While to deny the existence of an unknown kingdom is bad, to pretend that we know more about it than its bare existence is no better,' says Mr McElrie, regarding the chalets.

'Tomorrow,' says the physicist, who is a master butcher from Gore. 'we're all going over to the Mesopotamia side for photographs and then in the afternoon Professor Hankie is going to give the keynote address. If the weather holds, we'll tramp the Butler Pass the next day; well at least the fit amongst us. Do you know much about the great man?' Mr McElrie has his smile and quotation ready before Slaven can reply.

'Life is one long process of getting tired,' he says.

Mrs McElrie's speciality is personal and rather salacious material. 'Lucie Dumas was the mistress he shared with Jones. Butler visited her once a week for many years.'

'Dumas. How wonderfully appropriate,' says Slaven. By what chance are they here, the four of them, in the barren beauty of the glacial valley, gateway to a mirror image of Butler's Utopia. Slaven draws satisfaction from the thought that the peaks, the headwaters of the Rangitata, The Garden Of Eden, will all be the same after the CCP rally, after the elections, after the four of them have moved on as Butler moved on. McElrie is smiling.

'Every man's work is always a portrait of himself.'

'A young student at Heatherley's art studio once asked him if New Zealand was not the place where the hot water grows wild,' adds Mrs McElrie.

'Samuel was born on December 4th,' says the physicist. He thinks that Slaven as a stranger to the life, should first be acquainted with a sound historical context, rather than anecdotal material. 'His grandfather was the famous Samuel Butler of Shrewsbury — the school not the biscuit.'

Slaven can feel the warmth of the weatherboards of the old building behind him and the sun shines on his face so that his eyes lower before it. If he'd stayed at the Coalition office rather than coming with Miles, he would most likely be deciding with Kellie and the executive the endless questions generated by the run-up to the elections. Some matters of grand political strategy, others as trivial as the slavenisms for bumper stickers — Politics Is Not A Party, People As The End And Means.

'To live is like to love,' quotes McElrie. 'All reason is against it, and all healthy instinct for it.'

'When Butler travelled from Bologne to Basel by train in 1887 it was so cold between Chalons and the Swiss frontier that snow drifted in from the windows and piled up on the window seats so that Butler, alone in the carriage, had to huddle in the middle.' The physicist's description gains a greater impact by its contrast with the Erewhon in which it's told. The shimmer of heat past the helipad which makes the figures of the red deer vibrate behind the high wires fences, a hawk drifting across the blue. Yet closer to the sun are peaks of snow.

'Samuel had no normal family instincts,' says Mrs McElrie. 'He particularly hated his father and continually wished him dead. Not just for the inheritance either.'

'Is that right.'

'But a true sense of humour,' protests the physicist, who is a successful landscape gardener from Nelson. The sliver of his tongue works in the dry air. 'At one meal with his two helpmates here, no one else for scores of miles, he was suddenly struck by the coincidence of their three names — Butler, Baker and Cook.' In perfect timing the physicist and the McElries burst into laughter. It's obviously a treasured joke amongst the enthusiasts. Slaven looks across to Mesopotamia and imagines the young Butler making his witticism there in the hut, determined perhaps that it would survive to bear repetition in just such a way.

It is noon of this week day and Slaven is here at Erewhon with the deer, the Lodge, the long valley road empty for as much of its length as he can see, and three literary pilgrims. Well, isn't he? Is he at the Coalition headquarters at the Chenny Centre now that they have outgrown the rooms of the Charismatic Cambrian Church, weighing up offers which have been made which involve electoral endorsement in return. Is he in the West Wing lounge of the Beckley-Waite, pitting his wits against those of Philip Mathieson for the last wine biscuit, while Neville Kingi sneaks out a fart. Has he stayed with Mr Ng and Miles in the top chalet, listening to the understatements of commercial power and glancing down the slope to the physicist and the McElries who are still mute and anonymous. Is he in his own surgery with a patient open-mouthed before him and none of the other things begun, or necessary. He uses the new medication to inhibit salivation and is a master with the laser drill, but his most innovative work is with polymers which he uses against gum-level notching. From his swivel seat at the patient's head he can look up to see his Modigliani print and enjoy the elongated colours of the cat's eyes again. Is he with his wife in their garden, thinking of Erewhon amidst the foliage and flowers; with the Hoihos' *Half Moon Bay* and Kellie's watchful care. Is he lying in the Earl of Athlone rhododendron with the smell of sparks and something happened to his heart.

McElrie smiles. 'Childhood and old age hold the citadels of extremes and between them stretches the low landscape of compromise.'

'Oddly enough,' says the physicist, 'John Baker, who had explored the upper Rangitata with him, met up with him again by accident in a hotel in Rome, in 1892. Well, we'd better go down for the talk on The Fair Haven before lunch.' He invites Slaven to go with them, but when he refuses the three move away, though Mrs McElrie darts back for a moment to give Slaven a last insight into Samuel's mind.

'He said that the three most important things a man has are his private parts, his money and his religious opinions.' She doesn't wait for his thanks, but follows her husband and the physicist, turning her head to say, 'I know who you are,' as she goes.

Slaven is content to have some time to himself. It's the reason in fact that he's come, the reason he argued so vehemently that his minders weren't necessary in such an impromptu wilderness. Soon now he will face a great crowd again; will draw out of himself to feed them all. He walks up the pump creek behind the Lodge buildings and finds a flat, warm rock in the tussock to sit on. There are lichens on it, some yellow and very close-pressed, some blue-grey and offering purchase for Slaven's fingers as he sits and thinks. He has committed himself and the movement to one last, great rally before the elections and while the parties are most susceptible. His supporters are entitled to that surely. There are paradise duck in pairs scouting up the valley and a lone person lying on a towel behind the dormitory. A Butler enthusiast with the sort of individual perversity that Samuel had himself, or one who insists on a harder political reading of the works than Professor Hankie is willing to provide.

Power has to be exercised in order to be retained, displayed to prevent its usurpation. Slaven understands that. Having made the decision not to run candidates itself, but develop electoral pressure to gain the adoption of its policies by existing parties, the CCP has to demonstrate massive voter endorsement dramatically and regularly. And once the election is over the impact of that will be lessened. Kellie and the other leaders consider that the mood and the time are right for the big one. Even Miles has said that if you have a whip then you might as well crack it.

A degree of risk has to be taken — the risk that the power of the crowd prove finally incorrigible, that the serpent aroused choose sooner or later to serve its own ends.

It's tempting also to accept the apparent distancing that Erewhon provides by the permanence of elemental things, for Slaven to persuade himself that all human action is petty, that one more political rally before one more election will not alter the scheme of things a jot. That's always been an easy out, hasn't it, and there is enough cynicism in Slaven for him to feel the blandishment of the idea, but not enough for him to be convinced. That the oceans, mountains and stars maintain a set configuration isn't proof that an individual's actions are futile. That the effects will be minimised, trivialised, forgotten, or taken as inevitable in any case should be no consideration either.

Slaven thinks of Athol on the cherry leather of his Harley Hog and the goose girl's simple pleasures. He imagines the Caretaker discreetly latching the window of the room two down from the emergency ALW, or standing in the darkened courtyard late at night to smoke his pipe and plan improvements at Mahakipawa Hill, the entreaty man who is convinced marvellous things will be achieved and has told everyone so, the hundreds who besiege his office and camp at his road gate, the thousands who send letters with their lives smouldering on the page, the tens of thousands who come to his rallies, the thirty-three who have martyred themselves to date by electrocution. The CCP staff who have taken up its principles and obligations as a way of life. The personal friends who trust him — Thackeray Thomas, Eula, Sheffield, Miles, Paul Hurinui. Kellie, above all.

Slaven walks down to the chalets, careful not to slip in the burnished tussock grass. He is quite resolved that the Hagley Park rally will be his best. He can't entirely repress a sense of pride that he alone is responsible for an event that will focus the country's attention. The sense of potential, of latent power, is like a grip on his breathing as he walks through the peace of Erewhon towards Mr Ng's chalet. He sees that the sunbather behind the dormitory is their pilot and not a Butler devotee after all. The forty-five of those must still be at their devotions.

Yet maybe Mrs McElrie scampers out just long enough to tell Slaven of Samuel's tumescence in colonial Christchurch, of some comment from Mrs Boss overhead, of the last words of old Pontifex, 'Good-bye, sun; good-bye, sun.'

Mr Ng and Miles are drinking fruit juice and reminding themselves in an understated way of past financial coups and mutual acquaintances while they wait for Slaven to return for lunch. The valet brings a quiche, some blue vein and gruyere, a local botrytised Riesling. Slaven half expects to hear chanting from the Butlerites, but there is just the flat bed on the Rangitata and the mountains of bulwarks on either side.

Mr Ng is interested in the effect the electricity has had on Slaven, but doesn't want to pry. Is there an altered consciousness perhaps; an opportunity for new personality development. 'In acupuncture such changes are documented,' he says. 'I wondered if there was any similarity, any connection even, in the way the nervous system responds.'

'My friend Marianne Dunne's convinced that sometimes an electric shock can open up unused neuron pathways in the brain. Like a flash-flood changes the channels in the Rangitata river-bed out there. It can also do a certain amount of damage of course. Anything from a tingle to a killing depending on the charge and the circumstances.'

'Chuang Tzu said that lightning is beautiful to watch, but must strike somewhere.'

'The scans showed some localised and random activity,' says Slaven. He is comfortable talking of it with Mr Ng, for his interest is caring, yet impersonal. 'The specialists said there were similarities with some types of epileptic patterns. I've had behavioural responses as well, but nothing too accentuated.'

'Just sufficient for opponents to have him committed to the Beckley-Waite Institute,' says Miles hoarsely.

'Beckley-Waite?' queries Mr Ng.

'I'm joking.'

'I sometimes think that the burns themselves were just as much a reason for the change in me,' says Slaven. 'Not being able to use my hands, when doing so had become so much tied up with my identity. Something psychological there it seems, but so much is supposition isn't it?'

'May I see your hands?' asks Mr Ng. He takes each in turn within his own light, rustling grasp. The gold of his glasses catches the light as he bends forward. His fingers travel lightly over the topography of scars and grafts.

'They're okay now,' says Slaven.

'In the Analects it's said that the final indication of a fortunate man is that he's spared a death by fire, or water.' says Mr Ng.

'There's a thousand unlucky options then all the same.' Miles is taken with this comparative view of death. 'Mitten was the best futures broker in Sydney and he was killed by a shot-put at his daughter's school sports and Hannah Devanne was thrown from her bay gelding during a Hawkes Bay hunt and broke her back on the discarded axle of a straight eight Buick.' Mr Ng nods, but has had trouble following what Miles has said.

'How clear the atmosphere is in your country,' Mr Ng says. 'Everything can be seen to the limit of one's own eyes.'

He comes as far as the entrance to the chalet to make his farewell to Miles and Slaven. A man whose people originally came from Linping, whose grandfather began a fortune in Hong Kong and who now has a proprietary investment in companies of eleven countries. Mr Ng looks at the mountains of the Southern Alps and politely asks for some information of this Samuel Butler. 'He was a speculator in both an economic and an intellectual sense,' says Miles. 'I don't think he liked it much here, but some oddballs lay claim to him.'

'I'm told that like any good Victorian he hated his father,' says Slaven. He sees Cardew walking through the departure gates within the airport, bearing away two hundred thousand family dollars and a degree of malice which will gather interest long after the money has been squandered.

'One may as well hate oneself,' says Mr Ng.

The pilot hears their voices and gathers his things as Slaven and Miles walk down to the pad below the lodge, to the flat, dry ground before the gravel of the Rangitata, with the deer far enough away so that they won't get spooked. Before the pilot starts the motor, Miles makes an enquiry about Slaven's time by himself. 'Well,' he says, 'did you enjoy goofing off in the sun?'

'Just gathered some energy for the rally. I'm beginning to get quite pumped up about it; about the possibilities.'

'I think you might as well ride the tiger all the way. It's time for a pay-off. Another dose of what you gave them at Western Springs and I reckon the government will just about cave in.'

'Well, it's now or never, isn't it.'

The helicopter begins its retching ascent. There's no sign of any of the Samuel Butler party, just a muscular, bald-headed man in shorts and tramping boots carrying cartons of beer to a cross-country vehicle and the deer in an other-wise empty land. As they gain height and turn again over Erewhon to swing eastwards, Miles and Slaven have a final view of the alpine valley, the desolate screes, the pristine Garden Of Eden and the clouds still banking up on the western side of the Alps.

Slaven has come a long way since the winter meeting in the drizzle at Tuamarina. The rally in Hagley Park has been almost completely set up by professional consultants com-missioned by Kellie. Thackeray Thomas and Slaven joke about the truck deck at Tuamarina which had to serve as a stage. Les Croad and his Angel Hire chairs, the portable loos which overflowed, the Gay Riders' false rendezvous, the fires in the night, the gum nuts inside the railings of the Wairau memorial.

Today Sarah is at hand to put a cramoisy scarf around Slaven's neck whenever he is off stage, despite the sunshine of the afternoon, and accredited officials come and go in shifts. Sunday, and the park is like a Latin Fiesta. The Hoihos, direct from their Asian tour and by special invitation, as the promoters say, sing *Capetown Races*, *Remember Greenpeace* and of course *Half Moon Bay*. The media are everywhere, eager for spectacle, hopeful of drama, alert to disaster. This is where the action is, isn't it? *Baby, baby, come again and live with me upon the shore of Half Moon Bay* .

There's no genie such as that which swayed at St Kilda and Western Springs, even though the technology is not daunted by a bright sun. Rather it is a decision of principle on Slaven's part. There is already enough appeal to emotion and he wants most to advance the cause of reason. Thousands and thousands from the city, and far beyond it, cover the green of Hagley Park, those in the open ground mainly seated, others standing beneath the English trees and along the sloping banks of the Avon. The colours of the clothes, faces and arms even, are stipples and ripples, hues that from the stage seem to undulate in acquiescence when the band is playing and vibrate with the applause when it pauses. It is difficult to hold in the mind the reality of the rally — a direct challenge to the political establishment.

Slaven has excelled — he knows it himself. With the rally underway he experiences a mood which has in it both relief and anticipation. A sense of something vital begun, of life in the hazard. He speaks more simply, more openly, more poetically, than at any of the earlier rallies, yet with a greater consciousness of control and effect and throughout the afternoon there grows in the swelling audience a mood close to exultation, of joy without frenzy. People are amazed and stirred that they are part of an exhibition of public will on a scale so magnificent.

See the summer sky, blue as a computer screen, and Banks Peninsula bulked in its eastern quarter. If Slaven looks for his friend's tower house in Cashmere he can't pick it out, but Miles from his den can see the movement which marks the rally in the park; an ant-like swarm that shimmers in the sun. See far to the west the mountains which hide Erewhon and The Garden Of Eden. See too, the planes dipping down to the airport, or climbing from it on a steeper angle, hardly a time when one or other isn't visible in the sky. The colours of life are yellow and blue, as the failed preacher Van Gogh knew.

Even for Slaven and Kellie and Thackeray it is incongruous that this gathering, like some gargantuan gala amidst the trees and buildings, is also a deliberate exercise of political power, with calculated threat and intent. Who could possibly take exception to such open and self-assured expression of the people's wishes.

See the cardboard boxes of braised chicken bones and the clear plastic bottles gently bob and amble on the Avon and muster for parade past the river steps of Christ's College and past the gardens at the back of the museum. See that the people have taken common sense into their own hands and filled the cricket pitches with cars. There are great chestnuts and sycamores and oaks safely above the clasp of the crowd and so close, so much in harmony, that their leaves inosculate. Beneath the oaks, lying amidst the leaves and grasses, are old acorns — like fat, copper bullets which have never struck home. Are all manner of people here?

See the PhD from Ottawa who married a local guy and thinks she's in at a turning point for a country she wishes to understand. A group of Thackeray Thomas acolytes shriek at the sight of his Cambrian sons, Iago and Dafydd, with their fat, poetic cheeks and the daughter of the music critic of 'Speak Up' finds a hedgehog to beat with a stick. See by the bridge a man with delicate features and not long back in the community, given plenty of personal distance despite his smile, because of the stains of long use around the pockets of his yellow trousers and the scurf on his pin-stripe collar. And the Hoihos are playing *Glasnost Galaxy*, ah, lovely and *After Tiananmen Square*.

You recognise the bosomy, smiling woman whose free and easy hair has scents of clover seed? Come, come, some-one of whom you have abundant information. That's right, it's Croad's Blenheim babysitter and only a hundred or so away is Gebrill who turns his own gaze from the cynosure of other eyes with a downward, envious smile and he licks blood from his lip. See Roland Purcell, Anna Fivetrees, and Mr Garrity. See the Aucklander who has come from the carpark of the Burlesque Hotel for easy pickings in the south. See Alice grown old and long since parted from her Tigger.

Let the polar storms go bowling by, as long as we're still seeing eye to eye.

'That we are here is the candid expression of our unity. And not just a common purpose, but a unity of heart. A belief in the community of our fellows; faith that collaborative concern is the best way to benefit us all. What our presence shows,' says Slaven rather grandly, 'is that the people of this country are now individually committed to it again and collectively prepared to take responsibility for its direction. We see the promised land and the charter marks the road to it. We are on the march.'

'No charter, no vote. No charter, not vote,' is the crowd's chant and 'All six. All six,' as Slaven vows that the party who wishes CCP support must accept the complete charter of reform.

'There's no time now for wriggling on the hook,' he says. 'No time for evasions and half-promises, negotiations and commissions. No more time for dirty tricks — I'm not in the

Beckley-Waite Institute any longer. No more time for wait-it-out, tough-it-out policies. The election is here and we are here. We are HERE.'

'All six. All six. All six.' See the great multi-coloured audience like a froth over all the surface of the ground and beneath the summer foliage of the large, English trees.

'In two hours,' and Slaven deliberately checks his watch for the cameras and his supporters. 'Yes, at four o'clock, if we haven't heard from the Government that the full charter is accepted for implementation within the next Parliamentary term, then the CCP will be asking you and all those with us in spirit today, to vote for the Democratic Socialists who have already pledged support.'

As he finishes the line, Slaven hears the echo of his own words from the sound system, then the chanting begins again and the rush of that makes him catch his breath, as if he were high on a headland and the sea wind gusts into his face. He has learnt to play to the cameras as well as the crowd, to prolong a pose, or smile, long enough for effect, but without it becoming unnatural. Even as his skin tightens because of the great roar of the people, he leads the cameras with a sweep of his arm to pan over the crush which covers Hagley Park and spills out far beyond. He knows that the PM will be watching and Alan Warden, Fassiere and Tonkin. Dr Meelind will be appreciating it, all the politicians and advisors in fact and absent friends such as Miles and Marianne Dunne who sit together in the tower. Jocelyn Piers, his old classmate from primary school perhaps, Ayesbury, the CD Officer, from professional habit assessing any crowd risk if there is panic. The Caretaker he hopes, in the staff quarters even though it's a Sunday, absent-mindedly reaming out his pipe as he watches the screen — debts will be paid. Slaven's mother even, as long as there is no cricket on the all sports channel and enemies such as Pollen, Marr and Aristeed, the Director with his book and a carpet thankfully cleansed. Doctors Bliss, Eugene and Collett who are neither friends nor enemies and consider no doubt that they have done all that can be expected of them. But not Professor Hankie who has returned to Swansea, not Buffle the cartoonist who has finished his earthly portfolio at last, not Cardew who capitalises some of his two hundred thousand in the canting of a blonde across a hand-tooled leather humpty in the window alcove of the Sydney El Dorado Motels.

Not Athol and the goose girl, for nothing of general significance can break the individual focus of hand-to-mouth, moment-to-moment, which is the nature of life there. The river flows upon the ceiling still, Athol's nose-stud glitters, the grizzle of the pit-bull terriers at a section's remove is almost as loud as the sounding of the Hagley crowd at a distance. Athol is cutting up a hogget, perhaps, liberated from a Lincoln College field in the previous dusk. See the deft knife-work. The goose girl is lying on her bed, perhaps, watching the Heathcote flow time as beauty on her ceiling. Her long neck rests on the pillow, her compact head tilts back with her mouth open a little as she rests and her golden beak left to legend. The pueblo carving has its colours muted by dust where dust can lie, but other surfaces are agleam with vermilion and Prussian blue. The embroidered owl still contains its wisdom and disguises function on the bedside table and the turn down of the sheet is finely-creased and gentle, free from the stiffness of any recent washing. The goose girl is comfortable in this Sabbath afternoon which is no more, or less, than any other, with her knee-length calfskin coat behind the door, the sound of Athol's knife in the flesh, the whine of the pit-bull terriers who may yet get a share if Athol feels neighbourly.

Miles on the other hand has both the long and the short view. From his eyrie in Cashmere he sees the rally at a distance like a spawning ground, all congestion and multi-coloured intensity. On the screen however is detail enough in close-ups for him to recognise the scars on his friend's hands, sweat on his high forehead, the veins in his throat swollen in the delivery of his beliefs. 'Stick it to them,' murmurs Miles. Almost he wishes that he could still care for anything as much himself.

Foveaux storms are fading, baby, within the calm of Half Moon Bay.

See the advertising blimps tethered to strong points around the perimeter of Hagley Park. They drift in the empty space thirty metres above the press below and each one on its sides proclaims the charter points of the CCP. And Kellie has been careful to do well from the franchises for the day. Jumbo Pies has its particular territory and so despite the sun, the hot meat and pastry is ferried in. Kiwi Juice and Freeze Throws, whole hospitality tents as Lager Bars, rosettes with Slavenisms at their centre, perspex-embalmed badge photos of Aldous and Kellie in their garden, 'Crav'n for Slaven' bumper stickers, cardboard bookmarks with a treated surface superficially resembling leather and embossed with the koro and cambrian motifs — and the outline of Half Moon Bay.

Is this it? The context in which decisions of our welfare should be made, judgments concerning the efficacy of political ostracism and the reduction of the Presidential term, or is this the justifiable celebration of achievement in the palm. Miles is in some pain again, but he is delighted by everything he sees in this amalgam of the admirable and derisive. In the absence of Georgina he calls aloud to Marianne to share with him a vision of the high-wire act which is democracy.

See dapper Raymond Boydd who teaches Art History at Elmwood High School and each night paints the great canvases of his early ambition with no recollection at all on waking. He shouts, 'All six. All six,' with a sudden, inexplicable fury which appalls him, then adjusts the top of his walk-socks with shaking fingers. And Steven Wybrow is here of course, having become a computer historian and a follower of Jung. Georgina Kitson has come with Sarah and her beauty is remarked upon and Vivien Castle is with us, rather than examining the Montana meadows. See Nicholas Halley whose story this may just as easily have been, and Izzy Paycock, Majorie Usser, Simon Adderley, old Ger with his lolling, gap-toothed smile is only one cunt from our view. Madeline Shields is here, with her bulk and jandals as badges of discrimination. She has saved from several weeks' housekeeping to be able to afford a Slaven cassette and standing monolithically amongst the crowd she is certain that Slaven has caught her eye with special affirmation. See the entreaty man who glories in the fame Slaven has established and has his own secret pride at his early recognition of such power. People expect like with like, but an ordinary person can live an extraordinary life, and an extraordinary person can live an ordinary one.

There is a place in the south, in the unfashionable south of the city where the rain-mist comes in from the harbour — a fine and silent touch on the bare legs of the students. Two young men kiss in the park and a young woman stands alone with her pockets inside out and a calculus text. The old trees ramify above the park, their tops undulate while it's quiet beneath, as an ocean surface crests above the peaceful depths. Come past the park into the unfashionable south, where the rentals are lower, the foot traffic less intense, the premises more representative of individual enterprise, or ineptitude. The Holistic Health and Acupuncture Clinic is in the old office of Acme Dry Cleaners. It has a gilt oriental symbol on the window, an anatomy chart to show the points and meridians, it has dried flowers and joss sticks as ancillary supplies and Buddhist calmness in fine calligraphy. Don's New and Used Sportsgoods holds promise for fresh whims and the accoutrements of those long gone. Come past the Cascade Die Casters, the Housie and Mah Jong Hall with hours for three nights of the week, the engraving service, the Power Body Gym, the Hydroponics supplies, the tool hire and The Salvation Army Clothing Shop. The Lefage Beauty Salon has all its services listed and beside each is a small, pink cupid: electrolysis, facials, depilatory waxing, red vein treatment, manicures, pedicures, skin tag removal, Danish massage, lash and brow tinting, sculptured nails, sunless tans, steam baths, cellulite protection, body wraps, colour and image consultation, lobe dedowning, bikini line clearance.

Between Morten's Pallet Racking and the radiator repair shop is the factory showroom for gas beds. Between Trevor's International Cornish Pasties and the water-blasting firm is Fifi's Escort Agency with quotations from enthusiastic customers pasted to the glass of the door.

Above Controlair Systems (NZ) Ltd, who are agents for dual directional air handlers and Belissimo damper motors, are the same day couriers and Bubbelas Antiques. There's the Zealandia Business and Art College of course, founded you will remember by Wyeth Knox ASSW, PSN, BA. There's the security specialists, the computer firm, the Community Legal Advice Bureau, Ducati Parts and Servicing, Equestrian Leathers, the stall of coloured transfers on glass, economy rental cars, the Baha'i Meeting Room, retirement planning, Simmon's Marine Upholstery and the Seven Day Twenty-Four-Hour Lightning Breakdown Service with an Alsation chained to its door. And all our friends are present — some making money, some making conversation, some making just prints on the ground. In such places are our lives passed and past.

Slaven feels little fear as four o'clock nears and he's surprised by that. Anticipation and excitement are what he's aware of on the stage in Hagley Park. All his decisions have already been made, now the responsibility for outcomes lies with those invisible politicians that he knows are watching. The mood of the great crowd is just that balance between fervour and common sense which he has hoped for, as if they too realise that all that can be done for their beliefs is being done and done well. Soon it will be over. He feels a free sweat on his face and the base of his neck, but it's the sweat from the energy of his performance and the afternoon sun, not anxiety. The sun glosses the scene and draws a light wind from the sea which stirs the advertising blimps at their moorings and the leaves of the chestnuts, sycamores, oaks, limes and willows. A macrocarpa even, massive and relegated to the less scenic margins of the park and generating from such bulk, reduced, careful cones for its seed. All these trees seemingly grow not from the ground, but from the dense, endless mulch of people spread amongst them in a shifting and pointillistic array of colours.

'One hour to go,' exclaims Slaven.

'All six. All six. All six. All six.' So extensive is the audience that a true unison isn't possible and the shout sweeps through a mass many of which are too far away to see Slaven. The cry is sinuous and buffeting, racing in division at some times, catching up with itself at others in redoubled strength.

'What do we want.'

'All six. All six.' The red and yellow blimps heel in pleasure at the turbulence beneath them.

'What do we demand.'

'All six. All six.' In the crowd Sarah is reduced to tears and Georgina catches her breath at the enormity of the people's will.

'No charter, no votes.' The Hoihos join Slaven on the stage again: time for *Welfare Heaven* and *Blowing in the Wind.*

The PM and others sit in the Cabinet Room and watch the Christchurch rally on screen. Also they are in touch with the consultants one floor below and their own observers at Hagley Park.

'How many do you reckon are there?' says the PM.

'Too many,' says Alan Warden.

'Far too many,' adds the Minister of the Environment who did not at all enjoy watching the hands go up from his St Albans electorate when Thackeray Thomas was asking for an indication of the constituencies.

'Too bloody many,' he says.

'You can never trust the South Island voter, Neil,' says the PM. 'You should have moved up to Te Tarehi when we offered it to you.'

'Who let the bastard out of the Beckley-Waite. That's what I'd like to know,' says Neil. And who facilitated his entry? Has the deputy Prime Minister a special smile. 'He went in there because he was a nutter, didn't he, a stirrer of the first order, and he should've stayed there. Also he should have been stuck straight back in when he surfaced in Christchurch.'

'And you would be happy to explain that in St Albans?' asks Warden.

It isn't that Brian Hennis and his Government have been caught napping, not at all. They have had ample warning of the rally and the ultimatum it carries. It is in any case the obvious political play immediately before the elections. The United Party has already given the PM power to make whatever decision he thinks best. Going right to the wire is what this is about and Hennis doesn't concede key points until he must. Who knows what can happen? Each day there is hopeful advice to him that Slaven and the CCP are losing momentum, backing down, riven by internal dissension, modifying their stance, seeking a compromise, about to be discredited, or suffering a crisis of conscience.

None of these things has happened. The PM watches the screen. 'All six. All six.' There's a long shot of the endless audience over the lawns and beneath the trees and the streets clogged with cars. Slaven achieves attention with impressive ease and begins speaking again, distorted by the sound systems, but with the passion evident nevertheless.

'It's Western Springs all over again,' says Warden. 'Jesus, must be 300,000 there.'

'Bugger the man,' says Neil. 'He's got no concern for the careers of those of us who are professional politicians. He's appallingly ignorant of how things should be done.'

'Has anyone got a bright idea?' asks the PM. There are only grumbles and indistinct murmurs. Hennis has known all along where the buck would stop. 'I'm going to speak directly to Aldous Slaven and the people too, if he'll let me.'

'And?' says his deputy.

'All the polls tell us that we need CCP support, so I'm going to congratulate him. I'm going to say that the Government and the United Party are enthusiastic to adopt all the charter points and implement them when we're re-elected. I'm going to say that this is a great day for democracy and the common people in this country. The people have spoken and our party has responded, I'm going to say. I'm going to kiss enough arse to ensure that we're all back in power and that way we live to fight another day. That's my pleasant duty as PM. Right?' No one in the Cabinet Room denies it. 'Then I'm going to be asking some hard questions about the quality of advice and briefings that I've had over several months on this whole Slaven and Coalition thing. Some hard questions. Some of you may like to consider that, and in the meantime I'll talk to the dentist.'

See the people of Canterbury and beyond, standing close

together in the summer afternoon and singing *Capetown Races*, *Remember Tiananmen Square* and *Ice Cathedral* — so popular after the Antarctic pickets. But most of all, like any proud people, they love their own special *Half Moon Bay* sung by their own Hoihos. Those close enough to watch Slaven's face, do so as he joins in, for the significance of the song is part of the folklore which has grown-up since his near electrocution on the barge-board of his house. Can it be claimed that the Hoihos have any intrinsic commitment to the CCP and the six point charter? Certainly they know how magnificently they benefit from the association, bow to their guitars and keyboards with a will and the lead singer tenses her thighs against the blue leather skirt and sings it all again.

Baby, baby, come again and live with me upon the shore of Half Moon Bay.

The music critic of 'Speak Up' even, admits that it's splendid of its genre and his daughter leaves off beating the hedgehog and resumes innocence with the melody. One of the Thackeray Thomas acolytes cries in Gaelic between the riffs, dapper Raymond Boydd sees the sunlight play upon the coruscating branch of an oak in an epiphanic moment of texture, Madeline Shields sways her body blissfully, a movement not dissimilar to the nodding of the Coalition blimps, Norman Proctor has lilies in his hand and delights in scents and sights which logic would have him denied.

Kinder hearts are waiting, baby, amongst old friends at Half Moon Bay.

The wonder and the power, the implication, of it are nothing in Guatemala of course, in Sedalia, Missouri, the Sierra de Gata, Schleswig, Ogbomosho, or the reed beds of the Yevpotkin, nothing in the air conditioned subterfuge of the Beckley-Waite Institute, or Cardew's Sydney El Dorado Motels, nothing even so close to home as the rear flat by the Heathcote with the river flowing on the ceiling, Athol washing the hogget blood from his hands and the goose girl asleep beside her embroidered owl.

Within its own orbit though, within the political awareness of our small country, Slaven's rally is a mighty enough thing, sure enough. This immense crowd, Slaven, Kellie and her fellow leaders, the PM and all the other watchers, have no doubt of it.

Let the polar squalls go bowling by, as long as we're still seeing eye to eye.

See the Right Honourable Brian Hennis, Prime Minister, make his call before the deadline. The AV people cast his face from the vidphone link to the screen at the back of the rally stage. The definition is poor in a bright afternoon, but who doesn't know this face well enough to refurbish it from their own recollection. You are experienced enough to know how he carries it off: the mixture of warmth and sincerity in his voice, the trick of combing his hair back with his fingers as he speaks and its lapse again to the side of his face. 'All six charter points,' he says. 'Let there be absolutely no mistake about that and I'm thrilled that after prolonged discussion I carry all my colleagues unanimously on this pledge.'

The Avon ducks and scavenging birds scatter in fright before the great shout of triumph. The non-committed and tardy in the surrounding streets leave their cars static in the traffic lanes and hurry to the park, stranger talking to stranger in the freedom from inhibition that such unusual circumstance begets. One thinks that scaffolding has collapsed, another that a UFO has landed. There is a wildfire rumour that the PM has offered Dr Aldous Slaven the Presidency. People press on to see whatever there is to see, so that in years to come they can say that they were here at the great rally, and so gain the floor while others give way before such first-hand authority.

A trio of thieves runs through a street of abandoned cars as if the world is ending, snatching bags and purchases as they go. Someone in a mood of celebration cuts a yellow blimp loose and it rises above the people and the city, moving slowly away from the sea. Hundreds of people wade into the Avon to cool themselves, but more sub-consciously to prove that this is a day on which anything is possible. All of the CCP leaders come out on to the stage and as the PM continues with his message, Kellie pins a spray of Powys Hayhoe flowers to her husband's damp shirt.

So many grounds for pleasure and satisfaction, relief,

congratulation, even joy, but the response which surprises Slaven with its intensity is the sense of vindication in the call made to the conscience of the people. In his heart have been two contrary instincts: one is the belief in an open appeal to common action, the other a fear of the ancient perversity of the mob. Each time he raised the serpent to overcome those who opposed his cause he glimpsed the otherness of the pulse within its eye and caught the sulphur on its breath, but each time when the purpose had been served the creature swayed, looped down, as bidden.

Slaven's shoulders ache with the release of muscular tension. His hands tremble and beneath the soft skin below his left eye where the suture marks are just visible, a tic is like the small movement in the pouched throat of a tree frog. Ah, Jesus, there is nothing now that can go wrong on any terrible scale. He tightens his hand in Kellie's and in response she turns with a quick smile of excitement. This at least, at last, he can give her. The PM is praising him from a distance, the people press close to the stage.

To Slaven's right the driver is steadily making his way through the crowd, no more self-consciously than if he were still on the landing beneath the Lyttelton wharf. See the beak of his nose and deep eyes, head up so that he can pick his way better. He is not at all furtive and stops to apologise for treading on Walter Tamahana's foot.

Thackeray Thomas leans towards Slaven, taking his upper arm and shaking it in triumph. 'This is the start of a new era,' he shouts. 'I believe that. I really do. This is the way that things will be decided from now on. It's an irony that here we are in the technology of the twenty-first Century and yet democracy has come the full circle.' Kellie is passed a phone from an aide and after speaking into it, she points to it amidst the hubbub and then at Slaven who reaches for it.

'We're watching it. We can see it all.' Marianne Dunne's voice has for once lost its professional calm. Slaven imagines her, elegantly tall and dark, in the tower house overlooking the city. 'And the statement's come over about the Government's unconditional acceptance of all charter points. My God. The PM is going to announce it on national news too. What a thing for you and Kellie apart from anything else.

Miles is right beside me. He pretends it's all nonsense, but wants to talk to you anyway. You know how he is.'

The driver finds a place which suits him, the sun at his back and the ventillated cover of a Kiwi Juice storage unit for support. He leans there and watches Slaven with the suggestion of a smile. Not an expression that's meant for communication, rather the look of one who has come across an old class-mate who has done well. 'So there you are, old son,' he murmurs.

'Hello, Demosthenes,' says Miles in his husky way. His voice seems to come from a place very quiet and far away. 'The bastards have caved in I hear. Good for you. Good for you. Push home the advantage while you can.' The driver calmly lifts the supposed vid-camera, steadies it on the cowling and fires twice. The noise is nothing much at all amongst the clamour that is everywhere and attention focuses on the consequences of the shots not their origin. 'Come and see me when the world allows you a moment,' Miles asks, not knowing that the white phone is already falling from his friend's hand.

The first bullet passes through Slaven's left zygomatic arch into the brain and the shock of it stands his hair on end, the second strikes through the eye socket on the same side.

Do you doubt that everyone gives voice to exorcise the terror and the threat of what they see, blasphemies and screams, protestations and blessings, and various odd puffings, gruntings and groans which are quite beyond words, beyond consciousness even, the jerk of one soul at the passing of another.

Everyone gives voice — except that Aldous Slaven and the driver, those two most intimately concerned, make not a sound. Slaven has fallen with his legs strangely folded beneath him and the driver keeps his camera on target as would be expected and begins backing slowly through the tumult.

Slaven has, as you know, very straight, black hair, like that of an Italian, or a Slovak, and it lies across the pallor of one cheek despite the damage elsewhere. He has large feet, with thin ankles seeming a poor connection to them.

What description is necessary though, when you have come so well to know him, haven't you, in the same way as all your acquaintances are perfectly open to understanding?

Miles and Marianne can't get all this from television. They don't hear the vast droning as if from bumble bees, don't see the coursing blood like the Earl of Athlone flowers, but there are scenes of the supporters separating Kellie from the body and carrying it to the Square, shots of the rioting and looting within the inner city, the torching of the Town Hall and murder of a score of people separately identified as the assassin. Miles and Marianne continue to watch, but have no comment. Miles might admit to sorrow perhaps, but not surprise, for he understands that none of us has the price of the most precious things. Marianne Dunne takes the old man's hand and he doesn't move it from that consolation, or turn away from the screen, but he has begun to move his thoughts back to places where life had been bearable.